My Fairly Dangerous Godmother

D0807899

Also by Janette Rallison

My Fair Godmother
My Unfair Godmother
Blue Eyes and Other Teenage Hazards
Just One Wish
Masquerade
My Double Life
A Longtime (and at One Point Illegal) Crush
Life, Love, and the Pursuit of Free Throws
Playing The Field
All's Fair in Love, War, and High School
Fame, Glory, and Other Things on my To Do List
It's a Mall World After All
Revenge of the Cheerleaders
How to Take The Ex Out of Ex-boyfriend
Son of War, Daughter of Chaos
Slayers (under pen name CJ Hill)
Slayers: Friends and Traitors (under pen name CJ Hill)
Erasing Time (under pen name CJ Hill)
Echo in Time (under pen name CJ Hill)
What the Doctor Ordered (under pen name Sierra St. James)

My Fairly Dangerous Godmother

Janette Rallison

My Fairly Dangerous Godmother
By Janette Rallison
Copyright © 2015

This is a work of fiction. The characters, names, places,
incidents and dialogue are products of the author's
imagination and are not to be construed as real.

No part of this book may be reproduced in any form
whatsoever without prior written permission of the
publisher except in the case of brief passages embodied in
critical reviews and articles.

ISBN: 978-0-9906757-2-3
Cover design © 2014 by Janette Rallison
Formatting by Heather Justesen

To me, because I did most of the work. Besides, it's about time I was in a dedication. Hey Janette, you're awesome! And also to my family, friends, and readers. You're awesome too!

For Master Sedgewick Goldengill

Dear Professor Goldengill,

Here is yet another report of my fairy godmother awesomeness in action: I rock, plain and simple. And, I'd like to add, I appreciate all the extra practice I've had using my people skills while tromping around exciting places such as cheap hotel rooms, the Atlantic Ocean, and the borders of the Unseelie Court.

At this point you might be detecting sarcasm in my tone, although I doubt it because I'm convinced no one actually reads these reports. If you did—if anyone at the Fairy Godmother Affairs Office did—you certainly wouldn't keep teaming me up with the one assistant I specifically asked *not* to have. That's right. The FGA gave me Clover T. Bloomsbottle again, even though he already messed up three of my assignments.

In case anyone at the FGA is casually skimming through my report, let me say once again that I don't ever want to work with Clover T. Bloomsbottle. Ever.

Clover T. Bloomsbottle + Chrysanthemum Everstar = No. Do not do it.

Now that I've got that out of my system, I'd like to point out that even with the current rationing of magic, this assignment went extremely well—probably because I kept Clover's involvement to a minimum. Okay, I admit my client was nearly killed a couple of times, but mortals know their lives can be snuffed out at any moment, so they're prepared for those sorts of contingencies. And if mortals aren't prepared . . . well, a few brushes with death are just the thing to perk them up and make them appreciate their simple and frequently dull pleasures.

When I finished helping my client, she was quite perky. Again, if you're skimming:

Client + Me as her fairy godmother = All sorts of perk and happiness.

Here is my five-page report, complete with side notes showing my mastery of human culture. I so get them. I think this assignment proves beyond a shadow of anybody's doubt that I'm more than ready to enter Fairy Godmother University.

Sincerely,

Chrysanthemum Everstar

HOW I USED MY HIGHLY HONED AND TOTALLY ADVANCED-LEVEL FAIRY GODMOTHER SKILLS TO FIX ANOTHER MORTAL'S SADLY PATHETIC LIFE.

By Chrysanthemum Everstar

Subject: Mercedes "Sadie" Ramirez, age eighteen
Place: Greenfield, Kentucky, early twenty-first century

Some girls are born with beauty and grace clutched in their soft newborn hands. Sadie Ramirez wasn't one of those girls. As a toddler, she did nothing remarkable except bang into furniture and gather a collection of bruises.

Her parents thought her awe-filled brown eyes and smooth black hair were darling, and her older brother Alanzo, if pressed, would concede she was cute. But the world at large took no notice of her.

To the daycare providers who watched her from seven in the morning to seven at night, she was just another child to tend, herd, and supply with graham crackers. While Sadie fell off monkey bar ladders, her parents busied themselves climbing corporate ones.

Through elementary school, Sadie was plain and overlooked except when she did things like get the answers wrong in class. This always mortified her—both being called on and producing a wrong answer. In middle school softball games, she was permanently assigned to the outfield. In volleyball, she stepped aside and let other girls hit the ball. During Sadie's first couple years of high school, she was tall, gangly, and acne prone. It didn't help her social life.

Fairy's side note: Beauty is a harsh task master, but one humans worship anyway. Humans often don't make sense, which is why other species rarely ask them for advice.

Sadie wanted to fit in at high school, and since she had no athletic skill, she joined the marching band. During the first halftime performance, she dropped her flute and had to grapple for it on the ground before anyone trampled it. This caused a traffic jam and enough confusion that instead of spelling out 'Go Titans!' the band stood on the field displaying 'Got it ons!' This made them look like they were trying to be cool but didn't have the grammar skills to pull it off.

During the next game, Sadie wandered too close to the color guard and managed to get clubbed by a twirling flag.

Fairy's side note: This is the reason marching bands wear those big awkward hats. They double as helmets.

After two halftime fiascos, Sadie quit band and joined choir. The choir members stood and sang, which rarely produced chances for accident. Unless you were prone to tripping, and then you might step on your performance gown during the winter festival concert and cause a domino-like avalanche in the soprano section. Which Sadie did.

All of Sadie's awkwardness might not have been so bad if she had friends to console her, or at least help her laugh it off, but Sadie's luck with friends was similar to her luck with blunt objects.

Fairy's side note: Luck is often eerily consistent.

Sadie's best friends had the habit of moving to distant cities. At school she was left with the sort of friends who were friends if no one better happened to be around.

Nature isn't always as unkind as she first appears, and during Sadie's sophomore year, she filled out so she looked graceful and willowy, even if she wasn't. Her face cleared and she learned how to do her hair and apply makeup. In short, she waddled out of her ugly-duckling years and spread swan-like wings.

Fairy's side note: If Sadie had been a bird instead of a teenage girl, this story would have a happy ending right now. Unfortunately, Sadie was not only a teenage girl, but she lived in a town where girls had a pecking order harsher than any flock of birds. When someone was branded "unpopular," the mark clung there more stubbornly than a tattoo. Trying to shed the label annoyed the popular set. Once they'd decided where a person belonged, they didn't like to be contradicted. It made them look bad.

Sadie would have escaped notice from the popular girls if her singing voice had been as uninspiring as the rest of her talents. Her voice was a gift, though—a piece of magic. She made notes glide and hover, then land as softly as snowfall.

Over the next two years, Sadie learned how to play the piano and the guitar, and they became her best friends. Music could take her away from the clang of slamming lockers and the incessant noise of people talking. She made up lyrics as she walked to class, invented tunes as she drove home, and decorated her bedroom with posters of singers. They were her people—the ones who understood her—even if they didn't know her.

She dedicated an entire wall to teen rock star, Jason

Prescott. He had dark brown hair, a square jaw, and smoldering brown eyes that, even in poster-form, looked into her soul. She stared at him while she sang, pretending he heard her. Her songs grew stronger then, sweeter and deeper.

When Sadie sang solos in choir performances, the audience drank in her voice. It was as if the entire world opened up to welcome her. Each clap was a cheer of approval.

If her parents had known Sadie better, they wouldn't have been surprised when Sadie announced she wanted a singing career. College wasn't necessary. In fact, if an opportunity presented itself, she didn't care that much about finishing her senior year of high school.

Her parents, unfortunately, didn't know Sadie very well.

Fairy's side note: This wasn't completely her parents' fault. Sadie never told them what school was like. When someone is branded "unpopular," it's not a label they're eager to show off. Sadie didn't want her parents to think less of her. Deep down, she feared the brand was true.

Mr. and Mrs. Ramirez insisted their daughter go to college and get a practical major. Accounting, engineering, business. Something that would allow her to earn enough money to do a few nice things—like eat and pay rent.

Sadie and her parents talked, and disagreed, and Mrs. Ramirez applied to colleges for her while Sadie researched talent agents and recording labels.

And then Sadie got her break.

Fairy's side note: Mortals should be cautious when wishing for big breaks, but generally aren't. It never occurs to them that the word 'break' has several meanings, some of which are quite painful.

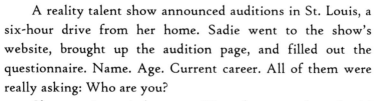

A reality talent show announced auditions in St. Louis, a six-hour drive from her home. Sadie went to the show's website, brought up the audition page, and filled out the questionnaire. Name. Age. Current career. All of them were really asking: Who are you?

She wasn't entirely sure. Was she an awkward girl destined to be overlooked her whole life, or was her talent worth more than that? Sometimes when she sang, the music seemed to reach inside and tug at her soul, stretch it into a taut line connecting to the sky, to hope, to a dazzling future.

She wasn't just searching for an audience clapping politely. She was looking for redemption.

A couple months before school ended, Sadie and her mother drove to St. Louis for the first round of auditions. Her mother read off descriptions from college catalogs during a good portion of the trip. She also muttered things about Sadie's grandparents who "came to this country with nothing and worked hard their entire lives so their children could have an education." This was inevitably followed by the instruction "Don't throw that gift away chasing after a silly dream."

Sadie had learned to tune out those sorts of comments.

Fairy's side note: Children are as careless with their parents' sacrifices as they are with slinkies. Both will only stretch so far. Both are easily tangled and ruined by people who don't know how to use them.

Sadie passed the preliminary audition round and was asked to come back that night to participate in the show, and thus she stepped out onto the tightrope of hope. It was a tiny tenuous chance for fame, for escaping the pecking order. And it was a long way to fall if the rope didn't hold.

Fairy's side note: Ropes made from hope rarely hold.

This time was no exception.

Falling is hard for teenage girls: falling from grace, falling in love, falling to pieces. All hurt on impact, which is why mortals need fairy godmothers to help put back together the shattered remnants of their lives. And if fairies can help the fairy realm at the same time, all the better.

In other words, I think you'll agree I have mastered the fine and extremely important art of multitasking while being a godmother. Please accept this extra credit project as proof I will make a valuable addition to Fairy Godmother University.

From: the Honorable Sagewick Goldengill
To: Mistress Berrypond

Dear Mistress Berrypond,

 I received Chrysanthemum Everstar's report on Sadie Ramirez, and despite her assertions, I read it. I can't help but notice that her reports continue to grow shorter and offer less detail, which makes it difficult to properly assess her role. I'm afraid I must ask you to have the Memoir Elves delve into Sadie's memories and write a more detailed report.

 With the utmost enchantment,
 Sagewick Goldengill

 PS: Many thanks for the nectar and crumpets. No one can crumpet like you, my dear. I'm so refreshed I can almost forget Miss Everstar. Almost.

The Department of Fairy Advancement
To the Honorable Sagewick Goldengill

Dear Professor,

As you requested, I sent Memoir Elves to Sadie Ramirez's home and had them delve into her mind while she slept. The Memoir Elves bravely faced this task, even though they have a resolved distaste of submerging themselves into teenage girls' minds. The elves inevitably come out of the experience feeling insecure, hating their hair, and feeling fat. Also, they have an unhealthy desire to spend hours texting and surfing the internet. The Memoir Elves are currently in detox and doing well, although Blinka Ruefeather continues to laugh about several unflattering memes she created of members of the Unified Magical Alliance. We are doing our best to speed her recovery. Their report follows.

Twinkling regards,
Mistress Berrypond

PS I so enjoyed our soirée. You'll be happy to know that the bluebells you sent chime beautifully every hour.

Chapter 1

My prerecorded number for *America's Top Talent* followed two tap-dancing grandmas and a bowling pig. This would probably not be my proudest singing moment, or one I hoped would define my career, but hey, when you're chasing fame, you can't be picky where you start.

While Peppy the Porker pushed a bowling ball across the stage with his snout, I stood in the wings doing relaxation exercises. *Deep inward breaths. Calm thoughts. Don't think about the slightly carnivorous crowd out there. Don't consider that a TV audience can turn faster than a figure skater.*

A buzz cut through Peppy's bowling music—the sign the judges had Xed the pig. Peppy wouldn't advance to the next round in Las Vegas. I hoped his short-lived show biz fame didn't mean he was destined to become bacon.

A flurry of stagehands went out to clean up the bowling props. I couldn't see them. From where I stood, only a slice of the black gleaming floor was visible. I wondered if it was slippery. And then I wondered why I'd thought three-inch spiked heels were a good idea. I'm not used to them.

The show's host, Rudger Zeeland, a bald guy with hipster glasses and no patience, motioned me to come closer to the entrance. "Ten seconds," he said. "Are you ready?"

No. How could anybody ever be ready to face TV cameras? Millions of people watched this show. Millions. I couldn't conceive how big of a group that was. My whole city only had eighteen thousand. Could you fit a million people in twenty football stadiums? Fifty stadiums?

I nodded at Rudger. I was as ready as I could be. I'd practiced my song so much, I could belt it out in any key, any tempo, with half my vocal chords tied behind my back. And right now I even managed to look the rock star part.

Before Mom and I came to St. Louis, we'd stopped at an upscale mall. I tried on twenty outfits, all outrageously priced, before I found one that looked glam enough—black leather pants, red heels, and a loose black mesh top over a tight red shirt. Putting on the clothes had been like putting on a new identity. I could be someone else. Someone better.

I'd styled my long black hair into loose curls. Even though I used half a bottle of hairspray to keep them curled, I knew they would fall out in approximately fifteen minutes. But it would be long enough.

Rudger didn't notice my nod of agreement. He was staring out at the stage. "Five," he told me.

Crap. I only had five seconds left. Five seconds of safety. If I tripped on the way out, the girls at my school would never let me live it down.

"Three."

Three? What happened to four?

"Two."

Why had I done this to myself? More importantly, how could I want to do this for a living when even walking out on a stage seemed excruciatingly painful?

"One." He waved me on my way.

I took a deep breath and made my legs carry me forward past the curtains, out onto the stage. Unbidden, a memory of yesterday's lunch period flashed into my mind. While I'd stood in the lunch line, I'd heard my name. Not called, just spoken about in one of the conversations behind me. Macy and Brooklyn, girls from drama, were talking loud enough that they probably meant me to hear.

"I don't know why she's trying out," Macy said. "What does she expect to happen? Like, does she think she's going to be discovered just because she played the lead in a few school musicals?"

I didn't want to listen, but what else could I do? Leave the line? I did what I always did—pretended I was invisible and deaf.

"Her voice isn't that good," Brooklyn agreed. "Mr. DiCicco only chose her because he felt sorry for her."

"He knows she doesn't have a social life, so she has lots of time to devote to rehearsals."

Then they both laughed.

I tugged myself away from the memory and concentrated on walking across the stage. "I'm good enough," I told myself. "I can do this. I just need a chance to prove it."

The auditorium was cavernous. The seating went on and on, layering the audience in balconies. I usually sang for a small group of parents in the school theater. Could my voice fill this place even with a microphone?

I strode, legs trembling, toward center stage. The lights' glare made it impossible to see the closest audience seats. The cameramen had completely disappeared in the haze, leaving only the gaping lenses of the cameras visible. They seemed like black holes capable of sucking people away.

I smiled anyway and hoped I looked natural and not horrified. I'd never had trouble smiling before but my lips quivered, unable to hold the weight of the moment.

I caught sight of the judges' table. A large unlit X sat in front of each judge. If none or only one of the Xs lit up, I would move on to the next round of performances. Two Xs meant I was out. Three meant I was laughably bad and would likely show up on the TV show. At least, that was what everyone told me while I waited to do the preliminary auditions. The really good, the quirky, and the pathetic acts got advanced so the TV viewers could watch them.

The problem was, I wasn't positive which category I fit into.

Before the taping, Rudger told the contestants a guest judge would be sitting in. I'd assumed it would be someone like the rest of the judges—a star who hadn't produced a hit in the last decade. Someone who had time to do this show because he wasn't touring.

Instead, Jason Prescott sat at the judges' table. My poster crush was here, live. Suddenly, breathing became hard. Jason—*Jason*—was looking at me.

I managed to tell the judges my name, age, and hometown. I refrained from offering Jason my number. I couldn't decide if cracking a joke would make me seem likeable or just really desperate. Besides, if I said something like that and it aired on the TV show, Macy and Brooklyn would never let me live it down.

The first notes of my accompaniment came over the speakers. I'd written this song with Jason in mind, a lilting melody about unrequited love. And now he was sitting here listening to me sing it. That was a good omen, a sign this was meant to be. Maybe Jason would like me so much, he'd talk to me after the audition. I didn't hope for more than that. Jason only dated supermodels, actresses, and rock stars—people whose fame clung to them like perfume.

Usually when I sang, I focused on people's foreheads. It looked like I was making eye contact, but it wasn't nearly as nerve-wracking. This time I gazed into Jason's eyes. I wanted him to feel a connection, to know this song was for him.

The intro ended, and I sang the first line. "Your smile is easy, but you never see just what that smile is doing to me."

Jason watched me lazily, bored almost. He picked up a cup from the table and took a drink.

"Love at first sight is real, so they say . . ." My voice wavered as I went into the next line. That wasn't supposed to happen. Couldn't happen. Why was it happening now, when I needed everything to go perfectly?

"But you've never even glanced my way." I sang louder to make sure my voice stayed steady. Unfortunately, performing louder made me run out of breath sooner. I quickly took a gulp of air to sing the next line. "Tell me what I'm supposed to do." It sounded like a gasp. Unprofessional. Jason's eyes weren't encouraging, or understanding, or any of the things I saw when I sang to his posters. He looked like he was on the verge of an eye roll.

"When I'm the one who's staring for two." I was grabbing at the notes, wrestling them into the melody. I noticed how low-budget my music sounded blaring across the auditorium.

Since I wrote the song myself, I had to do my own minus track—me, playing the piano. Suddenly it seemed so "school talent show." Not much better than the tap dancing grandmas and bowling pig.

My voice wavered again. I couldn't stop it. My vocal cords had decided to abandon me. Jason glanced at the ceiling in exasperation.

I sang louder to stop my notes from sliding. If Jason would just look at me encouragingly, everything would turn around and my voice would flow out to the audience the way it was supposed to.

Maybe it was the stress, or the strain of singing louder, but when I went for the highest note, my voice cracked. A horrible yodeling sound flung from my mouth.

A rumble of laughter went through the audience. I felt dizzy, clammy. My stomach clenched like it had folded in half. I kept singing, because that's what you do during a performance.

Jason reached over and hit his X button. As soon as he did, the other judges followed suit. They did it cheerfully, like this was all a joke and they were having a great time.

The music abruptly stopped, allowing me to hear scattered applause and calls from the audience. Were they clapping for me or clapping because they were glad I'd been Xed?

The worst part about this show, I now realized, was that they made the contestants stand there and listen while the judges told everyone why they thought you were a no-talent hack.

The other judges gestured to Jason, deferring to him as the guest judge.

He leaned forward, his eyes finally connecting with mine. "Listen, you're a pretty girl—"

A few people in the audience hooted at that. I felt my cheeks burn with embarrassment.

Jason held up a hand to stem the interruption. "But the problem with pretty girls is they're used to getting a pass in life. They're handed things so often, they come here and think the same thing will happen. In the music business, you can't get by on looks. You need actual talent and you need to practice. My advice is to spend less time doing your nails, and more time doing your scales."

He leaned back in his chair, done with his critique. The audience cheered and clapped, happily shredding my apparent singing method of not practicing and then expecting things to be handed to me.

On the TV show, sometimes people yelled out angry retorts before they walked off the stage. Other times they thanked the judges for their time. I'd told myself that if I got Xed, I'd be gracious. Instead I stood there aching to tell him I practiced all the time, I usually sang better, and this was the first time I'd done my nails in a year.

If the judges would only give me a second chance . . .

I knew they wouldn't, though. My dream was over. And worse, if my audition made it on the show, every catty girl at Greenfield High would tell me how badly I'd sucked.

The lights felt painfully bright, and a wave of nausea washed through me. I opened my mouth to thank the judges. That's when things got worse. My wave of nausea went tidal. I stood in the middle of the stage—too far away from the wings to run for cover. I couldn't do anything to stop this. My stomach lurched uncontrollably, and I threw up on the floor.

Chapter 2

Mom met me backstage, took Kleenex from her purse, and helped me wipe off my now not-so-beautiful red heels. I was numb with embarrassment. It was all I could do to fight the tears burning at the back of my eyes. I'd already embarrassed myself enough. I didn't need to make it worse by crying in front of everyone.

"It will be okay," Mom said with forced cheerfulness. "I'm sure they'll edit that part of your performance out of the show."

Rudger, who stood nearby waving his hand and yelling at a group of stagehands to go sanitize the stage, didn't confirm or deny this theory.

"My shoes are fine," I told Mom. "Let's get out of here."

That's when Rudger sliced a glare at me. "You shouldn't have come here if you were sick. That's why we specifically ask on the release form if you're healthy enough to perform." He mumbled something to a passing stagehand, then added, "The last thing this show needs is a flu outbreak."

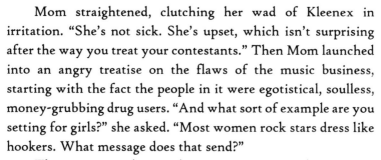

Mom straightened, clutching her wad of Kleenex in irritation. "She's not sick. She's upset, which isn't surprising after the way you treat your contestants." Then Mom launched into an angry treatise on the flaws of the music business, starting with the fact the people in it were egotistical, soulless, money-grubbing drug users. "And what sort of example are you setting for girls?" she asked. "Most women rock stars dress like hookers. What message does that send?"

The message the producer sent my mother, in an increasingly clipped tone, was that she needed to leave immediately, and neither of us were to come within a five-hundred foot radius of the show's staff again. Although, I don't think you can really issue restraining orders without some sort of paperwork, so that was probably an empty threat.

I didn't say much to Mom during the car ride back to the hotel. I was too busy reliving every horrible moment of my song. The audience's laughter. Jason rolling his eyes. The way a bunch of people shrieked after I threw up. It made me feel sick all over again.

As we neared the hotel, Mom finally calmed down, no longer gripping the steering wheel like she was trying to strangle it. "This is for the best," she said. "Now you've learned what a singer's life is really like—the complete jerks you have to deal with. You don't want that. You're a smart girl. In honors classes," she added to prove her point. "You'll go to college, get a good job, and then people will treat you with the respect you deserve."

I couldn't bring myself to argue with her, but even now when I felt horrible, I still wanted to sing. I just didn't want to ever do it in front of people again.

I slumped in my seat and didn't answer.

Our hotel came into view, squatting on the street with the

other buildings. It seemed rundown and plain. A shrine to averageness.

"I don't think we should even watch the show when it airs," Mom said. "There's no point."

"I have to watch it." That way when everyone at school slammed my performance, I'd know whether they were exaggerating or not.

Mom drove into the parking lot. Instead of pulling into a space, she looked at me tentatively. "Are you hungry? Do you want to get something to eat?"

I shook my head.

Mom sent me an encouraging smile. "I bet I could find a place with chocolate ice cream."

I shook my head again. This was not the type of problem ice cream could solve. "I smell gross. I want to take a shower."

Mom handed me a key card for our room. "All right. You go clean up, and I'll get some food."

I climbed out of the car and headed to the hotel, the dull ache of resignation settling in my chest.

It wouldn't matter what I said to my mother about needing to follow my dreams now. This audition was proof I couldn't succeed. Some people were born for greatness and others were cursed with mediocrity. Time to admit it to myself: the mediocrity troll had settled under my bridge.

Tears filled my eyes. This time I didn't stop them from coming, couldn't. By the time I reached our room, I was sobbing and hoped people wouldn't open their doors to see what was wrong.

Keeping my head down, I slid the key into the slot, then pushed the door open. Why did things always turn out badly for me? Why couldn't—just once—something go my way? I walked inside, slammed the door shut, and kicked off my heels so hard they flew across the room.

A voice across the room said, "I don't think you fully understand the problem."

My gaze shot in that direction. A teenage girl with long pink hair lounged on the far bed, talking on a cell phone. She wore a jean miniskirt, a bright purple shirt, and matching purple flats. She had an air of effortless confidence, the sort of attitude beautiful people always have. She glanced at me and then went back to her phone, more concerned with her conversation than with my arrival. "Did anyone even read my last report?"

Oh crap. I was in the wrong room. This sort of thing was bound to happen since the front desk used programmable plastic cards instead of actual keys. They'd messed up and programmed one that worked on the wrong room. What must this girl think of me? I'd barged in here crying, slammed the door, and then kicked my heels across the room. "I'm so sorry," I stammered. "I thought this was my room."

She held up a hand in an I'll-be-with-you-in-a minute sort of way. "How is an assistant actually assisting if he tries to sabotage the mission?"

I hurried across the room to grab my shoes. "I didn't check the door number before I came in and . . ." As I reached down to pick up my second shoe, I noticed my suitcase sitting by the bathroom door—a turquoise one Mom bought on a shopping spree.

Wait, this was my room after all, and some strange pink-haired girl was sitting on my bed. Had she not noticed our stuff around the room when she checked in? I straightened and took a step toward her. "Excuse me—actually, this *is* my room."

She gave me the I'm-busy hand again and spoke into her

phone tersely. "You might as well assign an ogre to help me. At least an ogre would be up front about trying to kill people instead of pretending the whole thing was my fault."

I took a step back. "Uh . . . are you talking to the front desk?" Another step back. "Maybe you should speak with them in person."

"She's griping to the FGA," a small male voice said in an Irish accent. I spun around to see who'd spoken. I didn't see anyone. No one else stood in the room. This was getting decidedly weird.

"As though," the man continued, "anyone at the fine and fancy Fairy Godmother Affairs cares a trot for what either of us has to say."

Godmother Affairs? Weirder still. I peered around the room, trying to figure out where the disembodied voice came from. "Where are you?"

"Directly in front of you."

Only if he was invisible. "No, you're not."

"I'm here on the ruddy bed, lass."

I still didn't see him. Was this a joke? I ran a hand through my hair, nearly getting my fingers stuck in the hairspray. "Look, I'm sorry about this whole room mix up, but I've had a really bad day and I'm not in the mood for—"

And then I saw him. A man who couldn't have been more than six inches tall. He stood on the end of the bed waving his hand to get my attention. He wore a green suit and bowler hat that he tipped in my direction. "My name is Clover T. Bloomsbottle. And don't be asking for me gold, as I'll not be giving it to you."

A leprechaun.

I let out a startled scream, stumbled backward, and

smacked into the dresser. I looked at the pink-haired girl and screamed again. A pair of shimmering butterfly-like wings had opened across her back. Not costume wings. These were real moving wings with intricate glimmering veins running from their center.

Impossible. I put my hand to my mouth and took frantic breaths. This couldn't be happening. I was having some sort of post-traumatic psychotic episode. If I blinked, it would go away.

I blinked. It didn't go away.

"You're not real," I sputtered. "Now leave. Leave. Leave. Leave."

The girl let out a humph and gripped her phone harder. "Do you hear that?" She gestured in the leprechaun's direction. "Clover has already done something wrong. He spoke to Sadie for all of two seconds and now she's hysterical."

Not only were magical creatures in my hotel room, they knew my name. I didn't know why a fairy sat on my bed talking to someone about ogres killing people, but I wasn't about to stick around and find out. Ogres were never good news. I backed toward the door, heart pounding in overdrive.

As I reached the door, a shower of sparks zoomed past my side in a burst of light and glitter. At first I thought the fairy had shot something at me and missed. I yanked at the doorknob, trying to get out before she shot again.

The knob didn't move, didn't even turn. She'd locked me in. I pulled at it uselessly, then pounded on the door. "Help!" I glanced over my shoulder to see if the fairy and leprechaun were closing in.

Clover still stood on the bed, tilting his head and rubbing his beard as he considered me. The fairy shoved her cell phone into a pink sequined purse and let out another humph. An air of frustration accompanied every flutter of her wings. "I can't work under these conditions. What is the FGA thinking?"

"Maybe it isn't the FGA," the leprechaun said. "Maybe it's the damsels you're choosing. They seem a wee bit bockety in the head."

Choose? Choose for what? For ogres to kill? I rattled the knob again. It was still locked. I slammed my hand into the door. "Somebody help me!"

The girl stood up from the bed, gripping a silver wand with exasperation. "We're *trying* to help you, but it's hard to do with you screaming and flailing around. Honestly, haven't you ever heard of a fairy godmother before?"

I stopped pounding on the door. "Fairy godmother?" I repeated, only slightly calmer. My breaths were coming out deep, fast. "Is that what you're supposed to be?"

The leprechaun let out a laugh. "It's what she's *supposed* to be. Unfortunately for you she's only a *fair* godmother. Her grades weren't high enough to get into Fairy Godmother University." He hooked his thumbs into his belt. "But she'll keep practicing on the likes of you until they let her in."

"Shut up!" The girl flicked her wand in the leprechaun's direction and a stream of sparks shot out, hitting him in the chest. He flew backward into the air and landed on the bedspread with an "Umph!" His hat tumbled from his head, flipping over.

The little man sprang to his feet, grabbed his hat, and stalked back toward her. "It's a breach of the Magical Creatures Treaty to attack a leprechaun. I'll be reporting you to the FGA!"

The fairy tossed her long pink hair off her shoulder. "Good luck with that. They obviously don't read their reports because if they did, you'd be doing time with the Keebler elves."

She turned her back on him and glided to me, moving with the grace of a dancer. Her wings had a pearl-like shine that made everything in the hotel room look cheap and rundown. "So anyway," she said with a smile, "I'm your fairy-godmother-in-training, Chrysanthemum Everstar. You can call me Chrissy for short."

"You're my fairy godmother?" I repeated. "You're not going to let ogres kill me?"

"Well, not on purpose." Her wings flapped lazily. "I did mention I was still training, didn't I?"

I twisted the doorknob again. Still locked.

She let out a sigh, took hold of my hand, and led me away from the door. "You don't need to be so nervous. I'm here to grant you three wishes. It's a good thing."

I gulped, unsure I'd heard her right. "You . . . you want to grant me wishes?"

The leprechaun eyed me, shaking his head. "She keeps repeating everything you say—a sure sign her brain is banjaxed. Blame me all you please for the troubles in our last missions, but I tell you this: you can't grow lilies from a scrub brush, now can you?"

Chrissy smiled at me again. "Ignore Clover. That's what I usually do when we're forced to work together." She dropped my hand and tapped her wand against her fingers. "Now let's talk about your wishes. As I understand it, you want to be a star. I could whip you up something along the lines of singing and dancing talent."

I kept staring at Chrissy in disbelief. She was real. Standing in my hotel room. Talking to me. "I have a fairy godmother?"

Clover gave Chrissy an I-told-you-so look, then pointed in my direction, and mouthed, "Scrub brush."

"I'm not stupid," I told him. "I'm in shock. I didn't know people actually had fairy godmothers."

"Most people don't." Chrissy said airily. "Usually you have to do a selfless good deed to a beggar who happens to be a fairy in disguise. You, however, qualified for help on the FGA's pitiable and wretched damsel outreach program."

"Oh." It's never good news to hear your life has become so wretched that other species feel sorry for you.

Bits of glitter fell from the tip of Chrissy's wand, fluttering onto the floor. "I guess I should warn you that when the show airs, not only does it show you splattering the stage, the next three people who get Xed express their disappointment by imitating your event. By the end of the show, the judges pretend to vomit every time they think an act is bad. You go viral."

Oh no. I put my hand to my throat. "How many people are going to see it?"

Chrissy looked upward, calculating. "Do you mean when the show airs or after the segment hits the internet and people make remixes of your audition?"

My legs felt weak. I sunk onto the nearest bed.

Clover disappeared from his spot and the next moment reappeared next to me. He patted my arm with his tiny hand. "Look on the bright side, lass. You always wanted to be famous for your singing."

"And," Chrissy added, opening her purse, "your crush said you were pretty. So, you know, that's cool."

Well, it might have been if he hadn't also said I had no talent and then watched me puke on my shoes.

Chrissy dug around in her purse until she pulled out what I thought was a lipstick tube. It grew longer and thicker, becoming a scroll of ivory paper covered in elegantly written handwriting. "You'll be able to improve your life with your wishes." She took hold of one end of the scroll and unrolled it. "Just as soon as you sign this waiver." The scroll kept unrolling until the end lay on the ground. "It's the standard fairy godmother contract."

Fairy godmothers had contracts? Somehow I'd missed that part of the Cinderella fairy tale.

"Make a careful reading of it," Clover muttered.

Chrissy waved away his words, deeming them unnecessary. "Most of the contract is written in longwinded legalese that's hard to understand. Basically what you need to know is this: Wishes are permanent and their consequences are real and lasting. You can't wish for more wishes or vague generalities like being popular or happy.

"Your wish has to be something tangible. Something I can actually make happen. Oh, and I wouldn't recommend wishing for magical powers. My last charge asked for the ability to change things into gold and then got all upset when she had to face an evil, megalomaniac fairy who wanted to kill her because of it. Seriously, sometimes mortals are so hard to please."

"Um . . ." I said. "What was that about an evil, megalomaniac fairy?"

"Don't worry about him. He's not a problem anymore." Chrissy kept unrolling. "One more thing. Since you didn't earn your fairy by doing a good deed, you have to pay attention to the honesty clause. While I'm acting as your fairy godmother, if you tell a lie—" She stopped unrolling and ran a finger down the words on the scroll, searching. "They just changed the consequences again because a bunch of tree nymph lobbyists worried about fire hazards . . . oh, here it is. 'If thou tellest a lie, thy nose shall grow and stay protruded until thou doth correct thine untruth.'"

I touched my nose gingerly. "Does that hurt?"

She shrugged. "Why? Are you the dishonest type?"

"No," I said quickly. I wasn't. But everyone tells white lies occasionally. The no-I-don't-think-your-boyfriend-is-a-jerk sort of thing. It would be horrifying if my nose randomly grew an inch during a casual conversation. "How long will you be acting as my fairy godmother?"

"That depends on how long it takes you to use your wishes."

Even with the threat of possible nose growth, I didn't want to turn down her offer. I mean, having magic wishes could solve so many of my problems. I would just have to be careful to be completely honest.

Chrissy reached the end of the scroll and handed it to me. While I scanned the long looping words, she pulled a quill from her purse and handed it to me too.

I hesitated for a moment, but only for a moment. Any dangers magic might present were dwarfed by the thought of my audition going viral. People were going to do remixes of my audition. I couldn't let that happen. I signed my name and handed the quill and contract back to Chrissy. She tugged on the end of the scroll, and it rolled up like a window shade.

"Now then," she said, tucking the scroll back in her purse. "What do you wish for?"

Easy. "Can you change something that's already happened? Can you make me do great on my audition—so good, I win the show?"

Her lips pursed in dissatisfaction. "That sort of time travel is tricky. If I change the audition, you would no longer qualify under the pitiable and wretched outreach program, which would mean I couldn't be your fairy godmother, which would mean I couldn't grant you that wish in the first place. Do you see the paradox that creates?" She fluttered pink fingernails in my direction. "Please spare me the paperwork. The paradox office is a hassle to work with."

There had to be a way to get around that. "If I wished it, could you make the tape of my audition self-destruct, then make the show give me another audition, and make my voice perfect from now on?"

"Yes." Chrissy raised her wand. "That's three wishes. Is it what you want?"

Behind me, Clover cleared his throat. "Psst. Scrub Brush, you might want to think that over a wee bit more carefully."

"No, those aren't my wishes," I answered. I hadn't realized how fast I could spend them. I needed to phrase things better so I only used one wish. If I said "I wish to win the *America's Top Talent* competition," Chrissy would have to work whatever magic necessary to make that happen, and I would only use one wish.

Then again, what if my wish made the audition go so viral the show offered to make me an honorary winner as a publicity technique. That wouldn't actually make things any better.

"Listen, lass," Clover padded across the bed until he stood in my line of sight. "Don't just think on what will make you happy now. Choose something that will still be making you happy ten years from now." He nodded knowingly and looped his thumbs through the buttonholes of his jacket. "Gold is a popular choice."

Clover was right. I needed to look at the big picture. I didn't want to just win the *America's Top Talent* show. That had always been a stepping stone to my real goal—being a successful singer.

Chrissy glanced at her bracelet, and I noticed a watch face nestled among the twisting beads. "I hate to rush you," she said, "because I'm the kind of godmother who is compassionate, thorough, and understanding—and please remember to use those words should you be contacted by the FGA with a customer satisfaction survey—but I've got to go soon. I have a job interview."

Clover let out an amused scoff. "What is it you'll be interviewing for this time? Another stint as a tooth fairy?"

"No," she said with an offended sniff. "Used teeth are totally disgusting. I'm applying for a part-time position as an insomnia fairy."

"Insomnia fairy?" I asked. "There are fairies for that?"

Chrissy's wings spanned open and closed. "It's not widely known among mortals. People who know about us get all uppity and do totally unreasonable things like bar their windows with iron and try to zap us with dark magic."

She smoothed her shirt and flecks of glitter sprinkled on the floor. Housekeeping would wonder what I'd done in this room. "People always wish they had more time to get things done, but no one is ever grateful when we give it to them."

Probably because no one wants to get anything done at 2:00 a.m. except sleep. I didn't say this. I just made a mental note never to wish I had more time.

Chrissy checked her watch again. "I can only stay a few more minutes."

I opened my mouth to wish to be a famous rock star and then decided on different wording. I'd heard a few rock stars whose voices weren't that great. They had to rely on autotune to produce decent albums, and every time they performed live they sounded bad. I needed more talent—so much talent I never had to worry about messing up during a number again.

"I wish to have such a beautiful voice," I said slowly, "that I'm famous, adored for generations, and . . ." I hadn't meant to add the next part. The words came out impulsively, as though they wanted to be said. ". . . loved by Jason Prescott."

Granted, the guy had criticized me on national television, but he'd only said those things because he didn't know me. I wasn't the type of girl who had things handed to her. I practiced long and hard. If he got to know me, he would see that.

Chrissy lifted her wand. "You don't want to use a wish to erase your audition tape? It will go viral if you don't."

I shook my head. "I can live through that as long as I know I'll have a voice I'm famous and loved for." A sort of giddy excitement filled me, warming my thoughts. I would not only become a rock star, I'd be one with real, lasting talent.

I suddenly regretted not giving a timeframe to my wish. It wouldn't do me a lot of good if I didn't become a great singer until I was sixty. As Chrissy waved her wand, I called out, "How long will it take?"

Hundreds of sparks burst from the tip of the wand, surrounding me until the hotel room disappeared behind the winking lights. "Not long," she said.

The tingle of magic brushed against my skin. Everything seemed weightless, as though I was floating. Cloudlike wisps curled around me, and ribbons of sunrise-colored steam twisted through the lights. What would it be like to be famous? How was it going to happen? I could hardly wait to try out my beautiful new voice.

As the lights cleared, I had one glimpse of a cloudy sky above me, and the next moment I plunged downward into cold water.

Chapter 3

I had expected many things from my magic wish. None of them involved falling into a giant body of water. Tiny bubbles whooshed around me, licking my skin. I couldn't see the bottom or sides of a pool. I was in something bigger—a lake or an ocean. I held my breath and swam upward toward the light wavering on the water above me. I swam fast, filled with the adrenaline of surprise. I broke through the surface, sputtering. "What in the—" My voice didn't sound any different, which was another surprise. I thought it would.

Steel blue waves lapped around me, stretching out as far as I could see. An ocean. Several clouds roamed through the sky, but the air felt warm. As I became used to it, the water did too. I pushed strands of wet hair away from my eyes. Why had Chrissy put me here?

I turned around and I noticed a ship a few hundred feet in the distance behind me. Several white sails billowed from its towering masts. The ship was midsized, made from weathered wood, with a silhouette of a woman carved into the prow. Some sort of odd decorations rimmed the side. Over all, the ship looked like something out of a pirate movie. I hadn't realized anyone still made boats like that.

A tour ship? A yacht owned by an eccentric history buff? Whatever it was, it was the only boat within sight, and I needed help.

"Hey!" I yelled and stroked toward it. Chrissy had probably meant to put me on the ship and she'd missed. That was the downside, I supposed, of having a fairy godmother still in training. "Hey!" I yelled again. "Woman overboard! Help!" The boat wasn't moving fast. I could catch up to it, but I wasn't sure which end to swim to. I didn't see any sort of ladder. Hopefully someone had a long rope they could throw down.

A man appeared at the ship's rail. He was round-faced with a scraggly blond beard and a bandanna tied around his head. He saw me, did a double take, and called to someone behind him. A tall man joined him at the rail. He had a bushy brown beard and wore a wide-brimmed hat over his tangled hair. Both men stared at me in puzzlement.

"What's a wench doing out 'ere in the ocean?" the man in the bandanna asked.

I couldn't tell them my fairy-godmother-in-training had bad aim and missed the boat. "I fell in the water," I called back. The honesty clause in my contract stopped me from providing more details. "Can you help me get onboard?"

The man in the hat leaned further over the rail, eyeing me suspiciously. "She couldn't 'ave fallen overboard. We ain't got no women on the ship."

The man in the bandanna cocked his head. "Unless the prince brought one along that we know nothing about. Royalty does what they likes. I'll go tell the captain." To me he yelled, "You hang on, m'lady, and we'll drop the longboat for you."

Prince? M'lady? I took a better look at the men. The grayish long sleeve shirts they wore seemed old-fashioned. Just like the ship. Now that I was closer, I could see the decorations rimming the side weren't decorations at all. They were the ends of cannons.

Little bursts of alarm pumped through me. This couldn't be right. Had Chrissy sent me back in time?

No, she wouldn't have. There weren't any rock stars hundreds of years ago.

The man in the hat squinted at me. "Blimey. She ain't got no clothes on."

Oh no! Had Chrissy messed up my wish so badly she'd dropped me naked into an ocean?

I crossed my arms over my chest and looked down. I wasn't naked. My wet hair covered most of it, but I wore an odd plastic bikini top made out of large pale shells. I guess I should have expected someone with pink hair to come up with this sort of outfit. I sunk lower in the ocean so less of me was visible. "I'm not naked," I yelled back to the man. "I've got a bathing suit on."

Three more scraggly men arrived at the ship's rail. "A naked wench?" the first asked.

"Where?" the second added.

"Let me see."

The first man cocked his head. "What's she doing out 'ere in the ocean?"

One of the men pulled out a spyglass and pointed it in my direction.

I sunk lower into the water and gritted my teeth. "If you don't mind, I could use some help."

The sailor with the spyglass lowered it. "She's got on naught but her unmentionables."

Another leaned over the rail, gawking at me. "She must have taken off her dress. Them skirts women wear—they could drown a whale, they could." He cupped his hand to the side of his mouth. "Keep swimming. I'll ready the longboat."

"Nay, don't." A man with stringy black hair crossed himself once, then twice, as though the first time might not have worked. "The wench is a mermaid. Mark my words, seeing one is always a portent of trouble."

The man with the hat put his hands on the rail and smiled an oily smile. His teeth were yellow and crooked. "Seems more like a piece of luck to see such a pretty thing out here." He motioned to me. "Swim closer, dearie, and tell us your name."

Eww. Creepy. The guy was old enough to be my father. Were all the men on the ship like this? I looked to the left and to the right, out at the waves that sloshed in every direction. "Um, are there any other boats nearby?"

The wind caught the men's shirts and rippled them like a row of dirty gray flags. The sailor with stringy black hair shook a scolding finger in my direction. "Don't listen to anything she says. Mermaids lure men to their destruction."

I glared back at him. "I'm not a mermaid. See, I'll prove it. I've got legs." I leaned back in the water and lifted up my feet.

Only, they weren't feet anymore. Where my legs should have been, glistening teal scales spread upward, each as intricate and interconnected as feathers on a bird's wing. They tapered into a tailfin that spread out at the top like a lace fan.

I let out a startled scream, which was nearly as loud as the men's startled screams. In disbelief, in horror, I moved my tailfin up and down. It felt so natural, so much a part of me, that I hadn't even noticed I didn't have legs. What had Chrissy done to me? I was half fish.

"I told you she was a mermaid!" the man with the stringy black hair yelled. He stumbled back away from the rail. "We'll have bad luck now!"

"You think *you'll* have bad luck?" I coughed out. "I'm the one without legs. *That's* bad luck." I submerged my tailfin in the water again. I didn't want to see it anymore. Shallow, panicked breaths pumped through my chest. A scream of indignation was fighting to come out.

Chrissy had to fix this. She had to. I gazed upward, as though I might see her lounging about in the air. "Chrissy!" I shouted. "I need to speak to you!"

She didn't show up. Only clouds and sky lolled about above me. "Chrissy!"

The man with the stringy black hair followed my upward gaze, checking to see what I was looking at. "Now she's yelling something unholy!"

By that point I was yelling quite a few things, many of which were definitely unholy.

The man crossed himself again and returned his attention to the water. "Soon we'll be surrounded by an entire school of fish folk. Surrounded, and us still not in sight of shore."

As soon as he'd given this pronouncement of doom, two dark shadows rippled underneath the water below me. I didn't know what they were and didn't want to put my face underwater to find out. *Please*, I thought, *not sharks*. Let them be seals, or dolphins, or friendly passing turtles.

I headed sideways, darting out of their way. I was fast in the water, slicing through the waves effortlessly. The shadows followed, then sped up and circled around me. Whatever they were, they weren't just randomly passing by. They were after me.

My heart pounded in a frantic rhythm. I swam toward the ship, tail pumping so urgently I didn't need to use my arms to propel myself. The ship was the only shark-free place around and I was ready to climb the side using my fingernails. Before I could enact this plan, the shadows cut around in front of me. They were coming up to the surface.

I braced myself, ready to fight. But instead of gaping, serrated mouths, two teenage girls popped out of the waves. Water streamed from their hair, down their shoulders, and past their shell bikinis.

The closest girl had long blonde hair decorated with shells and starfish. Her blue eyes had a tint of purple in them, and she had the pretty, perky look of a cheerleader. The second girl was beautiful in a more angular, sophisticated way. Rows of pearls twisted through her long brown hair like jeweled streamers. Her green eyes regarded me disapprovingly. "That's it. We're staging an intervention."

"What?" I'd had so many shocks I couldn't think straight. It barely registered these girls must be mermaids too.

The blonde folded her arms and made a gesturing nod at the ship. "Don't pretend you weren't just talking to those humans."

"Blow me down!" a sailor exclaimed. "Two more of them showed up!"

The black-haired sailor scanned the waves. "I told you they'd attack the ship. Dozens are probably circling us."

The sailor in the bandanna motioned for the spyglass. "Are all of them dressed in their unmentionables?"

Both girls ignored the men and waited for my answer. I

swallowed, feeling helpless. "There's been a mistake. I'm not supposed to be a mermaid."

The brunette girl rolled her eyes. "Oh, not this again. Look, I don't care how handsome that prince guy is. You're not human and never will be. And if you think—"

The blonde girl held up a hand to stop the other mermaid's words. "Let me handle this, Daphne."

The brunette, Daphne, let out a humph.

"The prince . . ." I repeated weakly. The pieces fell together, interlocking in my mind to reveal a picture—a story. It couldn't be coincidence, could it? I put my hand to my throat. "I'm in love with a prince?"

The blonde mermaid let out a sigh. "I think the correct term is infatuated. I mean, you can't *really* love him. The guy doesn't know who you are."

I said several things at that point, all of them completely unholy, and all of them directed at my absent fairy godmother. Underneath the water, I flicked my tailfin back and forth angrily, stirring up a current. "I'm the Little Mermaid, aren't I?"

The other mermaids—my sisters, I supposed—exchanged a patient look. Daphne swam over and put her hand on my shoulder. Her large green eyes turned sympathetic. "Just because you're the youngest, that doesn't mean Marina and I don't take your feelings seriously."

Marina, the blonde mermaid, nodded. "Interspecies crushes never work out. Trust us on this one." She took hold of my hand and pulled me a few feet farther away from the ship. The water made parting ripples around us, blue and sparkling. "You need to come home now," Marina said. "If you stay out here too long, you'll get sunstroke."

Daphne glowered in the boat's direction. "Or netted by those vicious barbarians."

"Or speared," Marina agreed.

I couldn't go home. I was half fish. And in a fairy tale. And none of this was supposed to happen. But if I said this to the other mermaids, they'd think I'd already succumbed to sunstroke.

I took deep breaths, trying to calm myself. When lost, it was best to stay put until someone found you. I was lost now, and Chrissy needed to find me. She had to undo this, to change me back.

I pulled away from the Marina and Daphne. "I can't leave yet. I need to talk to someone. It's really important."

My sisters exchanged another look, this one not so patient.

Before either of them spoke again, a loud voice rumbled from the ship. "What the—what's going on? Who are you people? Where am I?"

The guy wasn't close enough to the side of the ship that I could see him, but he sounded familiar. I listened, drifting closer to the ship.

"You—yes, you—get me a latte and a cell phone." There was a small pause and then a moan of frustration. "I don't even remember leaving a party last night. How did I get here and why is the floor moving?"

The sailors at the side of the ship turned toward the voice and bobbed their heads in curt bows.

"Your Highness," a simpering man near the rail ventured. "Beggin' your pardon, Sire. I would happily get you a latte and . . . whatever the other thing was you asked for . . . if I only knew what they were and where to fetch them."

The prince let out an unsympathetic grunt. "Have you

been living under a rock? How could you not know what a latte is? It's coffee, only better. Go get one."

A sinking feeling took hold of my stomach. I recognized the voice now. It was Jason. He was the prince.

A lot of apologetic murmuring came from the men on the ship, and then Jason's voice rang out again. "Where is my assistant? Gordon! Gordon—get out here!"

I put my face in my hand. This was how Chrissy was fulfilling my wish? She'd kidnapped Jason Prescott and made him the prince in a fairy tale? Yeah, that would make him love me for sure. What guy wouldn't fall for a pathetic fangirl turned mermaid?

"My contract," Jason yelled, punctuating each word, "states I only stay at five-star hotels. This dump doesn't rate one star. It doesn't even rate one of the pointy parts of a star. And what is that awful smell? No—don't come closer. *You're* the smell." A smacking noise came from the boat as though Jason was batting someone away.

Marina glided over to me, barely disturbing the water around her. "So *that's* the guy you like?"

Daphne joined us. She shook her head slowly. "Sorry, there's not enough handsome in the world to make that guy look good." She leaned closer to the boat, sunlight glowing across the shells adorning her head. "You can't actually believe you're in love with him."

"Um . . ." I answered. I didn't know what else to say.

"Sire!" one of the sailors motioned to the water. "What are your orders concerning the mermaid infestation?"

"Mermaid infestation?" Jason asked with a scoff. "One of us drank too much last night, and I'm beginning to think it wasn't me."

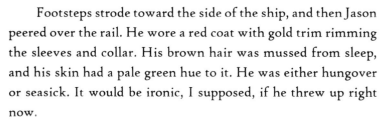

Footsteps strode toward the side of the ship, and then Jason peered over the rail. He wore a red coat with gold trim rimming the sleeves and collar. His brown hair was mussed from sleep, and his skin had a pale green hue to it. He was either hungover or seasick. It would be ironic, I supposed, if he threw up right now.

He stared blankly at us. "Is that water down there?"

Daphne and Marina both laughed. The sound was musical, like lilting bells. "He's charming and *smart*," Daphne said.

Jason's gaze narrowed in on me, as though he recognized me but didn't remember from where.

Marina grabbed my arm. "We've seen enough. Let's go." Her grip tightened and she dived downward, dragging me into the depths of the water.

I struggled, twisting as I tried to swim back toward the ship. But then Daphne took hold of my other arm, and the two of them pulled me along with them. They were strong. I could only wave my tailfin in protest, watching the sunlit surface grow more distant.

I was afraid I was going to drown, which would have been just my luck—to drown while being a mermaid.

Chapter 4

I didn't dare take a breath. One part of my brain knew mermaids must be able to breathe underwater, but I wasn't a real mermaid. I was a girl that a fairy godmother—no, a *fair* godmother—turned into a mermaid. What if she'd forgotten to give me mermaid lungs, or gills, or whatever they used?

I gestured wildly upward.

Sign language is something I'm apparently not good at. The mermaids only glanced at me and kept dragging me deeper.

"What's with her?" Daphne asked Marina. She actually spoke the words, though I wasn't sure how she'd done it underwater, or how I'd heard her.

"I think it's human dancing," Marina answered. "You know how the savages shake their arms about when they're making merry."

Daphne and Marina didn't use their hands to swim. Their tailfins waved in smooth arcs, propelling us downward. "Humans are a bad influence," Daphne muttered. "Next she'll be strapping heels on her fins and wearing a corset."

"It's sad how humans torture their women." Marina shot me a reproving look. "Really, what do you have to say for yourself?"

I said the only thing I could, which was "Mmrrr mm eemm mm!" It meant "Let me go now," only it didn't come out sounding that way, and they kept dragging me deeper. The water was warmer and clearer than I expected, or maybe it just seemed that way because I was a mermaid. I could see so much. Bits of seaweed drifted peacefully in the current. Gray fish lumbered by without paying any attention to us.

Below in the distance, a huge rock city spread out along the bottom of the ocean. Hundreds of buildings—some made from tan stone, others from black, orange, and white—glistened in the streams of sunlight that fingered down from the surface. A white castle sat in the middle of the buildings, its rock towers piercing the water. Gleaming blue flags waved lazily back and forth from its spires. It was probably my mermaid home.

I couldn't hold my breath any longer. My lungs ached. The remaining air went from my mouth in a rush of fleeing bubbles, and I gasped inward. I expected pain, choking, something. Instead, breathing the water felt like breathing air.

I gulped in and out several times, amazed and relieved. I wasn't going to drown.

As intriguing as the city below me looked, I didn't want to go there. I was afraid if I agreed to any of this, I would be stuck in the fairy tale forever. Perhaps if I explained the situation to the other mermaids, they could help me. Maybe they knew how to get a hold of fairy godmothers.

"Listen, I don't know how to say this . . ." I glanced up at the distant water of the surface. It seemed like a dark blue sky, cloudless and shining. "This is all a big mistake."

"I'm glad you finally realize that." Marina kept pulling me toward the white castle, her tailfin effortlessly pumping back and forth. "If Dad finds out you were prince-gazing again, he'll go tidal."

Daphne nodded, brown hair streaming behind her. "Remember how he stormed around, throwing waves everywhere after he heard that song you wrote about the prince?"

Marina pursed her lips at the memory as though it tasted sour. "We were picking palm trees out of the coral gardens for days."

"What song?" I'd written more than one song about Jason Prescott, but I'd never told anyone they were about him. Had Chrissy known somehow? Had she used my songs in this fairy tale?

"What song?" Marina repeated incredulously.

Daphne gave an extra hard tailfin kick and sang: *If I had feet, I'd use them for pace'n, because I'm so crazy about my Prince Jason.*

I had definitely never written those lyrics. I still blushed though, because the Little Mermaid version of me had. It was probably a bad sign that I was pathetic in more than one world. "You don't understand," I said over the next stanza.

His eyes are so dreamy, I'd love to be his queenie.

"I'm a human who was accidentally turned into a mermaid."

At least I hoped it was an accident. I hoped Chrissy wasn't so completely bad at granting wishes she thought a wish for a beautiful singing voice was a request to live out a Disney movie.

Daphne slowed down enough to regard me. "Great. She must have been in the sun too long. Now she's delirious."

"No," Marina said with a frustrated sigh. "She's in love. It makes girls act like they're delirious."

On our way to the city, we swam toward a large school of silver fish. They turned to go around us, prodded by two larger, yipping fish with long whiskers. I hadn't realized fish could yip, and I stared at their mottled brown bodies and flapping fins.

This place was so odd.

"Ho there, princesses!" A merman with a braided black beard appeared behind the school, carrying a hooked shepherd staff. His tailfin was curved and gray like a dolphin, and he wore a bag strapped to his waist. He swam casually in our direction, giving us a quick bow of deference. "Are you checking on your father's herds?"

"No," Marina answered with a dainty wave of her free hand. "We're just out taking a morning swim."

"Fine day for it." The merman noticed my sisters' grip on my arms but didn't comment on it. He motioned to one of the yipping fish, and it directed the rest of the school to swim by.

When we'd passed them, Marina looked over her shoulder at him. "Do you think he suspects anything?"

Daphne snorted. "You mean from the girl who sang, *Pace'n Over Jason* a few days ago and is now being hauled home by her sisters? No, I doubt he suspects a thing."

I tried again to explain my situation again. "You see, I made a wish. The magic must not have worked right—"

"Magic?" Marina cut me off, alarmed.

Daphne stopped swimming and drew herself up so that we were vertical. Her hair swirled upward like the flame of a candle, and her tailfin twitched in agitation. "You didn't make a deal with the sea witch, did you? You know magic causes nothing but trouble."

Yeah. I was beginning to realize that.

Marina put her hand to her lips and blinked in worry. "You'll end up as sea foam before your time. Tell me you didn't bargain with the witch."

"I didn't." This was true. I'd signed a contract with a fairy.

Satisfied, Daphne and Marina pulled me toward the city again. "If you really care about your prince," Daphne said, "the best thing you can do is stay away from him. Even if you found some magical way to bring him here without drowning him, well . . . how do I put this delicately?" Without attempting to be delicate, she said, "Someone would kill him."

"Dad especially would kill him," Marina agreed. "Humans are just a bunch of nasty fish thieves."

Daphne lowered her voice. "Dad would've already locked you up somewhere, except we told him the reason you keep going to the surface is so you can practice luring ships to their doom."

Luring ships to their doom? Seriously? I'd always thought mermaids were nice creatures.

"Which reminds me," Marina put in cheerfully. "Dad is having one of his advisors look into the Siren Foreign Exchange Student Program for you."

"Your singing is amazing," Daphne added with a note of pride. "You'd make a great Siren."

In Greek mythology, Sirens were creatures who sang so irresistibly that sailors blindly followed their voices. The sailors then crashed their ships onto the rocks and drowned.

I decided right then not to tell my mermaid sisters I was actually human. Even if I found a way to convince them it was the truth, I doubted they would take the news well.

As we drew closer to the city, I saw street-like swimming

channels twisting through the buildings. Kelp as big as trees grew everywhere, their broad leaves swished rhythmically, bending and swaying in the currents. Merfolk in an assortment of colors swam through the channels. Several glided slowly, talking together. Others shot through the water with eel-like grace. A few mermen rode near the castle in dolphin-harnessed chariots. They wore turtle-shell armor around their chests and carried spears.

Curved white lampposts lined the street, each with a large luminescent jellyfish tethered at the end, drifting up and down. As I swam past one, I realized the posts were bones—probably rib bones of a whale.

Even though I was seeing all of this, I could hardly believe it. Were there mermaids in my time period too? Could there be?

Daphne and Marina swam toward a window in one of the upper turrets of the castle. Once there, they deposited me inside the room. A large stone bed sat in one corner with puffy anemone pillows and a blanket made of woven seaweed. Elaborately-carved stone chairs sat at the other end of the room, each with thick algae for cushions. A chandelier made of small glowing jellyfish was tethered loosely to the ceiling. They drifted this way and that as they swam.

"We need to tend to the oyster gardens now," Daphne told me, her hands on her hips. "You'd better hurry and get ready to join your school."

I thought of the schools of fish I'd seen swimming around the city. Which was I supposed to join, and what was I supposed to do with them? "Uh, what school?"

Daphne gave me an exasperated look. "High school."

"Oh, right. I don't want to be late for that." Mermaids had high school? Who knew?

Marina glided over and put her hand on my forehead, feeling for a temperature. "Are you sure you didn't get too much sun? Maybe we should take you to see Doctor Gills."

"No, really I'm not sick." Freaking out, yes. Panicked, definitely. But not sick. The last thing I wanted was someone asking me a lot of questions I couldn't answer without lying. It was bad enough having fins. I didn't want an oddly long nose too. "I'll be fine. I'm just . . . not feeling like myself."

Marina dropped her hand away from my forehead. "All right. Go to school, behave, and we won't tell Dad about your latest surface excursion."

Daphne sent me an encouraging smile. "Tonight there's a party at that new shipwreck. We can cruise around for cute mermen. I bet we'll find someone you like."

Yeah, no matter how cute the guy, I wasn't going to be able to get past the whole scaly tailfin issue. I know, call me a hypocrite.

I glanced around the room again. I needed to get out of here. I knew what happened in *The Little Mermaid* story. The prince's ship had an accident, and the Little Mermaid saved him drowning. Would that event happen soon? Later tonight? Tomorrow maybe?

A closed door stood behind me, most likely leading to other rooms in the castle tower. The window offered my best bet for escape—although with so many merpeople swimming around the city, it wouldn't be easy to swim back to Jason's ship unnoticed.

If Chrissy didn't show up soon, at least I knew how to get out of being a mermaid. In the story, the Little Mermaid traded her voice to the sea witch in exchange for being human. Not being able to talk would sort of suck. Ditto for living in a century without electricity or indoor plumbing, but at least the story ended well—with me being human, getting back my voice, and the prince falling in love with me.

At that moment I remembered an important fact. When Disney made The Little Mermaid into a movie, they changed the ending of the story. In the original version, the prince married someone else, the Little Mermaid died brokenhearted, and angels carried her soul away. I'd only read that story once—been horrified—and then pretended the Disney version was the real story.

My heart was beating so hard I thought it might start rattling my clamshell bikini. Which version had Chrissy put me in? She wouldn't have put me in the sad version, would she? I'd wished for Jason to love me.

But then, loving someone and marrying them were two different things. I vaguely recalled that the prince loved the Little Mermaid in a platonic, totally unsatisfying, let's-just-be-friends sort of way.

How could I figure out which version I was in? I drifted closer to Daphne, brushing away a couple passing clownfish that had taken an interest in my hair. "Um, do I have any friends who are singing crabs?"

Daphne raised her eyebrows. "I don't know. Do you?"

No good. I would have to come out and ask a direct question. "What's my name?"

Marina put her hand back on my forehead. "The sunstroke must be worse than I thought."

"It's Ariel, right?" My voice went higher, as though hope and the right inflection could make it true.

Daphne frowned. "Last time I checked, it was Sadie."

Sadie. My name. Had Chrissy changed the story so now

the Little Mermaid had my name? Or could Sadie have possibly been the mermaid's name in the original story? Now that I thought about it, the author only ever called the main character the Little Mermaid . . . which meant her name could have been anything—even Sadie.

Crap.

I was *so* not selling my voice to the sea witch if it meant I would die a tragic death, unloved by Jason. Hello, I was already unloved by Jason in my real, normal life. I didn't need to live it in fairy tale form too.

Daphne and Marina were still regarding me, worry etched on their expressions. "Maybe we'd better have Dr. Gills stop by."

"No need," I said quickly. "I totally remember my name is Sadie . . . and I should be getting ready for school." I glanced around the room again. I had no idea what mermaids did to get ready for school. Did they wear uniforms? Carry backpacks? My eyes stopped at a mirror hanging on the wall, and for the first time I caught sight of myself as a mermaid.

Strings of pearls twined through my hair along with flower-like pink anemones. Weirder still, several clownfish were poking through the anemones. They followed the movements of my head like little orange fish groupies.

I moved my tailfin forward and back, searching for any sign of my legs underneath it. I couldn't get used to the shiny teal scales. My scales had a ridge where my fish half connected to my hips—as though the tailfin was a size bigger than the rest of my body. That didn't seem right.

I twisted so I could see my back. "Does this tailfin make me look fat?"

"You're right," Daphne told Marina. "She's delirious."

"Maybe I should rest instead of going to school." I attempted to look wan and tired, slowly floating toward my bed. I also let out a sputter of a cough. Coughing is not lying, so my nose didn't grow.

Marina eyed me suspiciously. "Is that why you're spouting off nonsense? You want to skip school?"

Daphne folded her arms, tapping her nails against the crook in her elbow. "If you need to rest, you should. And to make sure you stay in your room all day, we'll ask one of castle guards to keep an eye on your window." She raised a challenging eyebrow. "Still want to skip school?"

I nodded even though I felt like a mermaid juvenile delinquent. What else could I do? I needed to contact Chrissy. It was better to do that alone in my room than to try and fake my way through whatever subjects they taught in aquatic high school.

Daphne sent me one last disapproving look, then she and Marina turned, scales glinting in the water, and swam out of my window. I put my elbows on the windowsill and watched as they made their way to the castle's courtyard. Rows of coral and kelp trees lined the square, interspersed by stone archways. A dozen large mermen with turtle shell armor were patrolling the castle grounds, hefting hooked spears on their shoulders.

Daphne and Marina swam to the nearest guard and pointed in my direction. He turned his gaze at the window, surveying me. I half expected him to leave his post, swim to my window, and stand watch there. Instead he moved a few feet so he had a better view of my window. He leaned against one of the archways in a bored manner, every once in a while glancing in my direction.

I retreated back into the bedroom, out of his sight, and sat on a stone chair. One thought repeated through my mind: I needed to get hold of Chrissy and tell her she'd made a mistake. My mother was going to come back to the empty hotel room and assume something horrible had happened to me. Besides, I couldn't just leave my whole world and live out a mermaid fantasy. I had homework due on Monday. I had to rehearse for the end-of-the-year choir concert. And I had a phobia of sharks.

I called Chrissy softly, letting her name drift upward on the water currents. I called her sternly, pleadingly, desperately. I hung out of my window and searched for her among the swaying kelp trees and coral gardens.

Nothing. I knew she had a job interview, but really, how long could that take?

In between calling, I explored my room, hoping to find something that would help me. I found a harp and a flute. Not much help. Inside a shell-encrusted dresser, a dozen stiff bikini tops waited to be worn. Another drawer held jewelry and hair combs. I slipped on a pearl bracelet to see how it looked. Pretty. I may be a mermaid, but at least I was a rich mermaid with style.

A jumbo snail made its way—leaving a trail of slime—across the top of my dresser. Was it a pet or just something that had wandered inside? Really, those were the sorts of details Chrissy should have told me before dropping me into a story.

A metal cup with an English insignia sat on the dresser. Probably from a shipwreck. It held quill pens whose pale feathers undulated in the current. Did quill pens work in the water? I picked one up and realized it wasn't a pen. It was some sort of thin spiny creature that let out a tiny shriek, pulled its feathers inside its shell and squirted black liquid from its bottom. I quickly dropped the thing back into the cup and wiped black stuff off my fingers. Gross. Butt ink.

You know, mermaid life seemed more quaint and charming in the movie.

A short knock sounded on my door, and then the door swung open revealing a large merman. He didn't look like Disney's King Triton. Instead of white hair, his hair and beard were a brownish green, as though algae had taken hold there. He was also younger than his cartoon version, but I still knew he was the undersea king.

A coral crown sat atop his head, and he wore a gilded breastplate. But even if he hadn't worn these adornments, I would have still pegged him as the Little Mermaid's father. It was in the look he sent me. Half concern, half frustration.

He swooshed into the bedroom with one flick of his powerful tailfin. "Your sisters said you were sick."

I sat down on the bed and attempted to look ill. "I threw up earlier."

He cocked an eyebrow like he didn't believe me, but didn't press the subject. Instead he sat beside me and put an arm around my shoulder. "Are the mermaids at school still giving you a bad time about your . . ." He sounded uncomfortable saying the words. ". . . your crush on that human fellow?"

I was getting mocked at mermaid high school? Honestly, how did Chrissy think this life was an improvement on my real one? I shrugged nervously. Anything I said would be a lie.

"Are they?" he prompted.

I gave him another shrug. "You know how mermaids are." He knew better than I did.

The king patted my shoulder consolingly. "It'll all wash over soon and they'll forget. Especially if you go study with the Sirens for awhile."

I shifted away from him. "I don't think I could do that. I

mean, it just seems cruel to lure sailors to their doom. They probably have families and stuff."

The king made a low, disapproving sound in the back of his throat. "Humans are nothing but selfish, arrogant creatures. The fewer of them, the better."

"They're not all like that." I wasn't. Although, come to think of it, when Chrissy offered me three wishes, I'd never even thought about asking for something altruistic. I vowed to change that. Next wish I'd do something good for the world.

The king let out an unhappy sigh. "Prince Jason is like the rest of his kind. What you feel for him is infatuation, not love. You need to learn the difference or you'll never be happy."

I wanted to say I did know the difference. I wasn't in love with Jason. I just thought the possibility for love existed.

"You don't really know anything about that boy," the king went on.

The Little Mermaid might not have known much about her prince, but I'd seen Jason interviewed. I knew all sorts of things about him. He loved snowboarding, dancing, and his dogs. He wrote his own songs, worked hard, and did charity benefits. He'd always seemed so nice. Back on the ship when he'd yelled and acted like a prima donna—he'd just been in shock. And who wouldn't be?

"How can you tell the difference between infatuation and love?" I'd meant the statement as a challenge. It tapered off somewhere in the middle, becoming a question instead.

The king dropped his hand and looked at me solemnly. "When you can tell me the difference, I'll believe you're really in love."

I couldn't reply to that. What did I know? I'd never even had a boyfriend.

The king gave my shoulder another pat and stood. "I've meetings to attend, and you need your rest." He swam toward my door, but turned back before he left. "Think about what I've said." Then he was gone.

I did think about what he'd said—especially the part about me living with Sirens. I had to get out of here, had to get Jason out of here too.

I called Chrissy again.

Still nothing.

I floated around my room in a pacing sort of way and wondered what Jason was doing. Had he realized he was now the prince in the Little Mermaid? Had he figured out who I was? Did he know he needed to kiss me to break the sea witch's hold on me?

I'd never kissed a guy before, although I'd imagined more than once what it would be like to kiss Jason Prescott. Was it possible he'd be my first kiss? Instead of feeling expectant and dreamy, the thought prickled me with anxiety.

I knew you were supposed to shut your eyes when you kissed a guy, but if I shut my eyes, how could I tell where to put my mouth? What if I missed his lips altogether? Like most things I did the first time, I'd probably be horrible at it.

I called Chrissy again. She didn't come. My anger built as minutes stretched into hours. I circled around my room so fast the clown fish hovering near the anemones in my hair had a hard time keeping up. "You can't leave me at the bottom of the sea." I muttered. "My contract says I have three wishes."

Another knock came at the door, sending a spike of hope through me. Maybe Chrissy had come.

An older mermaid with a seal tail glided inside. "I thought you might be well enough for lunch."

"Oh. Thanks." I was hungry. I hadn't eaten since breakfast, and I'd deposited most of that food on the *America's Top Talent* stage.

A large sea turtle swept into my room, carrying a covered dish on his back. His eyes were half-lidded, like he was bored or sullen or both. He stopped by my bed, sunk to the floor, and sat there like a grumpy coffee table. He had been carrying utensils in his mouth but dropped them to nibble on the edge of my seaweed blanket.

Well, that was another difference between the mermaid world and mine. Unsanitary room service.

"Thanks," I told the woman.

She curtsied, swam back to the door, and shut it behind her.

I drifted over to the turtle table and lifted the dish lid to see what was for lunch. Fish slices. Raw fish, I supposed, since a fire would be impossible in the ocean. Even from where I stood, the fish smelled oily. The meal came with a seaweed salad, sprinkled with something I hoped weren't fish eggs.

I was going to starve here. The only seafood I liked was breaded, fried, and dipped in sauce. I took a spear from the floor and jabbed one of the slices. Maybe now that I was a mermaid, fish would taste good.

Lots of people ate sushi. And caviar was an expensive delicacy. Ditto for escargot and oysters. Instead of regarding the food here like it was something my cat would refuse, I should pretend I was in an exclusive, elitist restaurant.

"So," I said to the turtle, delaying taking a bite. "How long have you worked as a table?"

The turtle only stared back. Either he wasn't the talkative type or, despite what the Disney movie depicted, sea creatures weren't actually capable of speech. I didn't know which.

Sheesh. If someone had asked me yesterday if I thought crabs and fishes could perform song and dance numbers, I'd have laughed along with everyone else. Now that I knew fairies, leprechauns, and mermaids existed, anything seemed possible.

I turned the spear, peering at the fish slice from a different angle. "Is any of the castle food better than this?"

Again, no response.

"Okay, I'm ordering you to speak. I'm using my royal power and all that."

The turtle turned its attention to the food in my hand.

I tried again. "If you understand me, blink."

He didn't blink, in fact his head squished backward like he was trying to shrink into his shell.

This was not a reaction to my words. A shadow had blocked the light coming in from the window. Someone was there. Probably my guard. And he was most likely wondering why I was having a conversation with my table. I was going to end up with Dr. Gills for sure.

I turned to face him and stopped short. Instead of a merman, a huge squid was squeezing through my window.

Chapter 5

Maybe I was still jumpy because I hadn't fully adjusted to my mermaid surroundings, but having a giant squid invade my bedroom didn't seem like a good thing. I let out a startled scream, dropped the fish, and shot upward. This might have been a good way to escape if it hadn't been for the ceiling. I thunked my head into the stone there.

By the time my brain processed that I should have dashed out the door, the squid had slithered inside. He was enormous, eight feet tall at least, and coming toward me with unfurling tentacles. Each arm was covered in rows of suction cups; made for grabbing things.

I trembled and edged toward the door. Slow movements were best, weren't they?

The squid's overly-large black eyes surveyed me with interest. His beak looked like it could snap a hand off.

What, I wondered, was the point of having a guard watch my window if a huge squid could get by him? How did someone not see an eight-foot-long sea creature swimming toward my window?

I decided it would take too long to open the door. I should go around the squid and dash out the window—or maybe I should just throw my turtle table in the squid's direction and hope squids preferred shelled creatures to mermaids.

I was inching toward the window, when I noticed one of the squid's reaching tentacles held an envelope. There were several odd things about the envelope—odd beyond the fact a large squid clutched it. The envelope looked like it came from my century, it wasn't soggy, and my name was written on the front.

Was this how mermaids delivered mail? I drifted downward, warily keeping my eyes on the squid's still-waving tentacles. Either Chrissy or a mermaid must have sent it, which meant the squid was tame and wouldn't eat me. I supposed that was the reason the courtyard guard hadn't stopped it from coming inside. He was used to squid post. I put my hand to my chest, waiting for my heart to resume its normal rate.

The squid, determined to deliver the letter, advanced toward me, arm fluttering the letter in my direction.

I plucked the envelope from his tentacle and hoped he would leave now that his task was done. Instead, he hovered in front of me. Either his arms were drifting in a current, or he had no concept of personal space because his tentacles kept brushing against me, wavering like streamers in a strong wind.

I backed away, opened the envelope, and unfolded the letter. In a bouncy sort of handwriting, it read:

Sadie,

I hope your first day as a mermaid is everything you dreamed it would be!

Oh yeah, I'd always dreamed of abandoning my own culture in favor of dwelling in the bottom of the ocean and eating raw fish. And the squid that kept frisking me—bonus.

I pushed one of the squid's arms off my waist and kept reading.

The fairy godmothers' guild has proudly served the Deserving Mortals Community for more than fifty centuries, and each of us strives for excellence in meeting our charges' magical needs. However, as the ocean depths are out of the realm of forest fairies, I can't visit you in your new home, despite the fact that you keep sending me messages, like, every two minutes."

Even though I moved away from the squid, he followed me. His arms fluttered over me like he was trying to brush the water away from my skin. I slapped a tentacle off my shoulder and kept reading.

When you're ready to discuss your next wish, simply call from the surface and either Clover or I will attend to your request.

Remember, this is your time to make a big splash!

Magic is my business,

Chrysanthemum Everstar

The surface. I needed to go there so Chrissy could fix this mess. But how could I leave the city when I was under guard? My family wasn't about to let me go off by myself.

I untangled one of the squid's tentacles from where it was stuck in my hair. The clown fish that had been darting around my anemones were suspiciously absent. I hoped the squid hadn't eaten them.

PS In case you didn't know, mermaids of good breeding always tip a postal squid with food.

Well, that probably explained why the squid was still hanging around trying to eat my hairpiece. I swam to my lunch plate which now lay on the floor. The turtle had abandoned it and was hiding underneath my bed. I could see the tips of his green flippers sticking out one side. Coward.

I kept half of the fish slices in one hand and tossed the rest to the squid. Several of his arms shot out, grabbed the slices, and brought them to his beak. While he devoured the fish, another arm slid, snake-like, over my hand to retrieve the food there.

It's hard to tell where to look while addressing a squid. I focused on his huge black eyes instead of his waving tentacles. "If you want the rest of the fish, you have to do something for me. Do you understand?"

He dropped his tentacles away from my hand, so I figured that was a yes.

"I want to swim out of here without being seen by the merman who's watching my window. Can I swim beside you so you're between me and him?"

The squid just stared at me. I don't know why I expected a response. It was, after all, a squid. I took hold of one of his arms, up near his cone-shaped head. Either he agreed to my terms, or the way I'd grabbed him had spooked him. He shot forward toward my window.

I held on, glad he was an invertebrate. Otherwise we wouldn't have both fit through the opening. As it was, my back banged against the window edge. I decided to give the squid the benefit of the doubt and assumed that was accidental and not an attempt to scrape me off.

The squid darted away from the castle, letting out a stream of something dark and inky that obscured us from the mermaids below.

He was either helping my cover, or he was completely

freaked out that I still hung onto him. "Take me to Chrissy," I told him. "Take me to the fairy who gave you the letter."

He shot away from the city, the opposite direction from the way I'd come. Squids have jet propulsion, and he was using it. We rocketed so fast that the water felt like liquid silver streaming across my skin. He was either eager to take me to Chrissy or he was trying to shake me off. It was odd not knowing whether I was with the ocean version of Lassie or whether I was tormenting an innocent postal squid.

The city grew smaller and smaller, disappearing behind us into a blur of blue. Then, perhaps because I still hadn't let go, the squid swam toward the surface. When we'd nearly reached the top, I put the rest of the food in one of his tentacles and let go of his arm. Without a backward glance, he zoomed away back into deeper water.

"Thanks!" I called after him and pushed the last few yards to the surface.

More clouds had crowded into the sky, rumbling, and restless—ready to storm. On my right side, the endless expanse of the ocean stretched out before me. To my left, I saw the back of a ship. By the looks of it, it was the same one I'd run into earlier.

Jason's ship. It was heading toward land. The shore beyond the ship spread out in a brown line with the faint shape of trees feathering the shoreline.

Hopefully, Chrissy could hear me now. I called her name several times, waiting while choppy waves sloshed around me, lifting and lowering me. I called her name again. Nothing happened. No sparkles, no glitter. The clouds above let out a warning drizzle, a mist that dissolved into the water.

Chrissy had said the ocean was out of her realm. Maybe it

was hard to get here. I might have better luck if I went in closer to shore. Besides, I had nothing else to do. I sunk back into the ocean and swam in that direction.

I wasn't worried about the ship seeing me. I was far enough underwater that even if the men looked down at the waves, they wouldn't spot me. I meant to swim by without pausing. As I neared the boat, though, I heard Jason's voice.

Mermaids must have good hearing. His words were clear even under the water. "All of you, get away from me! I don't know who you are, but you won't get away with kidnapping me like this!"

Apparently his day hadn't gotten any better.

"Sire," one of the sailors called. "Come down from there. You'll fall."

I stopped swimming and listened.

"Police everywhere will be searching for me," Jason insisted. "I'm platinum in every major country and some you've never even heard of—I'm a hit in Botswana."

"No need to hit anyone's Botswana," a nervous sailor replied. "We're only trying to serve you."

"Serve me with what?" Jason demanded. "If you've got a subpoena, show it to me."

I drifted upward, making sure to keep behind the boat. Thick raindrops pocked the surface of the water, churning what little they could of the ocean.

"Sire, we be decent men. We ain't got no diseases, nor subpoenas neither."

A general murmur of agreement went up from the rest of the men. "Mind your footing, Your Highness. The ship ain't steady."

"Don't come any closer!" Jason shouted. "I know how to use this!"

What was Jason doing? I lifted my head out of the water to see. The wind shivered across the waves, prodding them higher. I spotted Jason easily enough. He stood on the ship's railing, clutching the end of a rope in one hand and a sword in the other. Rain spattered into him, dampening his hair so it stuck, cap-like, to his head. The way he held the sword made me doubt he knew how to use it.

The sailors formed a distant semi-circle around him, out of the sword's reach. A man holding a cup and saucer took a tentative step toward him. "Sire, come down from there and 'ave a nice cup of tea." Another step. "You can get out of the rain and sit in your cabin where it's nice and cozy-like."

I let out a sigh. Hopefully when Chrissy fixed this, she could make Jason think this had all been a dream.

I was about to sink back into the water and continue my swim to shore, when Jason slipped. The railing was drenched, and as he took a step, his boot went out from under him. He let out a yell, struggled to regain his balance, and dropped the sword. It clattered against the rail then fell, spinning on its way to the ocean. A moment later, Jason lost the fight for balance and tumbled backward, off the ship.

At first, I thought he would be okay. He had a hold of the rope and it was tethered on deck. Certainly part of his brain was screaming: Don't let go of the rope!

He should have listened to that part. Instead he made a grab for the railing. The wet, slippery railing. As he fell, his pathway took him directly into a protruding cannon.

I suppose if Jason's specialty was gymnastics instead of singing, he might have been able to right himself and stick an impressive landing on the cannon. Not only did he not right himself, he managed to hit his head on the cannon before plunging into the water.

If he lost consciousness, he'd drown.

I dove after him, worried about his injury and frustrated the fairy tale was playing out even though I didn't want it to. The Little Mermaid saved the prince from drowning, and here I was speeding to save Jason from that fate.

He sunk downward through the water, unmoving. A twisting trail of blood ran ribbon-like from the gash in his head.

Above me, the sailors let out panicked cries. "Your Highness! Your Highness!"

"Do you see him?"

"Lower the longboat and we'll go after him."

"Nay, dive in and retrieve him or our necks will be in the noose."

"Who can swim?"

No one answered.

Really? Sailors who couldn't swim? And no one had seen a problem with that fact when they commissioned the crew?

I pushed through the water until I reached Jason. Wrapping my arms around his chest in a hug, I swam upward. The metal buttons on his coat dug into my skin. I hardly felt them.

We broke the surface, and I held his head out of the waves, ignoring the wind that pushed ocean spray into our faces. Jason's eyes were closed. He made no attempt to open them, didn't move at all. Blood trickled down his forehead, mixing with the water running from his hair. I put my cheek against his mouth to see if he was breathing. He wasn't.

Fear made my chest feel tight. I wouldn't let myself consider the possibility that he was dead—that my wish had killed him. In the fairy tale, the Little Mermaid saved the prince and brought him to the shore. That's all this was. The next part in the story. Only why wasn't he breathing?

"There he is!" one of the men on the ship shouted. "Look, a mermaid has him!"

In junior high I'd taken a CPR class for babysitting certification. I tried to remember everything I'd learned, to think logically. Jason had probably breathed in water. How could I get it out? Was it possible to do mouth-to-mouth resuscitation while floating in the ocean? With the hope that the Heimlich maneuver might help clear his lungs, I unbuttoned his wool coat, and pushed the front open.

I moved behind him, wound my arms so my fists connected under his ribs, and made quick upward thrusts. The motion jerked us about, bobbing us up and down. Jason's arms flailed and his head flopped from one side to the next.

Several sailors let out alarmed cries. They crowded together at the side of the boat, gawking at us. "What's she doing?" one asked.

"You down there!" another shouted. "Leave him be! You've got no cause to beat on a defenseless man."

The best dressed of the men—most likely the captain— simply shook his head. "Our prince is being roughed up by a mermaid. This is not our nation's proudest moment."

Someone else shouted, "You can take her, Sire! C'mon! Give her the old heave ho!"

I was too busy Heimliching Jason to respond to any of them. I thought he had expelled some water but I couldn't be sure. I leaned backward, let him lie against me, and slid one hand over his chest to check for the rise and fall of breathing. I didn't find it.

A voice in my mind kept repeating Chrissy's warning. *Wishes are permanent, and their consequences are real and lasting.* Real and lasting. This was real and lasting. How long could Jason go without oxygen before he died?

To administer CPR I needed to do thirty chest compressions and then two rescue breaths. I'd only practiced with the dummy on the ground. I couldn't use the floor's resistance here. I would have to improvise. I moved my hands so they covered his heart and pressed thirty times, hard and fast at a speed of a hundred compressions a minute.

Next I twisted around so he faced upward. His face was smooth, expressionless, and achingly familiar. This was Jason Prescott. Famous. Beautiful. And dying.

In all the scenarios where I'd imagined pressing my lips to Jason's, I'd never envisioned doing it in front of a ship full of sailors while I tried frantically to save his life.

I tilted his head back, plugged his nose so the air didn't escape, then blew a breath into his mouth. His lips were cold and tasted like the sea.

Several men onboard let out shocked exclamations. "What in the—now she's doing something unnatural to him!"

"She's trying to suck his soul out through his mouth!"

"Aye, mermaids have no souls, so they go about stealing them."

"Nay, she's having her way with him. Mermen are unsightly creatures, which is why mermaids can't resist a bonnie sailor. Drawn to us like bees to a flower."

The men quietly considered this for a moment. "Weren't we going to lower the longboat?" a sailor asked. "I volunteer to man it."

As if. This bee wasn't interested in any of those grimy, unwashed flowers.

In my arms, Jason stiffened, jerked upward, and coughed water all over me. It trickled down my chin and neck. Pretty much the most unromantic end to a kiss possible.

Jason's eyes fluttered open and then fell shut again. He sunk into the water, and I had to tighten my grip around him so he didn't go under. He was breathing now but still wasn't conscious. The lump on his head had grown to the size of a golf ball and blood still leaked down his cheek. He needed help.

I could stay around and wait for the sailors to lower the longboat. They would take Jason back on board and get him warm and dry. But I doubted they were the best people to treat an injured man, and besides, I didn't like the net a couple of the men were holding. They seemed to be judging my distance from the boat, getting ready to toss the thing at me.

Yeah, this sort of treatment was probably why mermaids didn't like humans.

The shore wasn't far away. In the story, the Little Mermaid took the prince there—a fact that made me not want to do the same. It felt like I didn't have any choice, like the outcome of the story would engulf me no matter what I did. And I didn't know if I was in the happy version of the story.

Jason was hurt, though, and it was my fault. My wish had done this. I needed to take him to safety. With one arm hooked around his chest, I swam toward the shore.

Chapter 6

The men called after me, shouting and threatening to catch and fillet me if I didn't return the prince forthwith. I didn't turn around.

A mermaid's strength comes from her tail, so it wasn't hard to swim while holding onto Jason. I pushed across the surface, carefully keeping his head above water. The rain continued to come down and the wind had picked up, frosting the waves with white foam.

The closer I got to land, the worse the idea of bringing Jason here seemed. How could I drag an unconscious guy onto the beach? I didn't have legs. And as soon as I didn't have the water to help support Jason's weight, I wouldn't be able to carry him.

I swam toward the shore anyway in hopes someone would be around.

A building came into sight—perhaps a lighthouse. No, it was too short for that. Someone's home, maybe? I headed toward it.

There was a natural break in the shoreline there, a curve of the land that created a cove. As soon the waves entered it, they lost their fury and settled into a lapping, tired peace.

As I swam into the cove, I realized the building was actually a gazebo set on the edge of the shore. Its closest side spread across the water acting as a dock. Jason wouldn't have walls to protect him against the wind, but at least the roof would keep off the rain.

Hoisting Jason up onto the floor proved tricky. I didn't have the strength in my arms to lift him out of the water, and I accidentally banged his head against the stone floor trying. He let out a low moan.

"Sorry," I told him.

He didn't answer back.

The answer to this problem, I realized, was my tailfin. I'd been lifting Jason like a human would when I had an awesome, mythical tailfin at my disposal. If dolphins could leap out of the water several feet into the air, I could too.

Still holding onto Jason, I swam away from the gazebo, then sped back toward it.

Dolphins make leaping look easy. You see them in nature movies gracefully arcing out of the ocean. Playfully. Happily. Dolphins, it turns out, are liars.

My arc out of the water looked like I was being shot haphazardly from a cannon. I skidded into the middle of the gazebo—farther than I'd intended. Unfortunately, I also landed on top of Jason, something that made him let out another groan.

I slid off him and turned him face up. My movements were strained now that we were on land. It felt like I was dragging around a hundred-pound sack on a pair of useless legs.

Jason lay on the floor, pale and barely conscious. His lips

looked more purple than red, and blood still oozed from the wound on his head. He needed a bandage. The only thing I could use was the sash around his waist. It wasn't clean, but the pressure might stop the bleeding. I pulled it off and tied it over the cut.

His eyes flickered open and he coughed.

"Are you all right?" I asked.

His head turned at the sound of my voice. He stared at me blankly. Without recognition, without surprise—I wasn't sure he even saw me.

"Say something," I prodded.

"I'll fight every one of you," Jason slurred. "You better get my manager." He shut his eyes again and went still. I ran my hand across his cheek, hoping it would elicit a response. It didn't. He showed no other signs of reviving.

I couldn't leave him like this—wet, shivering, and likely to get hypothermia.

A path led from the gazebo into the trees. I scanned the fluttering leaves for signs of a traveler, for anybody. Shadows grew and shrank with the branch movement, but no one stepped forward. "Chrissy!" I called. "Where are you?"

I didn't get an answer except for another low moan from Jason. I pulled myself closer to him, and draped my arm across his chest, covering his legs with my tailfin so my body heat could warm him.

It was risky to stay on land. People here thought mermaids were dangerous. When someone finally showed up, what would they do when they saw me lying half on top of their wounded prince? Every moment I stayed out of the sea I was vulnerable and exposed.

I kept my gaze on the path that led to the gazebo. If anyone came that way, I'd pull myself back to the water before they reached me.

"Chrissy!" I called again. "I want to make another wish!" She had to come. She had to help Jason.

I saw no telltale sparklers going off. Only rain plunked down, tapping at the edges of the gazebo. I laid my head next to Jason's, dejected. "I'm so sorry about this." He couldn't hear me, but I had to say it anyway.

"There you are." The Irish brogue came from behind me, clipped with irritation. I turned to see Clover, dressed in green with a matching bowler hat perched on his head. He held a green umbrella, shaking the rain off it. "What problem is so terrible important, that you needed to drag me away from me poker game and have me trolling about in the rain searching for you?"

"What problem?" I pulled myself up on one elbow. "The problem is that Jason is injured, unconscious, and I'm a mermaid."

Clover snapped the umbrella shut. "Yes, well, it's been a bad day for all of us. I'd a full house. Aces high." He vanished from the spot where he'd stood, just disappeared.

I looked around the floor, wondering if he'd left altogether. "Clover?"

"The lad'll be fine." Clover had reappeared by Jason's head and was lifting the side of the bandage to see the wound. "He has a thick noggin. It's a common enough condition among celebrities. Comes from having a big head." Clover dropped the side of the bandage and stepped toward me. "He'll have a right terrible headache, but outside of that, he'll be back to his own arrogant self by tomorrow."

I let out a sigh of relief. I hadn't killed Jason Prescott. "And what about me?"

"Ah now, you'll still be a mermaid. It's what you wished for."

I sat up straighter. "No, no, no." These words were followed by so many more no's that they transformed into a stream of N-n-n-n-n. "I never wished to be the Little Mermaid or any sort of mermaid. Not once did I ask for aquatic DNA."

I held up my hand to stop Clover from interrupting. "I know Chrissy is just training to be a fairy godmother, and everybody makes mistakes, so I can overlook this. Really, I'm sure one day it will . . . well, if not seem funny, at least it will blur into a jumbled memory of panic and squid tentacles. What I'm saying is have Chrissy put Jason and I back in the twenty-first century, and we'll start over again with the wish thing. I'll be super specific about what I want next time."

Clover let out a huff of exasperation, like I was the one being unreasonable. He reached into his breast pocket, and pulled out a scroll, small even by leprechaun standards. He tapped it with one finger and the scroll grew bigger, doubling size and then doubling size again. When it stopped growing, he took hold of the top edge and let the rest fall to the ground. It unrolled as it went across the floor. "No one ever reads the contracts when they should. You lasses are in such a blasted rush to make your wishes, you'll not even glance at the fine print. It's only after requiring me to traipse around the ruddy Atlantic Ocean that you want a better look at the deal. Alright then...It's in here somewhere...The first party, hereafter known as Chrysanthemum Everstar, fairy godmother in training, hereby agrees to grant the second party, hereafter known as the Doomed, three wishes—"

"What?" I twisted to better see the contract. "What was that part about the Doomed?"

Clover tilted his chin down. "Now you're regretting you didn't take the time to read the contract like I told you. No one ever listens to the leprechaun."

I put one hand to my throat. "I'm doomed? It says that in the contract?"

He let out a small chuckle. "I'm only pulling your leg—or in this case, your fin." He turned the contract so I could see it. "In all truth, you're known as the pitiable and wretched damsel, Sadie Ramirez."

I squinted at the scroll. Yep, my name was penned next to the words pitiable and wretched.

Clover skimmed through the contract, letting the top part fall to the floor, "Although with Chrysanthemum Everstar as your fairy godmother, doomed is implied. Ah, now, here it is—your first two wishes: I wish to have such a beautiful voice I'm famous, adored for generations, and loved by Jason Prescott."

"Two?" I sputtered. "It was one wish."

Clover held up a finger. "Number one, you wanted a voice so beautiful you're famous and adored for generations." He held up a second finger. "Number two, you wanted to be loved by Jason Prescott."

A gust of wind went through the gazebo, and I shivered even though I didn't feel cold. It was bad enough my wish had gone horribly wrong, but now Clover was telling me I'd used up two wishes? "Jason's love wasn't a second wish. I only wanted to make sure he was included with the group of people who adored me for generations." I waved a hand in frustration. "The phrase was a clarification. It's one wish."

"It's two separate action items, making it two wishes. And count yourself fortunate Chrissy didn't consider it three. Famous and adored for generations could be construed as two different things."

I let out a humph. I only had one wish left. One. Using magic for something altruistic was quickly slipping on my list of priorities. I needed to figure out a wish that would get me out of being a mermaid, bring Jason and me back to the right time period, and still leave me with something worthwhile.

Out above the trees, a streak of lightning lit up the sky, followed quickly by a protest of thunder. Jason opened his eyes and stared blankly at Clover. "Hey, tha's a little person. Or two. It keeps moving around." He reached a hand in Clover's direction, grasping at the air.

Clover stepped further away from Jason, rolling up the contract as he did. "You have the voice, you have the lad. We've fulfilled our part of your first two wishes."

Another bolt of lightning split the sky, this time closer. "Chrissy didn't change my voice," I said. "It's exactly the same."

Jason's gaze moved from Clover to me. He didn't seem shocked to find himself lying in between a leprechaun and a mermaid, which probably meant he wasn't completely conscious. "You look fery vamiliar," he told me.

Clover finished rolling up the contract. "If you doubt Chrissy's handiwork—and I don't blame you for that—give us a song. If your voice hasn't changed, then contractually you'll have a leg to stand on . . . so to speak."

I wanted more than a leg. I wanted two.

Jason squinted at me, trying to clear his vision. "I know ya from somewhere, don' I?"

Clover shrunk the scroll and tucked it into his jacket. "You likely recognize her from her movie. She's famous and adored for generations."

I took a deep breath and sang the opening notes of the song

I'd done for the show. I hoped more than anything my voice would be the same wavering one that had messed up the audition. Instead, the melody lifted effortlessly from my mouth. The notes sounded stronger, clearer, with a resonance that flowed through the gazebo with aching perfection.

Jason pulled himself up on one elbow, wobbling, and stared at me. "Whoa."

I kept singing, almost as entranced as Jason. I couldn't fault Chrissy for my voice—couldn't claim she hadn't changed me.

Clover folded his arms with satisfaction. "Beautiful voice: done."

"The wish still isn't valid." I pointed at Jason. "He doesn't love me."

"Yet," Clover said.

Jason smiled, clearly loopy. "Oh, I could love you, baby."

Clover made a gesture like he was checking an item off a list. "Done."

I lowered my voice. "Jason said he *could* love me, not that he *does*. And besides, it isn't real love if he says it while he's got a head injury." I patted Jason's arm. "Trust me on this. I'm not your type. For example, you might want a girlfriend who isn't part fish."

Jason reached out to brush a strand of hair away from my face. At least I think that's what he was doing. He missed the first time and had to wave his hand around a bit before he found my face. "I'm not that particular when it comes to beautiful girls."

Clover nodded smugly.

"Oh come on," I told Clover. "That's clearly the loss of blood talking."

A cloud of sparkles erupted a few feet away from us, shining in the air like bits of a falling star. When the light cleared, Chrissy stood beside us in the gazebo, wand in hand and wings fluttering. Her hair was pale blue this time, which perfectly matched her blue beach dress and sequined sandals. A pair of white sunglasses was tucked on top of her head. Whatever beach she'd been on, it must have been sunnier than this one.

"So how are you enjoying your fairy tale—or in this case, your fish tail?" She smiled at her own joke, then noticed Jason laying on the ground beside me. "You've already rescued the prince? That was fast." She cast a glance at the sky. "I didn't think the storm had hit the ship yet."

"It hasn't," I muttered. "Jason tried to get away from the sailors and he fell off the boat." I touched his makeshift bandage, making sure it was tight enough. "He hit his head and nearly drowned. He could have died."

Chrissy's wings spanned open. "But besides that it's going well?"

Clover tucked his hands behind his back and let out a grunt. "You know as well as I do that mortals are a perpetually unsatisfied lot. Sadie decided she doesn't want to be a mermaid."

"Really?" Chrissy asked, although she didn't seem surprised. "Not many singers are as famous or adored as the Little Mermaid. I mean, you've got product tie-ins that span generations."

I sat up as much as I could. I didn't like being stuck on the ground, legless, while she looked down at me. "Yeah, about that—am I in the story version where the prince marries someone else and I die heartbroken?"

Chrissy flicked her wand around lazily, and specks of glitter dropped on the floor. "Well, you never asked for Jason to *marry* you."

A sharp inward breath lodged in my throat. It was every bit as bad as I feared. "So you put me in the *tragic* version?"

Chrissy shrugged. "A story is what it is. I don't create versions. And speaking of the story, you've already stayed here too long. The prince is supposed to get a fleeting, romantic glimpse as you serenade him. You're not supposed to be here so long that when the two of you part you feel the need to sign each other's yearbooks."

Jason tried to sit up, winced, and lay back down again. "Wait, who's doing what tragically?"

I ignored him. I was breathing in and out so fast I was in danger of hyperventilation. "This isn't what I meant when I said I wanted to be famous. Fame doesn't matter if you're *dead*."

She shrugged again, unconcerned. "Most famous people are dead, and the ones who aren't are going to die someday soon. That's just part of mortality."

This wasn't an accident. This wasn't a mistake Chrissy made because she was in training. She did this on purpose. I blinked at her, stunned. "What sort of a horrible fairy godmother are you? You said you wanted to help me, and then you took me from my time period and put me in a story where I *die*?"

Chrissy lifted her chin and sniffed, clearly offended. "I just grant your wishes. What you wish for is your affair."

Jason held his hand in front of his face, and stared at it perplexed. "Have I always had six fingers?"

Clover made tsking noises as he regarded Jason. "And a charming affair it is. Who wouldn't want this fine fellow?"

I slapped my tailfin against the floor angrily. "I won't go along with this. I'm not selling my voice to the sea witch." Another slap. "What's the point of singing beautifully if I'm mute as a human?"

Chrissy's wings slowly slid closed. "I don't know why you're so concerned with losing your voice. It's not like you ever said much in your own defense anyway."

I bristled. "What is that supposed to mean?"

She rolled her eyes and let out a martyred sigh. "I know I'm your fairy godmother, and therefore, it's my job to help you have epiphanies, insights, and what not. Really, I don't mind trudging through your little mortal life, even though up to this point it's been as exciting as watching flowers wilt. But is it truly necessary to review it with you? I mean, you were there. Habitually silent. Wrapped up in your own world. Shall we talk about how your parents know nothing about what goes on in your life? Or would you rather discuss how you never defend yourself to the Macys and Brooklyns of the world?"

"I . . . I . . ." I stammered. She wasn't right about me, was she? Okay, maybe I would rather write songs than hang out with kids from school, but that didn't mean I was wrapped up in my own world. And ignoring bullies was the best way to deal with them, wasn't it?

"At least as a mermaid," Chrissy went on, "you can make some waves."

I didn't comment on that, just glared at her. Whether I liked it or not, she wasn't going to undo any of this.

Chrissy lifted her wand. "Now then, are you ready to use your last wish or would you rather continue on with this story and work your tail off?"

Clover wiped bits of stray rain from his jacket. "We're waiting with baited breath."

Apparently everybody loved ocean puns. "I haven't decided what to wish for next." I needed more time to think. I needed to find a loophole.

Chrissy stepped around to my side, fiddling with her wand. "Did I mention that you've stayed here too long?" She gestured to my hair. "Anemones can only be out of the water for so long before they dry out."

I didn't pay attention to her. I was drumming my fingers against the stone floor, running through different possibilities. "If I don't make a bargain with the sea witch, then I don't become human, and the prince will never grow to love me in any sense of the word. My wish won't be fulfilled, and you'll have to undo it."

Chrissy smiled, unworried. "I'd think about that carefully. If you change a storyline, you never know what might happen."

I slapped my tailfin against the floor again. "Would it be worse than dying?"

A gust of wind rippled through Chrissy's hair. The storm was picking up. "If you're not happy here, use your other wish to go somewhere else."

"The last time I wished for something I got a death sentence. What's going to happen next? Earthquakes? Floods?"

"It's possible. Or not. Life is all about decisions."

I heard shouts, close by, coming from the ocean. My head snapped in that direction. A longboat filled with half a dozen sailors paddled into the cove, cutting through the gray water. They must have seen where I'd gone and followed. Most of the men had their hands on the oars, rowing, but a sailor in the front wielded a sword and the man next to him held a net. He fingered it, getting ready to throw it.

I had to leave. Could I reach the water in time? I pointed

my torso that way and tugged the lower half of my body in the same direction. My tailfin flapped into Jason.

"Ouch," he complained, and then turned his head toward the boat. "Hey, look! It's the guys. The smelly ones." He waved at them weakly. "Did you get pizza?" The effort of raising his head seemed too much and he lay back down.

There's a reason why seals look ridiculous as they shuffle along the beach with their little useless flippers. It's impossible not to look that way if you don't have legs. I wobbled in break-dancing-like motion across the floor, only slower. Too slow. "Order the men to stay away," I told Jason.

"Okay." Jason waved at the men again, "I need an order! I want pepperoni and sausage!" He laid his head back on the floor and mumbled, "I told 'em before to bring me pizza, but they never did."

I kept making rocking motions with my body to push myself to the water. I was too far away. I wouldn't make it in time.

Clover eyed the boat warily. "You might want to hurry a bit, lass."

Chrissy said nothing. She just absentmindedly twirled her wand, waiting.

"Help me," I pleaded.

"Is that what you wish for?" she asked. "You want to escape from the net?"

"No." I wouldn't waste a wish on something that would only help me for a moment.

The men were almost in range of the gazebo. The one holding the net fingered it eagerly. "That wench standing with the mermaid is a fairy! Shall we catch her too?"

"Nay," another sailor insisted. "Nets can't hold fairies.

She'll only curse you. Just seize the mermaid. She's the one who took the prince's soul. Look at him—laying there all soulless-like."

I turned to Chrissy, imploringly. "You're my fairy godmother. Can't you help me without using my third wish?"

Chrissy tapped her wand against her fingertips. "I have helped you. I warned you twice that you needed to go. And when you said you were going to change the story, I told you it might not turn out how you wanted."

Clover put his shoulder on my tailfin and pushed. It made no difference in my shuffling speed. He was as nervous as Chrissy was calm. Clover let out a huff. "All right, miss high-and-mighty godmother. You've made your point. We all should listen to you. Now give the lass a hand and toss her in the water. I don't care for the looks of those men. Not one bit. "

Chrissy didn't move. Her wings opened slowly, her gaze intent. "Your wish?"

I didn't have a choice. A surge of anger ran through me. I didn't want to use my last wish to just undo the first two. Now that I'd heard my singing voice, I wanted to keep it—needed to in a way I couldn't describe. My songs would finally match what had been in my heart all along.

I'd have to be careful how I phrased my last wish. I couldn't leave room for interpretation that could keep me a mermaid.

The man on the boat swung the net into the air. It flew toward me like a reaching hand and landed with a heavy thud. I pushed at the ropes, attempting to free myself from them. It was scratchy and smelled of dead fish. As I struggled, the net tightened, tangling in my hair and catching on my tailfin.

The men on the boat let out a cheer. "We've got her!"

"Haul her in!"

I pushed away the fright that encompassed me every bit as firmly as the net. My wish. I needed to decide. First, I had to get out of being a mermaid. What could I wish for that would also require two legs? Turning to Chrissy, I called, "I want to dance so well with Jason that I'm famous for it—in my normal time period." I added the last part to ensure she took me back to the present.

Chrissy smiled, self-satisfied, and swished her wand in my direction. "Wish granted."

Chapter 7

The air around me shimmered with pulses of light. The gazebo, the water, and the sky melted away into a blur of blues and grays. The smell of the net and the weight of it against my skin disappeared. I felt weightless. Everything spun and twisted.

When the air cleared, I found myself standing in a lobby of a fancy resort—no, it was the grand entrance of a mansion. Sweeping stone arches were interspersed with stained glass windows as big as doors. A balcony with an intricate wooden banister wrapped around one part of the room.

Several hallways led into the entrance, and off to my side stood a pair of elaborately carved wooden double doors. A dozen multilayered candelabras were spread around the room, complete with glowing candles.

I wore a pale yellow gown with green sleeves and a flared skirt that split in the front to show a matching green underskirt. Yellow and green brocade trimmed the sleeves, hem, and collar.

Apparently I was either on my way to the Grammys or a masquerade ball. Even though I knew I was standing, I hiked up my skirt to see my legs. They were right where they were supposed to be, decked out in white stockings and yellow slippers with satin bows on top.

Whoever had designed this outfit had gone all out. I ran my hand along my sleeve, taking in the smooth, delicate material. I had kept one thing from my mermaid story: the pearl bracelet I'd put on earlier still circled my wrist.

Looking around again, I noticed Chrissy at my side. She wore a blue gown with a tight fitting bodice, a long flowing skirt, and puffy sleeves that tapered in at the elbows. The sort of dress fairies wore in elaborately drawn versions of Cinderella. Her hair, now platinum blonde, was piled up on the top of her head in ribboned braids, and her wings had vanished. I hadn't realized wings were accessories fairies could hide when they wanted.

"Where are we?" I asked.

"Your new home. You're not only famous, you're rich. I threw that in at no extra charge." She nodded with a knowing air. "You're welcome."

"My home?" This was better than I'd hoped for. I put my hands to my lips, suppressing a squeal of delight. Maybe I shouldn't have been surprised. Celebrities lived in mansions, and that's what I'd wished for. I cast another look at the stone arches and indoor balcony, nearly laughing at the grandeur. When Chrissy decided to do rich, she didn't skimp. "Where's my family?"

Chrissy pointed her wand at the double doors. "In there, sitting down for supper."

I hadn't been away from my parents for long, but I had an overwhelming desire to rush in and throw my arms around each of them. "Thank you!" I gasped out. "Thank you so much!" I was ready to take back everything I'd said about Chrissy being a lousy fairy godmother.

I hurried to the doors, pushed them open, and stepped into a huge dining room. Floor to ceiling carved oak panels spread across the room. Large oil paintings hung next to arched windows, and three long tables were draped in white flowing tablecloths. A middle-aged man and woman ate dinner at the middle table. The woman's light blonde hair was done up in a bun and covered in a lace cap. She wore a formal, long-sleeved crimson dress and looked effortlessly elegant and graceful.

The man sitting beside her was heavy. Not fat exactly, just broad . . . like he needed to eat five times a day because he bench pressed ponies in his spare time. He had receding blond hair, a bushy beard, and he wore a blue vest with a high collar over a shirt with oddly-puffy sleeves.

Two longer tables sat on either side of the middle table, each filled with young women. Eight of them looked enough like the man and woman at the middle table that they must have been related. They had the same wavy blonde hair, pale elegant skin, and high cheek bones.

The other three girls looked like guests. One had red hair and freckles, one was Asian, and one was black. Several people in old-fashioned servants' attire walked around the room with trays filled with fruit, bread, and cheese. Others carried pitchers or plates of meat. A mandolin player sat in a corner of the room, plucking his instrument and singing a tune.

There were two problems with what I saw. None of the people seated at the tables were my family, and they were all dressed in clothing that made them seem like they belonged in a Renaissance movie. I glanced at my dress again. I didn't have a mirror, but it probably could be classified as Renaissance too.

A cold trickle of dread crept down my back. I wasn't just in the wrong house. I was in the wrong century. Again.

The greeting that had been on my lips faltered and sputtered away. I couldn't do anything but gape at everyone uncomfortably. Servants and eaters stopped talking and stared back at me. Even the mandolin guy quit playing.

The man at the middle table furrowed his brows and set his knife down on the table. "Who let you in here? What is the meaning of this?"

I hadn't realized Chrissy stood next to me until she spoke. "This is your youngest daughter, Mercedes—Sadie, for short." Chrissy swished her wand in a circular direction, and a burst of sparkles spread outward, like magical mist. As it reached the people at the table, their expressions changed, relaxed. The diners turned back to the business of eating and talking. The servants made their way around the room again, placing food on the table. The clinking of silverware and the noise of conversation filled the room.

My throat felt tight and it was hard to swallow. "Chrissy, this isn't my family."

"It is now," she said brightly. "The important thing about family is not who they are, it's that you have a good one. I gave you the best possible—royalty."

She had done this as a favor? Did she understand anything about humans? Families weren't interchangeable. I took a horrified step backward. "I don't want royalty. I want my family."

Chrissy gave me the sort of look a teacher gives an unreasonable student. "You were willing to leave your family to go on the road to find fame and fortune. I've made it so you can have both. It's those special little extras I provide that make me an excellent fairy godmother—and please remember to use that wording should the FGA contact you with a customer service survey."

Chrissy waved her wand at the nearest table and it grew several feet longer. A silver plate appeared, flanked by gleaming silverware and a cloth napkin. She motioned toward the table with a magnanimous sweep. "Your seat awaits."

The king turned away from his conversation with the queen and sent me a disapproving look. "Mercedes, you're late for supper again."

The queen smiled and gestured toward the empty plate. "Sadie dear, it isn't proper for a princess to keep her family waiting."

The king picked up a turkey leg from his plate. "Which is why we didn't wait. Sit down before I decide lollygaggers should miss supper altogether."

I couldn't speak. I could only shake my head. The Queen's gaze turned to Chrissy. "Is your friend joining us?" She waved at a passing servant. "Set an extra plate next to Sadie's, will you?"

Chrissy made a small curtsy. "Many thanks, Your Majesty, but Princess Sadie is about to see me out. She'll come back and eat with you in a minute."

The queen nodded, dismissing us. The king no longer paid attention to me. He called to one of the serving girls for more to drink.

Chrissy turned and glided toward the large double doors, her gown swishing around her in waves of blue satin. How could someone who looked so innocent have completely messed up my life—twice? I caught up with her, bristling with frustration. As soon as we were out of the room, I started in on her. "I wished to dance in *my normal time period*. This is clearly not *my time period* unless Renaissance fashion has suddenly made a big comeback."

"Technically, that's not what you wished for."

"Technically?" I repeated.

"You said you wanted to dance so well with Jason that you're famous for it in your time period. You will be. You're one of the twelve dancing princesses and Jason is the prince you dance with. You'll be famous for generations."

"*The Twelve Dancing Princesses?*" I choked out. "You put me in another fairy tale?" The room's grandeur seemed cold and foreboding now. "You knew that wasn't what I meant." I was breathing so hard something in my dress—a corset probably—dug into my ribs.

Chrissy blinked innocently. "I'm a fairy godmother, not a psychic. Perhaps you should have said, "In my normal time period, I want to dance so well with Jason that I'm famous for it." She shrugged her shoulders. "Grammar. Who knew it would be so important in life, right?"

I gritted my teeth together. "Well, now I'm clarifying the wish for you. Shouldn't a good fairy godmother fix her mistakes?"

"Mine, yes. Yours, sadly, no. I've used up the magic allotted for your wishes."

"But . . ." The panic building in my chest kept growing, threatening to erupt in a hysterical scream. Jason was somewhere in this century too. Trapped like I was. What had I done? I had to fix this.

I quickly reviewed what I knew about the Grimm fairy tale. A king had twelve daughters who snuck out of their bedroom every night, went through a forest of silver, gold, and diamond trees, then danced at a ball with twelve princes. The king noticed his daughters' slippers were worn out every morning and was so upset by this fact, he offered his kingdom and one of his daughters' hand in marriage to anyone who could solve the mystery.

Princes and nobles came to the castle and stood watch in the princesses' chambers, but the princesses spiked their drinks with sleeping potion so the men wouldn't discover the secret.

One day a soldier did a good deed for a fairy, and in return she gave him an invisibility cloak. He went to the castle and pretended to fall asleep each night, but really followed the princesses, thereby learning the truth.

The soldier married the oldest princess, the other princesses married their princes, and supposedly everyone lived happily ever after. Although I always assumed the prince who had danced with the oldest princess was less than thrilled by that arrangement. A spying soldier with a slick invisibility cloak got to marry his girlfriend. Harsh.

On the positive side, none of the princesses died during the story, so it was a definite improvement over my last fairy tale. On the other hand, I was still in the wrong century, in the wrong family, and I didn't particularly want to get married soon. Jason would undoubtedly be just as unhappy about the whole arrangement.

How could I fix it?

Chrissy tapped her wand lazily against her palm. "However, if you want to go back to your old home—keeping the things you've gained from your wishes, of course—fairies do occasionally barter for magic."

"Barter?" I grabbed onto the word. "What do you want?" What *could* she want? She had magic at her fingertips. Rumpelstiltskin was the only fairy tale I could think of where a magical being wanted something from a mortal, and he'd wanted the Queen's firstborn child.

Not that, I thought. I put my hand to my throat. I couldn't give away a child.

Chrissy leaned toward me, speaking in a hushed tone. "You and your sisters dance every night for Queen Orlaith, ruler of the Unseelie Court. She has a special goblet. I want it."

A goblet, not a child.

Chrissy pulled a postcard-sized color drawing from a purse that hung on her belt. It showed a golden cup with a thick stem that curved into a wide base. "Here's what it looks like."

I stared at the drawing, trying to process all this. She wanted me to steal a fairy queen's goblet? Was this sort of request normal? I didn't recall any fairy tales where fairy godmothers encouraged their charges to take up a life of crime. Should I do it? Did I really have a choice?

Chrissy placed the drawing in my hand. "I made sure your dresses have especially large pockets, so concealing a goblet shouldn't be a problem."

I thrust my hand into my pocket. She was right.

"That's one of my special touches," Chrissy added. "Sewn in pockets weren't really in vogue until the eighteenth century." She reached into her purse again and pulled out two strips of white paper. "Once you give me Queen Orlaith's goblet, you can use these." She handed me the strips. They looked like plane tickets. Across the front were the words:

Magical boarding pass. Good to transport one mortal anywhere, any time. Simply contact your fairy godmother with your destination.

Void where travel creates time paradoxes. Cannot be used in conjunction with any other magical coupons. Sales tax applies in Michigan during most portions of the twenty-first century.

"Keep them," Chrissy said. "Once you give me the goblet, I'll activate your passes."

I fingered the slips of paper. I couldn't even lie without my nose growing, and Chrissy was asking me to steal something?

"Isn't stealing from other fairies illegal in your world?"

Chrissy waved away my words with a flick of her manicured nails. "Don't think of it as stealing. You're simply relocating an object to the owners who should have it. Queen Orlaith stole half of the things she owns. "

Chrissy pulled the drawstring on her purse tight. "The gold trees that are part of *The Twelve Dancing Princesses* fairy tale used to belong to the leprechauns. She swiped the silver trees from the tree nymphs. The goblet should belong to Queen Titania of the Seelie Court."

"Oh." I kept fingering the slips of paper nervously. "Then why don't you get the goblet from her? I mean, I'm just a teenager. You've got magic to help you." I didn't know a lot about fairies, but judging from the story of Sleeping Beauty, it wasn't wise to tick them off.

"I can't get the goblet *because* I have magic. Queen Orlaith cast a spell on her island and the forest surrounding it. No magical creature except herself and her son can enter there. Anyone else who tries is attacked by the plants."

Anxiety began to twine through my chest. "What do you mean the plants attack people? Plants don't move."

"Well, not when mortals ask them to. Plants haven't spoken to your kind in thousands of years, but fairies and plants have a special bond. If Queen Orlaith tells her vines to grab someone, they will. They hold trespassers until she decides how to dispose of them." Chrissy pursed her lips in disapproval. "It's usually something over the top to make her point. Once three leprechauns snuck onto her land to try and take back one of the gold trees." Chrissy let out a sad, resigned sigh. "They've been stuck on a cereal box ever since."

Had I heard that right? "A cereal box?"

"So you can see why I can't set foot in the place. I don't want to end up snap-crackle-and-popping for eternity. Mortals and animals are the only ones who can go there safely, and it's a bit hard to train animals to stealthily retrieve magical objects."

Chrissy surveyed me, then brushed a piece of lint from my dress. "Which reminds me, what in the world did you do to my postal squid? He came back all twitchy. The poor thing is a nervous wreck."

I ignored the question. A terrible, and likely, possibility had just occurred to me. "Wait a minute—did you mess up my wishes on purpose so I'd have to get the goblet for you?"

She let out an offended humph. "First of all, I didn't mess up your wishes. I delivered them with style and pizzazz. And second, it's not like you have anything better to do with your time. I mean, what are you missing out on? Calculus homework? Please. Like that's ever going to come in handy during your life."

I was right. She'd done this on purpose. I looked upward, eyes on the arched ceiling. "I don't believe this. I've been suckered by a fairy godmother. They always seemed so nice in the stories. Sending girls to balls, helping them find true love . . ."

"Exactly. I'm sending you to balls and helping you find true love. You know, Cinderella and Sleeping Beauty were a lot more grateful about our services. Maybe that's your problem— a bad attitude."

A bad attitude. My mind was stuck on a vision of vines wrapping around me, of green leafy ropes twisting around my arms and neck. "What will the queen do if she catches me stealing something?" I put my hand to my throat and gulped. "I don't know how to crackle, and I've never popped."

"That is why as a concerned fairy godmother, I'm officially advising you not to get caught. Once you come back through the forest, you'll no longer be in Queen Orlaith's domain. Call me as soon as you pass the last tree, and I'll come for the goblet." She tipped her wand in the direction of the tickets. "Then you and Jason can go home. He'll appreciate it— what with that pizza withdrawal he's suffering."

I gripped the tickets so hard they crumpled. There are a lot of stupid ways to die, and stealing something from a fairy queen seemed high on that list. But what choice did I have? It wasn't just my life I'd messed up. Jason was stuck here too. I had to at least try to get us home.

"What does the goblet do?" I asked.

"It's like a fancy glass," Chrissy said. "Rich people use them for drinking."

"I know what a goblet is. I want to know what's so special about this one that I'm risking my life for it."

"Oh, that." Chrissy straightened one of the ribbons near my collar, looking me over like my drama teacher used to do before she sent me on stage. She was making sure I was ready to play my part. "The goblet is enchanted. If you pour a special elixir into it at the stroke of midnight, you can ask a question, and it will answer you."

"That's it? It answers your questions? We already have that in my world. It's called Google."

Chrissy gave me a look that made it clear I'd missed the point. "The Internet can't tell you what your enemies are planning or the secrets of breaking spells, and it certainly can't tell you how to care for magical trees."

Voices interrupted us. Two people were coming from a hallway that connected to the grand entrance.

"I'm sorry," a female voice said, though there wasn't any sign of sorrow in her words. They were spoken lightly, triumphantly almost.

"I can't stay here for days," a guy said, irritated. "I've got to take care of my brother. I've got school assignments that are already overdue—and if my probation officer thinks I skipped out, he'll pop a vein. Seriously, he's an old dude. He'll probably have a coronary."

School assignments? Probation officer? Those were modern things.

Two people stepped into the room, both about my age. The girl wore a flowing green dress that showed off her shoulders and ruffled around her feet like trailing greenery. Her black hair was pinned up into a braided bun with green ribbons twisting around its folds. Her dark eyes were set, jewel-like, against flawless, pale skin. She moved with a grace and a bearing—not to mention a slight glow shining around her—that made me suspect she was a fairy.

The teenage guy walking with her was tall with sandy blond hair and a two-day-old beard. He wore scruffy gray clothing, a crumpled felt hat, and dusty boots with gaps in the soles. A sheathed sword hung on his belt, along with a leather purse and a wooden cup.

To say he wore the clothes well anyway seemed odd, but it was true. With his square jaw and blue eyes, he was attractive enough to make a girl look twice. Or three times. Not that I was counting.

Chrissy took in the scene and let out a huff. "Jade Blossom. What a surprise to see you here."

The dark-haired fairy stopped short, and her mouth made an indignant O. "What are *you* doing here?"

Chrissy squared her shoulders. "I'm here on official business."

"Official business?" One of Jade Blossom's dark eyebrows rose. "What official business do you have in *The Eleven Dancing Princesses* story?"

Chrissy casually tapped her wand against the side of her dress. "It's *The Twelve Dancing Princesses* now." She gestured to me. "Meet my client, Princess Sadie."

"*Twelve* princesses?" Jade Blossom let out a snort of disbelief. "You can't send more girls to this story. I mean really, what family has twelve daughters? It just screams magical tampering. Mortals are bound to get suspicious."

"Wait . . ." My gaze ricocheted between the fairies. "Hasn't the story always been about twelve dancing princesses?"

Chrissy patted my arm reassuringly. "Of course it has. Don't listen to her." She turned to Jade Blossom and lowered her voice. "It's not my fault. Being a princess is a popular wish."

Jade Blossom's eyes narrowed into glittering slits. "You're just after the goblet. Admit it."

Chrissy took a couple steps toward the guy, regarding him disdainfully. "And what are you doing here toting a mortal around?"

Jade Blossom fluttered her hand in the guy's direction, making the jeweled bracelets on her wrists clink. "Donovan asked for wealth, power, and an invisibility cloak. What else could I do?"

The guy—Donovan—had been studying Chrissy and me, measuring us every bit as carefully as we were measuring him. Now his attention turned back to Jade Blossom.

"For starters, you could have left me in the twenty-first century. What good is being rich if you're stuck someplace where you can't buy anything?"

He had an air of confidence about him, a careless swagger. I knew these types of people from school—guys who were effortlessly cool and spent their time mocking everyone else.

"Where am I?" he asked, "and what is The Twelve Dancing Princesses?"

He didn't know the fairy tale. And I was glad. Instead of answering him, I turned to Chrissy. "He's from my century and doesn't know anything about the story. That means I'm not famous, which means this wish didn't work and is null and void. Undo it and take me back home." Granted, it was only a thin straw of a hope, but I was ready to grasp at anything,

Chrissy waved her hand dismissively at Donovan. "You can't expect one of Jade Blossom's clients to know anything of importance or culture. He probably crawled out from the same rock she lives under. "

Jade Blossom glared daggers at Chrissy, then reached into a ruffled green bag at her waist and produced a white strip of paper. A magical boarding pass. Apparently he needed to make a bargain with a fairy too.

I didn't want to give up on the null and void angle so easily. "I'm not famous," I insisted. "I'm some nameless character in a fairy tale that never made sense to begin with."

It was true after all. The story never said why the princesses secretly went dancing every night. It didn't explain who the princes were or why they didn't just ask the king for the princesses' hands in marriage. It also didn't give a reason the soldier followed the girls for three nights instead of ratting them out the first night like any sensible person would do.

Chrissy was unmoved by my argument. "You'll be in

books, movies, and have a Barbie doll created in your likeness. That means you're famous. You never asked for your *name* to be famous. However, if you want to get technical, I can pull a few strings in your father's ancestral history so your last name will be Benz instead of Ramirez.

And then my name would be Mercedes Benz. Like I hadn't already heard enough car jokes. "No." I held up a hand to stop her from swishing her wand and rearranging my ancestry. "Don't do that."

Donovan finished reading the boarding pass and held it up between two fingers. "Hamilton, Ohio on the day I left." He glanced around at the unchanging scenery, then turned to Jade Blossom. "Well, that didn't work. What else you got?"

Jade Blossom took the paper from his fingers. With a smile that verged on flirting, she tucked the boarding pass into his pocket. "Your pass isn't activated yet. It will become magical as soon as you give me Queen Orlaith's goblet." She pulled another paper from thin air, it seemed, and handed it Donovan. "Here's a picture of the goblet. You'll see it later when you go to her court. When you're out of Queen Orlaith's lands . . ." She lifted her hand to the side of her face, mimicking a phone. "Call me."

This kept getting worse. Donovan was after the same goblet I was supposed to get. Every contest—every game in PE I'd played and lost—flashed into my mind. I was horrible at competitions. I was even horrible at singing competitions, and singing was something I was good at. What chance did I have to win?

Chrissy planted her hands on her hips, her lace cuffs draping over her fingers. "I already gave Sadie instructions to take the goblet, and we were here first."

Jade Blossom cast us an unconcerned look. "Then it's too

bad Sadie doesn't have an invisibility cloak. It gives my client a distinct advantage."

My stomach sank. With an invisibility cloak, Donovan could steal the goblet before I even got close to it. Besides, I suddenly remembered that the story said the soldier took a goblet from the ball. It was already decreed, and if I tried to take the goblet instead, I would most likely be considering that mistake from a cereal box.

I stepped toward Chrissy. "Isn't there another way I can go home?"

She didn't answer. Jade Blossom was speaking with a smile of cat-like smugness. "Think how grateful Queen Titania will be when she gets the goblet—oh, sorry, I bet you *were* thinking about that. You're still trying to find a way to get into Fairy Godmother University."

Chrissy's lips pressed into a tight line of pink lipstick. "The only reason they haven't already accepted me is because I dumped Master Goldengill's son. He blacklisted me."

Jade Blossom reached into her bag again, this time producing a thin, green wand. She fingered the end absentmindedly. "You know, maybe you should try for a less exclusive job. One more suited to your talents. A snail guardian, maybe."

Chrissy raised her chin. "Don't count your snails before they've hatched. My client has a few advantages over yours."

"Like what?"

"For one, she's . . ." Chrissy gazed at me, searching for a redeeming quality, ". . . very smart." Chrissy was obviously bluffing.

"Really," I said. "If there's another way to—"

Chrissy didn't even acknowledge I'd spoken. She was still

proving her point to the other fairy. "And Sadie knows the story. That gives her the advantage of foresight."

Jade didn't blink. "Donovan's a professional thief."

Chrissy let out a gasp, not of revulsion but of pure jealousy. My gaze flew back to him, seeing his mussed hair and confident swagger in a new light.

He wasn't the trendy type, the effortlessly cool guy who spent his time mocking everyone else. He was a rebel who skipped school altogether unless he was casing out whose car to steal. He was the type who fought dirty, a thief with an enchanted cloak. And I was up against him.

Chrissy recovered as best she could from the news, striking a pose of airy confidence. "Sadie may not be skilled in the criminal arts, but she has other abilities."

Of all the things I ever expected anyone would say about me, never once had 'Sadie may not be skilled in the criminal arts, but she has other abilities' crossed my mind.

"Sadie has . . ." Chrissy struggled for a moment to come up with a quality that might help me knick a goblet. ". . . hidden talents."

Jade Blossom smirked. "Hidden extremely well, apparently."

Chrissy turned her back on the other fairy with a sharp air of dismissal. She gave me a smile like cheerleaders wear during pep assemblies. "We'll win this. Call me when you have the goblet." She flicked her wand, and without any other sort of goodbye, she vanished. A trail of falling pink glitter wafted to the floor where she'd been.

I was stuck here until I got the goblet. That is, *if* I could get the goblet.

Chapter 8

I stood in the entryway. Just stood there. I didn't know what to do now, where to go. Was I supposed to join the royal family for dinner? Pretending things were normal seemed too overwhelming of a task. I needed time to pull myself together, to think. I needed to stay here in case Jade Blossom gave Donovan any sort of clues about how to get the goblet.

I was still grasping the tickets Chrissy had given me. I folded them and slipped them into my pocket.

Neither Jade Blossom nor Donovan paid any attention to me. The fairy launched into an explanation about the magic prohibitions surrounding Queen Orlaith's island that Chrissy had already told me. He regarded her, arms folded, his blue eyes cold with frustration. "Hold up a sec. Where exactly is Queen Orlaith's court? And what is this princess story you mentioned earlier?"

Jade Blossom let out a sigh, her shoulders dipping dramatically with the effort. "Haven't you ever heard the fairy tale about the dancing princesses?"

"Sorry. I'm not the Barbie-doll type."

"Your parents must have read you fairy tales when you were young."

He let out a grunt. "What can I say? It's just one more way my mother failed me."

Jade Blossom's lips twitched unhappily at this piece of news. "I can only tell you what the story allows. The king of this land has eleven—" she glanced over her shoulder at me. "I mean *twelve* daughters. Don't ask why he had that many. There isn't a good answer."

Jade Blossom went on to explain about the worn slippers and the king's proclamation, then said, "Once you figure out the mystery, you'll become the king's son-in-law and inherit the kingdom." She smiled, self-satisfied. "That will give you power, wealth, and your choice of a beautiful princess thrown in at no extra charge, because that's the sort of amazing fairy godmother I am."

Donovan rubbed at his forehead and looked at her skeptically. "Wait—the dude is offering up his kingdom just because he can't figure out how his kids keep sneaking out? My dad would have been kingdomless when I was ten years old."

Jade Blossom brushed flecks of dirt off the front of Donovan's coat in a fruitless attempt to make him more presentable. "The king is bothered that his daughters keep sneaking out, although that's not why he offered the reward. He knows magic must be involved, and nothing makes a mortal edgier than knowing magic is drifting through his home every night."

Donovan peered around the room, taking in the stairs, balconies, and chandeliers. "Ten to one it's the windows. Mine were on the fourth floor and that didn't stop me from leaving."

I wondered, but didn't ask how he'd managed to climb out a fourth floor window without plunging to his death.

Jade Blossom kept brushing Donovan's coat. She was either pointlessly optimistic about the dirt's grasp on the coat or she liked touching hot guys. "You'll have a chance to tell the king your theories. However, if after three nights, you haven't brought him proof your explanation is the right one, the king will order your execution."

"What?" Donovan took a step backward and swore several times. "You never mentioned this stuff when you offered me wishes."

He held up a hand, waving it for emphasis. "All I wanted was a decent ride and a home where the landlord wasn't breathing down our necks. You not only sent me back in time, you dropped me in a place with some homicidal king? What— was it too hard to conjure up a Toyota?"

Jade batted her eyes innocently. "The test is part of the story. Now calm down and listen up. This is what's happened so far: You're a Capenzian soldier returning from a war against Briardrake. The good news is your country won. The bad news is you're poor."

Donovan clenched his jaw, his expression dark. It only made him look more broodingly handsome.

"While you made your way through a nearby forest," Jade Blossom continued, "you came across a beggar woman who sat shivering from the cold. You gave her your coat, and she transformed into the most stunningly gorgeous and exquisite fairy a mortal has ever seen." Jade Blossom put her hand to her chest. "That would be me. As a reward for your selflessness, I gave you a magic invisibility cloak. Don't lose that, by the way. It'll take forever to find it again."

"Go on," Donovan said stiffly.

"The story allows me to give you one other important piece of advice: Drink nothing the princesses give you. They may be beautiful and lovely, but every single one of them wants you dead."

Donovan's gaze snapped to mine, astonished.

"Hey," I held up both hands, "I just got here too. I don't want anyone dead."

Jade Blossom leaned closer to his ear, her skirts rustling in satin whispers. "Remember, you can't trust her. She's after our goblet."

As Jade Blossom spoke, the clothes she wore changed, transformed from an elegant gown into a simple black dress and hair cap, the uniform of a servant.

Before I could guess why she'd done this, the dining room door swung open, and a middle-aged woman strode out. Her blue dress was crisp and spotless, her black cap perched tidily over her graying brown hair. She carried an air of authority in every step she took toward me. A lady's maid? A head servant, perhaps?

"Princess Mercedes, the king—" The woman stopped when she saw I wasn't alone. She regarded Jade Blossom and Donovan with brows furrowed in disapproval. "Why have you brought this beggar to the main hall? If the lad wants something to eat, take him to the kitchen entrance."

Jade Blossom gave a brief curtsy. "Pardon me, Madam Saxton, this man isn't a beggar. He's a soldier home from the war, and he's come to try his hand at solving the king's mystery. I was about to take him to see King Rothschild."

"Is that so?" Madam Saxton looked Donovan up and down more thoroughly. A flicker of sympathy passed through her eyes but was quickly replaced by a resolute firmness. "I'll take care of this," she told Jade Blossom. "You may attend to your duties."

Jade Blossom curtsied again, then walked back toward the hallway she'd come from. As soon as she turned the corner, a poof of green glitter fluttered to the floor. She must have gone back to wherever fairies went when they weren't throwing unsuspecting mortals into other centuries.

"I am King Rothschild's head housekeeper," Madam Saxton said, still regarding Donovan. "You wish to see him?"

Chrissy had told me it was dangerous to change things in stories. But I didn't see how it could be more dangerous than letting Donovan have the first shot at the goblet. I had to stop him from seeing the king.

"Madam Saxton," I said, mustering up a regal tone, "we can't allow this young man to see my father today. He should think about his request for several days to ensure it's what he really wants." I pointed to the hallway. "See him out, and make sure he doesn't return for a week."

Donovan's eyes narrowed at me. "Oh, I don't have to think about this. I want to see King Rothschild now."

"That's an order," I told Madam Saxton. "See him out."

Donovan took a step toward me. "The king said anyone could try to solve the mystery. Do your orders supersede his?"

Supersede? I hadn't expected a guy with a probation officer to use that sort of word. Was he smart? Smarter than my supposed smartness?

Madam Saxton held up her hands to stop our argument, then dipped her head in a deferential bow to me. "Princess Mercedes, your concern for the lad's safety does you credit. However, your father's decree can't be changed. Still, I've some leeway in weeding out those unsuited to the task."

She eyed Donovan's ragged clothing. "I suppose you think your life is so wretched, you've nothing to lose by attempting to uncover the secret of the princesses' slippers. Nonetheless, I won't admit you into the king's presence unless I know you're cleverer than your predecessors. I'll ask you three questions. If you don't answer each of them correctly, you'll be on your way forthwith."

Good. If Madam Saxton turned Donovan away, I would have time to scope out the goblet tonight. I might be able to figure out a way to take it. I fingered the pocket where I'd put Chrissy's tickets, a movement Donovan noted.

Madam Saxton went on speaking to him. "A moment ago when I came through the door, I uttered four words: 'Princess Mercedes, the king . . .' What was the rest of my sentence going to be?"

Donovan wasn't flustered by this new demand. Without hesitation, he answered, "The king wishes you to join the family for supper."

"And how do you know this?" the housekeeper asked.

"I smelled food when you opened the door, and King Rothschild is the sort of man who wants to know where his daughters are at all times. I'm sure it's bothering him not to know where Princess Mercedes is."

Madam Saxton nodded, satisfied by his explanation. "My second question is: What is one of the talents Princess Mercedes possesses?"

I inwardly groaned. The question was too easy. This was a story about twelve dancing princesses.

Donovan pretended to give the question thought. "Have the princess walk around me."

Madam Saxton prodded me to do so. I felt odd, but I circled

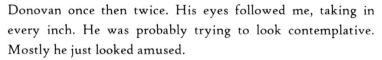

Donovan once then twice. His eyes followed me, taking in every inch. He was probably trying to look contemplative. Mostly he just looked amused.

"One of her talents?" Madam Saxton called as I made my third loop.

He lowered his voice so only I would hear. "With a name like that, I bet she's got a talent for driving."

"What?" Madam Saxton asked.

"Dancing," he said. "She's a beautiful dancer."

"How did you come to that conclusion?"

"She moves with grace and elegance."

"Or," I said under my breath, "you remember the name of the fairy tale."

"That too," he said.

I forced a smile. "Let me ask the third question." Without waiting for Madam Saxton's consent, I turned to Donovan. "What did I wear yesterday?"

It was the perfect question. He couldn't know the answer. If he said any kind of gown, he'd be wrong. And if by chance he guessed the right answer—jeans and a brown T-shirt—Madam Saxton would think he was crazy and dismiss him.

Donovan smirked, his blue eyes going full blast. "Clothes."

"What kind of clothes?" I asked.

"That's four questions," he said. "When do I talk to the king?"

Madam Saxton held up her hands again. "The task was to answer three of *my* questions. Come with me, please."

She headed down the hall, shoes tapping against the stone floor in a brisk rhythm. We followed after her, walking into a room that seemed to be an office. A wooden desk and an ornate chair sat in front of a large fireplace. Shelves along the wall held boxes, scrolls, books, and several abacuses.

Madam Saxton motioned for me to go to the desk. I did, noting a large painting on one wall that showed the king, queen, and twelve princesses sitting in rows beside them. There was something surreal about seeing my face among them.

Madam Saxton closed the door and addressed Donovan. "A keen and observant mind has helped you answer twice, but that alone can't uncover the secrets a lady holds in her heart."

She gestured at the quill pen on the desk. "Princess Mercedes will write one word—the thing she wants most in life. She'll then show me the paper. If you can tell me the word she writes, I'll let you have an audience with the king. If not, I'll send you on your way."

A happy swell of victory lifted me. I'd won. There was no way a guy I'd met ten minutes ago could guess what I wanted most. *I* wasn't even sure. I strolled to the desk, cheerfully contemplating it.

The word 'home' came to mind first. I didn't want to be trapped here. Although technically, I wanted my family back— my twenty-first century life, not just my house.

I picked up the quill pen, hesitating before dipping it into the ink bottle. The thought of my old life reminded me that once I went home, I would have to endure my *America's Top Talent* audition becoming a viral video.

The weight of all those opinions, all the sneering laughs— it was enough to crush a person, to squeeze the air right out of me.

As badly as I wanted to be with my family, I still dreaded enduring nationwide humiliation. So did that mean I desired respect the most? Is that what I'd really meant when I wished for fame—I wanted the world to respect me? I twirled the quill pen between my fingers, thinking. No, I'd wanted more than respect. I'd wanted sighs of admiration from fans and the glitter of camera flashes going off around me. I'd wanted to feel the wet cement under my palms in the Hollywood Walk of Fame. I'd wanted everyone at my school to regret the way they'd treated me.

Fame seemed so vain and needy when I thought of it like that. Certainly I desired more from life than the adoration of strangers. What did I really want?

When Chrissy had told me she'd give me three wishes, it had been easy to think of things to ask for. Ironic. Right now I didn't really know what would make me happy.

Donovan, unconcerned by my indecision, surveyed the painting, then the room's woodwork. It all spoke of wealth, of dozens of craftsmen doing the king's bidding. "If I get the answer right, I'll be a royal guest here, and I'll be given everything I need to solve the mystery?"

Madam Saxton sighed at his optimism. "Of course."

I dipped the quill into the ink bottle. Rivulets of black ink dripped off the end.

Back in the hallway, Donovan heard me tell Chrissy that since I wasn't famous in my century, my wish was void. He probably expected me to write something along those lines— fame or admiration. I needed something that he couldn't guess.

Freedom, I decided. It wasn't a lie. I wanted freedom from the bad things in my life.

I made sure Donovan was standing far enough away that he couldn't see what I wrote. I also checked to make sure there weren't any mirrors or reflective surfaces nearby that would let him see my paper. Then I put the tip of the quill pen to the paper and made an F.

There is a reason people stopped using feathers to write with. My F came out gloppy. I had to write slowly and in large script so the letters didn't bleed into an unrecognizable blob. I wasn't about to risk having to whisper my word to Madam Saxton.

Donovan strolled across his section of the room, hands clasped behind his back, studying me. He sent me a wide grin, one that probably made most girls melt. "I don't think Princess Mercedes is writing *riches* or *beauty*. People don't value what they've always had in abundance."

Yeah, right. Empty flattery wouldn't make me give him any clues. I rolled my eyes and went back to writing.

"It certainly isn't the word cooperation," he added.

It occurred to me that Donovan, like me, couldn't lie without magical consequences. Did he really think I was beautiful? I replayed his words and just as quickly, the compliment soured. Donovan hadn't said I was beautiful. He'd made two unrelated comments—I wouldn't write beauty or riches, and people didn't value what they had a lot of. He must have worded it that way because he *didn't* think I was beautiful and only wanted the appearance of flattery. Jerk.

Donovan noted my scowl and kept slowly pacing. "I doubt she wrote *kindness. Charity toward strangers* doesn't seem likely either."

If I folded the paper now, the ink would smudge and the word would be indecipherable. I leaned over the paper and blew on the ink to dry it.

"Are you almost done?" Donovan called. "It's a word, not a birthday cake."

I blew on the paper a couple more times. After the ink dried, I folded the paper once, and then twice.

Madame Saxton watched my caution with evident weariness. "You see the crux of the problem," she said to Donovan. "Despite the rewards the king offers, how can anyone discover the princesses' secrets if the girls remain unwilling to share them? It's fruitless to risk your life in such a venture."

She shook her head sadly. "Whatever dark spell is upon our dear princesses, I fear it will remain until a greater magic can overcome it."

I didn't comment on my hopeless status. "Move away from Madam Saxton," I told Donovan. "I don't want you reading over her shoulder while she unfolds this."

He smiled, clearly humoring me, then sauntered in my direction holding his hands up in surrender. His eyes were confident, though. He was far from surrendering. "I'll stay as far away from Madam Saxton as you like."

I kept watching his dark blue eyes, wondering at his assurance. Did he think I was so transparent he could guess my word?

I lifted my chin, met his eyes, and strode toward Madam Saxton. I was glad I wore a dress made for a princess. It carried its own confidence within its silk and brocade.

My eyes were on Donovan's, so I didn't see his hand move until it was too late. As he passed by me, he reached out and yanked the paper from my hand.

"Hey!" I yelled, lunging at him. "You can't take that! That's cheating!"

Donovan used his height to hold the paper out of my reach. He was stronger than I'd expected. He didn't budge even with me knocking into him, tugging at his arm. He unfolded the paper above my head. "Freedom," he called to Madam Saxton. "Princess Mercedes wants freedom." He flipped the paper so she could see it and then gave it back to me. "I expected it to say *goblet*. Go figure."

I clenched my fists and stamped my foot, something that

didn't make nearly the dramatic sound I'd hoped for. Slippers weren't meant for stomping. "That doesn't count. You cheated."

Donovan met my protest with another smile, this one triumphant. "Madam Saxton never said I couldn't cheat."

I glared at him. "It's obviously implied. Thus, the term *cheating*. She told you to guess."

He shook his head. "No. She said I had to tell her what you'd written. I did."

I looked to Madam Saxton for support, for agreement. I expected her to be angry. Instead her eyes shone happily. Her whole face was lit up with hope.

I marched to her, indignant. "He has no integrity. Is that the sort of man King Rothschild wants as a successor?"

"What King Rothschild wants," Donovan answered for her, "is someone who can figure out the slipper mystery. Someone who can free the princesses from their dark curse. All the guys who've come to the castle before, maybe they had integrity and chivalry, and they wore those—" He waved a hand as though it would help him produce the words he wanted, "—capes and fancy clothes, but how successful were they when it came to learning the truth?"

That seemed to decide the matter for Madam Saxton. She clapped her hands together with enthusiasm. "Well said. Perhaps you're just the one to succeed."

Her excitement irked me. She actually thought this cheating probation dude was some sort of savior. She strode to Donovan, all action now. With a contemplative "Hmm," she fingered the edge of his coat where buttons were missing. "I'll need to give you clothing befitting a royal suitor."

Apparently deeming the coat a hopeless cause, she tugged

it off his arms. "We mustn't insult Capenzia by letting the King Rothschild think only poor travelers and vagabonds value his daughters."

Underneath his coat, Donovan wore a coarse gray shirt that was stained and ill-fitting. Madam Saxton made huffing noises at it. "It's a good thing you're a handsome lad. The right clothes will transform you well enough. From here on, you're Prince Donovan from the kingdom of . . ."

"Hamilton, Ohio," he supplied.

She nodded, folding his coat over her arm. "That sounds sufficiently exotic."

I crumpled my paper, making freedom disappear in the creases. "That's because you've never been to Ohio."

"You're a fifth son," she continued, "so you've no chance of an inheritance from your goodly parents, but when you heard of King Rothschild's dilemma, you came straightway to assist him." She opened the door and stood aside so he could follow her out.

Donovan gave me a parting smile. All teeth and charm.

Madam Saxton turned back to me and made a shooing motion with her hand. "Princess Mercedes, don't idle about. You must go into supper now. Your parents await you."

I had no other choice really. I stalked off down the hallway.

Chapter 9

The dining room smelled delicious, like warm, roasted tastiness. The mandolin player barely looked up when I came in this time. The princesses were equally uninterested in my arrival. They glanced at me, and then went back to their meals and conversations.

Each wore an elaborate dress, all in pastel colors so they gave off the impression of rows of Easter eggs. Jeweled necklaces flashed and gleamed in the light—pearls, diamonds, amethysts, and pale blue stones I didn't have a name for. The blonde princesses looked as pretty as porcelain, as though they should be sitting in a doll cabinet somewhere surveying the lesser knickknacks.

The obviously imported princesses were as elegantly dressed, but less graceful in their manners. They didn't raise their pinkies while holding their glasses or dab their napkins to their lips with the same dainty flourishes.

As I walked to my place at the table, I wondered what

wishes had brought these girls to the castle. Were they glad to be here? None seemed particularly sad or upset. Although maybe that was because they were busy enjoying the feast. That's what it looked like—a Thanksgiving feast complete with savory dishes and more than one turkey.

I sat down at the empty seat, already worried that I would have the worst table manners. I'd never been the type who could tell a dessert fork from a regular fork. If it had prongs, I figured I could use it to eat. I would have to copy the BPs— blonde princesses'—mannerisms to figure out what to do.

The king set his goblet on the table with a loud thunk. "Lo, my youngest daughter arrives at last. Mercedes, you finally deign to dine with us?"

"Uh . . ." I didn't understand the question.

The queen looked at me with motherly concern, making the tiny wrinkles around her eyes deepen. "We worried your food would grow cold."

"Grow cold?" the king sputtered. "If I'd traipsed in late to supper at her age, my father would have given me nothing save a crust of bread, which," he slapped his hand onto the table so forcefully his silverware rattled, "is precisely what Sadie shall be given now."

"But I was . . ." taking care of fairy business and trying to circumvent your decree about suitors. I couldn't finish that statement. Instead I murmured, "I'm sorry."

"And you shall continue to be." The king motioned to a serving man who carried a wooden tray piled with cheese and bread. "Princess Mercedes will contemplate her punctuality while dining on bread crusts and water. Give her nothing else."

The man bowed. "Yes, Sire."

I hoped the queen would argue my cause, but she went

back to eating without any sort of comment. When the servant arrived at my seat, he took a loaf of bread from his tray and curtly ripped the end off. He set it on my plate where it lay, forlorn and dry-looking. It seemed oddly out of place on the fancy silver place setting. I picked up the crust and bit an edge off. It was as stiff as Styrofoam.

Great. In my last fairy tale, I was served seaweed and raw fish. Now I got bread crusts. I really should have made wishes with better dining choices.

King Rothschild went back to his conversation with the queen, my disturbance forgotten. The two princesses sitting at my side—both the blonde variety—were too wrapped up in a conversation about their new fur-lined cloaks to speak to me. The mandolin player crooned out a song about a knight and the ill-fated love he felt for his lady.

I wondered where Jason was and what he was doing. Chrissy had made him a prince, so hopefully he had servants attending his head wound. I would see him tonight when the princesses snuck out and went to the secret ball. What would I say to him? How could I explain I hadn't meant any of this to happen?

I tore off pieces of crust and ate them in silence. No matter how I envisioned the scenario, it always ended with me feeling pathetic and stupid, not to mention guilty for ruining his life.

I would just have to assure him I could get us out of this mess. I would steal the goblet and trade it for our passage home.

Several minutes later, when Donovan and Madam Saxton walked in, his hair was combed and his face shaved clean. He wore an embroidered black vest over a white shirt with sleeves that poofed from his shoulders in typical Renaissance style. Shiny black boots went to his knees and a wide leather belt hung around his hips, holding a sword much more ornate than the one he'd come with. He should have looked ridiculous—he was just a parrot shy of a pirate costume—and yet he had a swagger that made the outfit work. He caught my eye and winked, then he and Madam Saxton strode to the front of the king's table. Donovan bowed at the waist, making a show of it.

Madam Saxton gave a quick curtsy. "Prince Donovan of the Kingdom of Hamilton-Ohio, having heard of your daughters' beauty and the great mystery besetting them, has come to offer his services."

Half of the princesses giggled and leaned together to talk. The other half eyed Donovan with curiosity.

King Rothschild picked up a turkey leg from his plate and took a bite. "Hamilton-Ohio, eh? I've heard naught of that kingdom. Where is it?"

"Very far away," Donovan said. "It's next to the kingdom of Cincinnati."

"Cincinnati?" King Rothschild repeated with disapproval. "What sort of kingdom uses the word 'sin' in its name twice? Does it want to encourage ruffian behavior? What next? PlunderPlunder-ati?"

The queen patted her husband's arm reassuringly. "I'm sure it's a lovely place."

King Rothschild grunted, unconvinced, and turned his attention to Donovan again. "You believe you can discover the reason my daughters' slippers are worn to ribbons each night?"

The queen dabbed her napkin to her lips, then gingerly set the cloth on the table. "It's simply horrible. The cobblers can't keep up, and then my girls have nothing to wear—well, nothing that matches anyway, and you know how ladies hate that." She let out a small laugh, expecting Donovan to agree.

He nodded politely. "Have you tried sending them to bed without slippers?"

The queen frowned at the suggestion. "That doesn't seem proper. Well-bred ladies need footwear befitting each occasion. Isn't it the same in your land?"

"I wasn't suggesting anything, Your Majesty. I'm only asking what methods you've already used to solve the problem." Donovan was poised while he spoke. Not freaked out and fumbling like I'd been when I first found myself in the mermaid kingdom.

He glanced upward in thought. "Have you tried putting something else beneath the princesses' beds to see if other objects get worn out? Perhaps the beds are enchanted."

"Enchanted beds?" the king repeated, letting the idea sit in his mind.

"In my land," Donovan said, "some people think monsters live under their beds. Perhaps in your land you have monsters who suck the life out of shoes."

The queen put a hand to her chest, displaying an array of golden rings. "Is such a thing possible?"

"Very possible," Donovan said, though his expression remained unworried. "I've had teachers who assigned books that sucked the enjoyment out of reading."

The queen pursed her lips. "They must have been evil books."

"Evil, indeed." Donovan's gaze swept over the princesses, sizing us up, then returned to the queen and king. "What exactly have you done to solve this mystery?"

The queen pressed her hands together, careful to avoid draping her sleeves onto her plate. "We keep asking the girls to tell us what happens to their slippers. We constantly assure them of our love so they know they can trust us."

In the same motherly tone, she added, "We also lock their door from both inside and out, and set armed guards in their hallway and below their windows—for their good, of course."

The king picked the remaining bits of turkey from the bone. "I threaten them frequently with disinheritance unless these shenanigans stop. They're obviously doing something they ought not."

He used the bone like a pointer, jabbing it at one table and then the other. "Are you listening, daughters? I'll sell you all to the first gypsy troupe that comes by!"

The queen smiled tolerantly at us. "Of course we won't do that, darlings. Our children are our greatest treasures."

"Daughters," the king muttered. "Twelve of them." He tossed down the bone and picked up another turkey leg, sullenly chewing it.

The queen kept smiling at us, meeting each of our eyes as her gaze traveled around the room. "Remember my dear girls, you can do anything you set your mind to, because you're so *special*."

No wonder none of the princesses told their parents anything. They probably didn't know whether they would get a pep talk or be banished.

The princesses smiled at their mother and ignored their father's threat. They went back to eating and murmuring to each other, still eyeing Donovan coyly.

The queen called to a serving girl. "Set a plate for Prince Donovan. He'll join us for supper."

The girl curtsied and hurried toward a door that must have led to the kitchen. A stream of servants had been coming and going from it carrying trays and pitchers.

"To the business at hand," the king said, chewing a bite of

turkey while he addressed Donovan. "If you can tell me what my daughters do every night, I'll give you one of them to wife and make you my heir. Are you fit for the challenge?"

"I hope so, Sire."

Bits of turkey had fallen in the king's beard and he wiped them off. "I hope so as well. I don't like men traipsing around my daughters' chambers. If you can't solve the mystery within three nights, I'll assume you're a scoundrel—just here in the hopes of glimpsing royal nightgowns—and it's the execution block for you."

The queen leaned forward, smiling at Donovan. "I'm sure you're a very nice young man, and we'd love to have you as a son-in-law."

The king shook his turkey leg at Donovan. "And don't attempt more than a glimpse at my daughters' nightgowns, or I'll think up something worse than execution for you." He turned to the queen, picking up his goblet as he did. "We need to hire a wizard. One that can change eager young suitors into doorstops." He downed his drink in one swallow and then waved at a passing servant to refill his cup.

Another serving girl set a plate and utensils in the only available place, the spot at the end of the table next to me. The queen gestured toward it. "Please sit down, Prince Donovan. The girls love company."

Oh yes. The princesses clearly loved company, evidenced by the fact they drugged the men who came here, thus dooming them to execution.

Donovan bowed to the king and queen, then strode to the seat next to mine. Once the king and queen stopped speaking, the minstrel began his tune again and the volume of chatter in the room picked up. The clink of silverware reminded me I'd had precious little to eat.

Donovan dropped into the seat at my side with a smile. "Princess Sadie, isn't it?" His words held a mocking tone. He knew I was no more royalty than he was. "A pleasure to join you."

I was not about to be taken in by his blue eyes and easy smile. He had grabbed the paper out of my hand in order to get here. He was my competition.

I matched his smile. "You have good manners for a guy with a criminal record. Is that something they teach in reform school?"

"Of course not." He leaned back in his seat, unruffled. "I learned how to act around kings the same way every other twenty-first century guy learns—by watching movies and playing medieval computer games." He glanced at the bread crust sitting on my plate. "Although I always thought princesses ate better. Food allergies?"

"No. The king punished me for coming to dinner late."

"I guess you shouldn't have spent so much time trying to send me away."

Several servants arrived at Donovan's seat, all bearing trays of food. One servant piled slices of turkey onto Donovan's plate then drizzled gravy across them. Another servant spread butter on his bread and spooned steaming peas in garlic sauce onto his plate. A third came by and poured cider into his cup. The smell wafted over, flavorful and delicious.

I took a bite of my gritty crust, ripping it with my teeth. Dry crumbs fell back onto my plate. My stomach rumbled unhappily.

The servants finally left in search of more plates to fill, and Donovan dug into his meal, making happy "mmm" sounds. "This turkey is great," he said between mouthfuls. "You should try it. Oh, wait . . . I forgot. You can't."

"Listen . . ." I leaned toward him so none of the other princesses would hear our conversation. "I understand you want to go back to the twenty-first century and your life of crime there, but I was here first, and I need the goblet. So can't you let me have it? I mean, your probation officer won't miss you much, and if you stick around here, you'll earn riches, power, and your choice of princesses. That's better than anything you could steal back home."

"Sorry. I'm attached to indoor plumbing, electricity, medicine, Internet access—"

"You get an entire kingdom. That completely trumps plumbing."

He raised a disbelieving eyebrow. "People travel by horse here. Horses are slow, uncomfortable, and don't come with heating or air-conditioning."

"But horses are cute."

"Yeah, like that's enough to convince me to give up technology." He picked up his goblet and took a quick drink. "You can bat your eyelashes as much as you like. It's not gonna get you anywhere."

I snorted. "I wasn't batting anything. I just want you to see reason."

He took a bite of his turkey, watching me like I was a jigsaw puzzle he was trying to piece together. "I know your type. You flirt and guys give you whatever you want."

"You don't know me at all."

"Hello. You wished to be a *princess*. That says a lot about you, Tiara-Girl."

I leaned closer to him and dropped my voice. "I didn't wish to be a *princess*. I wished to be a famous dancer."

He let out a laugh, nearly spitting food from his mouth.

He actually choked a little and had to cough a few times. "A famous dancer? Well, I take back everything I just said about you. That's clearly a practical wish. Who doesn't want to be remembered among the dancing ranks of . . ." he laughed again. "Are there actually *any* famous dancers?"

I ripped off another piece of crust. "I'm not going to feel guilty for beating you to the goblet."

"Don't be sure you will."

I wanted to knock the smugness out of his expression. "Really? What do you think will happen if I tell the king you're misbehaving in his daughters' bed chamber?" I gazed upward, considering the idea and wondering if I could infer something to the king that would get Donovan thrown out of the castle.

Donovan's eyes narrowed. "If you accuse me of anything, I'll have eleven witnesses who'll say I'm innocent."

"I know you haven't read the story, but trust me. The princesses are on my side."

Donovan sent me a quelling look, then stood up and faced the king. "Your Majesty?"

The conversation at the tables halted as every jeweled head turned to see what Donovan had to say. "King Rothschild, you told me if I succeed in my task, I can have the princess of my choosing." He made a sweeping motion toward me. "I've picked Princess Sadie."

I let out a startled gasp. What was he doing? What could he possibly hope to achieve by choosing me? Besides, the soldier was supposed to end up with the oldest sister, not the youngest.

Several of the princesses giggled. A few of them sent me reproachful looks. I wasn't sure whether they thought I'd been fraternizing with the enemy or whether they thought it was cruel of me to encourage a suitor who wouldn't live longer than three nights.

The king dipped his bread into the gravy on his plate. "You decided the matter so quickly—you must be either decisive or foolish. Let's hope for the kingdom's sake it's decisiveness. We've enough fools around here already."

The queen smiled at Donovan, giving him her blessing with glowing contentment. "He's neither. True love doesn't always need days or weeks. It can call to people in an instant." She put her hand over the king's, caressing it affectionately. "I felt the same way when I first saw you. And years later, we're still as much in love as the day we wed."

The king grunted and took a bite of bread.

Donovan cleared his throat. "I wouldn't wish anyone to say anything improper happened before I marry Princess Sadie, so I ask that Madam Saxton chaperone us while I stay in the princesses' chambers."

That's why he'd chosen me—so he could enlist an ally and make sure I couldn't accuse him of anything that would banish him from the castle.

This wasn't part of the fairy tale, but Donovan didn't know how the story went and probably wouldn't have cared about changing it. We both wanted out of this place. If that meant rearranging the story, so be it.

The queen nodded approvingly. "Your concern does you credit. I shall bid Madam Saxton to accompany you each night."

Donovan sat down, smugly, and everyone resumed eating. The mandolin player began another song, and the clanking of silverware and the hum of voices filled the room again.

Donovan returned to his food. "Do you have any other strategies you'd like to share? It's much easier to counteract them when you tell me about them beforehand."

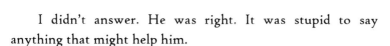

I didn't answer. He was right. It was stupid to say anything that might help him.

He took a bite of his peas. "Perhaps you could tell me why I'm not supposed to accept any food or drink from the princesses? Do you poison your suitors?"

I chewed my bread silently.

He shook his head, thinking. "No, that can't be it. Fairy tales aren't that dark."

Now it was my turn to laugh. "You obviously don't know where the word grim comes from."

"I bet you'll tell me."

I ignored the jibe. He ought to know things weren't always happily-ever-after. "Grim comes from the Grimm brothers who first collected the fairy tales and published them."

A serving girl came around with a pitcher to refill glasses. I stood and took the pitcher before she could refill Donovan's. "Here," I said sweetly, "let me do that. After all, I'm practically his fiancé." I poured cider into his glass with a flourish, then returned the pitcher, and sat back down.

The serving girl moved down the table, attending to the princesses' goblets.

Donovan eyed his glass warily. I knew he wouldn't drink it now. Good, let him worry. I was tired of watching his self-satisfied expression.

He leaned back in his seat and folded his arms. "Why do you want to go back to the twenty-first century anyway? You got what you wished for—you're a famous dancer."

"This is not what I wished for."

It was the truth, at least in the ways that mattered. I hadn't wanted to be separated from my family or time period. I'd never wanted to live in a fairy tale. But apparently my words weren't *technically* the truth. A strange sensation bloomed on the tip of my nose, a tingling pushing feeling. I let out a gasp and covered my nose with my hand. Had my nose just grown?

Donovan tipped his head to the side, a pose of vague curiosity. "Is something wrong?"

"No." That was definitely a lie and my nose tingled again, pinching as it pushed outward. This couldn't happen. Not in front of Donovan. He would know I was lying. How bad was it? I dumped the remaining bread from my plate and held it up, checking my reflection.

The silver surface distorted my image, making it impossible to tell how long my nose was. Would people notice? Did I look like Pinocchio?

I waited for Donovan to make the connection and accuse me of lying. Instead, he peered at me suspiciously. "Are you all right?"

I couldn't say yes, and I didn't want to say no. I kept holding the plate up, hiding my nose behind it. "Why do you ask?"

"Well, you dumped your food on the table and now you've got a plate in front of your face. It's just not something you see very often at formal dinner parties."

Did he not know about the lying clause in the contract? I kept gripping the plate. How had Chrissy said I could get my nose back to normal? Oh yeah—by telling the truth. "I did wish to be a famous dancer, but I didn't want to end up here." My nose tingled again, shrinking this time. "And yes, something was wrong a few seconds ago." I touched the tip of my nose. "But it's okay now." Slowly, I lowered the plate and put it onto the table.

Donovan was still watching me. "Do you have meds back home someone should know about?"

"No."

"Uh huh," he said, unbelieving.

He should know I was telling the truth, but clearly didn't . . . which meant he must not know about the clause. I put the biggest pieces of bread back on my plate, and wiped smaller crumbs onto my napkin. "Did you read your fairy's contract before you signed it?"

"What contract?"

"The fairy contract. Didn't Jade Blossom make you sign something before she gave you your wishes?"

"Nope."

He hadn't signed a contract? "How did you get a fairy godmother?"

He picked up his goblet and almost drank from it, then eyed it suspiciously and set it firmly back down. "How did you get yours?"

I wasn't about to relate the story of my viral video. Not when Donovan was already acting superior. "I asked you first."

Donovan picked up a piece of cheese from his plate and popped it into his mouth. When he finished chewing, he said, "If you want to know my secrets, you'll have to give me information in return."

"Sorry. I won't tell you why the princesses' slippers are ruined each night."

"All right. Tell me what you wished for besides being a famous dancer."

"Why do you want to know that?"

Another piece of cheese went into his mouth. "I'm curious."

That wasn't it. He was gathering information about me, getting to know his enemy's weaknesses.

"What person asks to be a famous dancer," he went on, "if she values freedom? Doesn't fame take away your freedom? Celebrities have to worry about hiding from rabid fans and even more rabid paparazzi. If you want freedom, obscurity is the way to go."

I hadn't thought much about the downside to being a rock star. I didn't linger on it, didn't want to admit Donovan had a point. "When I wrote the word freedom, I meant I wanted freedom from my problems."

He let out a short laugh. "It's a good thing you didn't wish for *that* from your fairy godmother. You're only free from problems when you're dead."

He was right, of course. I'm not sure which felt worse, that I'd said I wanted something so impossible or that I still wasn't sure what I wanted most from life. I didn't comment about it. I wasn't going to discuss my personal life with him.

Instead, I studied him with the same scrutiny he'd given me. If he was figuring me out, I needed to figure him out too. It would give me a better chance at stopping him. He was handsome, confident, and a professional thief. Why did a teenage guy need to steal things? Did he do it for kicks? Did he have a drug habit? Had he fallen in with the wrong crowd?

Maybe I could offer him a deal. "I'll tell you one of my wishes, if you tell me how you got your fairy."

"Okay," he said.

"I wished to have a beautiful singing voice."

Donovan shook his head, incredulous. "You really do want to be a celebrity, don't you?"

I didn't deny it, couldn't. My cheeks grew warm. "What's wrong with that?"

"With everything you could have wished for in the world, you went for pop star?" He made it sound so shallow, so stupid.

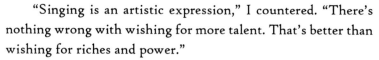

"Singing is an artistic expression," I countered. "There's nothing wrong with wishing for more talent. That's better than wishing for riches and power."

"What was your other wish? A band?"

That was a question I wasn't going to answer. "So how did you get your fairy godmother?"

Donovan pushed his plate away, apparently full. "Jade Blossom thought I was a nice guy and offered to be my fairy godmother, no contract required."

No contract? Perhaps no pitiable cross-species outreach program either. Maybe Jade Blossom was just looking for hot guys. Or ones with a talent for theft. "So what happened? She popped into your room wearing a sparkly dress and offered you three wishes?"

Donovan smiled. "If you want more details, you have to tell me what your other wish was."

"We made a deal that if I told you about my singing wish, you would tell me how you got your fairy."

"C'mon, you already know what I wished for." He cocked his head. "Why the secrecy? Did you wish for something even stupider than singing and dancing?"

Um, yeah. I crossed my arms. "I'm still waiting for details about you and Jade Blossom."

"Details weren't part of the bargain. If you want those, you'll have to give more information."

The king and queen stood, signaling the meal's end. The mandolin player stopped strumming, mid-song. The princesses stood almost as one, hushing their conversations as they looked at their parents. Donovan and I got to our feet last.

The king watched me stand with an aggravated sigh hovering on his lips, most likely because I should have gotten up when the other princesses stood. "I've business to attend to," he said. "The never-ending work of wrapping up a war. Be glad such matters don't fall to you, daughters."

Several of the princesses lowered their gazes. A few others swallowed guiltily. I didn't know what brought this reaction. The fairy tale never said anything about the war. It only mentioned the soldier had come home from it.

The queen motioned to Donovan to come forward. "Madam Saxton will give you a tour of the castle and grounds. If you're going to stay with us, you need to know your way around."

Donovan gave me a quick parting bow, then walked to the front of the room where Madam Saxton waited. Her calm stance didn't hide her eagerness. She was definitely on his side and would do everything she could to help him uncover the princesses' secrets. And tonight they would both come to our bed chambers.

Chapter 10

After the king and queen left, the princesses filed from the room in a dignified procession. A man by the door bowed when we passed and said each princess's name, as though our leaving needed to be announced. Rosamund, Beatrix, Clementia, Philippa, Isolde, Mathilda, Elizabeth, Catherine, Penny, Darby, and Kayla.

The OP—or other princesses—had the obviously-from-the-wrong-century names. With my dark hair and tanned skin, I knew I stuck out as much as the other transplants. It felt so odd to be here, like I was part of a play but didn't know my lines.

We retired to an empty sitting room to do embroidery. Retired in this case, meant we sat on uncomfortable chairs with handkerchiefs. I sat between Kayla and Darby, struggling with my needlework and wondering what I could say to the other princesses to get their help. I needed to find a way to keep Donovan from following us tonight. I couldn't just come out and tell them I was from the future and I knew what was going to happen because of a fairy tale. The BPs—blonde princesses— would think I was crazy.

I expected Kayla or Darby to ask me where I was from, comment on my arrival, something. But they seemed as unaware of my sudden addition as the BPs.

Kayla's smooth black hair was shorter than the other princesses' hair. She was probably the most recent addition. While the other princesses were busy talking, I bent my head toward hers. "How long have you been here?"

She didn't take her eyes off her embroidery. "I came in the room with you, Sadie. I've been here as long as you have."

"No, I mean how long have you been in this fairy tale?"

"Quiet," she murmured. "You shouldn't speak of fairies."

"Well, it isn't wise to speak *to* them, that's for sure. Especially if they ask you to sign a contract." I edged closer to her. "Did you have to sign one?"

She pushed her needle into the cloth, making it disappear among embroidered leaves. "I don't know what you're talking about."

I let out an indignant humph. "Am I the only one who had to sign a contract? Chrissy made them sound like they were standard."

"Contract?" Rosamund called over. "What are you prattling about, Sadie?"

All the princesses stared at me questioningly.

I swallowed. "Uh . . . never mind."

Mathilda lifted one of her delicate blonde eyebrows. "Methinks her time with Prince Donovan has addled her brain."

Beatrix giggled. Even that sounded elegant. "Prince Donovan is quite comely—addlingly so."

Philippa tsked as she drew her needle from the cloth. "Would you that your prince heard you utter such things?"

Beatrix stiffened and raised her chin. "I meant no disloyalty to my dear Frederick. I only mentioned Prince Donovan's countenance because it's a shame that such a fair lad must fail in his task. Many a woman would welcome his interest."

Philippa sent me a reproving look. "Yes, and Sadie's name shouldn't be found among that litany. You must have been free with your attentions or Prince Donovan wouldn't have asked for your hand."

Darby nudged me with her elbow. "Yeah, spill it, girl. What went down between you two?"

"I didn't encourage him." I jabbed at my handkerchief, attempting to turn my pink thread into a flower petal. "I was trying to get him thrown out of the castle."

Darby let out a disbelieving snort.

But several of the BPs nodded knowingly, loose tendrils bobbing around their chins. Clementia fluttered her hand over her embroidery in graceful arcs. "Some men think the unreachable fruit must be the sweetest."

I pulled my needle up through the cloth, managing to prick my finger in the process. "That wasn't it. He just wants Madam Saxton around so she can help him." How did I best explain Donovan to them without lying?

Catherine dipped her needle into the cloth and brought it up again in a smooth, fluid motion. "Prince Donovan should know our servants will be of no help. Nay, I fear he is smitten with you, Sadie." She held up a hand to stop my protests. "Perhaps you had no intention to use your womanly charms on him thusly, but for honor's sake you must behave with more decorum. What would Prince Jason say of your actions?"

I imagined Prince Jason was going to have a lot to say about my actions. Hopefully he wouldn't say it too loudly or with too much hysteria.

Isolde's eyes shifted to me. "Men grow weak in the presence of beauty. You may intend only to bestow a smile in friendship; however, to an eager heart it will appear an invitation."

When had I smiled at Donovan? I didn't recall ever smiling at him, at least not in a way anyone would think was inviting. But there was no point in arguing about it. The BPs already thought I was a tease. I had to steer the conversation, to warn them about Donovan. It was the only way to enlist their help in keeping him away from the goblet.

I peered around to make sure none of the servants had wandered into the room. "Look, Prince Donovan is different from the other guys who've tried to discover our secret. He won't eat or drink anything we give him, and he has an invisibility cloak. He's going to follow us tonight."

I had imagined this revelation would cause a stir of alarm. Instead the princesses calmly continued on with their needlework. "Nonsense," Rosamund muttered. "He ate well enough at supper."

"An invisibility cloak?" Kayla asked scornfully. "Are you for real?"

Beatrix crinkled her nose. "I've never heard of such a device."

"I have," Catherine said. Her voice took on the tone of a teacher. "Emperor Marcos of the Eastern Empire purchased such an outfit from some cunning tailors. They insisted all but fools could see the thread, and he was too ashamed to confess he saw nothing himself."

"Indeed," Isolde said, continuing the story, "Emperor Marcos was so taken in by the scoundrels that he let them dress him in the pretended clothes and then strolled down the street among his subjects."

Darby shook her head as primly as the other princesses. "That part of the story never made a lick of sense. If you know fools can't see the clothes, why would you put on the outfit? Who wants a bunch of fools watching you parading around buck naked?"

Mathilda let out an airy laugh. "Whatever his reasons, he made quite a stir among his subjects."

"To this day," Catherine added, "the emperor still insists the material was real and his kingdom is full of fools."

Clementia trimmed a piece of thread with a snip from her scissors. "Prince Donovan must have fallen victim of the same tailors. Poor, foolish, handsome boy."

"It's not an invisible cloak," I explained. "It's one that makes you invisible."

Penny threaded her needle with a red strand. "Did he seriously tell you that?" She had a valley girl accent. "That's like, so lame."

"He probably wanted to impress her," Kayla put in. "You know how guys are."

"Pray tell, where does he keep this cloak?" Elizabeth asked.

Isolde's silver needle flashed in the light. "On his invisible horse, no doubt."

Rosamund waved her hand dismissively. She was the oldest and her movements had the air of authority. "He's the fifth son and has no inheritance. All of his belongings are invisible."

It was clear I wasn't going to convince the princesses about the cloak. I pressed the other point. "He knows we're going to put sleeping powder into his drink. He'll dump it out into a planter instead of swallowing it." That's what had happened in the fairy tale.

Rosamund eyed me with sharp reproach. "And how, I might inquire, did he learn of our sleeping droughts?"

I met her gaze. "A fairy told him."

Elizabeth and Philippa shared a knowing look. "A fairy named Sadie, mayhap?"

"No, her name was Jade Blossom, and she . . ." I didn't mention the goblet. If I told the princesses I needed to take it, they might stop me. They probably didn't condone stealing goblets from fairy queens.

Mathilda put her hand to her chest in alarm. "Has a fairy betrayed our confidence?"

Elizabeth patted her arm reassuringly. "Don't fret. This is simply one of Sadie's wild tales. The fairies would do no such thing. Who amongst them would dare invoke Queen Orlaith's wrath? No one shall ever know of our secret ball."

Except for the hundreds of millions of people who would read the fairy tale in the future. "I'm not telling any wild tales," I insisted. But I had no way to convince them. They weren't going to believe I got the information from twenty-first century sources.

I looked to Kayla, Darby, and Penny for support. "You believe me, don't you?" I lowered my voice. "He's the soldier from the fairy tale. You know, *The Twelve Dancing Princesses.* Or eleven. It may have been ten or nine at one point."

Penny and Darby looked at me blankly . . . which went to show that, despite Chrissy's claim that the story was famous, not many people knew it. Kayla kept her attention on her embroidery and wouldn't meet my eye. She wasn't going to be of any help either.

"Positively addled," Mathilda proclaimed.

Beatrix tilted her head, examining me like I was a patient. "Or 'tis the effect of too little sleep." Her voice grew soft. "Do you wish to stay home tonight and rest?"

"No." I sounded petulant, not calm and reasoning like I'd intended. I took a deep breath and tried again. "The point is, Donovan knows not to drink anything we give him. We can't let him follow us. We need to come up with a Plan B."

I realized I'd used the wrong phrase when all the BPs stared at me questioningly. "What do you think we should plan to be?" Elizabeth asked.

"I plan to be dancing with Frederick tonight," Beatrix chimed. And the others quickly agreed, murmuring plans with various princes.

"That wasn't what I meant—" I started.

Rosamund gave me silencing look. "We'll have no more of your wagging tongue tonight. You've done nothing but stir up trouble since you came in for supper. First, you encouraged Prince Donovan to choose you above the rest of us, then you warned him not to take food or drink from our hand."

"I didn't warn him," I sputtered. My denial fell flat and unheeded. Her accusation that I had encouraged Donovan to choose me put the other princesses in a sudden and intensely offended mood.

They began complaining about my shortcomings—including the fact that my affections for Prince Jason were clearly not pure since I'd allowed myself to be swayed by Prince Donovan's charms and rugged looks.

Catherine punched her needle into her cloth, prim and

sharp. "Sadie has come to believe what so many people say: we are twelve princesses, each more beautiful than the last."

Isolde let out a humph. "You're no fairer than the rest of us, Sadie, so put on no airs."

Darby nodded. "And don't give us your sass, either."

And to think I'd always wanted a sister. Right now, I could do with eleven less.

Finally Rosamund raised her hand to quiet everyone. "You need not worry about Prince Donovan. I myself will ensure he drinks the sleeping drought."

She sent me a stern look. "And you, dear sister, will do well to consider your indiscretions. If you do more to help Prince Donovan, we won't allow you to come with us to the midnight balls."

After that, I didn't say much. Instead, I fumed and plucked at my needlework, taking out as many stitches as I put in. Not only had I failed to get the princesses' help, but now they were threatening to leave me behind tonight.

Well, Rosamund wasn't the only one who would be watching Donovan to make sure he drank the sleeping drought. I would too. If he didn't take it, I would insist that none of us go dancing. Donovan couldn't steal the goblet if he didn't leave the castle.

An hour passed, maybe more. The BPs were expert embroiderers. They barely glanced at their thread and were somehow able to make it do their bidding. Smooth, bright leaves appeared in their cloth, and delicate flowers bloomed under their fingers. The OPs weren't quite as good, but still passable. My stitching was uneven, didn't resemble anything found in a garden, and looked like a mistake from the beginning.

This caused a fair amount of head-shaking from the BPs, several attempts at instruction, and two predictions my prince would be embarrassed to carry any token I'd put my hand to.

I imagined when Jason saw me again, the state of my embroidery would be the least of his concerns. As I struggled with thread and needle, I made plans. If Jason and I worked together, we had a better chance of stealing the goblet. Perhaps he could distract the queen by serenading her. After all, he had that whole sultry, you-can't-break-my-gaze thing going for him.

In between plotting theft, I listened to the princesses' conversation, piecing together information about the country, our parents, and the princes. The more I knew, the easier I could pull off being a Capenzian princess. If the others realized I was clueless about everything, they'd undoubtedly realize something was wrong.

The war, I learned, started when Briardrake, one of Capenzia's vassal lands, decided it didn't want to be part of Capenzia anymore. They appointed their own king and led a revolt.

Fearing the loss of their own independence, Devanter and Salania, two nearby countries, joined with Briardrake's army. The resulting war lasted five years. Capenzia won, retaking not only Briardrake, but adding Devanter and Salania to the empire.

The war, like most, came at a great cost. Thousands of people died. Crops were burned and trampled, livestock taken to feed the armies. During a siege in one of the outer provinces, King Rothschild's brother and sister-in-law were killed, leaving their four daughters orphans—Catherine, Elizabeth, Isolde, and Mathilda.

King Rothschild adopted his nieces, which was why the king had eight blonde daughters around the same age. No explanation was given as to why the last four of us were also so close in age, or why we looked completely different.

After his brother's death, King Rothschild swore he would make the rebelling countries pay. He was in the process of doing that now—issuing heavy taxes on the people and stripping the nobility of their lands and titles.

"He's far too vengeful." Elizabeth sighed and her china doll features settled into frown. "Those who survived the war didn't start it."

Catherine nodded, a hint of tragedy finding its way into her expression. "If we can forgive the lands responsible for our parents' deaths, certainly King Rothschild should be able to."

Rosamund patted Catherine's hand soothingly. "Father's strong temper will eventually run its course. We must exercise patience."

"Love isn't patient," Catherine murmured sadly.

I didn't comment. I wasn't sure why the princesses were upset about the king's foreign policy or what it had to do with love. And besides, I had serious doubts patience would do anything to change King Rothschild's temper. It was one more reason to steal the goblet and get out of here as fast as I could.

Chapter 11

When the sun went down, we went to our bed chambers, although apartment would have been a more accurate term. The princesses had a sitting room complete with a fireplace, three couches, and more than enough chairs to seat us and several guests. I was relieved to see the room, as it meant Donovan and Madam Saxton wouldn't be hovering by our beds, watching us breathe while we pretended to sleep.

A door in the back led to another large room, this one with twelve ornately carved canopy beds lined in two rows. Sheer curtains draped each bed, see-through enough that anyone glancing into the room could still check to see we were there. Twelve dressing tables sat in front of the beds, complete with a pitcher, wash basin, combs, pins, ribbons, and mirrors.

Four closet doors interspersed the rows of beds, each closet bigger than my bedroom back home. Wardrobe rooms, the princesses called them. Skirts, bodices, and sleeves of every color and hue hung there, along with hooped skirts, long slips, corsets, coats, riding habits, hats, stockings, and things I didn't have a name for.

Honestly, how many layers of clothing did people in the Renaissance need to keep warm?

Lady's maids came into the bedchamber and unlaced, unhooked, and basically extracted us from our dresses. I was glad for the help. My bodice laced up the back, making it impossible to get out of by myself.

Underneath my dress and corset, I wore a cotton chemise and a padded pillow that gave my skirt its overflowing look. As my maid took it off, she called it a bum roll, which I thought sounded like a dance move.

I hadn't realized I wore a necklace until I was down to my chemise. Then I noticed the golden locket hanging at the bottom of my throat. I held it up, admired a tiny jeweled flower on the front, and flipped the locket open. A small painted portrait of Jason smiled back at me. He wore a yellow silk coat and an accordion-like white ruffled collar that pressed up against his chin.

I supposed Chrissy thought this necklace was one of the special little extras she provided as a godmother. I blushed and snapped the locket shut, worried Jason would see it. There is just something extra stalkerish about wearing a painted portrait of a guy you barely know.

I didn't want to wear the locket, but if I took it off, one of the servants might find it and show it to the king. It was better to wear it, hidden underneath my clothes.

After getting into my nightgown, I sat at my dressing table where my maid unpinned my hair, brushed it out, and fastened it into a braid. The lanterns on the tables and the glow from a fireplace in the back of the bedroom did a poor job of lighting the room. Everything seemed shadowed and watchful. The maids became more squeamish the later it got, as though the dark magic of ruined slippers might jump out of a corner and grab them.

Finally King Rothschild ushered Donovan and Madam Saxton into the sitting room and called for us to come out and greet our guests. The lady's maids left the room and the princesses spread out on the couches and chairs. Some talked with Madam Saxton or kissed their father goodnight.

Before the king left the room, he turned and surveyed us. "I expect the lot of you to behave and go to sleep like obedient daughters."

"We will," several princesses chorused back.

The king's gaze turned to Donovan. "I expect you to . . . well, I expect you to fail like every other man who's stepped into this room. See if you can prove me wrong."

"I will," Donovan said.

The king humphed, and shut the door with an authoritative bang. A moment later the outside bolt scraped against the door. We were locked in for the night. Rosamund went to the door and locked it from our side. The outside world was now locked out of the room as well. No one headed to the bedroom. Apparently it was our custom to socialize before sleeping.

I sat down in a chair that was a little farther than those around the fireplace. I didn't want to stare at Donovan. Enough of the princesses were already doing that—eyeing him with subtle and not so subtle attention.

My gaze only kept wandering to him because he was the enemy. I needed to see what he was doing. The fact that he wore the whole Renaissance thing well—his slightly long hair fit right in with the time period—was secondary.

Madam Saxton walked to the fireplace and put another log on. She'd brought a cloth bag with her, and she pulled out a ball of yarn and sat on the couch by the fireplace. "I've some knitting to do while I sit watch," she said with forced cheer. I imagined she wasn't thrilled to pull an all-nighter.

Donovan strolled around the room, examining it like a crime scene that might offer up clues. "So, how were your slippers when you put them under your beds?"

Our maids had actually placed our slippers under our beds, but no one corrected him. Several BPs innocently glanced in the direction of the bedroom and shrugged.

"They seemed well enough," Rosamund said.

Elizabeth adjusted the ribbon tied to the end of her braid. "Perhaps the cobbler made these pairs sturdier than our last."

Beatrix stretched her feet, enjoying the freedom of being shoe-less. "It's the cobbler to be blamed, certainly, and not—as our father suggests—mischief on our part."

"We're free of mischief," Clementia agreed.

"I don't know about her," Darby said in a confidential tone, "But I'm certainly free."

Penny sauntered past Donovan on her way to a chair. "Don't tease him. He already chose his favorite princess." She batted her eyelashes. "Without even meeting any of the rest of us. Your loss, Prince Donovan."

Several of the princesses giggled. Catherine murmured, "Sadie is a good choice for you."

"A very good choice," Kayla said.

Isolde and Mathilda both winked at me as though sending me a message—that I totally didn't get. My gaze went back and forth between them in an attempt to explain that I wasn't in on their facial gestures. Isolde rolled her eyes and Mathilda just laughed at me.

Donovan didn't comment on my suitability as a choice. "I'll check your bedroom before you go to sleep," he said, and headed there. The princesses went back to their conversations with each other, unconcerned.

When Donovan came back, he circled the room, still examining things, then finally sat in the chair beside me. "So," he whispered, "are you planning on killing me yet?"

"No, but there's always room on my agenda later."

His gaze drifted over the princesses. "This is just my luck. I'm locked in with a dozen beautiful women, and they all want me dead. I couldn't get to sleep tonight if I tried."

I leaned closer to him so our voices wouldn't carry. "To clarify, we don't want you dead. We just don't want you to discover our secret, and unfortunately, the byproduct of that may be your execution."

"I feel so much better."

"Although I'm not even sure about the execution. Is the king serious about killing you after three nights, or is that one of those I'll-sell-you-to-gypsies threats?"

"I don't plan on finding out." Donovan had picked up a brass coin from somewhere, and he fiddled with it while he peered at the door to our bedroom. "I thought being a princess meant you didn't have to share a room. Obviously your other wish wasn't for privacy."

I smiled despite myself.

He turned the coin from one finger to another in a practiced way. "What *was* your other wish?"

"Why do you keep asking?"

"Because I think you're interesting." His smile was too broad. He was trying to charm me.

"I'd rather be mysterious and not tell you."

He flipped the coin into the air and without looking, caught it. "There's got to be a secret passageway in here. It's the only way you could get out."

There was, and I didn't want him searching for it. Time to change the subject. "Jade Blossom has a lot of confidence in your stealing abilities, but it seems to me that the really good criminals wouldn't get caught and be given probation officers."

"I never claimed to be really good." He flipped the coin again. "Of course that doesn't mean I'm not."

Was he denying the claim or bragging about it? I couldn't figure him out. "How did you get caught?"

"I didn't. I just had some bad luck." He couldn't hide the grimace that flashed across his features. Whatever had happened, it wasn't pleasant.

Perhaps it was misery hoping for company, but right then I wanted to know his story. "I'll tell you how I earned my fairy godmother, if you give me the details of how you earned yours."

His eyebrows lifted with curiosity. "All right. You go first."

I told him about the audition, about how nervous I'd been, and how my voice cracked onstage. Until that moment, I hadn't thought about the incident with anything except horror, but somehow telling Donovan about it took out some of the sting— made it seem almost funny. Maybe being stuck in the wrong century put it in perspective. "Jason Prescott was one of the judges," I said. "After he Xed me, he told the entire audience I had no talent."

Donovan scoffed. "Like Jason Prescott would know talent if it walked up and punched him."

Or threw up nearby. Donovan was clearly not a Jason fan. A part of me felt relieved about that. Not everyone would care what Jason said about my singing. Another part of me wanted to defend him.

My hand automatically went to the locket underneath my chemise. "He's made millions of dollars and he's only twenty. You can't do that without talent."

"His music sucks." Donovan flipped the coin again, catching it with only two fingers this time. "The only reason his stuff sells is that stupid girls think he's cute. A singing cocker spaniel would do as well."

I repressed a shudder. "I think one of those was actually at the competition."

"Did it win?"

"I don't know, but I'm pretty sure it didn't throw up on the stage. So anyway you look at it, the dog did better than I did."

Donovan laughed. It had an easy, open sound to it. "I would have loved to see that."

"If you go back to the present, you will. Chrissy told me the video will go viral."

"Think of it as a commentary on the quality of the show's judges."

I shook my head, momentarily shutting my eyes against the memory. "The whole thing was so horrible that it qualified me for the fairies' pitiable damsel outreach program. That's how I got my fairy godmother."

Donovan bit back another laugh. "I'm sure it will be one of those here-today-gone-tomorrow videos."

Yeah, right. Donovan was too busy containing his laughter to convince me of that. I knew he would look up the video as soon as he got home . . . and then probably post it on all of his social media.

"When Chrissy showed up in my hotel room, having a

fairy godmother seemed like a good thing. I mean, who doesn't want three wishes?" I tugged at the back of my nightcap, adjusting the ruffle. "And then I wound up here."

"Exactly. That whole fairy godmother angle is just an excuse for fairies to mess with us."

"They should come with warning labels."

Donovan cocked his head. "Wait, did you just tell that story so I'd feel bad for you and let you have the goblet?"

"No." I hadn't even thought of trying to gain his sympathy.

"'Cause that's not going to work." He straightened, pulling away from me, then glanced around the room, to see what the other princesses were doing. Most of them sat talking in the chairs by the fireplace. Isolde and Clementia were passing silver goblets out to everyone. Catherine followed them with a bottle, filling each cup.

"I'm sorry you're stuck here," Donovan told me. "And I feel bad about your vomiting video problems, but I need to go back home."

"Yeah, to see your probation officer. It would be a shame if you missed that appointment."

"I have a brother who needs me, okay?"

"Fine," I said. "Clearly no one needs me."

"I never said that."

He didn't have to. I'd just thought it myself. Who at home needed me? Not my parents who were busy with their careers, not my older brother away at college, not anyone at school. No one needed me. I wasn't even sure how much anyone would miss me.

I forced a smile. "Now it's your turn to confess. How did you earn a fairy godmother?"

Donovan turned the coin between his fingers again. "It was nothing as dramatic as your story."

"Well, not everybody can splatter Jason Prescott's judging podium."

Donovan didn't say anything for a moment. "I'm not sure you want to hear it. It won't make you feel better."

I did want to hear it—all the more because of his secrecy, but Rosamund and Philippa didn't give me a chance to answer. They came over, carrying two goblets apiece, both already filled with drink.

"The time for slumber is upon us," Rosamund said, her voice as gentle as a lullaby. "Before we retire, we wish to toast you and your land. 'Tis our custom for visitors." She held out a goblet to Donovan. "Come stand with us by the fire."

He stood and took the goblet warily. "How thoughtful."

Rosamund looped her arm into his and led him toward the fireplace where the other princesses were waiting. Philippa handed me my glass and we followed. Madam Saxton still sat on the couch, her knitting in her lap and a goblet in her hand. I supposed her drink had sleeping potion in it as well as Donovan's.

The room was warmer near the fire, brighter, and yet it still felt like the room was cloaked in shadows. Rosamund held up her drink to get everyone's attention. "To Prince Donovan."

The princesses lifted their cups. "To Prince Donovan," they repeated and sipped their drinks.

I took a sip as well. A spicy apple cider slid over my tongue. It was room temperature and not as sweet as the apple cider from my century, but still, it was the best food I'd had all day.

Donovan raised his goblet to his lips and seemed to swallow, although I imagined when he lowered his glass, it would still be full.

"To the land of Hamilton-Ohio," Philippa called, and we drank a second toast, this one with entreaties that Donovan tell a story about his land.

"But not until we're done toasting," Beatrix added.

"To Capenzia," Kayla chimed. Everyone repeated the country's name, Madam Saxton the loudest.

After the murmurs of patriotism died down, Donovan raised his glass. "Allow me to make a toast." He smiled, and it had a challenging tilt to it. "To secrets and the curiosity that drives us to figure them out."

Rosamund laughed, a light giddy sound. "I know not if we should toast that. Haven't you heard the saying, curiosity killed the cat?" The look she gave him verged on feline satisfaction. "We wouldn't want that."

Donovan clinked his glass into hers anyway. "Fortunately, I'm not a cat." He took a step away from her and stumbled, sloshing some of his drink onto the floor. "Oops, sorry about that." He pulled a handkerchief from the bag on his belt, and bent down to wipe up the mess. As he leaned over, more drink sloshed from his cup onto the floor. "Oops again." He chuckled at himself. "I don't know what's wrong with me. My balance is off."

Or he was trying to dump his entire drink on the floor.

Rosamund took the glass from his hand before he could. "Here, let me refill this for you."

Strike one for him.

Donovan wiped up as much of the mess as his handkerchief could absorb, then straightened and tossed the handkerchief onto one of the chairs. "What were we toasting again? Cats, was it?"

He took his glass from Rosamund and lifted it. "To cats. Without them . . . the world . . . would have more mice."

"Perhaps you should sit down," Rosamund suggested.

"Perhaps." He headed toward a chair that stood by a planter. In the fairy tale, the soldier had dumped his drink there.

Rosamund looped her arm through his and led him past it. "You'll find one of these chairs more comfortable."

Philippa, taking her cue from Rosamund, quickly sat in the seat by the planter so Donovan couldn't make an excuse to return to it.

Strike two.

He turned from the chair Rosamund suggested and walked to the couch where Madam Saxton sat. No planters stood nearby, so Rosamund didn't protest the change.

Madam Saxton lifted her glass to Donovan as he sat beside her. "To less mice," she slurred. The sleeping potion must work fast. "They're nasty little vermin and they never clean up after themselves."

Donovan clinked his glass into hers. "But you've got to admit," he slurred back at her, "Mickey's got one fine theme park."

"What's a theme park?" she asked.

"Whatever a theme is driving at the time." Donovan tilted his head back, laughed, then raised his glass to his lips again.

Rosamund sent me a superior look, one that proclaimed, "See, he's drinking the potion."

I wasn't convinced. I watched Donovan for another moment, studied his too broad smile and half shut eyes.

Rosamund handed me a spare handkerchief. "Clean up the rest of the mess and hide the handkerchiefs with our soiled laundry. We mustn't leave any evidence father might find."

While I cleaned, the princesses talked demurely. A few took off their caps and undid their braids. Donovan hummed the theme song from the Pirates of the Caribbean. Madam Saxton laughed like a school girl, encouraging him to hum the tune again. She tried to join in. By the time I'd finished hiding the handkerchiefs, they were both silent. Madam Saxton's chin rested against her chest, eyes closed. Donovan's head lolled back against the couch and his breaths became deep and slow. The firelight made his features look warm, vulnerable somehow.

Rosamund strolled to the couch to check on them. "Prince Donovan, let me take your goblets from you."

Neither responded. She snapped her fingers near Donovan's face. Still no response. He seemed like the perfect picture of sleep.

Rosamund picked up the cup from Madam Saxton's lap. It had tipped over and a few drops spilled onto her dress, but beside that the goblet was empty. Next Rosamund took the cup from Donovan's loose grip. She looked inside, smiled, then tipped the glass upside down to show us it was empty.

"Well," Rosamund said, carrying the glasses to the nearest table. "That's done. Time to dress."

I still didn't believe he'd drunk it. Not when Jade Blossom had warned him not to. I padded to the couch to search for proof he'd dumped it out. I scanned the cushions for wet spots, the floor for puddles, then leaned over him and looked behind the couch. Nothing.

Donovan's breathing changed. He held his breath for a moment, then breathed in deeper as though wanting to move closer to me. I glanced at his face.

It was absent of any expression. His sandy blond bangs fell across his forehead, untouched. The lips that had so often twisted into a smirk were slightly open, relaxed. His dark eyelashes were closed, resting against his cheeks.

Perhaps his uneven breathing had been coincidence. Sometimes people breathed oddly when they slept. I kept leaning over him, checking for any twitch in his muscles that would reveal he knew I was there. "Can you hear me?" I whispered.

No response.

It felt odd to be this close to him, close enough I could smell a lingering scent of spices that clung to him. Close enough I could have easily run a finger across his cheek.

He didn't move. He kept breathing deep. Perhaps this was strike three and he really was out.

Chapter 12

Penny came up behind me. "Come on. If you make us late, Rosamund will totally flip out."

Kayla smirked as she walked by us. "Looks like Sadie can't take her eyes off Prince Donovan."

I straightened, moved away from the couch, and headed to the back room with the other princesses. "The king isn't really going to kill him after three nights, is he?"

"Of course he is," Clementia said with a laugh. "And then he's going to sell us to gypsies."

We went to the wardrobe rooms and helped each other get back into our gowns. I was especially slow. I'd never tied sleeves onto a bodice or laced a corset before.

We did our own hair. The others not only rolled and braided their hair into flawless coils, they managed to weave ribbons throughout them. I tried, failed, tried again, and finally managed to pin up a lopsided bun. It looked like a small animal was desperately clinging to my head.

When we finished getting ready, Rosamund lifted the edge of a tapestry by the window. A small silver key dangled from a hook on the underside. She inserted the key into a notch on the hearth, and the whole thing slid sideways, fire, smoke and all. The fireplace just stood there crookedly, apparently unaware of the change.

Impossible. No, not impossible, *magic*. The fairy queen wanted us to come, so she'd provided the portal.

The new doorway opened onto a landing. Shelves of lanterns lined one wall, and a row of black cloaks lined the other. The top of a wide staircase was just visible, leading downward.

Catherine pulled a stick from the woodpile, put the end in the fire, then lit the lanterns one by one. Philippa and Elizabeth handed them out to the princesses closest to the doorway.

While this happened, Kayla surveyed my hair, found it lacking, and undid my bun. "You can't go out like this. You look more like a trailer park princess than a real one."

Trailer park. The word meant she had memories from the twenty-first century. I lowered my voice. "You're from the future too, aren't you?"

"Quiet," she whispered. She took a section of my hair and coiled it. "I don't want anyone to hear I'm not their real sister."

I glanced at the BPs, all elegant copies of each other. "If they haven't figured it out by now, I don't think you need to worry."

Kayla pinned the first section of my hair up, and went to work on a second, coiling it as well.

"Do you want to be here?" I asked. "Did you wish for this on purpose?"

She let out a grunt. "Of course I want to be here. I used to be an overlooked, unpopular loser. Now I'm rich, pampered, and have my own Prince Charming. What's to miss?"

"Your family."

Another grunt. "Trust me. There's nothing to miss there."

"Computers. Cars. Phones . . ."

The other princesses put on their cloaks, adjusting the hoods. Rosamund lifted the edge of her skirt so it wouldn't trip her, then disappeared down the stairs. Beatrix followed.

Kayla worked faster, taming my long hair into an orderly row of coils. "You'll forget about modern conveniences after awhile." She said this as though comforting me. "Your old life will fade from your mind. That's the best part of the magic. Penny and Darby don't even remember the future. I find myself forgetting more each day."

"You want that?"

"Who wants to remember the stuff I put up with in high school? Pretty soon I'll only be Princess Kayla. Loved, revered, and admired. That's better than a phone."

I was so surprised, I didn't know what to say. You didn't have to abandon modern times in order to feel loved. Then again, what did I know about her life beforehand?

I hadn't always thought my life was so good. Hadn't I tried to escape high school through a rock star life just like Kayla had escaped by coming here? But still. "You don't mind being in a fairy tale?"

"What?"

"*The Twelve Dancing Princesses*," I clarified. "Or maybe it was eleven when you came."

She tipped her head to the side, still not understanding. "You sound as though you drank some of Prince Donovan's cider. Next you'll be toasting cats."

It was no use. If she'd ever known the story of the dancing princesses, she didn't remember it now.

Kayla slid a couple pins into my coiled hair. "Listen, Sadie, you need to behave tonight. Don't go acting strange around Queen Orlaith. If you do something that makes her cancel the balls, the rest of us will never forgive you."

I inwardly sighed. Kayla wouldn't be any help getting home.

She pinned up the last section of my hair, then stood back, admiring it. "Now you're presentable."

She went through the doorway, grabbed a cloak and lantern, and hurried down the staircase to catch up with the others.

I checked on Donovan one last time. He still sat where he had before, gently snoring. It was a low, grumbling sound.

I ducked into the magic doorway, picked up the only remaining black cloak, and put it on. If the story went the way it did in the fairy tale, Donovan would put on his invisibility cloak and follow us. I wished I could close the fireplace so it slid over the doorway, but I saw no way to do that and figured it could only be managed from the princesses' chambers. We needed the door open to get back to our room.

I took the last lantern and turned toward the stairs. It was only then I realized what a strange place I stood in. The princesses' chambers were on a top floor, so logically we should have descended into another room in the castle. Instead, the doorway had brought us someplace far away.

Stars spread out overhead, thick and bright. The white marble stairs stretching out below me seemed to go on and on. Even with the lanterns illuminating the way in front of me, I couldn't make out anything below us. Blackness stretched out on either side of me. The stairs were wide enough that three people could have walked side by side. The princesses, however, went down in single file. I didn't blame them. No railings lined the staircase, no walls either. Nothing seemed to be keeping the stairs up except magic.

I wasn't afraid of heights, but walking down these stairs in the dark while wearing a cumbersome evening gown had "bad idea" written all over it. I'd never been graceful, and it would only take one misstep to change this story to *The Eleven Dancing Princesses and Their Fatally Clumsy Sister*.

Lifting my skirt with one hand and holding the lantern with the other, I took a tentative step down, and then a second. What else could I do? I needed the goblet.

The marble glowed in the spots where the light licked against its surface. The air was still and breathless with a scent of leaves drifting up from somewhere.

Kayla turned to check on me. When she saw me gingerly padding down the stairs, she motioned for me to hurry. I did. A little. I also listened for Donovan's footsteps behind me. In the fairy tale, the soldier stepped on the hem of the youngest princess's dress. She reported the incident to her sisters, but they didn't believe her. No surprise there. These princesses hadn't believed me about anything.

I could change things. If Donovan stepped on my skirt, I would turn and snatch his invisibility cloak off. Not only would this reveal him to the princesses, I could use the cloak myself to get the goblet.

I made my way downward, waiting. Donovan didn't step on my hem. Of course he didn't. He couldn't be following me. He had nowhere to pour his drink, and when Rosamund took his cup, it was empty. He must have drunk it.

As I took the next step down, I was jerked backward. Donovan had stepped on my dress.

I spun around and grabbed at the air behind me, trying to catch hold of his cloak. My hand brushed against material. I tightened my fingers around it. For a moment I had the cloak, then he wrenched it from my grasp. I took a step upward, my hand making wide arcs, searching for the fabric again. I'd been so close.

"Sadie!" one of the princesses called sharply from below.

I jolted from surprise and lost my balance mid arm-swing. I hadn't expected anyone to check on me. At that point, I probably should have let go of my lantern and used both hands to catch myself—as tumbling off the stairs was a quick way to die.

But I could think of another more painful way to die. And it involved dropping my lantern, breaking it so oil spilled over me, and then having my dress go up in flames in the ensuing fire.

I held onto the lantern, realizing too late that if I fell, the lantern would break anyway. The only thing I'd accomplished by holding onto it was that I would now be on fire as I toppled off the stairs.

An arm grabbed hold of my waist and pulled me backward, steadying me. Donovan. It had to be him. He was the only one above me. As soon as I wasn't in danger of falling, his hand was gone.

Kayla darted up the stairs. "Are you all right? What were you doing waving your arm around?"

I put my hand to my heart, felt the pounding there. It was hard to catch my breath. "I . . . I thought someone was behind me."

"Who? A giant fly that needed swatting? You could have fallen."

Penny marched up the few steps separating us, lifted her lantern, and peered around. Yellow circles of lights spotted the marble. "No one followed us."

"Is everything well?" Philippa called from down the stairs. They'd all stopped and were trudging upward to see what the problem was.

"Perhaps she should return to our room and rest," Rosamund said. It was more of a threat than a statement of concern.

"No," I said hurriedly. "I'm fine."

The princesses gave me exasperated looks, then turned and descended the stairs again. After a moment, I followed them, going slower than the others. I knew that Donovan was nearby.

"Thank you," I said.

He didn't answer. Maybe he was afraid that if he gave away his position, I would make a grab for the cloak again.

I slowed my pace, curiosity tugging at me. "Why did you save me? If you'd let me fall, you wouldn't have any competition for the goblet."

"Yeah," his voice came from behind me. "That's pretty much the story of my life. Those good impulses always get me in trouble." Before I could comment on that, he added, "But if you grab my cloak again, I'll toss you over myself. And by the way—you hit like a girl."

"I wasn't trying to hit you," I said, offended.

Kayla turned and looked over her shoulder. "Who are you talking to?"

"No one—ow!" My nose had grown. Not a little bit like last time. It felt like the cartilage had pushed outward an inch.

Perhaps the bigger the lies, the more it grew. I put my hand to my face, as if I could push it back into place.

Kayla squinted at me in concern. "Are you okay?"

Donovan's voice was at my ear. "Whoa—did your nose just grow?"

"What I meant," I said to Kayla, hand still covering my face, "Is that Prince Donovan concerns me, and I spoke to him as though he was here."

All true. He was here, so technically I'd spoken to him that way.

Dealing with magic was all about finding the right technicalities.

My nose shrank down to its normal size. I dropped my hand and forced a smile at Kayla. "I'm fine. Really."

Kayla turned back around, her dress swishing around her feet. "Hurry. The boats are probably already waiting."

I picked up my pace. Apparently so did Donovan. His voice came near my ear again. "You wished to be Pinocchio? *That* was your other wish?"

"Of course not. Who in their right mind wants to be a wooden puppet?"

"Do you have a singing, dancing cricket for your conscience?"

"No. I have no conscience, so you should watch your step on the stairs. Ouch!" You wouldn't think sarcastic comments would count as lies, but apparently they did. My nose grew again. I raised a hand in disbelief. "It was a joke. I have a conscience."

I put my fingers to the tip of nose to make sure it shrunk again. It did. "Sheesh, whatever power is in charge of magic really should get a sense of humor."

"So, every time you lie your nose grows?" Donovan stepped beside me. "I'll have to remember that."

"And you can lie without any visible consequence. I'll remember that, too."

The front of the princess line had reached the end of the stairs, and Rosamund walked out into a meadow. The light from her lantern flickered over grass and scattered onto patches of clover. It was an odd thing to find at the bottom of a staircase, sort of like stepping off an elevator and finding a beach. Yet everything about this place seemed real, the stars overhead, the breeze meandering past, the sound of crickets. The night air was tinged with a scent of flowers. Jasmine, maybe.

A couple minutes later I reached the bottom of the stairs. I held my lantern high so I could see as much of the scenery as possible. A dirt path stretched out before us, leading through the grass toward a nearby pine forest. We headed down the path in our line of oldest to youngest, which made me feel like the caboose on a princess train.

Chrissy had said that once I went past the first tree, I would be in Queen Orlaith's domain. Other fairies couldn't go there, which meant if I got into trouble, Chrissy wouldn't be able to help me.

I'm not sure why the thought sent shivers up my back. It wasn't like Chrissy had done much to help me in the first place. But Queen Orlaith was a more powerful fairy, one who commanded plants to grab people and hold them until she decided their fate.

As we walked into the forest, I couldn't help searching the passing trees for random creatures they'd grasped in their branches. The trees all looked normal enough. Tall pines, growing so closely together their branches had never filled out. Sort of like a bunch of anorexic Christmas trees.

Fireflies blinked around us, making the whole forest appear to be strung with twinkle lights. Ten minutes later I noticed the other trees. They looked like deciduous trees at the end of fall when just a few leaves stubbornly held on. Only these trees weren't wood. The moonlight gleamed silver on their branches and the fireflies hovering around them made them glitter. The trees were beautiful, and yet there was a starkness to them—something that spoke of night.

I knew from the fairy tale that the soldier took branches from the trees to use as proof when he reported to the king. Of course, Donovan wasn't a soldier, he was a thief. He probably wouldn't be able to resist taking more than a branch. Perhaps if he kept busy stuffing his pockets, he'd miss the boats waiting to take us to the queen's island.

From beside me, I heard his sharp intake of breath. He'd noticed the silver trees. "Hey, Little Black Riding Hood, what's the deal with the trees?"

"They're real silver," I told him. "It's in the book."

He didn't speak again. I assumed he was entranced by all the wealth sitting out in the open. The branches of a couple of the pine trees on the path up ahead swayed as he pushed them aside to reach the silver ones.

Not long afterward, I heard the crack of a branch breaking. Several large gray owls took flight from hidden boughs, letting out hoots of protest and circling the trees as they hunted for the offender.

I didn't see whether they gave up the search. The path took me away.

Not long after, we reached the golden trees. They had a glow of their own, as though they were too proud, too fine, not to show off a little. What few leaves they had, shifted in the breeze, making the moonlight wink off of them. One grew so close to the path, I stepped into the forest to touch it. The trunk felt smooth and cold, like touching glass. As I examined the delicate leaves, a large brown owl swooped from the sky, screeching angrily. It dived at me, pecking my hand with its beak.

"Ouch!" I jerked away from the branch and jumped back on the path before the owl could strike again.

It glared at me with angry yellow eyes, shot back up into the forest, and disappeared into the darkness of the branches.

Stupid bird. I'd never realized owls were so touchy. I rubbed the back of my hand. A small bloody welt had formed between my knuckles.

Apparently people weren't allowed to touch the trees. I envied Donovan again for his invisibility cloak. Judging by the owls' behavior at the silver tree, they suspected someone was skulking around but didn't know how to find the culprit.

Next we passed the diamond trees. Mixed in among the pines, they seemed like normal trees—rough brown bark, spindly branches, patches of heart-shaped green leaves. But nestled among the leaves at the end of the branches, were cherry-sized diamonds.

I wasn't a greedy person, but if I hadn't known I'd be swarmed by angry owls, I'd have filled my pockets. After all, the pearl bracelet I'd put on as a mermaid had traveled with me to this world. Wouldn't the diamonds come home with me too?

For the next minute I had a heated conversation with myself. The sensible part of me insisted that trying to grab a diamond wasn't worth the risk. I'd come for the goblet. I shouldn't do anything that might jeopardize that—like being pecked to death by owls.

The un-sensible part of me persisted though. I had to tell myself firmly: *Angry magical creatures are dangerous. Have you learned nothing from fairy tales? Has Walt Disney's life's work been in vain?*

When I saw a small, stunted diamond that must have fallen from a tree and rolled near the path, I couldn't help myself. I reached down and picked it up. No owls sprang from the air or dived toward me.

I hadn't touched the trees or gone off the path, so the owls hadn't been alerted.

The diamond was only pea-sized instead of cherry-sized. Still, it was a diamond. I slipped it into my pocket, suppressing a smile.

How could my parents ever hope for me to become a sensible person, when being un-sensible had just totally paid off? As I walked, I worried the diamond might clink into the goblet once I'd stolen it, and I took the diamond from my pocket and slipped it into my stocking instead.

A few minutes later, the forest opened up, and a dark lake spread out before us. An island was barely visible in the night. It was perhaps a mile from the shore, and would have blended into the sky and water if it hadn't been for a lit pavilion that stood there, partially obscured by trees.

Twelve narrow boats sat along the edge of the lake—half in the water, half on the land. They were the size of large rowboats, decorated with ornate curving prows that reminded me of giant snail shells.

Twelve guys stood by the boats, each holding a lantern. To say the princes wore brightly-colored jackets with matching pants wouldn't be quite accurate. Pants go down to the feet. Theirs ballooned out and ended at the knee.

Each guy wore colored hose and leather shoes with heels like a woman's. But perhaps the oddest things in their ensembles were their ruffled collars. They were so thick they made the guys look like their necks had gone into hiding.

I stopped walking and searched for Jason. Which boat was he standing by? And more importantly, what should I say to him? I'd thought of dozens of things, but wasn't sure what would be best. How does one properly apologize for sticking a complete stranger in a fairy tale—twice?

I heard a muffled laugh behind me: Donovan's commentary on the scene. "So," he said, "every night the princesses go and hang out with elaborately dressed clowns? That's the big secret?" Another laugh. "No wonder you don't tell your father about this."

"They're not clowns. That's Renaissance fashion for noblemen."

"Call it what you want. They're still wearing poofy capris."

"Your pants go to the knee too," I reminded him. "The only reason you don't look ridiculous is you're wearing boots."

"And I'm better looking."

That too, but I didn't admit it.

Donovan let out another low chuckle. "All those dudes look like their heads are stuck on platters."

"No one claims that fashion makes sense."

A row of lampposts stood at the end of the trail. The other princesses hung their lanterns there and then headed toward the princes. I walked slowly to the posts, still searching for Jason.

I spotted him at the end of the row of boats, closest to the trail and the lamppost. He was half leaning, half sitting on his boat's prow, eyes shut. Instead of carrying his lantern, it sat on the ground by his feet.

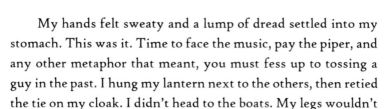

My hands felt sweaty and a lump of dread settled into my stomach. This was it. Time to face the music, pay the piper, and any other metaphor that meant, you must fess up to tossing a guy in the past. I hung my lantern next to the others, then retied the tie on my cloak. I didn't head to the boats. My legs wouldn't move in that direction.

Beside me, Donovan drew in a low breath. "Is that Jason Prescott?"

"Maybe." *Ouch.* "Yes."

"*That* was your other wish? You made Jason Prescott come here to be your boat rower? Sheesh. Remind me not to get on your bad side."

"It wasn't like that. I wished for him to be here because I liked him."

Donovan paused. "In that case, remind me not to get on your good side."

A couple of fireflies circled around me, flashing as they chased each other. I waved them away. "You can't go any farther toward the lake. Sadly, you didn't have the forethought to wish anyone here who has their own boat. Bring one with you tomorrow night. And don't forget the oars."

I headed toward Jason. I doubted my instructions would have any effect on Donovan. In the fairy tale, he snuck onto the youngest princess's boat.

Most of the princes left their boats, and strolled toward the princesses, their strides filled with anticipation and gallantry. The princesses glided happily to their boyfriends, as poised as a ballet troupe. They called out happy greetings and curtsied demurely. Each girl held out a hand to her prince, and each prince took his girlfriend's hand and kissed it.

I imagined my greeting from Jason would be quite

different. I trudged toward him, words tumbling uselessly around my mind. *I'm really sorry. Completely, thoroughly, mortifyingly sorry.*

Jason had finally noticed me. He watched me, eyes narrowed, trying to place me. I didn't know whether to be relieved or insulted he didn't recognize me. Was there any way I could get through this night pretending we hadn't met?

No sign of his head injury showed on his forehead. I supposed I should be grateful to Chrissy for fixing that, but right now it was hard to be grateful to her for anything.

When I drew close, Jason's eyes went wide. He gasped in surprise and took a startled step forward. "You!" he said, waving a finger in my direction. "You're that girl from the audition."

Chapter 13

My throat went dry. I cleared it uncomfortably. "Yeah . . . um . . . hi again."

His eyes, which had always looked so kind and understanding in his pictures, now glared holes into me. He kept waving his finger. "You're responsible for all of this, aren't you?"

"Sort of." Chrissy was responsible for part of it. I held out my hands, a gesture asking him to hear me out. "This will sound crazy, but I have a fairy godmother, and I made a few wishes. I didn't know she would send you here. I didn't even know she would send *me* here. I wouldn't have—"

"What kind of crazy stalker are you?" he shouted. "You come to the show, make a mess, have a bunch of smelly sailors kidnap me, then I end up in a place where everybody dresses like the Three Musketeers." He took another step toward me, his finger nearly jabbing me. "Take me home right now!"

Everyone was staring at us. I imagined the princesses

would have plenty to say about this when we got back to the castle, and none of it would be good.

"You're making a scene," I whispered.

"A scene? You haven't seen the scene I'll make if you don't get me out of here. I have people, you know."

I raised my hands in an attempt to calm him. Several princes shot him disapproving looks before turning their attention back to the task of escorting their princesses to their boats.

"I'm trying to get us home," I said. "But I need your help." Behind Jason, our boat wobbled back and forth on the shore, a telltale sign Donovan had climbed inside.

"Help? You want my—" Jason stopped. His eyes went over me, once, twice. "Wait a second, did you . . ." He shook his head as though clearing it. "Were you a *mermaid* at one point?" His gaze zeroed in on my shoes, checking to make sure I had feet.

I cleared my throat again. "I need to explain a few things."

Jason's lips clamped together, and his nostrils flared. He didn't look like he wanted to stay here for two more seconds let alone stand around and hear what I had to say.

The other princes had finished escorting the princesses to their boats and were exchanging whispered words before helping them step inside. I didn't have much time. I quickly condensed the last day of my life into a minute-long report, emphasizing I'd never meant to involve him. He listened in sullen silence.

"So it was an accident," I emphasized. "All we have to do is get the queen's golden goblet, and we can go home."

"Fairies did this," Jason said flatly. "That's your explanation."

"Yes."

He stared at me for another moment, then smiled with dawning realization. "This is a prank, isn't it?" He glanced around, nodding his head as though he had the whole thing figured out. "Did my manager okay this? 'Cause I'm going to kill him if he did."

Jason put his hands on his hips and forced out a laugh that sounded more relieved than happy. "When he told me I should dive into reality shows, I didn't expect him to take things this far."

"It's not a prank."

Jason scanned the shoreline. "Where are the cameras?"

"Look," I said, trying to recapture his attention. An idea had suddenly occurred to me. "We might be able to get out of here on a technicality. You don't love me, right?"

He reached out and patted my shoulder patronizingly. "I love all of my fans. They're the best." He said this too loudly. "No hard feelings." He glanced around again, still searching for cameras. "You got me good."

I inwardly groaned. He didn't love me, but now that he'd said he did, Chrissy would consider it proof she'd fulfilled her part of the contract.

"I can be a good sport about this." Jason gave a thumbs up to the prince at the boat next to ours. "Hey, guys, we're cool now."

Finally Jason turned back to me. He lowered his voice a whisper. "You tell your people they have to cut any footage of me yelling. In fact, I want editorial approval of the whole thing, or you'll be dealing with my lawyers."

I would take lawyers over fairies any day.

"It's not . . ." I started, then didn't finish. Maybe it was for the best Jason thought tonight was part of a reality show prank. It would keep him on his best behavior, and I didn't feel like listening to him yell again. I stepped toward the boat. "Do you know the story *The Twelve Dancing Princesses?*"

"Sounds familiar." He snapped his fingers. "They're an indie rock band, right?"

Really? Was I the only one who ever read fairy tales as a child? I couldn't tell Jason the story, not with Donovan nearby listening. I took the last few steps to the land's edge. "We'd better go, or we'll be late for the dance."

Jason seemed to remember a boat sat behind him. "Right. The other guys mentioned the midnight ball. We're supposed to dance for some queen chick."

The land was damp here, and I lifted my skirt to avoid getting it wet. "Right."

"Here's the deal," Jason said, voice still hushed. "I don't care what my manager agreed to. I'm not staying the entire night. I'll do two numbers. Maybe three if I like the band. That's it. And I'm not signing autographs for anyone."

"I wasn't planning on asking." It would have been nice if Jason offered to help me climb into the boat since my skirt weighed about twenty pounds. He didn't offer, so I climbed in as carefully as I could and made my way to an intricately carved wooden bench at the back of the boat. I half expected to bump into Donovan. Where was he sitting? I knew the answer as soon as I thought of the question. He was in the only place where Jason and I wouldn't run into him—sitting on the top of the back edge of the boat.

I saw nothing that indicated his presence. No telltale glimmer from the moonlight hitting his cloak. I could have ordered him to get off the boat, but even if he listened—and that was highly doubtful—he would just climb into one of the other boats. They were still lined up on the shore.

Besides, I didn't think it would improve Jason's confidence

in me if I suddenly yelled at the empty space behind the bench. I had to think of something else—something that would prevent Donovan from getting to the island. If he came, he would get the goblet and Jason and I would be trapped here. The thought made me feel prickly with panic.

I couldn't stay here. And I couldn't let Jason be stuck here either.

The other princes gave their boats a powerful shove, sliding them into the lake. Then the princes took a few strides and leaped inside, barely getting the bottoms of their boots wet.

Jason pushed our boat. It only moved an inch. He pushed again with little better results. He probably wasn't as strong as the other princes, and Donovan's added weight wasn't helping matters. Jason turned and pressed his back against the prow, using his legs to push. "The boat . . . must be . . . caught on something."

The prince closest to us let out a mocking chortle as his boat glided away from shore. "This is what becomes of those who grow lax in their training. Next, you'll be unable to lift your sword."

Another nearby prince dug his oars into the water. "Did Jason lift his sword today? I only saw it knocked from his hand. Repeatedly."

"Last in swordplay," a third prince called, "and he'll be last in rowing too!"

Jason put his shoulder to the boat and grunted with effort. "I'll beat both of you losers across the lake!"

The princes had more to say, but by then they were too far away for us to hear. Finally, Jason managed to scrape the boat across the shore and into the lake. Huffing, he sloshed through the water and flung himself inside.

To Donovan's credit, he didn't laugh at this performance, at least not that I could hear.

Breathing hard, Jason picked up the ends of the oars, and paddled them into the water. "They couldn't give us a motor? What's the deal—are they turning this into some sort of triathlon?"

I figured it was a rhetorical question and didn't answer. I looked out at the lake. Small waves lapped against the boat, as dark and shiny as black oil. The moonlight made a trail across the water like a path leading to the island. This place was probably beautiful in the daytime. It was a shame we only got to see it at night.

I didn't know what to say to Jason. His fame still awed me. I was sitting in a boat with Jason Prescott—the real him, not the posters that lined my room. I felt stiff and awkward and completely ordinary.

I expected him to make small talk—maybe ask me why I wanted to be a singer, or why I currently had eleven sisters. He didn't. He kept his gaze on the other boats, trying to catch up with them. "I'm only behind," he panted, "because I got a late start."

After a few more moments of watching Jason strain at the oars, I said, "So where are the princes from?"

The fairy tale never said anything about them beyond the fact that they danced with the princesses every night. As a child, I'd always wondered why twelve princes happened to be hanging around a secret ball, why their parents were never concerned about the state of their footwear, and why one of them didn't ever show up at the castle and tell the king he could solve the riddle. If one of the princes wanted to marry his princess, hey, problem solved.

Even though I was now living the fairy tale, thus far I only knew the answer to one of my childhood questions. The princes didn't have to worry about their footwear because they wore leather shoes. Leather was sturdier. This, I supposed, is why nobody wore silk slippers in the twenty-first century. Say what you wanted about the discomfort of high heels, at least they lasted more than one night.

"Where are you staying?" I added.

Jason strained against the oars. "I'm staying with four other guys in a castle in Briardrake. Don't ask me where that is because I've never heard of it. They keep saying I'm their brother. Must be part of the show. We met up with the other guys when we got here. They all know each other."

"Briardrake?" I repeated. And another part of the fairy tale made sense. "Capenzia went to war with Briardrake. Along with Devanter and Salania."

"Devanter and Salania," Jason said. "That's where the other princes are from."

And that explained why the princesses didn't tell their father about their suitors. The king wouldn't be happy to learn his daughters were in love with the enemy. I gazed across the water at the other couples. "I wonder how the princes and princesses met?"

Jason didn't have an answer to that. The muscles in his arms strained with effort. He nearly stood up while he rowed, attempting to gain distance on the other boats. I doubted he'd make any ground. The other princes were used to rowing. Jason had spent his time playing guitar.

"If the princes love the princesses," I continued, "I wonder why they didn't call a truce years ago." Maybe it meant their relationships were recent.

Jason grunted. "I think we've got a defective boat. This

thing isn't moving." He obviously wasn't going to be any help in solving fairy tale mysteries.

He let go of the oars and rubbed his palms against his pants. "Explain again how we win this thing—we're supposed to get a goblet at the dance?"

"The queen's golden goblet. She can't know we're after it. When we give it to my fairy godmother, she'll send us home."

He picked up the oars and rowed again. "So how do we get the goblet?"

I wasn't about to discuss strategy while Donovan sat behind me, listening. From here, it was about a ten-minute swim back to the shore. Not too bad. It was a lot closer than the distance to the island. "We'll make plans to take the goblet in a minute. First, I've got to do something."

Without explanation, I pivoted and lunged with outstretched arms in Donovan's direction. If I'd been wrong about where he sat, my momentum might have made me topple from the boat. But I wasn't wrong. Donovan let out a muffled exclamation, and a moment later a huge splash of water sprayed the side of the boat.

I sat back down, folded my hands in my lap, and calmly smiled at Jason.

He peered at the water then back at me. "What did you just do?"

I shrugged. Shrugging is not a lie, so it was safe.

Off to our side, the water stirred, splashed some more. A string of muttered curse words seemed to hang, disembodied, in the night air.

"Row faster," I told Jason. I didn't want Donovan to swim to the boat and hang on.

Jason applied the oars to the water with extra urgency.

"Did you see that?" He looked over his shoulder. "What's living in this lake, anyway?"

After a moment's thought, I decided Jason should know about our competition. After all, Donovan might swim to the island instead of the shore.

"Actually, that splash was an invisible guy who stowed away on our boat."

"An invisible guy?" Jason repeated doubtfully.

"His name is Donovan, and he's after the queen's goblet too. You'll need to watch out for him."

Jason's eyebrows rose skeptically. "How do I watch for an invisible guy?"

"I didn't mean *literally*."

Jason cocked his head to the side. "Why does an invisible guy want the queen's goblet? Doesn't he have enough invisible goblets at his house?"

This was just what I needed. Jason thought I was crazy. I let out a frustrated sigh. "Don't any guys know the story *The Twelve Dancing Princesses*? What were you all doing during your childhood?"

"What was I doing?" Jason asked, taking offense. "I was practicing. While the rest of you wannabes goofed off, I took guitar, piano, and voice lessons." He went on for the rest of the trip across the lake talking about how everyone thought his success was a fluke—when actually he'd worked his butt off *for years*.

I nearly told him I was impressed to meet someone who could play musical instruments with his butt.

Wannabe. Honestly. I was taking his posters off my walls as soon as I got home.

As we neared the shore, I broke into his rant. "We need to get back to our plans for the goblet. The queen asks it a question at midnight. After that, she might not notice if it goes missing. So here's what I think we should do: We'll dance for awhile. A few minutes past midnight, go up to the queen and tell her you want to sing a song in her honor. Turn on the charm. Keep her attention on you. Can you manage that?"

Jason let out a snort as though it was ridiculous to even ask. "Hey, when I sing to a woman, she doesn't take her eyes off of me."

"Good. While she's watching you, I'll swipe the goblet. After your song, we'll fade into the crowd. When no when is looking, we'll leave and head back to the boat. Hopefully we'll be long gone before the queen notices that her cup is missing. Once we're through the forest, we can contact Chrissy. She'll take us home."

It sounded easy enough, and I desperately hoped it would be.

Jason's speed had picked up once I'd pushed Donovan from the boat, and we weren't far behind everyone else now.

The first boats were reaching the island. The trees there had an unearthly beauty, shining faintly, as though holding bits of sunshine in reserve. In between them, rows of lampposts lined a stone path leading to a large columned pavilion.

The other princes rowed as far as they could onto the shore, then hopped out of the boats and dragged them further onto the embankment so their girlfriends wouldn't get their slippers wet. The princesses accepted these attentions with smiles, eyelash flutters, and beaming looks of approval.

Jason rowed our boat as far as it would go onto the shore, then mopped his forehead with his coat sleeve. He shook out the cramps in his hands took off his gloves to check for blisters, and seemed to be waiting for me to disembark.

I tried not to hold his lack of gallantry against him. He

hadn't been born in a time when women needed help hauling their dresses around. I gathered up my skirts, holding as much fabric in my arms as possible, and attempted not to trip while stepping out of the boat. My slippers partially sunk into the wet ground. I took careful steps to drier land.

Overhead, a raven sailed through the moonlight, circled us, then glided down to the stone path. Before it landed, it transformed into a young man. He was perhaps in his early twenties, although it was hard to tell. He was handsome in an ageless way, in a fairy way. His dark hair was pulled back into a sleek ponytail, accenting a pair of equally dark eyes that oversaw our arrival.

He wore black pants, boots, and a loose black shirt—not modern but not Renaissance either. His wings resembled raven feathers and seemed fierce somehow. Warlike. So different from Chrissy's silky butterfly wings.

He spread his wings out, then drew them together and with a flash of magic they disappeared. He waited for us on the path, arms crossed. I'd been standing in front of the boat, blocking Jason's view of the man, which was perhaps for the best. Jason might have worried if he'd known our hosts weren't human.

Jason stepped onto the shore after me, glancing around and still stretching the aches out of his hands. "Who's that?" he asked, gesturing toward the man.

"I don't know."

"Must be a show worker. Good."

Instead of looping his arm through mine like the other princes had done with their princesses, Jason strode up the stone trail, not caring that I had to struggle to keep up with him. The other couples were a little ahead of us, chatting as they strolled toward the pavilion. They hardly glanced at the fairy guy, and he didn't pay any attention to them.

His gaze slid to Jason and me. I noticed a scabbard hung at the fairy's side, revealing the hilt of a sword. Was he here to guard against intruders?

"Only eleven couples have graced the ball before," he said. "And yet now comes a twelfth. How is it you found your way here?"

"I rowed." Jason wiped sweat from the back of his neck. "And it's harder than it looks. Can you have someone get me a drink?" He fluttered his hand. "I don't care what it is, as long as it's chilled."

I stared at the fairy and gulped. I hadn't expected him to realize we were new to the story, and I didn't know what to say. I couldn't lie, and I couldn't tell him the truth—at least not the part about Chrissy sending me here to get the queen's goblet.

He turned to the couple passing him, Catherine and her prince. "Who is yonder maiden?"

Catherine let out a laugh of surprise. "Do you not recognize her? 'Tis Sadie, our youngest sister."

"Your sister?" The fairy's gaze skimmed over the group, checking their responses.

Elizabeth sent me a teasing look. "Perhaps you don't recognize her because Kayla did her hair tonight. Sadie looks presentable for once."

The fairy smiled genially at the couples. "Very well. Go eat and drink. The music has already started." He turned to me, and the smile faded. "I'll take you to meet the queen. She wishes to speak with you."

"Thank you," I said, though the ominous tilt of his brows suggested he wasn't doing me a favor.

Chapter 14

The fairy motioned for me to follow him. Before I did, I curtsied politely. If we were all polite to each other, the queen might not . . . say . . . get mad at me for crashing her ball and turn me into a topiary bush. "May I have the pleasure of your acquaintance?" I tried to sound royal, but the tone sounded false in my ears, like play acting.

His lips quirked up, humoring my attempts. "I am Kailen, Queen Orlaith's son."

That made him a prince. Fairy royalty. I curtsied again. "I'm pleased to meet you, Your Highness."

"Yeah, pleased," Jason added absently. "Drinks are waiting for us, right?"

Kailen swept his hand toward the pavilion. "This way."

I followed the others up the trail, listening to the orchestra music. Violins, flutes, cellos, oboes, clarinets, and instruments I couldn't place. The sound of running rivers and the hush of wind twisted into the music, playing the tune along with the brass and strings. "What are those instruments?" Jason asked. He'd noticed them to. "Cool sound. I like it."

I adjusted my grip on my dress. "I guess we'll see."

He didn't speak to me after that. The rest of the way to the pavilion, he tapped his hand against his pants to the rhythm and hummed along with the song as though committing the tune to memory.

After a couple of minutes, we reached the pavilion. Although the word pavilion didn't do the place justice. It wasn't the sort of structure found in a park. It was more of an open-air cathedral with a high arched roof made of white stone.

Marble columns were etched with silver vines so detailed I nearly expected them to sway in the breeze, to stretch and grow. Each buttress, each roof panel was decorated in patterns of leaves and flowers, making it seem like an overhead garden. The flowering bushes surrounding the pavilion were so laden with blossoms that in places they dripped onto the dance floor in splashes of color.

On one side of the room, two long tables were covered with platters of food and pitchers filled with pastel drinks. A dozen chairs sat nearby, waiting for couples who wanted to rest. I couldn't tell where the music came from. It was just there—drifting about the dance floor.

My attention was drawn to the back of the pavilion. Two large wooden thrones stood behind a white marble table. A beautiful, dark-haired woman sat in one of the thrones. Queen Orlaith.

Jason saw the refreshment table and made a beeline toward the drinks. Kailen didn't call him back. Instead he motioned for me to follow him toward the queen. She didn't look old enough to be Kailen's mother. No wrinkles lined her face, no signs of

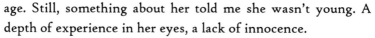

age. Still, something about her told me she wasn't young. A depth of experience in her eyes, a lack of innocence.

She wore a long green dress and a white crown. It wasn't silver or gold like I'd expected. Instead the crown was made from rows of sharp curving teeth. What sort of animal had those teeth come from? A huge wolf? A bear? I had to tear my eyes away from it, make myself stop staring at it in horror.

I did a quick scan of the table, looking for the goblet. Only a box lay there, wooden with ornate carvings of deer, birds, and flowers. How was I supposed to steal the goblet if I couldn't find it?

Kailen stopped in front of the table. "Mother, may I present Princess Sadie." The way he emphasized princess made it clear he knew I wasn't one.

I curtsied nervously.

"The other princesses believe she's their sister," Kailen went on. "Magic must have influenced them."

Queen Orlaith's eyes were bright with interest, studying me like I was a dress she might buy. I noticed small green vines grew up the side of her throne. They wrapped around the arm rests and trailed over the back. I gulped, remembering that Queen Orlaith could command plants to capture people. The flowering plants and vines overflowing onto the pavilion suddenly seemed sinister and dangerous.

"Which fairy sent you?" she asked. "For what purpose have you come?"

For what purpose had I come? I swallowed hard, felt nerves stinging my stomach. I'd come to steal her goblet. This was such a bad time to be unable to lie. "Chrysanthemum Everstar is my fairy godmother, Your Majesty. I wished to be a famous dancer so she sent me here." I swallowed again. "Your pavilion is beautiful. Thank you for letting me come here."

"Chrysanthemum Everstar?" the queen repeated. "I don't recollect a fairy of that name."

Kailen gazed out at the dance floor, bored. Most of the couples had ventured there, and the princesses' gowns flared out in a kaleidoscope of colors as they twirled. "Chrysanthemum is of the Seelie Court—one of the younger fairies. She's training to be a godmother."

Queen Orlaith ran her hand along the end of her armrest, and a vine tendril wrapped around her finger like a pet snake. "What else do you know of her?"

He shrugged. "Like most fairies in the Seelie Court, she's silly, vain, and pointless. She hasn't even finished her schooling. She's as harmless as a trinket."

Queen Orlaith lifted her hand and the vine tendril retreated. "Then why do you know of her?"

He gave a reluctant smile. "I never said she wasn't pretty."

Queen Orlaith didn't comment on her son's answer. He went back to watching the dancers, and she turned to me, her expression a mixture of suspicion and disdain. "Was that the only wish your fairy godmother granted you?"

"I also wished for a beautiful voice."

"And?" she prompted, sensing I was holding back.

I dropped my eyes, staring at my slippers. If I kept my gaze on them, I wouldn't blush. "Um, I wished Jason Prescott loved me." I glanced at the refreshment table. He stood by Isolde and Clementia, talking with them while he poured himself another drink. "Jason is from the twenty-first century too."

A smile bloomed on Queen Orlaith's lips. "You wished for love?"

I nodded.

She turned to her son. "The girl loves the boy so fervently

she used a wish to ensure her feelings were returned. Perhaps that is the sort of love that will feed the trees."

What was she talking about? "Trees?" I eyed the large diamond trees flanking the thrones. They grew all along the edges of the pavilion, and had thicker foliage than the trees I'd passed in the forest. My mouth went dry. All sorts of horrible visions presented themselves in my mind. "Wait, you're not going to feed us to them are you?"

"Don't be ridiculous," Kailen said, sparing me two seconds of his attention. "Trees don't eat flesh. You would give them indigestion."

Queen Orlaith leaned back in her chair. "Bring your prince hither so I can meet him."

I curtsied, relieved that *feed* wasn't a literal term. "Yes, Your Majesty."

When I reached the refreshment table, Jason was standing close to Clementia, a drink in his hand. He was trying to get her to throw grapes in the air and catch them in her mouth. "Come on," he told her, in that teasing tone guys use when they're flirting. "I know you can do it. Your tongue has talent."

"And my tongue?" Isolde asked, tapping her fan against Jason's arm. "Has it also talent?"

Jason wagged his eyebrows at her. "Maybe I'll find out sometime."

Isolde giggled and flipped open her fan, making slow, demure strokes. Her prince stood at her side, scowling.

Clementia tossed a grape into the air, and opened her mouth like a baby bird waiting for its mother. The grape hit her chin and ricocheted at Jason, an event that made her shriek with laughter. Her prince stood on her other side with his arms crossed, forgotten and sullen.

Maybe that was the point of Jason's flirting. Maybe he was getting back at the princes for their earlier jibes. Or maybe Jason just loved doll-like blondes.

I didn't care. At least not much. The fangirl feelings I'd had for Jason were quickly dying. I was at the ball for one reason: to steal the goblet. I looped my arm through Jason's to get his attention. "The queen wants to see us."

Jason put his drink down and winked at Clementia. "You may not be able to catch grapes, but I'll catch you later."

Nice. He was handing out pickup lines to my sisters. So classy.

Clementia giggled and waved goodbye to us. I pulled Jason toward the queen's table.

"She's a cool girl," Jason said, glancing back at Clementia, "She's got a weird name, though. Clementia. Isn't that some sort of a disease?"

We didn't have time for small talk. I leaned close to his ear. "Don't mention the goblet to anyone. No one can know we're after it."

"Oh yeah. The all-important gobletto. Where is it?" Jason glanced at the queen's table for the first time.

"I don't know. Maybe it's inside the box."

We didn't say more. We'd walked within earshot of the table.

Kailen was seated in the other throne: dark, aloof, and looking like the cover of a brooding romance novel. His gaze slid over Jason, unimpressed.

Queen Orlaith smiled at us, her fingers absently caressing a leaf that twined around her wrist. There was something about her that reminded me of a cat. Specifically a panther. "Welcome to my ball, Prince Jason. It will give me great pleasure to see you dance."

Jason dropped my arm and stretched his shoulders, all celebrity and smiles now. "This isn't my usual kind of music, but I'm game. I can work any beat." He took off his collar, tossed it to me to hold, and swaggered a few feet onto the dance floor. "Hey everybody, let's get this party going!" He threw his hands in the air, adding a couple of Woot! Woots! and fist pumps.

Several people peered around the pavilion in confusion as though wondering if Jason was warning them of impending danger.

Jason didn't notice. He was in his own world, one of stages and spotlights. He hip-hopped through the song, spinning, arms waving. Each swish of his hair was practiced, each thrust of his hips precise. During a concert, it would have been a great performance. Here, it looked borderline crazy.

The other couples stopped dancing altogether and stared at him—something that only egged him on. At that point he seemed to be channeling Elvis.

I put my hand to my mouth as I watched him. There was no graceful way to stop him.

Beatrix sidled over to me, her dress rustling in satin whispers. "Is something wrong with Prince Jason?"

"Many things, probably," I said.

"Should someone fetch a physician?"

"No, just clap when he's through, and he'll be fine."

At last the song ended. Jason slid across the floor on his knees, hands stretched into the air for a grand finale. I clapped. Beatrix joined me, worry etched on her face. The others just kept staring.

Jason stood up, brushed himself off and smiled triumphantly at the other princes. "See if you can beat that, bros."

Rosamund's prince cocked his head, perplexed. "Is that what you were doing? Beating something?"

Another prince nodded. "I suppose that explains your gyrations. I'm sure whatever you stomped on is quite dead."

Jason let out a huff of offense. "You posers are just jealous." He stalked to the refreshment table, shaking his head and using his sleeve to wipe perspiration off his forehead.

While the next song started, he downed a drink, then strode back over to me, muttering about critics. I held out his lace collar. He didn't take it. I couldn't blame him really. It looked like a doily on steroids and must have been nearly as uncomfortable.

Queen Orlaith steepled her slender fingers together and spoke to Jason patiently. "That was quite an entertaining performance. However, when I told you to dance, I meant for you to dance with Princess Sadie. You're familiar with the waltz, yes?"

"The waltz?" Jason repeated. "Does anybody do that anymore?"

I glanced out at the couples flowing across the dance floor. They were smiling and speaking in hushed tones, wrapped up in each other, yet still doing every step perfectly. Jason and I wouldn't look that way. "I don't know how to waltz either. Perhaps we should sit out and watch." I surveyed the chairs on the side of the pavilion. They weren't far from the queen's table. If Jason and I sat there until midnight, we'd be able to see the goblet as soon as she got it out.

Queen Orlaith stood up with a sigh. "Another couple from one of those uncivilized centuries. Well, I suppose we must teach you." She glided around the table, her long green dress trailing across the floor. She held her hand out to Jason, reaching for him with fingernails that looked like they'd been dipped in gold. "We'll see if you're a fast learner."

I was surprised the queen wanted this job—dancing with a mortal. I only had time to consider what odd dance partners they were when I noticed Kailen at my side, hand out to me. He'd moved so quietly I hadn't heard him.

He smiled, but there was something disapproving in his eyes that looked anything but happy. "It will be my pleasure to instruct you."

"Oh." Flustered, I took his hand. His fingers around mine were firm and warm. I'd expected them to be as cool as his demeanor.

He led me to the side of the dance floor and pulled me into formation. He smelled crisp and woodsy, without any of the heaviness of cologne. I'd slow danced with a few guys before, and they'd always had casual stances, as though—even while dancing—they were kicked back and slouching. Kailen stood straight, poised. I wasn't sure if that was because he was a fairy or because he was royalty. Whatever the reason, everything about him was so imposing I doubted I'd be able to remember anything he said.

This prediction proved to be true for the first ten minutes of his lesson. One wouldn't think waltzing would be hard. It only requires you to count to three and step in the shape of a box. Of course, both of those things become more difficult while dancing with a guy who could turn people into garden ornaments.

Every time I got one move down, he immediately added something else. Instead of stepping in a stationary square, we went forward in a line, then backward. We twirled, broke apart, and came back together.

I kept forgetting things and bumped into him several times. It didn't help that Kailen kept throwing out derogatory comments such as, "Pray, try to step to the beat."

Prayer wasn't likely to help.

"You need to follow your partner's lead," he told me for the fourth time. "The women of your century have forgotten that art. You always want to be in charge."

Should I pretend this was true or admit that no, I just couldn't count to three in my mind and also pick up the subtle clues he was about to swing me outward?

"I'm not used to dancing this way," I said.

Kailen nodded in Jason's direction. "Your prince is doing well enough."

He was right. Jason and the queen twirled on the floor, doing a step with ease that Kailen hadn't taught me. An elegant rise and fall accompanied their movements, like the sway of waves in the ocean. Jason wasn't as graceful as the queen, perhaps mortals couldn't achieve that, but he was still an excellent waltzer. Much better than me.

The incongruity of that struck me. "I wished to be a good dancer. I should be picking this up easily." A piece of hope welled inside me. If Chrissy didn't fulfill my wish, then I still had a wish coming, and I could use it to take Jason and me home.

The corner of Kailen's lips lifted in a smirk. "Perhaps Miss Everstar's powers aren't what they should be. Or," he said, pulling me back toward him after I'd misstepped, "perhaps her standards of good are lower than one would suppose."

A nice guy wouldn't have agreed so quickly that I was a bad dancer.

I was so busy thinking about what I would say to Chrissy,

I missed Kailen's signal to turn and had to take a quick step to catch up.

Kailen shook his head. "You should choose your fairy godmother more carefully next time."

As if I had a choice. "How well do you know Chrissy?" If he knew her, he might guess why she'd sent me here.

"The Unseelie Court doesn't mingle much with those from the Seelie. At the best of times we have an uneasy truce. Some fairies, however . . . well, I'll just say if Chrysanthemum showed the same enthusiasm for her studies that she shows for socializing, her precious university would have accepted her long ago."

"You don't like the university?" It was better to keep Kailen talking about other subjects than have him give me more dancing instruction.

"Fae of the Unseelie Court don't become fairy godmothers."

"Why not?"

He raised an eyebrow, surprised that I asked. "Mortals destroy and plunder the forest realms. We don't grant wishes to your sort."

There are several ways to make your dance partner uncomfortable. I'd thought Kailen had already hit upon the major ones by pointing out I sucked at dancing and insulting the women of my generation. But no, this kept getting worse. "I love forests," I mumbled. "I wouldn't ever destroy them."

Kailen casually pulled me out of the way of a passing couple. "You'll have children and they'll have children. Among your descendants will be those who would gladly destroy every tree and blade of grass for enough coins."

What was I supposed to say to that? "Sorry. I recycle whenever I can."

His dark eyes fell on me again. In the dim light they seemed almost black. "The people of your century no longer believe in magic. You think of yourselves as builders and creators, yet not one of you can create a tree. You fail to see the magic lying within every seed."

When was this song going to end? As soon as it did, I would claim I was thirsty and escape to the refreshment table. "If you don't like people, why invite us to come here every night?" His "feed the trees" comment still sat in my mind, worrying me.

Kailen didn't answer for a moment, and I wondered if he would ignore the question all together. Then he said, "Doesn't Chrissy know the answer to that question?"

"If she does, she didn't tell me."

Kailen twirled me under his arm. My skirt spun, making the material bloom outward. He pulled me back, recapturing my hand. "I suppose there's no harm in discussing our trees with a girl who loves forests. Surely on the trail here, you noticed how poorly the trees fare."

"They're not supposed to be silver, gold, and diamond?"

"It's summer. They're supposed to have leaves."

"Oh. Right. I knew that. I just thought magic ones were different." I could tell I'd lost all credibility as a nature-loving person. But really, how was I supposed to know what time of year it was? I wasn't even sure what continent I was on.

I gazed at one of the diamond trees near the edge of the pavilion. Small leaves lined its branches—the way spring leaves look before summer changes them to full dress attire. These trees were either stunted or behind schedule.

"The trees here," Kailen said, "are only kept alive by my mother's magic. She believes if her orchard basks in the air of lovers, the fruit will grow again. Every night the couples come and dance. Yet still, their fruit remains unripe and unusable. It's a fool's errand, this dancing, and we the fools for it."

"You can't fertilize them somehow?"

He made a scoffing noise. "So speak the fools."

Okay, maybe I should have known that if the queen could fertilize them, she would have already, but Kailen didn't need to be rude. I was just making conversation.

The music wound down and he dropped my hand. "I won't venture to teach you more steps tonight. Practice with your prince and perhaps tomorrow I'll show you others."

Only if I didn't manage to snag the goblet tonight. I curtsied in return. "Thanks for your help."

Queen Orlaith and Jason strolled over to us, her arm linked through his. Even in that position, they didn't look like a couple. The queen was too otherworldly, too mature. She seemed to be walking Jason like she might walk a dog. She deposited him in front of me. "It will give me great pleasure to see you dance with your lady. Enjoy the night."

"Remember to let your partner lead," Kailen added to me. He and the queen sauntered back toward their thrones, moving with effortless poise. A fairy thing, I supposed. No wonder Kailen thought I was a failure at dancing. I couldn't compare to his kind.

The music started up again and Jason took my hand so that we could waltz. "This place is wild, don't you think?"

A good word to describe fairies. Wild and undoubtedly dangerous too. It wasn't a comforting thought. Before the night ended, I had to steal a magical object from them.

Chapter 15

Jason and I danced for a few songs. I wasn't any better with Jason than I'd been with Kailen. Worse maybe, because Jason's leads were vague. He would move his hand upward, and I would think he wanted me to twirl when he actually wanted me to go forward.

Every time I apologized for messing up, he said something like, "Don't be so uptight. That expression won't go over well on camera." Or "You don't need to be so starstruck around me, babe. I put on my pants one leg at a time like everybody else—except for this pair. A butler named Archibald dressed me. I could get used to that, actually."

I nearly told him I stopped being starstruck around him after he called me a wannabe, but I figured there wasn't a point to bringing that up.

Every once in a while Jason asked me where I thought the cameras were or how the show had rigged up the sound system. I always shrugged or said, "Beats me." Which wasn't a lie, so my nose thankfully remained unchanged.

While we danced, Kailen strolled around the pavilion, hands behind his back, impatiently checking the trees for changes. Every so often he returned to the queen's table to speak with her.

She sat in her chair, haughty and cat-like, sometimes stroking the vines that swayed near her like fawning pets.

A large crystal clock hung from the ceiling at the far end of the pavilion. I kept glancing at it, waiting for midnight. At eleven forty, Jason and I made our way to the refreshment table. He poured himself a drink then plucked a yellow rosebud from a platter and popped it into his mouth. "Mmm. That one tasted like caramel."

I poured myself a drink and examined the platters. Besides the fruits that I was used to, bouquets of lilies, roses, and daisies lay across them. The blossoms looked real. "They're candy?"

"Either that, or I just discovered the reason women like flowers." He picked up a white daisy and bit off a few petals. "Vanilla. Not bad."

I picked up a red rose, hesitating before I brought it to my lips. "What if this is like the story of Persephone, and we'll have to come back here if we eat the food?"

"Who's Persephone?"

"You know, the Greek goddess."

"I thought this place was Renaissance themed. What are you doing in Greece all of a sudden?"

Jason was apparently lacking in Greek myth trivia as well as fairy tale knowledge. I took a bite of my flower because I didn't want to talk about it anymore. The petals tasted like hazelnut chocolate, and were therefore worth six months of my life, should it come to that.

We stacked fruit and blossoms onto plates and went and

sat in the chairs closest to the queen's table. Just before midnight she snapped her fingers and a wand appeared in her hand. I had expected something ornate and regal, but it looked like a thin branch plucked of leaves. She tapped it against the box, and the sides stretched and bent backward like clam shell opening.

The golden goblet sat inside. It was smaller than I expected, more like a tea cup with ambitions than a goblet fit for a fairy queen. She placed it in front of her and lifted her hand to Kailen. "The elixir?"

He pulled a vial from his shirt pocket, fingering it reluctantly before handing to his mother. "Don't waste the magic tonight. No matter how you phrase the question, the answer remains the same. It's time to ask something else. Ask what Queen Titania plots against you. Ask if you have enemies in your midst."

No, I thought. Don't ask that.

Queen Orlaith popped the vial's stopper off and poured the liquid into the cup. The first bell tolled the hour. Midnight. Picking up the goblet, she swirled the liquid around and around. "Magic cup within my hand, make me wise to understand." Her tone was pleading, desperate almost. "What more of love is now required, to cultivate the fruit desired?"

"Huh," Jason whispered to me. "Do you think you have to speak to the goblet in rhyme? 'Cause that would totally suck if your question ended in orange."

"Luckily, very few questions end in the word orange."

A voice emanated from the direction of the goblet, at first with a softness like wind rushing through trees, then growing louder like a storm picking up speed. "For lack of love your trees do pine. Give them this and the fruit is thine."

The queen showed no emotion to the answer. Her eyes had the same firm resolve they'd shown all night. But she slammed the goblet down so hard it clanged and sloshed drops of liquid onto the table.

Kailen lifted his chin, coldly triumphant. "You can bring twelve couples here or twelve hundred. It matters not. While we sit and watch dancers, our enemies will move against us."

"Which is why we need the fruit to ripen." She picked up the goblet as though it might tell her more information. After a moment, she put it down again with a frustrated thud. "How could the trees lack love? The princesses love their suitors enough to defy their father in order to see them. It must be true love."

"Or the thrill of rebellion," Kailen uttered. "Mortals don't know why they love." He gazed out of the pavilion to the night sky. "The goblet is giving you riddles, not answers. We love our trees more than these silly girls love their princes, and still not a leaf grows without your magic aiding it."

Queen Orlaith's dark eyes grew even darker. "It isn't my love the trees need. The goblet has made that clear enough. The trees require true love between mortals." She picked up the cup again and sipped its contents. "Perhaps we just need patience. Love, like fruit, requires time to ripen."

Kailen folded his arms. "Fine. Then let the couples' love ripen on its own for the next month. Tomorrow we should return to court and use the goblet for more productive ends. Ask what plans Titania has set in motion."

Queen Orlaith frowned tightly. "Am I not still queen? I decide where and when I'll hold court."

Her words silenced him.

She leaned back in her chair, clicking her golden

fingernails against the armrests. "You must learn to take counsel instead of giving it."

I'd stared at the goblet for so long, when I turned my gaze I still saw its outline everywhere my eyes went. I put my hand on Jason's arm. "Should you ask to sing to her now, or wait a few minutes and hope she's in a better mood?" If she blew him off now, we'd lose our chance, but if we waited too long, she'd put the goblet away. Once the goblet was in the box, it wouldn't fit into my pocket.

Jason bit off half a carnation. "Trust me, women are never in a bad mood when I sing to them."

The music from the current song wound down. Worry swirled in my stomach. If this went badly—no, I didn't want to think about it. I tightened my grip on Jason's sleeve. "Remember, keep the queen's eyes on you." That way, I'd only have to worry about making sure Kailen didn't see me.

Jason shoved the rest of the carnation into his mouth, not bothering to swallow before he answered me. "Don't worry. Charming is my middle name."

Well, so far it hadn't been his last name. He stood and walked over, all strut and swagger. I trailed after him, nerves shifting into overdrive. I had to tell myself not to wring my hands. Too conspicuous.

When Jason reached the queen's table, he bowed with a flourish. "A most excellent party, Your Majesty. It's only missing one thing."

She arched one dark eyebrow, regarding him. "What, pray tell?"

"One of my songs." He unbuttoned a few coat buttons. "Have your people sync up *Baby, You're the One For Me* and we'll get this place rocking." He winked at the queen, and pointed in her direction. "I want to sing it to you, because I have a feeling, baby, you're the one for me."

Queen Orlaith's eyebrow didn't move. "Rocking?" she repeated.

"It's a term from our time," I clarified. "It means people will enjoy themselves a lot."

No movement from the eyebrow.

I stepped between Jason and the table, skirt rustling as it bumped into the marble. "Jason is a famous singer. People from our time pay a lot of money to hear him sing. It's a great honor."

The queen picked up her wand, repeated the name of Jason's song, and tapped her wand with one finger. A perfect rendition of Jason's song rolled through the pavilion.

The couples dancing out on the floor didn't seem to know what to make of the change of music. They did their best to waltz to the faster beat.

Jason moved so he stood directly in front of the table. He nodded confidentially at Kailen. "If you have someone special in your life, pay attention to how I sing this song. The ladies love it."

Kailen didn't grace the advice with an answer.

Jason's smile gleamed in the queen's direction, suddenly boyish and adorable. His voice rang out, with the clarity that had won him fans around the world. "Baby, I need to tell you what's in my heart."

I wasn't sure whether it was impressive or tacky that he could turn on the charm like that. He put his hand on his chest and sang, "I see you standing there and know you're the one for me. With everything I have, girl, it's still you I need."

Both Kailen and the queen watched Jason, curiosity pinned to their expressions. I stepped toward the side of table, putting myself in a better position to take the goblet.

Jason held his hand toward the queen, imploringly. "Yeah, you saw in me, what no one could conceive."

"He does have a lovely voice," Queen Orlaith commented to Kailen. "One wonders where mortals find such gifts."

I could have given her the rundown I'd heard on the boat ride over, but I spared her the details of Jason and all the work his butt did.

Hand trembling, I reached across the table. I didn't breathe for fear it would draw attention. Kailen and Queen Orlaith were still looking at Jason. I leaned into the task. Almost there. As my fingers closed around the stem, the goblet moved, lifted slightly off the table.

At the same time, I caught a scent of Jason's boat. No, not the boat—the lake. I smelled the watery odor of something lake-drenched. Donovan. He was near, trying to steal the goblet out of my hand.

I tightened my grip. Donovan was stronger, but I had a better hold. We struggled over the cup, each pulling, lifting it farther off the table. For two seconds, we were at a stalemate. Then the goblet tipped, spilling the last few drops of elixir onto Queen Orlaith's arm.

Immediately, I let go and straightened up. Just as I did, the queen's head spun around. Fortunately, her gaze went to the goblet, not me. She saw it hanging suspended in the air, and raised her wand, a swift automatic action that put Donovan in her line of fire. He must not have liked his chances. The goblet clattered to the table.

Jason kept singing, but Queen Orlaith no longer paid attention to him. She grabbed the goblet and sprung to her feet, wand outstretched. "What mischief is this?" Her gaze darted around the table, then scanned the pavilion. "My cup floated off the table."

Kailen drew his sword with one hand and his wand with the other. He waved his wand and a shaft of light leapt from the wand's tip, arching over the dance floor in a long white rainbow.

The light sizzled and bits of glitter fell through the air, burning like embers. Several of the princesses took note of them, smiling like they were a new party favor the queen had added to the unusual song.

The glitter must not have hurt. No one flinched as pieces landed on their shoulders. At least they didn't flinch any more than the song was already making them flinch. Jason turned in the dancers' direction, aiming the song at them, full force. Instead of gracefully gliding around the room, the couples were off beat, taking unsure steps, and laughing at their own efforts.

The glitter falling near Kailen and Queen Orlaith turned black, became pieces of ash that gathered around their feet. Some of the glitter fluttering behind them turned dark as well. I watched a column drift closer to the table. By the time Kailen turned to check behind him, it was indistinguishable from the black glitter around him.

He turned back to the dance floor and lowered his wand. "No magic has crept in, save the magic here at our table." He kept scanning the pavilion though, searching.

So that's what the glitter was—a litmus test for magic. The dark column behind the table had marked Donovan's cloak. He had moved between Kailen and Queen Orlaith so they wouldn't notice him.

The queen turned to her son, her lips pulled into a tight, thin line. "True enough, as my wards keep away all magic folk but us. So I'll ask you why you attempted to take my cup."

"Me?" Kailen's head snapped back. "I never touched it."

Part of me wanted to point to Donovan and turn him over to Queen Orlaith to get rid of my competition. I didn't, though. She would undoubtedly do something horrible to him, and he didn't deserve that. Besides, he had kept me from falling down the stairs. Now we were even.

Queen Orlaith's dark eyes were still trained on her son. "You told me to use the cup to ask of Titania. And lo, minutes later, the goblet levitated off the table."

A flush of angry color spotted Kailen's cheeks. "If the cup did, indeed, levitate, it wasn't my doing."

Queen Orlaith sat down, stiffly imperial. She placed the goblet in front of her. "If? You doubt what I saw?"

He shoved his sword back into his scabbard. "It is inevitable that at times, even queens are mistaken." His words had too much emphasis. Apparently he thought she was mistaken about more than the cup.

If Queen Orlaith was in a bad mood before, she was doubly so now. Her eyes practically glittered with anger. "Then you won't object when I place a spell on the goblet." Before Kailen could comment, she touched her wand to its rim. "Until I speak otherwise, only a woman's hand shall move the cup. It will be slippery unto all others."

She firmly placed the goblet into the middle of the box, tapped the table with her wand, and the box pieces reconfigured themselves into the right shape.

Kailen's jaw clamped tight. "You insult me, Mother. I leave you to your dancers and your foolishness and won't be back."

He turned and strode into the trees behind the thrones with long fast strides. A moment later, a raven took to the air and sped through the night sky.

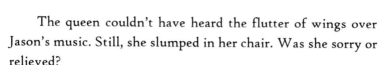

The queen couldn't have heard the flutter of wings over Jason's music. Still, she slumped in her chair. Was she sorry or relieved?

Jason finished off the song with a long-drawn out "Ohhh-ohhh-ohhh" that would have made modern girls swoon. The princes and princesses, however, only clapped halfheartedly.

Jason nodded, a smile plastered on his face, and held up a hand to acknowledge their applause. I could tell he was miffed at the lack of appreciation. "That song has been in the Top 40 for thirty weeks straight," he announced, as though that might change its reception.

"Let's have another waltz," one of the princes called.

The queen wordlessly swished her wand and a slow, lilting melody filled the area. "The two of you should also dance." The queen gave us one bare glance. "Before long the night will be spent. Enjoy each other's company ere then."

We followed her orders, although I can't say I enjoyed Jason's company much. He led me out on the floor and grudgingly pulled me into position. As soon as we danced our way out of earshot from the other couples, he said, "Just tell me this: How hard is it to pick up a glass without flinging its contents all over the place?"

"It wasn't my fault. Donovan grabbed the goblet at the same time I did."

"Donovan?"

"The invisible guy."

Jason tilted his chin down. "Okay, let me get this straight. An invisible guy kept you from taking the cup?"

I could prove I was telling the truth. I could show him what happened when I lied. I didn't do it. Jason thought this night was part of some reality show. If random body parts of mine started to inexplicably grow, I was pretty sure Jason would freak out and scream things like, "Gross! What is wrong with you?"

I didn't need a freaked-out celebrity to worry about right now, and I didn't want everyone to know I couldn't lie without having a Pinocchio experience.

"The night's not a total loss," I said. "Thanks to the queen's new spell, only women can hold the goblet now. That means Donovan can't steal it. We'll just have to find a way to distract the queen tomorrow so I can take it."

While I tried to think of a new distraction, Jason looked upward and made whiny-coughing noises. "I can't stay in Briardrake for another day. Where's my manager? Seriously. I need to talk with him."

I rolled my eyes. "How bad can you have it? You're a prince living in a castle."

"The place has no plumbing, no Internet, and do you know what the thermostat in my room is? A pile of logs by the fireplace."

"Pretend it's camping—except you've got better food and servants at your beck and call."

"I don't like camping." Jason's hand moved on my shoulder. I thought it was one of those dance cues that signaled he wanted to switch directions. He didn't move that way though, so I stumbled and knocked into him.

He made more coughing noises.

"Sorry," I said. "It's hard to dance and think."

"Yeah, I bet it's hard for you to walk and chew gum too."

Which was really too much. I stepped on his foot on purpose. "Oops," I said sweetly. "Clumsy again."

That's pretty much how we spent the next two hours. I

was so over Jason. Why had I ever thought I wanted him to love me? He wasn't the soulful, understanding person I'd imagined when I sang songs to his posters. He was vain, egotistical, and had no patience for anyone.

In fact, it may not have actually registered in his mind that other people existed. If he'd paid more attention to Kailen or Queen Orlaith, he would have noticed their magic. Instead, Jason was too busy wondering where the show's cameras were hidden so he could be sure they got his good side.

I absolutely couldn't be stuck here forever with him.

Chapter 16

As the night progressed, some of the couples stole off into the darkness, walking hand in hand through the grounds around the pavilion. Jason and I never did. Although he did take several breaks to go to the refreshment tables. At four in the morning, the music finally ended and the queen thanked us for coming.

As we walked en masse down the path toward the lake, I didn't speak to Jason. I climbed into our boat, folded my arms, and waited for him.

The other princesses seemed as energetic as when they started the ball. I was tired and my feet hurt. My slippers were not only worn through at the edges, the bottoms were dirty from trudging around the forest earlier. Anyone who saw them would know we'd left the castle. No wonder our slippers bothered the king so much.

Once again, Jason struggled to push the boat into the water. I supposed that meant Donovan was stowing away in our boat again. That was what happened in the fairy tale.

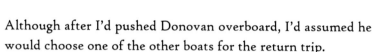

Although after I'd pushed Donovan overboard, I'd assumed he would choose one of the other boats for the return trip.

Around us, the princes pushed their boats into the water, picked up their oars, and rowed with long practiced strokes. "Last yet again!" one called to Jason.

Another yelled, "Don't blame Jason. His boat is sentimental. It's attached to the ground."

All the other princes laughed at that.

I slumped in my seat and then straightened when my corset bit into my ribs. The clothing here didn't allow for slumping. I wished I could take the thing off, curl up on the seat, and go to sleep. Or cry. Maybe both.

Jason gave one last concerted push and detached the boat from the shore. He sloshed a few steps through the water and heaved himself into the boat. With a few muffled complaints, he dropped down on the bench across from mine and dug the oars into the water. His stamina wasn't nearly what it had been on the way here. The other boats quickly pulled ahead of us.

"You've grown weak!" One of the princes yelled to him. "That's what comes of singing much and working little!"

Jason strained against the oars. "Sadie just weighs more than your passengers!"

"Thanks," I said. "Thanks a lot."

Jason glanced at me and pulled harder. "Seriously. How much do you weigh?"

This is not something a guy should ever ask a girl, especially one he is supposedly in love with. I folded my arms tighter. "I weigh as much as I'm supposed to. Maybe the other princes are right and you're just not that strong."

Jason let out a grunt, either due to effort or disbelief. "I have my own gym and a personal trainer." He then went on to tell me how he worked his butt off every day exercising.

I nearly told him his butt was extremely talented since it could lift weights and play music, but I didn't bother. Were all celebrities this shallow? I didn't like the thought. I wanted to be more than just my talent.

We were silent most of the way across the lake. By then the other boats had long outpaced us. They'd already landed at the shore, and the princes and princesses had disembarked. The couples were saying their goodbyes, their silhouettes bending together to steal kisses.

I leaned around Jason to see the shore better. "I wonder if the other princesses will wait for me." As I watched, they headed to the lantern post and then continued up the trail. "Nope," I muttered. "I guess not." I let out a sigh and hoped there weren't places in the trail where I could get lost.

The princes climbed back into their boats and set off, rowing to the left side of the lake. Their portal back home must have been somewhere over there. Several called out to us.

"Perhaps you'd be faster if Sadie rowed!"

"Jason needs to harness snails to pull him!"

I leaned around Jason again and watched the princesses' lanterns trailing off into the forest. "Is this as fast as you can go?"

Jason panted and dipped the oars into the lake again. "Until someone else rows, yes."

Behind me, Donovan whispered, "He probably couldn't row and chew gum at the same time."

Great. Not only was Donovan weighing down the boat so that I lagged behind the people who knew the way home, but he'd also eavesdropped on Jason and me at the ball. Had he listened to all of Jason's complaints?

I didn't like the thought. It made me feel like a scolded child.

Donovan's voice came in my ear again. "By the way, that dancing wish of yours was obviously magic well spent."

Dealing with Jason had drained my patience. I wasn't in the mood to deal with Donovan too. "Aren't you worried I'll push you off the boat?"

I thought I said the words quietly, but Jason cocked his head. "Why would you do that?"

Into my ear, Donovan whispered, "Because he's a dufus. Go ahead. Push him over."

I smiled at Jason apologetically. "I wasn't talking to you. Donovan is on the boat with us."

Jason stared at me blankly.

"Donovan. You know, the invisible guy I told you about."

Jason gave the oars a yank. "So now you're talking to your imaginary friend?"

"He's not imaginary. He's invisible. There's a difference." I automatically gestured to the back of the boat where Donovan sat, then realized it was a pointless gesture. "Donovan, introduce yourself."

He remained silent.

Jason pressed his lips together. "Okay . . ." He glanced at the shore longingly.

"Real mature," I told Donovan. "Make me look like the crazy girl who talks to imaginary people."

The last of the princes headed away from us. "Ho! Are you waiting for the tide to take you in? Hurry or it will be noon before you reach home."

Jason pulled the oars harder and yelled back, "Whatever. I'll beat your sorry—" Then he added the name of the body part he'd worked off so often.

I leaned back and my shoulders hit Donovan's knees. It

was one more item on my list of aggravations. He'd kept me from getting the goblet, made me late to shore, mocked my wishes, and now I couldn't even get comfortable in my own boat. I turned to him and hissed, "Why do you have to keep making everything harder? I really ought to shove you out of the boat again."

"Don't try it," he whispered. "I'm prepared this time."

It was as good as a challenge, and I was already frustrated, angry and irrational. In one quick move, I lunged toward him, arms stretched.

As it turned out, I should have controlled my temper, or at least believed Donovan when he told me I wouldn't get away with pushing him out of the boat again. My hands made contact with his chest. As he fell backward, he grabbed hold of my arms. If he went over, he was taking me with him. I gasped in alarm and fought his pull. My legs flailed against the bench in an attempt to find something to hold onto.

This was another disadvantage to silk slippers. It's hard to grab onto a bench with your feet while wearing them. In the end, my feet lost the battle. I flew over the side of the boat and into the lake. The water hit me with a slap, then embraced me with a cold, heavy grip. I plunged downward, into the darkness. I wanted to scream but had to hold my breath.

The weight of my cloak and gown pulled me deeper. I yanked off the cloak and let it sink. I couldn't undo my skirt. I struggled with the lacings, still sinking, then gave up on that. I lifted up the edge of my skirt and pulled my slip off. It fell away like a giant dying jelly fish. The bum roll came off next, rolling down to its final resting place. My lungs ached, but at least I was lighter now. Kicking upward, I managed to break through the water's edge. I gasped, coughing and sputtering. "Jason!" I called. "Help me!"

He peered over the side of the boat, oars raised midstroke, and let out one of his whiny noises. "Why in the world did you jump overboard?"

"I didn't jump. Donovan dragged me over." I looked around, even though I knew I wouldn't see him. So many ripples and waves sloshed near the boat, I couldn't tell where he'd landed.

"Yeah, sure," Jason said. "I saw you dive overboard."

I swam toward the boat, teeth chattering. Each stroke took effort. The weight of my dress felt like a hand tugging me downward. "Would you just help me?"

Jason reversed his strokes, guiding the boat to me. One of my coils had come loose and strands of hair clung to my neck and cheeks. Water kept sloshing into my face.

Jason held out an oar. "Here."

I grabbed the end and he pulled me toward him. I reached for the edge of the boat, but it was too high. My hands slapped uselessly against the side.

"I'll pull you up." I took a hold of Jason's hand. That's when I realized I was in trouble. Every time Jason lifted me, the boat rocked dangerously, nearly capsizing. With his weight at the side and my added weight, we made an unbalanced load.

After three attempts, Jason let go of my hand. "This isn't going to work." He looked back at the shore. "You're not that far from land. Why don't you just swim there?"

I treaded water, fighting to keep my head above water. "You want to leave me here?"

"It's only a few pool lengths. You can make it. You must be a good swimmer or the show wouldn't have chosen you to do that mermaid bit earlier."

I sunk downward and kicked harder to keep myself from

going under. "The water is freezing, and my gown weighs a ton."

Jason dipped his oars in the water, guiding the boat away from me. He looked over his shoulder in the direction the other boats had gone. "You'll be fine." Another pass of the oars, this time with more strength. "I'm already way behind the other guys, and I don't know the way home."

"You can't just—"

"You'll be fine," he called again, picking up speed.

Jerk.

Jerk. Jerk. Jerk! I tread water for a moment longer, shivering while I watched the boat recede. "Jason!" I yelled. He had to come back. Had to. But he didn't. I smacked my hands against the water in aggravation. "Being your date is *so* overrated!"

He didn't answer.

I tugged at the lacings on my skirt again. My fingers felt stiff and cold. I couldn't grip the lacings, let alone undo them. Groaning, I turned toward the shore and swam that direction. What other option did I have? I sunk with each stroke. *Don't panic,* I told myself. I didn't need to stay above water the whole time, just once every minute to take a breath. I could push myself to the surface for that.

Part of me knew I'd never make it. My strength would give out before I reached land. But I was too angry to be afraid yet. I wasn't going to drown because Prince Not-So-Charming had refused to help me. It was a tacky way to die—dragged to a watery grave due to the lack of zippers in the Renaissance age. I would make it to the shore on determination alone. And then I would never speak to Jason again.

While I took a breath, a wave sloshed into my face. I coughed and started swimming again. What sort of guy left a girl in a frigid lake? It served him right that he'd be stuck here in the past forever.

I glanced back to see if I could spot his boat. It had disappeared into the shadows of the night, leaving nothing but dark ripples in its wake. The shore didn't seem any closer though. Was it possible that a current was pulling me the other direction? Did lakes even have currents?

I thought, ridiculously, that if I'd studied harder in school, I would know those sorts of details. I would know what I was up against. I kicked, pulled numbly at the water. I'd only swam for a few minutes, and my strength was already giving out. I couldn't last much longer, and the shore was too far away. My throat felt tight, not from lack of air but from fear. Tears pressed at the back of my eyes. My parents would never know what happened to me. I wouldn't get to tell them goodbye. This was how my life would end. I was going to drown.

Chapter 17

Cold, dark water splashed into my face. I struggled against it, coughed some more.

"You'll sink unless you take off that dress." Donovan's voice came from my side.

I saw him swimming toward me, the invisibility cloak wrapped around his neck. His head seemed to be floating above his torso.

"I can't get it off," I sputtered. "It took two women to tie me into this thing."

"I'll help you."

My legs burned with the effort of keeping afloat. My chin kept dipping below the waterline. I glowered in the direction Jason's boat had gone. "Jerk."

"Hey, I'm sorry." Donovan swam behind me to reach my lacings. "I didn't consider that you were wearing a deathtrap when I pulled you in. Besides, I didn't think Rockstar Boy would ditch you like that."

"Not you. I meant Jason."

"Oh." Donovan felt along the fastenings on my back. I hoped he could figure how to loosen them in the dark. It was my only chance. "You've got lousy taste in men," he said. "Jason's not worth a concert ticket, let alone a wish."

I sunk downward and managed to swallow a mouthful of water before I kicked back up to the surface. I coughed, choking until I could get enough air. Fear rattled around my chest. How much longer could I last? "This is just my luck. I used my last wish to get rid of my mermaid tail, and now I'm going to drown."

"No you're not. Keep kicking." Donovan's voice sounded too taut, like he wasn't confident that what he said was true. He yanked the lacings on my skirt, momentarily making them go tighter. "I'm going to save you, and then we're going to work together to get the goblet."

"What?" I glanced over my shoulder. Donovan held a pocketknife and was cutting through the ties. I was so relieved I wanted to cry. Of course Donovan had a knife. Soldiers carried that sort of thing.

"You saw how well tonight went," he said. "In order for either of us to get the goblet, we have to work together."

He only wanted to team up with me because I could touch the goblet and he couldn't. Still, it wasn't wise to argue with someone while he kept you from drowning. I didn't comment.

The skirt loosened around my waist and fell away. I felt instantly lighter. The lake had given up part of its grip.

Donovan moved to the lacings on my bodice. "Don't be stubborn about this. You need me. Queen Orlaith will watch that goblet like a hawk from now on. You don't know how to steal things, but I've got a plan that will work."

More lacings snapped and gave way. "And then what? We leave Jason?" I didn't like the idea, even though Jason had left me. It was still my fault he was stuck here.

"No, we force our fairy godmothers to take all three of us back to the right century. They want the goblet badly enough. They'll do it."

The bodice loosened, and I peeled it off. I still wore my chemise and corset, but those weren't nearly as heavy. "Okay. We've got a deal." I dropped the bodice. It brushed past my legs as it sank, a final silky goodbye.

Donovan gazed at me and smiled.

"What?" I asked.

"Just seeing if your nose grew. It didn't."

I thought about asking Donovan to slice off my corset too, then decided against it. I could swim now and the sooner we got to land the better.

"Thanks for cutting me free," I said. "See you at the shore." Without another word I stroked in that direction.

Donovan swam beside me the whole way. He was a strong swimmer and could have outpaced me. He kept checking on me, though. Perhaps he had reason. I was tired, cold, and my energy was spent. My arms slapped stiffly into the water. After a few minutes I could barely move them and relied on my legs to propel me forward.

Finally the shore grew close and my feet touched ground. I dragged myself out of the lake, shivering. My chemise clung awkwardly to me and water streamed down my legs and filled my slippers. Like everything else, they'd been laced on, but they were light enough that I hadn't kicked them off. Now with rocks crunching underneath my feet, I was glad for them.

Only one lamp hung on the lamppost, sending out a

welcoming halo of light. As we walked toward it, Donovan pulled off his shirt and wrung the water out. I couldn't help but notice his build. He was all shoulders and hard muscles.

The wind picked up, and a fresh set of goose bumps lined my skin. Bits of seaweed stuck to me. I didn't bother wiping them off. As I walked, I wrapped my arms around myself trying to hold onto some warmth. Water still dripped down my legs, leaving dark puddles behind me.

We reached the lamppost. While Donovan put his shirt back on, I fumbled with the lantern handle. I was shaking too hard to get a good grip and was afraid I would drop it. If I did, we wouldn't be able to find our way through the forest.

Donovan saw my trouble and took the lantern. He held it up, scattering light around us. "The trail is this way."

He started in that direction and I stumbled after him, arms still wrapped around my torso. "Thank you," I muttered. With my teeth chattering it sounded more like, "Haiku."

I considered repeating the phrase, but my teeth kept chattering, so I decided to let him think I had a sudden interest in poetry.

Donovan paused and held the lamp closer to my face. "I think you're getting hypothermia. You don't look good."

I didn't look good? I was soaking wet and dotted with seaweed. "No one looksh good afer being dunked in a la-ake."

His gaze went over me, concerned. "Shivering, pale skin, slurring your words. Next is mental confusion. We'd better find a place to start a fire."

I watched the water dripping from his clothes and wondered how he planned to do that. "You got waterpoof ma-atches?"

"Nope. So it's a good thing we have a lantern. Let's get out of the wind."

Right. The lantern. The lantern used fire, not electricity. Maybe I really was getting hypothermia. I couldn't think straight anymore. I felt as though my bones had frozen.

As we walked through the forest, Donovan gathered dried twigs and branches that littered the path. He carried them in his cloak, adding to the pile as we went. He also surveyed the forest floor searching for dead branches. Every once in a while owls let out a warning hoot from somewhere in the forest, warning us not to go near the magic trees.

I gathered dry branches too. The bark and knobby ends bit into my skin, but I didn't care. All I could think about was a fire and warmth.

When we had enough wood, Donovan arranged the kindling in the middle of the path. He lit a twig, and then ignited bits of the pile. I sat and watched him, shivering so badly I was shuddering. Little flames leapt on the tinder, tiny specks against the vast dark forest around us. The heat was just a whisper, a promise. I would have given anything right then for a hot shower or an electric blanket, but no, I couldn't have those things because I'd used magic to wish for a better life. And now I was a princess. Suddenly the whole situation seemed so ridiculous that I started laughing.

Donovan lifted his gaze from the fire. "Why are you laughing?"

"On my eighth birthday," I said through still chattering teeth, "I had a princess party. Now that I'm actually a princess, I realize Mom got the decorations all wrong. Our house looked nothing like this."

Flames kept jumping through the kindling, flickering light into the night. Donovan nodded and put one of the larger chunks of wood on the fire. "Yep. You've got hypothermia."

"You never see paper plates depicting drenched princesses in their underwear."

Donovan sat beside me and put his arm around my shoulders. At first I only felt the chill from his clothes, then the warmth of his skin replaced the cold. I leaned into him.

My teeth kept knocking against each other. "You never see princess balloons with dark foreboding forests in the background."

"You'll be fine as soon as you warm up."

"And if anyone ever tells me they want a fairy tale life, I'm going to laugh."

"People say stupid things."

"Being a princess totally *sucks*."

Donovan wrapped both arms around me, held me tighter. "You'll be okay in a few minutes, Tiara Girl."

I didn't say anything else for a while. The heat from the fire had grown, and I tried to soak it in, to hold it inside of me. I wanted it to hurry, to melt my icy bones. Slowly, my shivering subsided. I thought of Donovan having to swim all the way to the fairy ball. He must have been so cold. Pushing him into the lake was such a mean thing to have done, especially since he'd kept me from falling off the stairs earlier.

"I'm sorry I pushed you off the boat," I mumbled into his shoulder.

"Yeah, I bet you'll think twice about shoving the next guy over if you're wearing half a ton of fabric."

"I meant I'm sorry for both times."

"Ah, you're still delirious." Donovan didn't let go of me, and I didn't move away from him. It was nice sitting with him like this, nice that he wanted to work with me instead of against me. Nice that he was hot—*I mean, warm.* It was nice to have the warmth of him next to me. And, okay, the hotness thing was nice too.

Wisps of smoke blew toward us. I didn't mind. It reminded me of a camping trip my family had taken once. We'd toasted marshmallows over a fire. Mine were soft, gooey, and tasted of smoke and happiness.

"How come I got hypothermia and you didn't?"

I felt him shrug. "You spent your energy keeping from drowning. When you're exhausted, you can't fight the cold."

"Oh."

"And besides, I'm used to the cold. That's what happens when the city keeps turning off your electricity."

I lifted my head to check his expression. He was serious. "Really?"

Another shrug. "Don't feel sorry for me. I learned how to take care of myself early on. That's a good thing."

It didn't seem like a good thing. I laid my head back against his chest. "Don't your parents have jobs?"

"My dad took off when I was twelve. Haven't heard from him since."

"I'm sorry." He'd just told me not to say that, and I chided myself for saying it. "What about your mom?"

"It's hard to hold down a job when you spend most of your time drinking."

My heart broke a little for him then. I didn't see my parents a lot, but at least I knew they cared about me. They would never drink away their money instead of paying the electric bill. And if they ever couldn't take care of me, my grandparents would have. "Isn't there anyone else in your family?"

"Yeah. My brother, Shane. He's fourteen."

Fourteen. Not old enough to help. "You take care of him?" I knew it was the truth even as I asked the question. "That's why you need to get home."

Donovan didn't answer right away. When he spoke his voice was low, asking me to understand. "I didn't start a life of crime for the thrill of it. When you're a kid, you don't have a lot of options when it comes to paying the bills."

"Sorry," I said, once again ignoring his instructions not to be. How could I not feel sorry? He'd had such a difficult life. And I'd pushed him into a cold lake. Twice. I gave his hand a squeeze. "We'll get back. And if your probation officer is angry, I'll vouch for your story."

He didn't let go of my hand. "My story that I was detained by fairies?"

"We can come up with something better. My Pinocchio thing ends as soon as I'm done with fairies." And a good thing too. I had no idea what I'd tell my parents about all of this. If I told them any sort of story that involved magic, they would think I'd had a nervous breakdown.

Donovan squeezed my hand back, keeping it loosely twined with his. His gaze went over me, soft and considering. Weighing me somehow.

Then he dropped my hand and moved away to pick up one of the dead branches in our wood pile. I had no idea what he'd been weighing, or what decision he'd come to. Which bothered me. I should have asked Chrissy for mind reading.

Donovan tossed the branch onto the fire. The yellow and orange flames licked the sides of the wood, making it crackle. He leaned back, his tone business-like. "We need to talk about the goblet. You can't just take it like you tried tonight. Queen Orlaith will notice it's missing and search everyone. She'll catch you. This is what you need to do instead: in the morning, go to the castle goldsmith and give him our drawings of the goblet. Order him to make a duplicate. You can tell him it's a surprise gift for the king."

I shivered and Donovan put his arm back around my shoulders. I laid my head against his chest. I liked the feel of it against my cheek. Strong. Warm.

"Bring the fake goblet with you tomorrow night," he continued. "After the queen asks her question, have Jason distract her, and make the switch. She won't be any the wiser until the next night, and by then we'll be long gone."

In theory this seemed like a safer plan, but I wasn't sure it would work. "How can I have the goldsmith make a copy that will fool Queen Orlaith? The pictures don't give specifications. We don't know the exact height, weight, or diameter."

"Most people don't check things too closely. I imagine fairies are the same."

It seemed like a lot to hope. Especially now that Queen Orlaith knew someone had tried to steal the goblet. I turned the problem over in my mind, imagining different scenarios. If Donovan let me borrow his cloak, I could use it to steal the goblet. However, when the queen discovered the theft, she would notice I'd disappeared and know who'd taken it. She would undoubtedly take her fury out on Jason. As angry as I was at him, I couldn't inflict that on him.

"How big is your cloak?" I asked. "Could it hide more than one person?"

"I doubt it." Donovan picked up the cloak and draped half of it over me. It was damp—cold enough that I flinched and leaned closer in to Donovan. He wrapped the rest of the cloak around himself. Our heads both stuck out, visible along with half our torsos. "Nope," he said and set the cloak on the ground. "But that's okay. You won't need to be invisible to make the switch. You just need to wait until she isn't looking."

Another idea occurred to me. "Rosamund has sleeping powder. We could find it and slip some into the queen's drink. If she passes out, we'll be able to take the goblet."

"Or Kailen will know someone has drugged his mother, and he'll turn every mortal there into a lawn ornament. He seems like the strike first, ask questions later sort of guy."

Donovan had a point, but I still worried his plan wouldn't work. "If Queen Orlaith even glances at the fake goblet, she'll know it's not the same one."

"You'd be surprised. People see what they expect to see."

"Most people would notice."

"Trust me on this one. I've gotten by for years because I know how to fool people."

The fire crackled, spitting out sparks that dimmed and blackened as they fell. "Maybe you're just used to being around . . ." drunk people. Only I didn't want to say that. "People who aren't very observant."

"You mean like you and the other Tiara Girls?" He shifted his arm so he could see me better. "Have you figured out how I got rid of my drugged cider?"

I hadn't, even though I'd replayed the scene in my mind several times. Donovan's cup was empty, and yet he hadn't sat by a planter or any place he could have dumped the contents— not without leaving telltale damp spots.

I shook my head reluctantly. "What *did* you do with your cider?"

"While no one was watching, I poured it into Madam Saxton's glass and she drank it."

And Madam Saxton was too drugged to notice her glass had been refilled. I tilted my head back and groaned. The answer seemed so easy now. Why hadn't any of us considered that possibility?

Donovan nodded, making his point. "People see what they expect to see."

"Let's hope you're right."

He shifted his hand on my back, holding me looser now that I'd stopped shivering. "I'm always right. Well, except in my choice of stowaway ships. On the way to the ball, how did you know I was in your boat?"

I wished my answer made me look clever. "It's part of the fairy tale."

"Seriously?" His head jerked in surprise. "Since you knew I followed you, I figured the last place you expected me to go was in your boat. Sheesh. What a waste of reverse psychology."

"Why did you get in my boat on the way back?"

He shrugged. "It was fun to watch you and Jason fight. After all the stupid things he said to you, I expected you to tell him off. I figured you were just waiting for the boat ride."

I hadn't told Jason off, though. Instead I'd taken out my frustration by pushing Donovan into the lake. Stupid. Maybe Chrissy was right about me. Maybe I did keep my mouth shut when I should be standing up for myself.

Donovan tilted his head to see my expression. "You don't still have a thing for Jason, do you?"

"If by 'thing' you mean admiration or respect— then no, I don't have a thing for him anymore."

Donovan laughed. It was a nice sound, low and masculine. "So what else happens in the fairy tale? How does the soldier explain to the princesses he's not in the outer room when they get back?"

"They don't notice he's gone. I guess they never check on him when they go back."

Donovan let out a grunt. "Who wrote this stupid story anyway?"

"Hey, we're tired, and we drugged you. I guess it never occurred to anyone you might do something besides sleep." I nudged him because he still wore a look that implied princesses were innately idiots. "The fairy tale has been passed down for generations. It's classic literature."

"Girls just like the story because it involves princesses, ball gowns, and dancing."

"Yeah, and?"

He let out another grunt. "Girls have unrealistic expectations about life. You realize that, don't you?"

"Is it our fault there aren't enough princes around?"

Donovan picked up the last of our branches and added them to the fire. He didn't put his arm back around me. Perhaps he didn't think I needed his warmth anymore. Parts of my chemise were dry.

We gazed at the fire and neither of us spoke. It was cozy sitting here. Flames wavered between orange and yellow, lazily spreading over the wood. The tiny embers that flew upward reminded me of the fireflies we'd seen earlier.

Suddenly I was conscious of how closely I sat to Donovan, how our shoulders still touched. I stole a glance at his profile, secretly watching him from the corner of my eye.

In the warm light, he looked even more handsome than he had earlier. My eyes traced the curve of his cheek, the dip of his eyebrows, the fringe of lashes over his eyes. His eyes were blue, I knew—blue like the sky on a clear day. The night had darkened them, but the firelight reflected stars into them, making them look mysterious.

Maybe I'd been wrong to want a prince. Maybe a thief was the way to go.

I forced my gaze back to the fire. Was it normal to think this way about a guy who'd been my enemy a few hours earlier? Maybe I was still a little delirious. Or maybe I was just responding to the hot guy who saved my life and then put his arm around me in front of a glowing fire.

I glanced at Donovan again. He was watching me now, those same scales weighing me. I waited, holding his gaze, feeling my heart beat faster. *Say something*, I thought. And then, *No, don't say anything. Bend over and hold me close again.*

His gaze lifted to the sky, and his eyes widened in surprise. The edges of the night were lightening, turning from black to grey. "It's nearly morning. We'd better get back to the castle or we'll be caught."

Chapter 18

Donovan stood and helped me to my feet. I blushed and was glad he couldn't see it. I shouldn't be embarrassed. I hadn't thrown myself at him. I'd just thought about it.

I brushed at a few bits of seaweed that stuck to my chemise. Dirt and pieces of bark covered my front, a result of carrying branches. I'd have to wash and change once I reached my room.

We put out the fire and then hurried along the trail, occasionally running as we raced to beat the sun. By the time we reached the staircase, the sky was nearing dawn blue and getting lighter every moment. What time did the king check on the princesses? Surely not at dawn. Kings probably liked to sleep in. Donovan and I sped up the stairs, our footsteps thudding on the marble. The meadow below us shrunk away with abnormal quickness. I felt like I was running through the sky and didn't dare look over the stairs' edge. My legs began to ache, but I didn't slow down.

When we got close to the top, Donovan put his invisibility cloak on. His image winked out, and we slowed our footsteps, quieting them.

The princesses had left the door open. I was glad for that. I snuffed my lamp, put it on the shelf with the others, then went into the sitting room. The fire had gone out, casting the room into darkness. Only pale slivers of light escaped the edges of the curtains—not enough to illuminate the couches. I supposed that was the reason the princesses hadn't noticed that Donovan was gone.

I gave the hearth a shove, and it slid back into place.

Slowly, I made my way toward the bedroom, hands out to keep myself from bumping into chairs. Once I reached the room, it was easier to see. The shutters across the windows let in more light. Each bed was occupied except for one. Mine. I could hardly wait to lie down in it.

Unfortunately I needed to change out of my filthy chemise and wash the dirt off my arms. I would use the pitcher of water that sat on my nightstand to clean up the best I could. My hair would take some work. Parts were twisted into coils, the rest hung damp and tangled around my shoulders.

I went through the closet trying to remember where I'd put my nightgown. Were there extra ones somewhere? There had to be, but it was hard to see what was hanging on the pegs.

I heard the faint sound of bolts scraping across wood on the outer room door. Someone was unlocking it. No. The king couldn't be here already.

A knock removed any doubts. "Unlock the door," King Rothschild called. "'Tis morning."

Only for overachievers. It was just past dawn.

"Coming!" Madam Saxton answered, with a half-startled, half-sleepy voice.

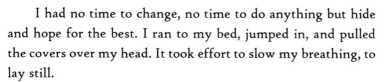

I had no time to change, no time to do anything but hide and hope for the best. I ran to my bed, jumped in, and pulled the covers over my head. It took effort to slow my breathing, to lay still.

I heard footsteps. The bedroom door swung open, and the queen's voice trilled across the room, "Rise and shine, girls. A new day is upon us."

One of the princesses let out an exhausted groan. "It can't be morning already."

"I'm too tired to get up," another protested.

I huddled farther down into my bed.

"Nonsense," the queen insisted. Her footsteps tapped across the room to the windows. "You must be well-rested. Two chaperones attended you last night to ensure you went to bed early." The queen opened the shutters, flooding the room with light. "Madam Saxton, did the girls sleep well?"

Madam Saxton didn't answer immediately. "I never heard any of them stirring."

"What a relief," the queen said. "King Rothschild will be so happy."

"I feel unwell," one of the princesses murmured. "Perhaps I'm ill. Let me sleep longer."

Several voices joined in, agreeing that they were ill too.

Heavier footsteps strode across the room, making their way between the rows of beds. "Why are my daughters lying about like lollygaggers?"

I pressed my eyelids together and willed him to go away.

"Arise at once," the king boomed. "All of you."

The princesses moaned in complaint. I heard the sound of their covers rustling and their feet hitting the floor. I couldn't join them, not dressed like I was. I feigned sleep. With so many daughters, perhaps the king and queen wouldn't notice me missing.

"Line up and show me your slippers," the king ordered, heading toward the outer room.

I stayed huddled underneath the blankets. A rumble went through the room, girls retrieving their shoes from underneath their beds. Surprised exclamations flooded the room. "Why, my slippers were fine when I put them under my bed last night!"

"Mine as well."

"I don't know what's happened to them."

The whole group was awash with astonishment. Totally overacted. After going through the same thing night after night, wouldn't everyone expect their slippers to be worn out? A patter of footsteps filed out of the room. Apparently the inspection took place in the outer room.

"Present your shoes," the king barked, and then a moment later added, "Where is Sadie?"

I pressed myself into the bed. *Be one with the mattress*, I told myself. *Stay hidden.*

Heavy footsteps marched back into the bedroom. "Sadie, out of bed! Line up this instant."

So much for mattress Zen. I had to face the king, face everyone. I sat up, took off my slippers, and slunk into the outer room. The princesses were standing as stiffly as soldiers in formation, six on one side, five on the other. All were primly dressed in clean white nightgowns and caps, their hair braided down their backs.

I was dirty, bedraggled, still wearing my corset, and my hair looked like it had endured a natural disaster. Everyone stared at me as I took my place at the end of the line.

Donovan stood by the queen and housekeeper, making a show of stretching and yawning. Madam Saxton pursed her lips and wrung her hands in worry.

The king took slow, heavy steps down the line of princesses, checking each pair of slippers they held out. "Worn, worn, worn, worn, worn, worn, worn, worn, worn, worn, worn." He stopped in front of me. "And damp."

The queen glided over to inspect my slippers. They weren't just damp. Their pale yellow had turned into dirty, ground-in brown. She turned them in her hands. "My heavens, child. These look as though you strolled across the bottom of a lake."

Close, actually.

The king looked me up and down, glowering, then pulled something from my hair. He showed it to me. "What is this?"

"Um, a twig."

He plucked a piece of limp green seaweed from my shoulder. "And this?"

I blinked, and tried to match the shock in the other princesses' voices. "I can't say . . ." *because it would get me in a lot of trouble.* It's amazing how much you can lie without lying.

"I see." The king's grip on the seaweed tightened. "Can you perhaps say how you went to bed last night and rose up this morning wet, dirty, and covered in plant life? How exactly does one accomplish such a feat?"

I gulped. "I . . . I can't explain it, Father."

He leaned closer. The fine lines around his eyes seemed to deepen, and a vein near his forehead bulged. "You will tell me, or you'll have nothing but bread and water for the rest of your days."

I lowered my head. Anything I said now would cause my nose to grow.

"Still all of you remain silent." The king's voice filled the room. "Shall your sisters have your diet as well?"

Beside me, a couple of the princesses whimpered. Several others said, "T'isn't fair, Father. We know not how Sadie soiled her clothes."

The queen put her hand on the king's arm. "The girls clearly remember nothing. They're victims of some curse or spell. We mustn't punish them for someone else's devilry."

The king flung the seaweed to the floor and strode over to Donovan. "Well, what have you to say about this? What transpired in this room last night?"

Donovan ran his hand through his hair. I wondered if he was checking to see if it was damp. Considering my state, that would have been especially bad. His hair fell back into place, mussed but dry. Donovan's vest and pants were dark colors, hiding the dirt that was certainly on them. His boots were most likely wet. They were black too, though, so it wasn't apparent.

"My journey yesterday must have tired me out." Donovan shook his head sheepishly. "I fell into a deep sleep last night—so deep I don't remember anything from the moment I sat down until this morning." He rubbed his jaw in thought. "But don't worry. I have two more nights to discover the secret of your daughters' activities. Certainly I'll solve the mystery tonight."

The king let out a low grumble of disapproval and turned his attention to Madam Saxton. "And you? What did you see last night? How often did you check upon my daughters?"

Madam Saxton's hand-wringing went into overdrive. "Forgive me, Your Majesty. I too, fell asleep."

The king let out another grumble, this time louder. "So says everyone who passes the night in this room. I almost believe the sandman has taken up residence and holds nightly revelries with my daughters' shoes."

Without another word, King Rothschild turned and stormed toward the door. He shot us one last exasperated look and flung the door open. "I shall disown all of you and turn you out onto the streets!"

The queen let out a sigh and pressed her hands together patiently. "Of course we won't disown you, my darlings. We're just worried about your welfare. I shall bid the cobbler to make you new slippers, forthwith." Peering at my hair more closely, she lifted a tendril, then dropped it as though it was too distasteful to touch. "And I shall tell your maid to draw a bath."

She looked as though she wanted to wipe her hand on something to clean it, but finding nothing, let it drop back at her side. "Very well." Her tone implied the inspection was officially over. "Take what rest you need, and then see to your duties."

She gave us one last encouraging smile, and sailed out of the room, her gown trailing along the floor. The housekeeper went with her, apologizing the entire time.

The princesses headed back to their beds. A few cast glances at me like they wanted to ask what had happened—or criticize me for coming home so bedraggled—but their gazes went to Donovan, and they didn't speak.

I wanted to join them, to skip the bath and curl up in bed for a long time. Donovan walked over to me and took hold of my hand to keep me from going. "You need to go talk to the goldsmith," he whispered.

I gestured to my soiled chemise and sooty arms. "I can't go anywhere like this."

He placed his picture of the goblet in my hand. "You're the one with the royal power. A goldsmith isn't going to listen to me."

"I can't just pull on some clothes and go," I said. "In the Renaissance, I need an entire committee to make me presentable." I went to my dressing table, took my drawing of the goblet from a drawer, and handed both pictures to Donovan. "Show these to the goldsmith, and tell him I want the goblet finished as soon as possible. Say I'll come later to discuss the project."

Donovan took the pictures, satisfied, and left.

I went to the back room and collapsed on my bed, barely noticing that the sheets were dirty from where I'd laid on them before. They could get dirtier.

It seemed like only moments later that my lady's maid shook me awake, insisting that my bath was almost ready. I followed her to a small room where a procession of maids were pouring buckets of steaming water into a metal tub. A dressing table stood nearby, holding bottles of perfume, lotions, combs, ribbons, and other bits of finery.

While I waited for the maids to finish filling the tub, I pulled pins, bedraggled ribbons, and bits of seaweed from my hair. Once the tub was full, a maid unlaced my corset and peeled it off of me. She handed it to another servant, holding it between her thumb and forefinger like it was something that had recently died.

The maids were prepared to stay, wash my hair, and scrub me off. I told them I would take care of that myself and dismissed them. A girl from the twenty-first century needed her privacy.

As I took hold of the ties of my chemise, a cheerful voice behind me said, "So how did the ball go? Did Jason kiss you goodnight?"

I turned and saw Chrissy perched on the dressing table, her wings flowing over the back. She wore a jean miniskirt, thigh-high black boots and a T-shirt that read "Team Sadie." Clover ambled across the table beside her, kicking through some scattered pins. His Team Sadie T-shirt was pulled over his other clothes, making it look like a rumpled afterthought.

"More importantly," Chrissy added, "Do you have the goblet?"

That was the thing that really mattered to her, the reason she'd come. I walked slowly toward her. "No, I don't."

A spark of worry flitted through her eyes. "Donovan didn't get it, did he?"

"No. We both went for it at the same time and tipped it over. Queen Orlaith immediately locked it up."

Chrissy relaxed. "Well, there's always tonight. You'll have to find a way to get to it before he does."

I folded my arms. "Look, we need to talk about my wishes."

Clover sat down on the table and sighed with an air of martyr. "Ah, she has that tone mortals always use when they're about to complain. You made me come here for this?"

Chrissy waved her hand at him dismissively. "We're being supportive, remember?"

"Right." He lifted his hand like he was giving me a high-five. "Go Team Sadie."

I ignored him. "I wished for Jason to love me. He doesn't." I held up a hand to stop Chrissy from speaking before I finished. "I'm not complaining about that. In fact, I would rather use that wish to take us all home."

Clover leaned back, resting against a jar of ribbons with marked resignation. "Do you know why we call you mortals? It's because you always want something more."

I shot him a dark look. "I'm just asking you to fulfill your part of the contract."

Chrissy picked up a perfume bottle and absentmindedly sniffed the scent. "Jason does love you. He said so himself."

I gave her a dark look as well. "Yeah. He said so, but he doesn't love me. Last night he talked non-stop about himself, except when he yelled at me for not getting the goblet. He was patronizing, rude, and left me stranded in a lake because he wanted to catch up with the other princes' boats."

Chrissy set the bottle down and lifted another to her nose, testing its scent. "You didn't wish for Jason to have a great personality; you just wished for him to love you."

I gritted my teeth in frustration. "I almost drowned."

Chrissy picked up the last perfume bottle, one made of blue glass. "Jason loves you. He just loves himself more." Chrissy sniffed the contents and wrinkled her nose in distaste. "Some guys are like that. It can't be helped."

"Then it's not *real* love."

Chrissy let out a tinkling laugh, one that said I was being ridiculous. "Real love, like real magic, is open to interpretation." She put down the blue bottle and draped her hands across her knees. "So I guess this means Jason didn't kiss you? Bummer."

"Let's talk about wish number three: my dancing ability."

Clover let out a groan and pulled his hat over his eyes. I suspected he was attempting to sleep.

"I wished to be a good dancer. I'm not. Even Kailen said so."

"Kailen?" Chrissy's expression brightened. "Prince Kailen was there?" She sent me a knowing look, one that verged on sympathetic. "No wonder you weren't impressed with Jason. Other guys fade in comparison to Kailen Emberwater. Was he dressed in black?"

"Yeah."

"Did he have that wicked cool sword?"

"The one with the hilt that looks like a twisted tree branch?"

"That's the one." She smiled dreamily and spread her hands out on either side of her. "He's such an irresistible bad boy. At my high school, he was voted hottest enemy combatant. I voted for him twice."

Clover pulled his hat down further.

"Back to my wish about dancing," I said, taking control of the conversation again. "Clearly I should have a magical refund coming. I'm supposed to be a great dancer, but I'm not."

Chrissy shrugged, sending her hair—pink again—sliding off her shoulder. "Technically, you wished to dance so well you'd be famous for it in your century. Your wish didn't ask for quality, just fame." Another shrug, this one apologetic. "As it turns out, a lot of people are famous on very little talent. I suppose that says something a bit unflattering about your society."

Technically. Always that word. No matter how poorly my wishes turned out, she wouldn't take responsibility for them.

Steam no longer hovered over the bath. It was growing colder. I sat on the tub's edge and pulled off a stocking, frustration making me yank extra hard. "Doesn't the intent of my wishes count for anything?"

"You know what they say about intentions. They're good for paving roads, but not much else."

I tugged my other stocking off. The diamond I'd found in the forest fell out and rolled across the floor. I'd forgotten about it.

The gem lay sparkling guiltily on the floor until Chrissy slid from the table and picked it up. "Pilfering wishes from Queen Orlaith's tree? That's dangerous."

"I found it on the ground. I thought—" I didn't finish the sentence. "Wishes? It's not a diamond?"

Chrissy turned the stone over in her hand. "The fruit from our magic trees is close enough to diamonds that your kind can't tell the difference. That's why you humans like diamond jewelry so much. It's like wearing wishes that are waiting to happen." Her usual carefree manner slipped away, leaving her expression solemn and wistful. "The trees are dropping a lot of their fruit lately. This one is stunted and will never ripen. I'm afraid it's doomed to be just a diamond."

My mind flicked back to the forest, back to the glittering trees. "All that sparkly fruit I saw last night—those were actually magic wishes?" I straightened, hope rising. "If I got one, could I use it to wish my way home?"

"Only *ripe* wishes work," Chrissy emphasized. "When they turn soft and white, then they've got magic." She dropped the stone into my hand. "If you ate this, it wouldn't do anything except give you indigestion."

I put the stone on the table, disappointed. I didn't remember seeing white fruit on any of the trees last night. "None of the fruit is ripe?" Donovan had an enchanted cloak. If there were any ripe wishes hanging around, he could manage to steal one.

Chrissy shook her head sadly. "Now you understand why Queen Orlaith is so desperate to find a cure. Can you imagine running out of magic? It would be like being mortal, except, you know, better looking." Chrissy let out a small laugh and put her hand on her chest. "Sorry. For a moment I forgot you're one of the magicless."

She returned to the dressing table and sat primly on the stool, pressing her hands together like a teacher starting a lesson. "Let's get back to the important stuff—the goblet. What question did Queen Orlaith ask it?"

"She asked why the trees weren't growing."

Chrissy leaned forward eagerly. "What answer did the goblet give?"

"It said the trees needed love. Apparently it's given that answer for awhile."

"That's all it said?" She frowned. "That can't be the solution. No one loves the trees more than the fairies."

Her attention to this detail, hinted at what she hadn't said. "Are the Seelie Courts' trees in trouble too? Is that why you want the goblet?"

Chrissy didn't answer. Instead she picked up her wand from the table and fiddled with it.

"They are, aren't they?" The thought of more barren magical trees was sad. All those wishes withering and dropping.

"Our trees aren't as bad as the Unseelie Court's," Chrissy admitted, "but they're struggling too. The goblet should disclose the solution. I wonder why it's saying the same thing." Her brows furrowed together and she tapped her wand against the palm of her hand in thought. "Maybe it's a riddle. Do you remember the exact wording?"

I shook my head.

"Tonight, remember it." Her brows were still drawn in a perplexed line.

"What will happen if your trees don't grow?"

Chrissy's wings slowly swept open and closed, reminding me of the princesses' lacy fans. "Mortals shouldn't bother themselves with fairy matters. It leads to temptation, which leads to mortals trying to work magic for themselves, which leads to either quick deaths or lives of wizardry."

She stood, walked over to me, and patted my arm. "You don't want either of those. You'd look horrible with a long, scraggly beard."

From the dressing table, Clover let out a long snore. His chin jiggled against chest, making his beard quiver.

Chrissy let him sleep. "So what's your plan to get the goblet tonight?"

I didn't want to give details about that. Vagueness was my best approach. "I'm working on it today. Any suggestions?"

"Don't let Orlaith catch you. She's not the forgiving type." Chrissy glanced back at the dressing table. "Oh, and don't go with the perfume in the blue bottle. It smells like something horrid lives inside. And speaking of unpleasant smelling things . . ." She pointed her wand at Clover and a poof of sparkles knocked into his chest.

Clover swatted at the glitter, sputtering, "I'm awake. I'm awake." He stumbled to his feet, still batting the air. "Go team Sadie." A yawn. "We believe in you."

Chrissy turned back to me. "Call me as soon as you have the goblet, and you're out of Queen Orlaith's land." She gave me a sly smile, leaning toward me conspiratorially. "I bet Jason kisses you tonight. That's something to look forward to."

No, not really.

Hundreds of tiny lights appeared in the room, swirling around Chrissy and making her wings glow incandescent. When the lights cleared, she was gone.

Clover took off his bowler hat and wiped glitter from it. "Fairies. They can't leave without making a production of it."

He placed the hat back onto his head, giving it a tug to hold it in place. "Do me a favor, lass. If Queen Orlaith does catch you, leave my name out of your confessions. It's always been a goal of mine not to be changed into anything unnatural." He adjusted his hat one last time then departed too.

I thought of his words the entire time I bathed.

Chapter 19

After I washed off the traces of the night, I put on a clean chemise and stockings. My lady's maid dressed me in a corset, slip, bum roll, a green bodice, and matching green overskirt. She tied blue silk sleeves to the bodice, which matched a panel sewn onto the underskirt, and also matched the stiff triangle of material attached to the bodice, called a stomacher.

She hooked on a metal belt that hung decoratively around my skirt—and didn't hold anything up—then finished off my outfit with a necklace, bracelet, and set of earrings. After that was done, she braided my hair and weaved blue ribbons into it.

When I was sufficiently beautified and royalified, I paid a visit to the goldsmith. The smithy backed up to a far wall on the castle grounds, a gray stone building tinged with moss. The clang of a hammer and smoke from the forge greeted me long before I got there. I stepped inside the doorway, enjoying the warmth that curled around the room, as cozy as a sleeping cat. It was a welcome change from the morning chill.

The goldsmith was bent over a table, studying something with a frown. He was a middle-aged man with calloused hands and biceps as big as my thighs. He wore an apron that may have once been beige but was now smudges of different shades of black. A younger apprentice stood in the back of the smithy, beating some poor, helpless piece of metal. When the goldsmith straightened, I saw he was examining Donovan's picture of the goblet. Good. That meant he was working on it.

I cleared my throat to get his attention. "Excuse me. I came to ask when the goblet will be finished."

He grunted like I'd insulted him. "I'll tell you the same thing I told Prince Donovan, his royal impatience. These things take time. I can't have it to you faster than tomorrow night, no matter how much you pay me."

I tried not to panic at the news. Donovan only had two more nights until he had to either rat out my sisters and me, or face execution.

My sisters and me. When had I started thinking of the other princesses as sisters? We weren't really related, and yet it was beginning to feel like we were. It seemed like I had known them for far longer than a day.

I thought of Kayla's words and realized what was happening. The magic was taking effect. I was starting to lose my memories of my twenty-first century home.

"Make the goblet as fast as you can," I told the goldsmith. "And send for me as soon as it's done." I left the smithy, focusing my mind on images of my real family. Mom, Dad, Alanzo. Our lazy cat, Pepper. I recited my phone number and locker combination. I pictured my house, my street, my school. It was hard to think of my old life clearly. I was too tired. I went back to my chambers in the castle, walked past my sleeping sisters, and climbed into my bed. Someone had put on clean sheets. I was glad for that. Moments later I fell asleep— corset, shoes, hair trappings and all.

• • •

When I woke up, my sisters were gone. Someone had left a drink, cheese, and a meat pie on my nightstand. I ate it hungrily, thankful the king hadn't followed through on his threat to feed me nothing but bread and water.

After my lady's maid repaired the damage I'd done to my hair by sleeping on it, I went downstairs to find Donovan. Madam Saxton told me he was having a lesson with the fencing master in the pasture near the stables.

I traipsed outside for the second time that day, slightly bothered by the fact that I knew where the stables were. The knowledge was just there, inserted by the magic of this wish. More proof that I was turning into Princess Sadie.

I strode toward the stables, flipping through memories of Kentucky, trying to keep them firmly in mind. The twenty- first century was home, not here. If it was summer like Kailen said, it must be a cold one. Instead of the humid eighty-five degree days I was used to, the temperature felt about sixty-five. I was glad for my layers of clothing.

It wasn't hard to find Donovan practicing in the field. If I hadn't heard the smack of wooden swords ringing across the grounds like a drum beat, I would have still noticed the audience. All eleven of my sisters stood beside the pasture fence, watching Donovan. Several of them had their fans out, demurely waving them back and forth.

I walked toward the group, wondering at their interest. Wondering, that was, until I got close enough to see Donovan better. Both he and the fencing master had stripped their tunics off, apparently too hot even for sixty-five degrees. They darted at each other, all gleaming muscles and testosterone. A grace accompanied Donovan's movements—an easy strength. And for a guy who was a thief, he had nice abs. I wondered where he'd gotten the physique: tall, lean, and well-defined.

He had enough stamina that he must be an athlete. Swim team maybe, or track. He didn't seem like the football players from my high school. They were a team off the court and on. Donovan struck me as the type who didn't try to fit in with a group.

Really, though, I knew so little about him. That bothered me now. It also bothered me that my sisters were gathered around him like some sort of fan club. Literally.

Rosamund glanced at me with disapproval. "Pray tell, where is your hat?"

Each of them wore a jeweled or feathered cap that matched their gowns. Apparently royalty wasn't supposed to step outside without one. I put my hand to my hair as though only now noticing I was hatless. "Oh," I said, "I forgot . . ." *that I should have studied Renaissance fashion before making any wishes.* I hated the way being honest made me look stupid most of the time.

"What are you all doing out here?" I asked to change the subject.

Penny didn't take her eyes off of Donovan. "We're seeing what sort of king the new suitor would make."

"I fear our military is in trouble," Isolde added, but she was staring at him as admiringly as the others.

"Kings aren't required to lead the charge," Catherine pointed out. "Father doesn't."

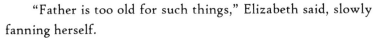

"Father is too old for such things," Elizabeth said, slowly fanning herself.

"Prince Donovan would lead the charge," Clementia murmured. "He's young. And strong." Her lips curled upward hungrily. "And . . . inspiring."

Philippa nudged her. "As inspiring as Eustace?"

Clementia put her hand to her chest, engulfing it in the rows of ruffles there. "Eustace shall always be my inspiration. I only meant that troops respect a man who is comely and well-built."

"Prince Donovan is quite well-built," Kayla agreed, letting her eyes roam over him.

"He knows nothing of sword fighting," Mathilda put in. "What sort of kingdom is Hamilton-Ohio that their prince has never had a proper lesson?"

"True," Beatrix said, her fan swaying lazily between her fingers. "But one can't fault the kingdom for producing handsome men."

Rosamund dragged her gaze away from Donovan long enough to give Beatrix a reproving look. "Would you say such a thing if Frederick were near?"

Beatrix fanned herself faster. "Prince Donovan has not tempted me away from Frederick. I only stated what nature has already made plain. I find it a pity that Father would execute such a handsome man."

Rosamund rolled her eyes. "Father won't execute him. Prince Donovan will run away on the third night like they all do."

Catherine frowned, worried. "What if he can't? He has no horse, and it's clear enough he couldn't fight his way past the castle guards."

"Bend your knees!" the fencing master yelled above the sound of swords clashing. "Hold your shield firm!"

Donovan lunged forward, his sword swinging at the fencing master's torso. The man blocked with a swing of his own, hitting Donovan's sword so hard it was knocked from his grip. The sword clattered to the ground, spitting up dust.

The fencing master bowed slightly. "Well fought, Your Highness."

Donovan shook his fingers to relieve the stiffness. "I'm afraid I'm a poor student."

"Just an untaught one, Sire. You've the reflexes and height to make a good opponent. Do you wish to go another round?" The fencing master glanced over at us. "Or perhaps not."

Donovan turned to see what the man was staring at. His gaze stopped on me. As his sort-of-betrothed, I suppose it wasn't surprising the fencing master thought Donovan would rather spend time with me.

I expected him to announce that, no, he'd rather keep practicing. Guys and swords. When my older brother played computer quest games, it took something along the lines of a house fire to break his concentration.

Donovan picked up his sword from the ground and handed it and his shield to the fencing master. "I guess that's enough practice for today. Thanks for your help."

The man bowed again, this time with a knowing smile. Donovan gathered up his shirt and jacket from a fence post, putting them on while he walked over.

My sisters fell silent. Several more lacy fans flipped open, rippling in the air like butterfly wings. Isolde and Kayla smiled. Catherine batted her eyelashes. The whole group was practically purring. For girls who were supposed to be in love with other guys, they didn't have any qualms about flirting.

When Donovan reached us, he put his hands on the top of the fence and swung himself up and over. He glanced at the fluttering fans and coy smiles then stopped in front of me and offered his arm. "Would you join me in a walk?"

It gave me an unreasonable jolt of pleasure to have him single me out. A silly reaction. He had only picked me because we were working together. We had strategies to discuss.

I slipped my arm through his. "Of course."

We strolled away from the stables following the path that led around the side of the castle. Above us, the sky was a careless blue with foamy clouds drifting here and there. The grounds smelled of animals, smoke from the forge, and breezes wandering over the castle walls. A few meandering chickens pecked at the ground by the path.

"You're pretty good with a sword," I said.

"Not nearly as good as King Rothschild's men."

"You won't have to fight them. I'll help you escape, if it comes to that."

We didn't say more because two men rolled a barrel by us. Donovan stopped and pulled me to his other side, out of their way.

"There are gardens behind the castle," he said. "Let's go there. It's a good place to talk."

The grounds were so large, it would take a while to reach the back. I didn't mind. I liked walking this way, with my hand on Donovan's arm. It made me feel elegant and protected. "I wonder why men don't offer their arms to women in our century?"

"You mean besides the fact that I look like a dork?"

"You don't. You look like a gentleman."

"I guess nobody wants to look like a gentleman in high school. Go figure."

I remembered I had resolved to get to know him better. "Do you play sports at your school?"

"Too busy. Especially now that I've got court-mandated service hours."

A few chickens scurried away from our feet, clucking indignantly at our intrusion. "I thought maybe you were on a swim team. You're a good swimmer."

"Growing up, the city pool was cheaper than air conditioning. I spent a lot of time there."

I felt a pinch of sympathy, an ache that he'd endured so much. "Was your entire childhood terrible?"

He blinked, taken aback. "Who said my childhood was terrible? Hanging out at the pool was more fun than the piano lessons I bet your parents forced you to take every summer."

"They didn't *force* me to take piano. Although they did pressure me to take some extra flute lessons so I could play with the school band."

"That's worse," he said. "The horrors."

"And I didn't take lessons during the summer. I went to camp."

He shook his head sadly. "Forced to leave home and bunk with strangers in primitive conditions."

"Okay," I conceded. "I guess happiness is a matter of perspective."

Across the courtyard, a couple men called to one another. A maid walked by carrying sloshing buckets of water. Such different sounds than our century. No whoosh of cars passing or distant rumble of planes.

Donovan glanced around to make sure no one was near enough to hear him. "Jade Blossom checked in on me earlier."

"What did she say?"

"Despite the fact that wishes are supposed to be confidential, someone leaked our situation to the Seelie Court." The Seelie Court—the one Chrissy belonged to. "The good news is the fairy bookies are giving three-to-one odds I'll manage to steal the goblet, and you'll be turned into a woodland creature by Queen Orlaith."

"I don't think you understand the definition of good news."

He laughed, teasing. "It's good news for me. I've never been a favorite. My ego needs the boost."

"Yeah, I bet." Guys as good looking as Donovan had fully-boosted egos. They just came that way.

"I decided to find out if giving Queen Orlaith sleeping powder was possible, so I asked Jade Blossom whether fairies can be drugged. She said they can't." He shrugged. "She may have said that so I didn't get any ideas about drugging her. She looked at me nervously after I asked."

Well, there went our only Plan B.

I told him about Chrissy's visit and what she'd told me about the diamonds really being unripe wishes.

"I'll look around for a ripe one tonight, " he said. "We could use a wish. "

I doubted he would be able to find one, not with the trees the way they were.

We rounded the corner of the castle. A garden the size of a football field greeted us, complete with trees, hedges, and bushes sculpted into geometric patterns. Flowered trellises stretched over orderly paths. Angel sculptures stood guard, wings folded, eyeing us. We strolled toward the main path.

"I talked to the goldsmith," I said. "He can't have the goblet done until tomorrow. That means we'll only have one night to get the real one. After that, you'll have to leave the castle so the king won't execute you."

"Or I could reveal the princesses' secret and marry you."

I raised an eyebrow at him.

"What?" he asked. "You don't think marriage would be better than my death?"

I hadn't thought about actually marrying him. Now that he mentioned it, the possibility seemed startling, and awkward, and intriguing all at once. "You can't tell the king where we go at night. If you do, he'll end the balls, and we'll lose our chance to steal the goblet."

"Which is still slightly better than my death," Donovan said.

"I didn't mean—"

Donovan held up his hand to stop me. "Look, there's no point worrying about King Rothschild killing me in a couple days, when it's much more likely that Queen Orlaith will kill us both tomorrow night. Let's worry about our deaths in the right order."

Donovan had spoken tongue in cheek, but he was right. If Queen Orlaith caught me, she would exact a fierce revenge.

"Stop frowning," he said, nudging me. "We can pull this off. You have two days to practice your thieving skills, and luckily, you'll be learning from a master."

He stopped walking and looked me over like I was a project that required a lot of work. "Ever stolen anything before?"

"Just cookies from the cupboard."

"Do you know any magic tricks?"

"Nope."

He lifted one of my sleeves. "Too bad. You could put a lot up these."

I tugged my sleeve away from him and slid my arm through his so we could walk again. "It's not as if I need a lot of skill. I'll just wait until no one is looking and switch the goblets."

Donovan let out a scoff. "That's the sort of attitude amateurs have. And do you know what they get?" Before I could answer, he said, "Caught."

"Wait, weren't *you* caught?"

"I've never been caught." We'd reached a gate leading to a pond and more flowerbeds. The air here was thick with the scent of crisp blossoms and lazy, waiting buds. He opened the gate and stood aside so I could pass. High school student or not, he had the gentleman thing down. I walked inside, waited for him to join me, and we sauntered over to a stone bench underneath a willow tree.

"If you were never caught," I asked, "how come you're on probation?"

He motioned for me to sit on the bench. "That's another story."

I sat down and smoothed out my skirt. "We've got time. Tell me."

"You need to practice first." He opened up the leather bag that hung from his belt, pulled a bronze coin out, and held it up. Tapping it with his finger, he said. "Here we have a coin with King Rothschild's face stamped on it. Completely solid. Nothing fake about it. Although really, probably not the most flattering picture as part of his nose seems to have worn off."

"Wait—you didn't steal that coin from someone at the castle, did you?"

"I borrowed it for teaching purposes. Heads or tails?" He flipped the coin into the air, caught it, and slapped it on the back of his hand. "If you call it, you can have my dessert tonight. If you're wrong, I get yours."

"Tails," I said.

He moved his hand. The coin was gone.

"Your first lesson is this: never bet with a thief. You'll lose every time." He reached behind my ear and the coin appeared in his hand again. "Ah, it's heads. I hope there's something good for dessert."

I folded my arms. "So what does cheating at a coin toss have to do with stealing the goblet?"

"Patience, Tiara Girl." He flipped the coin, caught it, and slapped it on the back of his hand. "Do you know the secret of this trick?"

"I'm guessing it's not that I have magical, wealthy ears."

"A sleight of hand. It's something good magicians and good thieves have in common." He lifted his hand, showing me that although it looked flat, the coin was cupped in his palm.

"The trick to palming a coin is you need to practice making your hand look normal." He brought his hands together, scratching the underside of his wrist. Then he held his hands apart again. "Where's the coin?"

I hadn't seen him transfer the coin to his left hand, but I couldn't be certain. I glanced at one hand, then the other.

He smiled at my uncertainty. "You need to learn how to redirect the mark's attention, moving so naturally that it doesn't seem like you're up to anything." He fisted his hands and held them out. "Double or nothing for dessert tomorrow night. Did I move the coin or am I just playing on your expectations that I would?"

I looked into his eyes, trying to read them. Couldn't. I slowly tapped his right hand.

He opened it. No coin. "Again, you've forgotten the all-important maxim about not betting with a thief."

He opened his left hand and gave me the coin. "You try. If you can pull it off, I'll give you tonight's dessert back."

It took me a minute before I could hold the coin by contracting my hand muscles. Then I flipped the coin, slapped it down on my other hand, and palmed the coin. Or at least I tried. The first four times, the coin tumbled to the ground. The fifth time it stayed fixed in my hand, but my fingers were stiff. They had to be for the coin to stay put. I made a fist with my empty hand, opened it to show it was empty, and with my other hand, produced the coin from Donovan's ear. "Ta da. I hope it's chocolate."

He shook his head, unimpressed. "No dessert. It's obvious you're palming the coin. Besides, chocolate was a New World food. It didn't become popular in Europe until after the Renaissance. Relax your fingers."

He knew chocolate's history? Who knew that sort of thing off the top of his head? Despite Donovan's whole bad boy image, the guy was smart.

He put the coin in my palm, then flipped my hand over and adjusted my thumb and fingers, moving them into a more natural position. I probably should have concentrated on that and not the fact that he was touching me. His fingers were warm, gentle, practiced.

Practiced because he's used to stealing things, I reminded myself. He wasn't someone I should get involved with. Even if he was funny and charming and smart. Even if his eyes were the same color as the sky and had that same open, limitless quality. I absolutely couldn't fall for Donovan, I wouldn't let myself.

Chapter 20

I spent the next five minutes trying to make my hands look normal. At best, they looked mannequin-like. Donovan patiently watched me fumbling with the coin.

When I'd picked it up off the ground for the tenth time, I handed it back to Donovan and slumped on the bench with a defeated thump. "What's the point of practicing this? We're not going to pull coins from Queen Orlaith's ears."

"The point is," he said, effortlessly flipping the coin upward, "you're practicing stealth." He plucked the coin from the air and tightened his fingers around it. "Tomorrow night you need to pull a heavy goblet from your pocket, set it on the table, pour any remaining elixir from one cup to the other, then pocket the queen's goblet, all without her noticing." He held his closed fist out. "Where's the coin?"

It had to be in his hand. He hadn't slapped—or pretended to slap—it onto the back of his other hand yet. "It's in your fist."

"See for yourself." Donovan slowly opened his hand, finger by finger. It was empty.

"Where did the coin go?"

"Check in your right pocket."

"It can't be in my pocket." He hadn't come near enough to slip something into my pocket.

"Look," he insisted. His blue eyes crinkled around the edges.

I slipped my hand into my pocket, and my fingers brushed against something small and circular. I pulled out the brass coin, astonished. "How did you do that?"

"Stealth, practice, and preparation." He motioned to the coin. "Now keep working."

"I watched you the whole time," I protested. "Neither of your hands came near me." I leaned toward him, looking him up and down as though I'd find some clue on his jacket. "Do the trick again. I need to figure it out."

He tilted his chin knowingly. "You're just trying to get out of practicing."

I took his hand, turned it over, and put the coin in his palm. "Seriously, it's going to bother me until I know."

Donovan held the coin back out to me, refusing to do the trick. "You've gone to magic shows before. I bet you didn't badger the magicians afterward and demand to know their secrets."

"But I would have if I could have."

Donovan laughed, flipped the coin in the air, and caught it. "Magicians don't tell their secrets. If you want to know, it will cost you something."

"What?"

"What are you offering?" He grinned, mischief lurking at the edges of his mouth. For someone who didn't do sports, he liked playing games.

"Well . . ." I tapped my fingers against the bench, thinking, "Jade Blossom already granted you money, power, and an invisibility cloak. I, on the other hand, received a good voice, a part in a famous fairy tale, and Jason's love. When you come down to it, I don't have much to bargain with."

The coin spun through the air above Donovan's thumb, light flickering off its surface. "When you put it like that, you are at a disadvantage."

"I'll trade you Jason."

"Not interested. But . . ." Donovan caught the coin and spun it into the air again. "If you agree to give me something I want, something small," Donovan added. "I'll tell you how I did the trick."

"You've already got my desserts. What else do you want?"

"I haven't thought of it yet. Eventually, I'm bound to want something—a drink of water, a foot massage . . ." He lifted his foot toward me on the bench. A layer of dirt covered his boot.

"Will your feet be clean?" I asked.

He didn't move his foot. "You know, I probably saved you from drowning last night. Doesn't that mean you're supposed to be my servant for life or something?"

I pushed his boot away. "Wrong fairy tale."

He chuckled and set his foot on the ground. "You at least owe me eternal gratitude."

"You already have that."

He flipped the coin up higher. It spun, turning into a brass blur. On the way down, Donovan's hand swooped out and grabbed the coin. With a closed fist, he held it out. "Were you paying attention that time?"

"I paid attention both times."

"Then tell me where the coin is."

I took hold of his hand in both of mine so he couldn't get rid of the coin somehow. He let me peel his fingers apart, revealing his empty palm. Impossible.

"Look in your left pocket this time."

I dropped his hand and scooted away. He didn't move. His hands lay motionless in his lap. A smirk was firmly planted on his lips. I reached into my pocket and groaned. The coin was there. I pulled it out and turned it over. "How did you do that?"

"Grant me that unnamed favor, and I'll let you know."

My curiosity wouldn't let me do anything else. "Okay, fine. But the favor can't be worse than a dirty foot rub."

"Worse than a dirty foot rub?" he protested, all offended dignity. "I bet there was a time when you would have paid to rub Jason's feet, dirty or not."

"Stop changing the subject. You're telling me how to do the trick."

"Stealth, practice, and preparation." He put his arms behind him on the bench and leaned back, smirk still going full force. "I think I want a foot rub now."

"Speaking of you promising to tell me things and then not doing it—you never told me how you got your fairy godmother."

"I believe I told you it wouldn't make you feel better, and you didn't press the point."

"I'm pressing the point now."

Donovan leaned forward and took the coin from my hand. "Okay, here's how I did the trick."

"Your story must be something really embarrassing if you don't want to tell me after I admitted throwing up in front of TV cameras."

Donovan held up the coin. "Stealth. Like most magic tricks, the secret lies in directing the audience's attention to what you want them to see." He tossed the coin into the air again, high and fast. "This time watch my left hand instead of my right."

The coin came down. I focused on Donovan's left hand. Both hands lifted, the left lower than the right, as though he wasn't sure which would be in a better position to catch the coin. When it got close, he made a swipe at the coin with his right hand. I saw what I hadn't before. His right hand closed, but not around the coin. It fell through to his left hand, which didn't close at all. He palmed the coin.

Donovan held out his right hand, fist closed. "Where's the coin?"

"In your left hand."

He held up that hand, revealing the coin. "Good job."

"How did you get it into my pocket?"

"Preparation." He moved his leg, revealing two brass coins on the bench. He picked them up. "I had three coins. I knew I would do this trick for you, so I slipped the first two coins into your pockets while we walked up here." He took my hand, turned it palm up, and dropped all three there. "Look at them. They're not exactly the same."

They weren't. One was darker, one was more worn, and the last wasn't as round.

"You didn't notice the coin changed," he went on, "because your mind expected there to be only one. That's why the goblet doesn't have to be an exact replica for our switch to work."

The trick seemed so simple when he explained it that I couldn't believe I hadn't noticed the differences in the coins before. "When did you put the coins in my pockets? My hand was on your arm the whole time."

As soon as I said it, I realized it wasn't true. He'd pulled me out of the way of the men rolling the barrel. He'd opened the gate door and then walked with me on my other side.

Donovan took hold of my hand and held it up, emphasizing his point. "Sleight of hand. You've got to have such good control of your fingers you could pick-pocket the name badge off a policeman." He let go of my hand. "Not that I did that . . . more than once."

He casually picked up a coin, made it disappear from one hand, then dropped it into my lap with the other. "Now you try. Toss the coin up high so your audience's gaze is focused on it. Look where you want them to look. Their gaze will follow yours. Then make a grand sweep with your right hand, but don't close your fist all the way until the coin falls through to your left hand."

I did my best to follow Donovan's instruction. I didn't catch the coin the first time, or the second, or the tenth. It thudded to the ground, sometimes lying sullenly at my feet, other times rolling off in an attempt to escape my doomed magic trick.

Donovan went after the coin those times. With my long skirts, getting up was a production of hauling lace and ruffles around. This was probably why you never saw magicians wearing Renaissance gowns.

While Donovan fetched my errant coin, I would toss one of the extras up in the air. The results were the same. Around the twentieth time, I threw the coin too close and it fell down the front of my dress.

"Hmm," Donovan said. "I suppose you don't want me to get that one."

I fished it out, blushing. "How long did it take you to learn this?"

"I don't know. I've been doing this sort of thing since I was a kid. Making things disappear was a necessity." He fluttered his hands dramatically, and both the extra coins vanished.

He could palm two at once? I couldn't manage one without it looking obvious.

"Why did you need to make coins disappear? Were you working your way up to dollar bills?"

"I didn't start with coins. I started with food. I went into the neighborhood grocery store and pocketed stuff. It didn't take long before I got caught. It's hard to hide cans of ravioli in your jacket."

He said it so casually, like it wasn't an awful thing. I couldn't imagine being hungry and having no way to feed myself. "Did you tell the police why you stole the food?"

"The store manager didn't call them. I guess he figured a kid stealing canned goods had his reasons. He just banned me from coming back."

"He should have helped you."

Donovan let out a laugh, not amused, just unbelieving that I was so naive. "My neighborhood was filled with kids like me. The homeless guys fought over trashcan territory. What was one manager supposed to do? He was trying to make a living."

The coin lay forgotten in my hand. "So how did you eat?"

"I realized I needed to be smart about stealing." He picked up one of the extra coins. Instead of flipping it, he moved it across the back of his fingers—not so much a trick as a nervous habit. "I'd seen restaurants on TV shows, so I knew how they worked. I got dressed in my best clothes took a bus to a good part of town, and walked into a restaurant during the dinner rush.

If anyone had asked why I was by myself, I would have told them my family was eating and I'd just gone to the car for something. No one asked, though. People are used to ignoring kids." The coin reached Donovan's pinky finger and he sent it back the other way.

"You know how people leave money on tables for waiters to take? Turns out, bills aren't much harder to palm than coins."

I wanted to tell him I was sorry his parents had failed him, sorry society hadn't helped him. He didn't want to hear it though, and it was pointless to say. The world was dark in places. You couldn't fix that.

"What will happen if you don't go back to Ohio?"

"The next time Shane needs money, he'll do something stupid. Probably steal another car."

"Another car?"

Donovan nodded. "I told you I'd never been caught." The coin moved around his knuckles. "Shane knew I stole things and figured he could too. You fence a car, and it keeps the rent paid for months."

Donovan stopped moving the coin. "The cops picked him up his first try. He got off with a hand slap. The second time he got caught, I took the rap. I didn't want him to go to juvie." Donovan put the coin back on the bench. "So those are the sordid details of my past."

I didn't know what to say. I gave his hand a squeeze. "We'll get back."

I practiced making coins disappear for a few more minutes. I didn't get much better. After that, Donovan put a goblet-sized rock into my dress pocket. I stood by the bench and practiced taking it out without rustling my skirt. I wasn't much better at this than I was at palming coins.

After a half an hour of failing at the task, I sank back on the bench with defeat. The rock sat despondently in my lap. This wasn't going to work. I couldn't learn the art of theft in two weeks let alone two days. I was kidding myself to think I could steal a goblet from underneath the nose of a powerful fairy. "So, what sort of woodland animal are the Seelie fairies betting I'll be turned into?"

Donovan motioned for me to get back up and keep working. "You'll be fine."

"If you wore gloves, you wouldn't technically be touching the goblet. Maybe the curse wouldn't affect you."

Donovan picked up the rock and held it out to me. "It has to be you."

I didn't take the stone. "Have I ever mentioned I'm naturally clumsy?"

"With more practice, you'll be able to do this."

"In PE after I ran hurdles, the track looked like a line of dominos had been knocked over."

Donovan took my hand and set the rock in my palm. "Then it's a good thing you don't have to jump over anything to move the goblets."

"At the winter choir concert, I lost my footing and fell into the row of girls below me. Think dominoes in sparkly red dresses."

"I'm sure it could have happened to anyone."

"Torsha Baker was accidentally standing on the edge of Nan Marie Swapp's dress. When Nan Marie went down, her dress ripped halfway off. She still won't speak to me."

"If you were clumsy before, Chrissy must have fixed it when you wished to be a dancer. I've been watching you. You're as graceful as the other princesses."

I would have liked to believe him. "Kailen said I was a lousy waltzer."

"No, he didn't. He said you needed to learn to follow your partner's lead. That's different."

"You heard him giving me dance instructions?" I suppose that shouldn't have surprised me. Kailen said it enough times. Still it was odd to think of Donovan, close by, watching my stumbling attempts.

He shrugged. "There wasn't much else to do. I figured I should learn how to waltz in case King Rothschild holds a ball. He'll expect a prince to know how to dance."

"Was it hard for you to pick up the steps?"

"I didn't have a partner who made me nervous."

In other words, no, it hadn't been hard. It was only hard for me because I was graceless. I let out a sigh. "I hope the queen turns me into a bird. At least it would be cool to fly."

Donovan stood up and held his hand out. "It's time for a dance break."

"You want to dance?"

He kept his hand outstretched. "Cocky fairies get on my nerves. We'll go over the steps and tonight you'll blow Kailen away."

Not likely. Still it was nice of Donovan to help me. And I was tired of practicing with the rock.

I took Donovan's hand and stood up. My skirt swished back and forth from the momentum, more eager than I was to start dancing. Donovan led me a few feet away from the bench and pulled me into position. I put my hand on his shoulder. He held me gently around my waist and took my free hand in his.

Last night at the campfire, we'd sat closer than we were now. While I'd shivered, Donovan had wrapped his arms around me. But I felt his closeness more now. A fluttering of nerves rumbled through my chest and made it hard to concentrate. His hand felt warm in mine. Did mine feel cold in his?

"We'll do the basic step for a few counts, then move to the spins and stuff." He stepped forward, smooth and confident, propelling me with him. "One . . . two . . . three . . . down . . . up . . . up . . ."

I moved my feet to the rhythm of his voice, doing my best to pay attention. He smelled faintly of leather. And something else. Something beckoning. I couldn't stop staring at the line his shoulders made in his jacket. I remembered him fighting shirtless, remembered the muscles in his shoulders. Taut. Tanned. Now my fingers rested on his shoulder. It made me feel like I couldn't breathe.

It was the corset, I told myself. I absolutely wasn't developing feelings for Donovan.

"One . . . two . . . three . . ."

I messed up on three. In my defense, it's hard to count and move your feet when your gaze wanders to your partner's blue eyes.

"Sorry," I said, and flushed. This was so stupid. Hadn't I learned it was a bad idea to develop crushes on guys I hardly knew? I'd known Donovan for what, twenty-four hours? And part of that time we'd been competing against each other.

Donovan kept counting off the beats. I concentrated on moving my feet in the right direction and swaying upward when I was supposed to. He had a nice voice. I wondered if he ever sang. My eyes went to his mouth, to the sloping letter M on his top lip. M was for magnificent and marvelous. I wondered what it would feel like to kiss that M.

Nope. Not a good idea to go there.

As I listened to the count, I listed reasons it was a bad idea to like Donovan.

1) Once we left this fairy tale, we'd never see each other again. He lived in a different state.

2) My parents wouldn't like me dating a guy with a criminal record.

3) Donovan could still betray me. I didn't know if he was telling the truth about working with me. He told me at the campfire that he'd gotten by for years because he knew how to fool people.

I tried to think of a fourth reason. Couldn't. I was stuck on the number three like the waltz. Donovan let go of my back, the signal to step out into a twirl. I did and he rewarded me with a smile. It tilted up at one side in an endearing sort of way.

Ohio wasn't really that far away.

"See," Donovan said. "Kailen didn't know what he was talking about. That's the thing about fairy guys. Have you ever met one that wasn't full of himself?"

The way Donovan phrased the question made me laugh. We both knew I'd only met one.

Almost against my will, a list of things I liked about Donovan formed in my mind.

1) He'd kept me from falling off the stairs even though we were working against each other.

2) He'd saved me from drowning and built a fire to warm me.

3) He was patient. He hadn't gotten frustrated with my lack of skill at palming coins, or working with rocks, or dancing.

4) He was smart and determined. He'd figured out a way to take care of himself and his brother.

5) He was loyal. He'd taken the rap for his brother and was still looking after him.

6) He wasn't a real criminal—he was like Aladdin from the Disney movie, but without the creepy monkey sidekick. He was a victim of circumstance. Big-hearted. And hot.

7) Hot probably deserved its own number.

I started plucking away the other reasons I'd put on my I-shouldn't-like-Donovan list. He wasn't going to betray me for the goblet. If he'd meant to get it at any cost, he would have let me fall off the stairs. And what did I care if my parents didn't approve of him? They didn't approve of me pursuing a music career, and that had never stopped me.

But what if none of it mattered? What if he didn't like me like that? None of the guys at my school had.

Donovan lifted my right hand and let go of my back, the signal to break away and do our next steps side by side. I did and returned to him again.

"Okay, let's try it with music now. Sing something."

I'd been contemplating the M of his lips and had to drag my attention back to his words. "You want me to sing?"

"Yeah. Let's see if your first wish was worth the magic."

I sifted through songs I knew, searching for one that would work with a waltz. The song I'd done for the auditions came to mind.

Nope.

I didn't ever want to sing it again. No doubt Donovan and I would both hear enough of it when we got back home. Spoofs and song remixes. No one would ever see it for what it was supposed to be: a wistful song about unrequited love.

Donovan hadn't heard it yet. I supposed he would be the song's only untainted audience. So there in his arms, I sang the tune. I didn't worry whether I'd be able to hit the notes while a corset constricted my diaphragm. Chrissy had taken the imperfections from my voice. The music lifted from my mouth, strong and clear, smooth and lilting. I meandered through the treble clef with ease, lingering on the hard, high notes and letting them flow off my tongue.

Donovan stared at me, impressed and then entranced. He hadn't expected my voice. I looked into his blue eyes and let every note caress him. This was what I'd wanted when I wrote the lyrics. This was what I'd tried for when I'd sung for Jason at the audition—the connection I saw in Donovan's eyes. He understood the struggle of standing when a person had already fallen down so many times.

Dancing was easier while I sang. I was concentrating on the notes, not obsessing about where my feet were. I finished the song and started another. Moving with Donovan through the garden felt as natural as talking with him. Fun, and a little bit exhilarating. This, I thought, is why people invented dancing.

As I finished my third song, Donovan slowed until we stopped. "You're amazing. I take back everything I said about singing being a useless, wasted wish."

"When did you say that?"

"Oh . . . maybe I just thought it. Intensely. But I've changed my mind." He dropped his hand from my back but kept hold of my hand. I liked the feel of his fingers intertwined with mine, liked the admiration in his eyes.

"I can see why you wanted that voice," he said, his own voice low and soft. "It's beautiful. Like the rest of you."

"Thanks." I didn't break our gaze. There was nowhere else I wanted to look.

"So . . ." Donovan rolled the word around in his mouth, tasting it. "I know the favor I want."

"What?"

He pulled me closer and lowered his head. He did this slowly, watching my reaction, giving me time to move away if this wasn't what I wanted. I didn't move away. I kept my eyes open until the last moment. Then I shut them and felt his lips press against mine.

My worries about my first kiss had been unfounded. Our teeth didn't bang together. My lips knew what to do. They followed his lead.

Donovan slid his hands around my waist, and I wound mine around his neck. His jacket lay open and as I leaned against his chest I felt the slow, steady rhythm of his heartbeat. It felt like music, and the words that sang through my insides were, "Donovan likes me *like that*."

I'm not sure how long we kissed. He wasn't in a hurry to end this and neither was I. Finally he lifted his head.

I smiled at him, my arms still draped around his shoulders. "You're right. That wasn't such a bad favor."

He kept his gaze on me, but didn't smile back. Worry tinged his eyes. "I'm probably not your usual type, am I?"

"I don't really have a usual type."

He stiffened, and the worry in his expression grew. "Because you see so many different types of guys?"

It was sweet he thought so many different types of guys were interested in me. I couldn't lie though, and didn't want to. If he liked me, he had to know who I was. "At your school do you have girls that are friends with guys, but never hang out with them except as friends?"

"Yeah."

"I'm one of those girls."

His eyebrows rose in happy surprise. "Score. The guys at your school are stupid."

I laughed at his assessment. "Yeah, exactly. So it turns out you can be my type."

He smiled, but it was still the shadowed with worry. "Will I still be your type when we go back to the twenty-first century?"

That was what was bothering him? He thought I was only interested in him as a fairy tale fling?

I drew out my words. "That depends. What's your usual type of girl?"

He pulled me closer. "Beautiful, talented . . . often clumsy . . . completely honest . . . oh, and over Jason."

"I think I'm your type."

"Good." He smiled, leaned down, and kissed me again.

Chapter 21

Donovan and I held hands on the way back to the castle. I don't remember anything about the walk—who or what we saw along the way. I felt like the sun had risen inside me, like a long dim chapter in my life had ended and everything was brighter now. It both amazed and frightened me how much a couple kisses could stir my emotions. No, it wasn't the kisses; it was the feeling behind them. It was Donovan seeing so much in me he couldn't imagine the guys in my school seeing less.

Most things hadn't changed since this morning. I was still stuck in the wrong century, and I had to steal a cup from a powerful fairy in order to return home. But I was grinning like none of it mattered because Donovan was holding my hand. What had happened to me?

By the time we got back to the castle, my lady's maid was searching for me so she could help me dress for supper. I hadn't realized I needed different clothes for that. Apparently in this time period the evening meal required its own attire. While she bustled me upstairs to change my clothes, a valet directed Donovan to his room for similar treatment.

I put on a dark blue dress with gold trim crisscrossing the underskirt and sleeves. My lady's maid's hands flew through my hair with practiced ease, braiding my hair so it resembled a ribboned Christmas wreath. My sisters were readying themselves for dinner as well, but they didn't say anything to me while our servants primped us into our finery. A couple sent me disapproving looks, though. They probably weren't pleased that I'd disappeared all afternoon with Donovan. I didn't care.

When I walked into the dining room, he was waiting by my seat. He wore a dark green jerkin with flared shoulders that emphasized his own. Sort of matador-ish and cool. He gave me a broad smile, and his gaze travelled over me in an approving way. Perhaps changing for dinner wasn't such a bad idea after all.

During the meal, we talked about school, swapping bad teacher stories. Donovan had me laughing in a very unprincessly manner about his chemistry teacher, who was occasionally careless in his demonstrations and at one point set his desk on fire.

"Mr. Mertz put out the fire right away," Donovan said, "but once the fire alarms go off, they make everyone evacuate anyway. We had to stand around outside while the firemen checked out the room for smoldering, combustible remains."

"At least you got out of class," I said.

"Yeah, and the best part was when Tyrone Wright carjacked the fire truck."

"Seriously?"

"The guy never should have messed with men who wield axes. That'll teach him to take a dare from me."

"You didn't!" With the smirk on Donovan's lips, I couldn't tell whether he was serious or not.

"Hey, the hood is an exciting place to live."

King Rothschild interrupted our conversation. "And what would you do, Prince Donovan, about the outer provinces?"

Donovan straightened and his voice took on a formal tone. "Pardon me, Sire. What is your problem with the outer provinces?"

The king ripped into his food with an enthusiasm that seemed out of place. "We won the war. Each province surrendered and swore fealty, yet they refuse to pay the reparations they agreed to. If you became King of Capenzia, what would you do about such defiance?"

Donovan hesitated. "Is it defiance, Sire, or are the outer provinces just unable to pay? Certainly the war must have been a financial burden to their lands as well as yours."

The king knifed the slab of meat on his plate, cutting it with gusto. "Their burdens aren't my concern. They caused the war and as such must pay for it. If I don't exact a price for their rebellion, what's to keep them from rebelling again?"

Several of my sisters glanced at one another uncomfortably. A couple looked like they wanted to speak, but none did. Donovan watched them, waiting, then spoke himself. "Have you considered marriages of alliance between your daughters and the provinces' princes?"

The clinking of silverware immediately stopped. Half of my sisters cast disbelieving looks at Donovan, the others cast hopeful looks at our father.

King Rothschild didn't see any of them. He made a grumbling noise in the back of his throat, like he was choking on Donovan's words. "Why would I give my daughters to the sons of conniving, treacherous men?" He set his goblet down with such a forceful thunk that the liquid sloshed onto the tablecloth. "Why not give them my silver, horses, and land too? That would teach my subjects not to cross me."

The king lifted his hand as though making an announcement. "Come fight King Rothschild. If you win, you'll take his possessions, and if you lose he'll give them to you." He lowered his hand and picked up his fork. "Nonsense. I'll give my daughters to allies, not enemies."

The king went on for several more minutes, insisting foes needed to be crushed not coddled. If he hadn't been so intent on his speech, he might have noticed several of his daughters let out disappointed whimpers and others stared forlornly at their plates.

I was glad the fairy tale ended with their marriages to the princes. Sooner or later the king would have a change of heart.

When the king finally stopped ranting about rewarding cutthroats, Donovan addressed him again. "Sire, do you want the provinces ruled by allies or enemies?"

"I want them to obey me. That's all."

Donovan should have dropped it. The princesses had never given him a reason to champion their cause, and the king had made it clear he didn't welcome differing opinions. But Donovan didn't drop the subject.

"Isn't a man more likely to want peace with you if he also calls you father? Those unions between your daughters and the neighboring princes would tie the lands together. A man as wise as you can certainly understand that."

The queen put her hand on the king's arm. "Prince Donovan makes a fair point. And you know 'tis not going to be easy to make royal matches for the girls—not when you keep threatening to kill every suitor who comes to the castle."

The king let out a grunt. "If a prince hasn't the wits to figure out where my daughters go each night, he would make a poor husband anyway. I'm weeding out the incompetent men. Which reminds me . . ." He turned his attention back to

Donovan. "You have two nights left to solve the mystery. Don't disappoint me. I don't reward that behavior either."

• • •

Our bedtime routine went the same as it had the night before. After our lady's maids combed out our hair, Madam Saxton and Donovan came into the room. They sat side by side on the couch and Rosamund and Philippa passed around drinks. I wanted to watch Donovan to see if I could spot the moment he poured his cider into the housekeeper's cup. Instead I talked to the others, doing what I could to keep their attention off him. After a half an hour, he and Madam Saxton both seemed to be asleep. My sisters and I helped each other dress.

While Philippa laced the back of my dress, she clicked her tongue. "Today, you carried on with Prince Donovan in a manner most unbefitting a woman whose true love awaits her in the forest."

I opened my mouth to say that any guy who left me in the middle of a lake wasn't my true love, but I stopped myself. My sisters might not let me go to the ball if they thought I didn't care about Jason anymore.

Penny fastened my stomacher to the front of my bodice. "Hey, don't deny it. You were totally checking him out at supper."

"Father will be less suspicious," I said, careful not to let any lies slip into my explanation, "if he sees me flirting with Prince Donovan. After tonight, Father would never guess I'm meeting someone else."

"True, perhaps." Philippa pulled the laces tight. "However, it's still unbecoming of one with our breeding."

"Really?" I asked. "You all paid close enough attention to Prince Donovan while he sparred with the fencing master."

"I didn't," Isolde said, breezing by to pick up extra pins from my dressing table.

From the table next to mine, Darby snorted. "If you'd batted your eyelashes any harder, you would have created a breeze."

Isolde lifted her chin and stalked back to her own table. "You're only vexed because Prince Donovan bid me a good day before he sparred, and he paid no heed to you whatsoever."

"Leave her be," Catherine said, coming over to help with my hair. "Prince Donovan has a body like our statue of Adonis. One can't help but appreciate art."

"His abs were quite a piece of art," Darby agreed.

Kayla weaved a yellow ribbon into her hair. "Artistically speaking, I liked the way his muscles rippled while he fought."

"Shh," I said. "You'll wake him." He was close enough to hear this whole conversation.

Beatrix picked up a green ribbon off a nearby table and tucked it into her golden curls. "No matter his resemblance to the garden statues, I shan't be tempted by his blue eyes, not when Frederick's brown eyes beckon me to remain faithful."

Mathilda let out a dreamy sigh. "Prince Donovan does have tempting blue eyes, does he not?"

"Wicked blue eyes," Elizabeth said.

Catherine and Penny giggled at the description. No one seemed to care about being too loud, and my annoyance increased with each of my sisters' comments. They were talking about Donovan like he was a high calorie dessert, not a person.

"He stuck up for you at supper," I reminded them.

When all eyes turned on me, I realized I shouldn't have spoken. My sisters didn't know that Donovan had followed us last night—that he knew we were meeting with the princes from the conquered provinces.

"Stuck up for us at supper?" Philippa repeated. She finished with my laces and checked her hair in the mirror. "Really, Sadie. Where did you learn these odd turns of speech?"

"What I meant is Prince Donovan thinks you should be able to marry whoever you want. You should be nice to him. He's . . ." I couldn't think of the right word and my sentence drifted off into happy contemplation. My expression must have said what I didn't.

Catherine momentarily stopped rolling my hair to study my face. "Heavens, you look positively smitten."

Rosamund was taming the curls by her face to hang as ringlets. "Perhaps Prince Donovan cast a magic spell on her."

Beside her, Mathilda giggled. "We had better take her to Prince Jason forthwith. True love's kiss will break the spell."

Not likely. And not going to happen. Even the mention of Jason's name made me inwardly groan. I would have to spend all night talking and dancing with him.

After we finished dressing, Rosamund opened up the secret door, and Philippa and Clementia passed out the lanterns. I'd lost my black cloak in the lake, so I had to take one from the closet, a brown one with a coarser weave.

With only a glance in Donovan's direction, I followed the others through the door and onto the landing. The white marble steps spread downward, as smooth as a keyboard, with each of our footsteps tapping out a rhythm. Above us, stars pricked the black night, glowing strong and bright. The air was still with a scent of leaves drifting upward. How did anyone ever get used to magic places?

Eleven lantern lights dipped down below me. I trailed them, listening for Donovan. I didn't hear him. I hung back, walking slower so he could catch up with me.

After a few moments I heard his voice in my ear, teasing. "Have I cast a spell on you, Princess Sadie?"

"You do know magic. I've seen you make coins disappear."

He let out a chuckle. I liked the sound of it, rich and secret. "Do girls always talk about guys that way?"

"Not always. Sometimes we talk about the fictional characters we wish guys were like."

"Do you think my blue eyes are wicked?"

"No, although you do have a wicked grin."

"We'll have to find that sculpture of Adonis in the garden. I want to see if it really looks like me."

I laughed and felt light and happy. I might have to spend the night dancing with Jason, but at least I could spend the day with Donovan.

When we came to the forest, Donovan left the path. The occasional eruption of owls, hooting and circling over the trees, let me know he was gathering twigs from the silver, gold, and diamond trees. He'd told me earlier he would get some for me too. It was one more perk of working with a guy who owned an invisibility cloak.

Finally the trees thinned revealing the lake. Twelve princes waited by their boats. Well, Jason was sort of waiting. He stood by a neighboring boat, talking to that prince.

My sisters hung their lanterns on the posts and happily made their way to their boyfriends. I hung my lantern last of all and grudgingly headed toward Jason. Just seeing him made a surge of hot anger flash through me. My footsteps became quicker, hard against the ground.

Jason saw me and headed back to his boat, reaching it the same time I did. Donovan arrived before either of us. I saw the boat tilt slightly, indicating he'd climbed inside.

The other princes took my sisters' hands and helped them into the boats. Jason either didn't see this custom or didn't care about it. Instead of getting into the boat, I stood in front of him, pinning him with a glare. "You know, I nearly drowned last night." I picked up a handful of my skirt and held it out to him as evidence. "This thing is like a lead suit with ribbons."

Jason walked closer, glanced around, and whispered, "Do you have a cell phone?"

"No. And you wouldn't get coverage here anyway."

His gaze travelled to the other boats. "Do any of the other girls have phones?"

I let go of my skirt. "Let's get back to the fact that I almost drowned last night—what kind of guy rows away and leaves someone in a freezing lake in the dark?"

Jason rolled his eyes. "You wouldn't have drowned. Someone from the show would have helped you if you'd been in real trouble."

Unbelievable. Jason didn't even feel bad. I planted my hands on my hips. "I think the correct thing to say at this point is, 'I'm sorry. Really, really sorry.'"

"I need a cell phone." His expression was devoid of its usual charm. A look of hard frustration was there instead. "I've got to get out of here. I don't care what my manager agreed to. I don't care what the ratings for this show will be. I'm done with cold drafty rooms and stinking toilets. I'm especially done with the crazed guy who thinks I should practice fencing for two hours a day."

There was no point waiting for an apology from him. It wasn't going to happen. I pushed by Jason and lifted my skirts to climb into the boat. I couldn't see past the material to tell where the edge of the boat was. My pride kept me from asking Jason for help. I didn't want to ask him for anything.

He followed me, pointing his finger at the ground to emphasize his words. "I will fire my manager if he doesn't have me on a plane to Los Angeles first thing in the morning. You tell him that."

Jason may have been immune to guilt, but I wasn't. It knocked around inside of me, reminding me it was my fault he was here. My wish had plucked him away from his life, his success, from everything he'd worked so hard for. He didn't even know all of this was real.

"We'll get home," I reassured him. "The castle goldsmith is making a replica of the goblet. Tomorrow night I'll switch it for hers. Then we'll be able to leave."

At the edge of the boat, I shifted my skirt from one hand to the other, peering around the mountain of material so I knew where to put my foot. It didn't help. My feet could have changed into live raccoons and I wouldn't have been able to tell. Why did I have to be here with Jason, a guy who couldn't notice I needed help?

It occurred to me that Donovan was here too, and he noticed everything. With a sort of curious hope, I held my hand out over the boat edge. He took hold of it and helped pull me inside.

He really was so sweet.

If Jason saw this odd maneuver, he didn't mention it. He tilted his head backward in aggravation. "Why wait until tomorrow? Why not just take the goblet tonight?"

"Shh." I glanced around to see if anyone heard him. The other boats were already pushing off, the princes busily chatting with my sisters. "If she doesn't know her goblet is missing, we'll have a better chance of getting away with the theft. Queen Orlaith is dangerous."

Jason put his hands on the side of the boat, leaning over it to glare at me. "You think *she's* dangerous? I'll tell you who's dangerous: my lawyers. And if I don't get a cell phone soon, this place will be raining subpoenas."

He said other things, but I couldn't understand them. By that point, Jason had put his back against the ship and was pushing the boat into the water. Once the boat edged into the lake, He jumped inside and picked up the oars.

One of the princes called, "You'll be last again tonight!"

Jason yelled back, "That's because I started later than the rest of you! Open your eyes!" He said a few more things— insults that made me think he spent way too much time thinking about rear ends and their functions.

"This isn't a race," I told him. "It doesn't matter if we're last."

Jason pulled hard on the oars, leaning into the motion. "It always matters if you're last. I work too hard to be a loser."

"So if you lose at something, it means you didn't work hard?"

"Not hard enough."

A cold prickle of irritation stiffened my spine. And this time, I wasn't keeping quiet. "Just like you, I practice music for hours every day. I play the piano or the guitar or work on my voice lessons. I still lost on your stupid TV show. Don't tell me only winners work hard."

Jason's eyes widened with surprise. Apparently it had never occurred to him that his thoughts about losers would offend someone who had bombed *America's Top Talent*.

He yanked at the oars. "I'm sure you'll get better someday." It was a pathetic attempt at consolation. "Or you'll find something else you're good at." He shrugged. "You're pretty. You could do something with that."

I held up my hands. "You don't need to offer suggestions. I stopped caring what you thought yesterday."

"You—" His jaw went a slack. "Have you forgotten who I am?"

"If I ever do, I'm sure you'll be the first to remind me."

Jason gripped the oars harder, dipping them into the black water with a hurried splash. "I could make you or break you in the music business."

Donovan's voice came close to my ear. "Do you want me to push him overboard?"

"Naw," I whispered back. "Then one of us would have to row."

I hadn't whispered quietly enough. Jason cocked his head. "One of you? Who are you talking to?"

"No one—ouch!" I slapped my hand to my nose. I'd lied without thinking about it. "I mean, I'm talking to my invisible friend."

My nose shrunk again.

"Great," Jason muttered. "That makes me feel better about being in a boat with you." He shook his head. "When I get my hands on my manager . . ."

I didn't say much else for the rest of the boat ride. Jason filled the silence with a nonstop rant about everything wrong with his castle. "Authentic is one thing, but they don't have a refrigerator. That's unsanitary. Even third world countries have refrigerators. I bet bushmen have refrigerators."

Behind me, Donovan chuckled. "I'll take that bet. After we get the goblet, have Chrissy send him to live with some bushman so he can find out."

I smiled despite myself. It was easier to listen to Jason when Donovan was nearby.

Chapter 22

By the time we reached the island, the other princes had already pulled their boats onto the land and helped their dates disembark. Arm in arm, they made their way to the dance pavilion, a picture of elegance.

Kailen was nowhere in sight. Perhaps he'd only come to the shore last night because he didn't know who Jason and I were.

I walked up the path toward the pavilion, listening to the strains of fairy music. Bell-like sounds were sprinkled through the song, chiming softly. Sometimes I heard the call of birds or the sound of waves. I swear a couple of times I heard the sound of starlight glimmering to earth. I wished I could make that sort of music.

Just like the night before, the tables were heaped with food and drink. Queen Orlaith sat in her throne in patient silence. Her dark hair was pinned up in an elaborate bun, and the crown of teeth glowed in the moonlight. Kailen wasn't with her. I wondered if I'd been wrong about his reason for not greeting us. Maybe he hadn't come tonight because he was still angry with his mother. I didn't mind the absence. The fewer fairies I had to deal with, the better.

The goblet was already out of the box. It stood on the table directly in front of the queen, waiting for her question. She fingered the stem absentmindedly, watching couples take the floor.

She hadn't been overly friendly last night, but tonight she looked even more severe. Her lips were set in a grim line and her dark eyes were cold. Was she upset about her fight with Kailen, or was I reading emotions into her expression?

She stood up, briefly welcomed the couples, and then sat again.

Instead of taking me to the dance floor, Jason walked to the chairs near the refreshment table. "I don't feel like dancing. I think I'll sit out for awhile."

He was sullen, pouting. I supposed he was used to girls who did their best to flirt and tease and plead him out of his bad moods. I wasn't going to be one of those girls.

"Fine," I said. "I'll walk around and see what's outside the pavilion." I headed in that direction, awash in the music and the scent of fairy trees. I had searched the branches on the way here for white fruit, for an overlooked wish. I hadn't seen any.

At the back of the pavilion, a garden spread out that put the castle's to shame. Lampposts lined alabaster paths, spilling gentle blue light everywhere. A mixture of flowers made the ground look like exotic bouquets were growing everywhere. Intricately-carved stone benches sat behind a pond with a fountain gurgling from the middle. I strolled around the pond, watching silver fish dart around the edges.

"Donovan?" I whispered. I didn't know if he'd followed me or was still inside the pavilion scoping things out.

No one answered. It was silly to feel disappointed. Donovan had kissed me, but that didn't mean he had to shadow me twenty-four seven.

Don't turn into one of those naive girls who meets a guy and thinks she's in love, I told myself firmly.

I'm not, I told myself back.

It's a good thing my nose didn't grow when I thought lies. I still felt a sort of shiny gladness at the thought of Donovan, a desire to hum a love song, an urge to write one.

Ridiculous. I couldn't be in love, not really, not this fast. I was more reasonable than that. But then, how did people know for sure? People talked about love at first sight. By that measure, love that took place the next day seemed downright reasonable.

My parents said they loved me before I was born. Clearly love came in many different shades. Was what I felt now one of them?

I kept walking around the pond. Diamond trees lined the path, glittering and wishless. Finally I sat on a bench and gazed at the golden light flecking the fountain water. It was such a beautiful setting, such a romantic one. Would it be so bad if Donovan and I had to stay here?

If I had to choose someplace to be stuck, this wasn't the worst place.

A noise to my side made me jump.

"It's just me," Donovan said. "Can you believe this orchard? There are more diamond trees here than in the forest."

I had noticed diamond trees rimming the pavilion. Apparently more grew in the surrounding gardens.

Donovan's hand appeared from underneath his cloak,

untangling three small twigs. A silver, a gold, and one with a diamond hanging from its end. "I didn't see any ripe wishes," he said. "Only diamonds." He let out a small laugh. "That's a phrase I never thought I'd hear coming from my mouth."

"Don't pick anything here," I said. "We don't want to set off any owls—and that's also a phrase I never thought I'd say."

He turned the twigs in his hand, making them glitter in the lamplight. "How do trees make silver, gold, or diamonds? I can't wrap my mind around it."

I ran my finger across a golden leaf, feeling its unbending ridges. "Is it any stranger than the way trees take water, dirt, and sunshine and make those into peaches, pears, and oranges?"

Kailen was right. Magic was all around us. We just didn't see it most of the time.

Donovan put the twigs back into his cloak. "Peaches are made through science, not magic."

"As my fairy godmother told me, 'True magic, like true love, is open to interpretation.'"

"I imagine the chlorophyll in the trees' cells help."

I couldn't comment on that. I'd forgotten what I'd learned in biology about plant cells. Donovan seemed to know more about most subjects than I did, and it bothered me I kept coming up short. I wanted to be one of those people who could talk about any number of subjects. But I wasn't.

Back on the dance floor, the princesses' dresses swirled across the room, colors swishing like blossoms in a breeze. Queen Orlaith sat watching them, waiting for their love to cure her trees. So far, the trees didn't look any different than they'd looked last night.

"What do you think true love is?" I asked.

"It's walking two miles to an all-night pharmacy to get medicine when your brother is sick."

I glanced at where Donovan sat, forgetting I couldn't see him. "You did that for Shane?"

"No, he did that for me."

And that was why we couldn't stay here. Donovan would never be happy here, not when his brother needed him.

"We'll get back," I said.

"Right." He didn't sound certain.

"What's the first thing you'll do when you get back home?" I asked so he'd think about happier things.

"I'll call you to make sure you got back home too. Which reminds me . . . you'd better give me your number."

I did and then asked for his. Once I'd memorized it, I said, "What's the second thing you're going to do when you get home?"

"Am I still on the phone with you?"

"Sure. And we've set up a date for next weekend. We'll do something we're both good at."

"What would that be? Stealing? Monster truck racing? Evading the police?"

I nudge him. "No, dancing. Seriously, have you really ever been monster truck racing?"

"There's always a first." His cloak brushed against my arm, then his fingers caressed the back of my hand. It looked odd—my hand had vanished. I didn't move away though. Just that small caress made me want to lean into him and disappear all the way.

"After I hang up with you," he said, returning to my question, "I'll buy planting supplies, graft my branches onto a normal tree, and see if they take."

"I can see wanting silver and gold trees, but the diamond branches? Do you actually want more wishes? They seem a lot more trouble than they're worth."

"Wishes, yes. But a tree with diamond fruit would be nice. I'll pick them before they're ripe."

"You never did tell me how you got your wishes."

He didn't answer. I didn't like that I couldn't see his face, couldn't read his eyes. "Come on," I prodded. "It couldn't be more embarrassing than my experience."

His clothes rustled a bit, indicating he was shifting on the bench. "Back in Hamilton, I was walking home from my job at the lumber store . . ."

He hauled lumber around. That, I supposed, explained his muscles.

"It had rained earlier," he went on, "and the night was getting cold. I saw a homeless lady sitting by the building, shivering, so I took off my coat and gave it to her. The next thing I knew the homeless lady vanished and Jade Blossom stood in her place. The rest, you know."

"You gave a fairy in disguise your coat?" I should have figured as much. That's how the soldier got his fairy godmother in the story. Still, it surprised me. Impressed me. Living in my suburban neighborhood, I didn't think about people shivering in the cold. Would I have given my coat to a homeless woman? Donovan had done it even though he had so little.

Donovan squeezed my hand. "I told you it wasn't going to make you feel better about your own story."

"But it makes me feel good about you."

Too good. Melting good. Maybe I wasn't a reasonable girl after all.

We talked about other things as we sat watching the fountain splash into the pond. School, family, what we planned to do in the future. Donovan wanted to go to college and major in business.

"You'll go to college?" I asked. "Even if you bring back gold, silver, and diamonds to live off of?"

"Money is gone once you spend it. An education stays with you. Besides, why shouldn't I know as much as everybody else?"

I opened my mouth to say I was skipping college to work on my music career, but the words didn't come out. I wasn't sure about that choice anymore. Suddenly I wanted to know as much as everybody else—or at least as much as Donovan. If I skipped college, would I end up like Jason, only talking about myself?

I could go to college and still work on my music. I could study Bach and Beethoven, learn how different composers approached music, and be well-rounded. And another plus—maybe people would forget about my viral video in four years when I tried a music career again.

"I haven't decided where to go to college yet," I said.

"You should visit the University of Cincinnati. In fact, tell me when you go to the campus, and I'll meet you there."

"I may need to go there multiple times to consider it."

Donovan chuckled. "With the gold and silver I'm bringing back, I bet my family could afford a better apartment. Maybe one closer to Kentucky."

"Maybe one in Greenfield," I said.

"We should both apply to—" Donovan broke off and he dropped my hand, shifted away from me. I looked at him—again forgetting I couldn't see him—then glanced around to see why he'd stopped talking.

Queen Orlaith was gliding toward us, as soundless as moonlight on the stone walkway. Her white dress flowed around her ankles like ocean foam sliding over the waves.

"There you are." She held her goblet casually in one hand, apparently unwilling to let it out of her sight. "Why aren't you dancing with your prince?"

I spoke slowly, careful not to lie. "Jason said he didn't want to dance."

She frowned. "Did you fight?"

No lying. "We said some unkind words to each other on the boat ride over."

"We must only have love here tonight." She smiled, impatience masquerading as understanding. "Your prince is bereft from the lack of your company. Go set things right. You'll both be happier."

I nodded and went back to the dance floor. Jason, far from being bereft of my company, stood at the refreshment table flirting with Penny and Kayla. I could tell he was flirting because my sisters were laughing and chatting to him while their dance partners stood nearby glaring.

No wonder Queen Orlaith came to get me. Jason wasn't helping the queen's true love goal. When I ambled up, Jason turned to me. "There you are. I wondered where you'd gone."

"You didn't need to wonder. I told you I was going to see what was outside the pavilion." I glanced at the clock, and did a double take. The hands stretched toward midnight. It hadn't felt like I'd talked to Donovan that long.

Four more hours and I could go home. If I stayed in the boat this time, I could get some sleep before the king came to check on us.

Jason popped a rose bud into his mouth and took my hand. "We might as well dance. Got to give the TV folks something to watch."

We went to the floor and waltzed, gliding across the floor

to the strains of the music. My practice with Donovan had paid off. Dancing didn't seem as hard tonight, and I was able to pick up on Jason's cues.

Sitting at her table again, Queen Orlaith looked on approvingly, all the while stroking the goblet's stem like it was a cat. Jason's gaze went to it as often as mine did.

"Let's get the goblet tonight," he muttered. "I don't want to spend one more day in that excuse of a castle."

"Be patient. We'll have a better chance of success if we switch the real goblet with a fake one."

Jason made a dissatisfied noise. "If you're not even going to try, I'll do it without you."

I leaned toward him, serious. "Don't. Queen Orlaith cursed it. Something bad will happen if you touch it."

"Yadda. Yadda. Nothing bad better happen to me. I've got lawyers, and I know how to use them."

Last night Jason had depended on the show workers to keep me from drowning, and now he was depending on his lawyers to protect him. I had to tell him the truth. He needed to understand the danger here was real. "Here's the thing." I cleared my throat uncomfortably. "This isn't a reality show. We're actually back in time stuck in a fairy tale. Queen Orlaith is a dangerous fairy queen."

"Save that look for your agent, sweetheart. I'm not buying it."

"Just don't touch the goblet, okay?"

He looked out across the pavilion, done with the conversation. "Whatevs."

Whatevs? Did it take too much effort to finish the word?

The clock struck the midnight. I ignored Jason's lead and waltz-dragged him closer to the queen's table so I could hear her question.

Queen Orlaith poured a vial of elixir into the goblet and swirled it once, twice, three times. "Magic cup within my hand, make me wise to understand. Two fortnights were spent in vain, and yet this night I ask again. To save my trees, once more I plead: How shall I find the love I need?"

A deep voice rose up, hanging in the air around her. "You mistake in trying to find . . ."

My mind raced ahead to finish the couplet, and I suddenly feared it would be, "Don't you know true love is blind?" Queen Orlaith would then blind us in an attempt to save her trees. Chrissy was so going to hear about this when—or if—I saw her again.

But the goblet finished, "What comes forth from human minds. Listen to fair wisdom's voice. Love's not a feeling. It's a choice."

"A choice?" the queen asked. "What choice? Who must choose?"

The goblet remained silent. Its answer was over.

The queen slammed the cup on the table and uttered the word "Brimstone!" as though it were a curse. Then she took a deep breath and put her fingers on the bridge of her nose in an attempt to regain her composure.

Jason dropped my hand, and without another word left me and sauntered to her table.

"Your Highness," he said, dripping his usual charisma. "You said you would teach me more steps of this dance." He held his hand out. "I'd love to have you as my partner."

Well, that left me standing awkwardly on the dance floor. Then again, if Jason danced with the queen, I could leave the pavilion and talk to Donovan again. I glanced around, wondering where he was.

The queen didn't move her hand away from her face. She

shut her eyes, fighting for inward patience. "No. Dance with your princess."

"Another time then."

I realized what Jason was doing a second before he did it. I had no way to stop him, no way to keep the queen's wrath from crashing down around him.

As Jason turned, he grabbed hold of the goblet. He didn't make it more than a step from the table before he froze, hand clenching tighter, spasming. His jaw went slack, and he shuddered as though electrocuted. The goblet tumbled from his hand, slow and spinning until it hit the ground with a clank.

The queen's head snapped up and her expression hardened. "Thief," she spat out. One word, spoken with the condemnation of a judge's gavel. She snapped her fingers and Jason disappeared.

I gasped in alarm, stepping toward the queen. "He didn't know it was magic. Please, you've got to bring him back. He didn't think any of this was real!"

Queen Orlaith eyed me placidly. "I didn't kill him. You'll find him on the ground."

I looked down. There, sitting on the white stone floor was a large green bullfrog. It held one webbed hand out in front of its face and shrieked—a human sound. A Jason sound.

I covered my mouth. "Oh, no."

Jason held up both webbed hands. To say his eyes bulged was perhaps unfair, but accurate. His voice, only smaller, came from the frog's mouth. "What happened to me?"

With an air of exasperation, the queen stood and strode around the table. She snapped her fingers again and the goblet flew from the floor into her hand. She set it on the table, then turned to Jason. "Why did you take my goblet?"

He peered up at her and jolted. "You're huge!"

She bent down to be closer to his level, and spoke the words again, this time with less patience. "Why did you take my goblet??"

I bit my lip. I couldn't answer for him, couldn't lie. I stared at Jason and hoped he had the sense not to tell her the truth.

Jason shrunk back. "Your glass was empty. I was getting you a refill."

The queen considered this, her expression an unreadable mask. Finally, she smiled. The movement was cold and smug. "I'll assume you're telling the truth because you couldn't be foolish enough to steal something from me. You certainly must value your life more than that."

She stepped back to her seat and sat down, giving me the barest of flicks with her fingers. "Be careful not to step on your boyfriend, my dear. That would make an ugly mess."

"Aren't you going to change him back?" My voice was high pitched with shock. "You can't just leave him a frog!"

Queen Orlaith raised an eyebrow, challenging me. "If you want to change him back, you'll have to break the spell with true love's kiss."

I gulped. If true love was needed, a kiss from me wouldn't be much help. I couldn't admit this. It would lead to questions. I bent down and cupped my hands so Jason could jump in them. "Come here. We're leaving."

Jason stopped staring at his hands long enough to gawk up at me. "What's going on? Why is everything so gigantic?"

"Climb into my hands, and I'll explain while I carry you to the boat."

He gave a small hop, then stopped, realizing what he'd just done. He lifted one foot and stared at it. "I'm a *frog!*" he sputtered. "A frog!" Then he toppled over in a dead faint.

Chapter 23

None of my sisters volunteered to leave the dance early and come home with me. You would think having your supposed boyfriend changed into an amphibian would be enough to break up a party. But no. All I got from the other princesses were questions about why I didn't kiss Jason there so the two of us could stay and dance. As if I wanted to stay.

When your hostess starts changing people's species around, it's time to row your boat back home. Which is what I did. Well, Donovan helped. He sat behind me, hands on the oars and did most of the work. "You don't want blisters on your hands," he said. "You'll have no way to explain them to the king."

Jason revived once we'd reached the other shore. Technically, this was because I dunked him in the lake. I wasn't being mean. I just didn't know how long frogs could be out of water and was afraid he might dry out.

Jason didn't appreciate this thoughtful gesture. He came

out of the water swearing and flailing his slimy little hands around. I held onto him, and tried not to laugh. I didn't mean to be insensitive about his suffering, but there's something absurd about a cursing frog.

Jason's big, googly eyes blinked angrily at me. "You think this is funny? Magic is *real*. I'm in a place with *fairies*. One just turned me into a *frog*. And you're *laughing*?"

"Sorry."

"That stuff you told me about your fairy godmother sending us here—that was the truth?"

"Yeah. Again, sorry."

He kept fidgeting in my hands like he wanted to jump somewhere. "Sorry? That's all you have to say?"

"I'm going to do everything I can to help you. Really."

Jason tucked his legs underneath himself and squatted down in my palms. "How?"

"Well, you're a frog prince, and I'm a princess. Sort of. So my kiss is supposed to break the spell."

Jason perked up. "That's right—the whole princess and the frog thing. Why didn't you already kiss me?"

Yes, why? I shifted Jason in my hands. His skin was clammy on his stomach and bumpy everywhere else. "Well, frogs aren't that attractive. Plus, I'm seeing someone else."

"You're seeing someone else?" Jason repeated incredulously.

"Yeah. The invisible guy."

Jason's eyes momentarily dipped down into his head. Freaky how frogs can do that. "You're seeing an invisible guy," Jason said flatly. "That must be tricky." His throat sack puffed in and out making him look like he was panting. "Stop making excuses and kiss me already."

Donovan was standing beside me, but he didn't offer a commentary on the situation. I lifted Jason closer to my lips. His bulging eyes stared back, waiting. Frogs don't have a lot of kissable real estate. I repressed a shudder and quickly kissed the top of his head. Then I set him on the ground so he could change back into a person.

Nothing happened. He didn't transform. Jason held up a hand and moved his wormy fingers back and forth. "It didn't work. Maybe you have to kiss me on the lips."

"Um . . ." Frogs probably have the least attractive lips in the animal kingdom. Wide and slimy. When you look at them it's hard not to think about the nature films where frogs zap flies and other disgusting things with their tongues.

Jason hopped toward me, his back legs stretching out like webby flags. "Go on, kiss my mouth."

Off to my side, I heard Donovan laughing. Yeah, it was easy for him to think this was amusing. He wasn't the one who had to put his lips on a frog.

"Don't say it," I told Donovan.

Jason cocked his head in question.

Donovan knew I was talking to him, though. "Don't say what?" he asked.

"Whatever frog joke you're thinking about right now."

"I wasn't thinking of a frog joke. I was thinking of a Jason Prescott joke."

Jason's googly eyes scanned the area around us and he took a step backward. "Who said that? Who's talking?"

I pointed in Donovan's direction. "The invisible guy."

Jason's mouth hung open. "Your imaginary friend talks?"

"Yeah. He's invisible, not mute."

Near my ear, Donovan said, "Don't tell him anything about me."

"Why?" I whispered back. "Don't you trust him?"

Donovan took my hand and pulled me a few feet away from Jason. "It's not that I don't trust him. I just don't think he's that bright."

"Hey," Jason said, throat sack puffing. "I heard that."

Who knew frogs had such good hearing?

Donovan ignored him. "He'll do something stupid to give us away, and we'll all be changed into frogs."

Jason's eyes bobbed up and down, blinking. "I resent that."

"I don't mind," Donovan said. "Go ahead and resent it."

I wasn't sure whether Donovan had a valid point. Jason wanted to go home as badly as either of us, so I doubted he would purposely do anything to jeopardize our plan; but that didn't mean he wouldn't accidently do something. I never should have told him about Donovan or even said his name.

Jason hopped over to me and stared upward. "I'm still waiting for you to kiss me the right way."

There was no way around it. I had to kiss him again. "Oh, all right," I muttered, picking up Jason. He opened his mouth—I suppose in an attempt to pucker. The inside of a frog's mouth is even less attractive than the outside.

"Stop that," I said. "Lips closed."

Jason rolled his bulgy eyes and clamped his mouth together. It was a good thing I already had my first kiss or this incident might have put me off kissing forever.

I lifted Jason to my mouth, shut my eyes, and gave him a peck on his slimy lips. Then I set him back on the ground, shivered with disgust, and wiped off my mouth.

Jason's throat sack flared in and out in indignation. "For your information, it wasn't that great for me either."

"Sorry," I said. "This isn't as easy as the fairy tales make it sound."

Nothing happened. No transformation. Jason slumped on the ground, a pathetic green lump, and eyed me resentfully. "Maybe it didn't work because you're not a real princess."

I couldn't bring myself to tell him Queen Orlaith had said true love's kiss would restore him. I didn't love him, and that sort of attachment wasn't likely to develop any time soon.

Could Chrissy help him? Would she? The words of the contract echoed in my mind. *The results of your wishes are real and lasting.*

There had to be more than one way to break a magic spell. I kneeled to be closer to Jason's eye level. "If you promise not to tell anyone about Donovan being here with me, I'll take you to my castle. We might be able to find someone there who'll know what to do."

Jason was breathing so fast he rocked back and forth. Could frogs hyperventilate? He gulped unhappily. "The other princesses live with you, right? So one of them should be able to break the spell."

"You have to promise not to say anything to them about Donovan," I repeated. "No one can know he's been here."

"I promise. I promise." Instead of waiting for my reply, Jason hopped in the direction of the lanterns, making arcs through the air.

"It's a long way," I called. "I'll carry you." I ran to catch up, then picked him up and slipped him into my pocket.

"Hey!" He thrashed around inside my cloak until I opened the edge of the pocket. "Why did you stick me in here?"

"Where did you expect me to put you? I'm not a pony."

He frowned, an expression that did nothing to improve his appearance. "You could carry me on your shoulder."

"I'm not a pirate either."

"Hey, Frog Boy," Donovan said, coming up beside me. "Pipe down and sit still. We're not out of the woods yet—pun intended—and wild animals live here. You wouldn't want one to see you and think you look appetizing."

Jason shrunk into my pocket so that only his eyes stuck out. "Wild animals?"

"Don't worry," I said. "You don't look at all appetizing."

Jason glowered at me and sunk back into my pocket. Muffled frog complaints came from that direction for the fifteen minutes it took us to walk through the forest. I ignored him and spoke to Donovan. Mostly we swapped stories about our high schools. It was easy to talk to him because he had a way of making me feel like my opinion mattered.

We went across the meadow, up the stairs, and finally tiptoed back into the princesses' chambers. Madam Saxton was still asleep on the couch, snoring softly. I filled one of the wash basins with water, placed it on an end table, and set Jason inside. Donovan took off his cloak and instantly became visible again.

Now that Jason could see him, he watched dourly as Donovan and I sat down, close together on a couch.

"You're supposed to be my princess," Jason called.

"Sorry," I said. "It turns out you're not my type."

Donovan put his arm around me. "Her type is awesome guys."

I nudged Donovan because he was being mean.

"You know," Jason called over, puffing up to make himself bigger, "I was really popular in high school. In fact, I still am. I'm loved in high schools across the world."

"They'll love you when we go back too," Donovan said. "Who could resist a singing frog?"

I nudged Donovan again.

He laughed and held a hand in Jason's direction. "What? The frog is moving in on my girl. He has it coming."

I liked the way Donovan referred to me as his girl and smiled despite myself. "Be nice. It must be traumatic being turned into a frog."

"I'll be nice for you." Donovan kissed my forehead.

I felt all glowy inside. Jason let out an angry croak, then sunk into the water so only his eyes peered out at us.

Donovan and I both laid our heads back against the cushions and talked some more. After a few minutes, he shut his eyes. He was tired and I knew I should leave him and go catch some sleep while I waited for my sisters to come home and untie me from my dress. Instead, I stayed on the couch. I liked sitting in the crook of Donovan's arm. It made me feel like everything would work out, like it was an adventure and not a horrible, magical disaster.

I watched him sleeping, traced the lines of his jawline and cheekbone with my gaze. His dark lashes looked like an artist's black pen strokes. I lingered on the slope of his parted lips and let the memory of his kisses warm me. If Donovan had been the one turned into a frog, would my kiss have changed him back?

What I felt seemed so genuine, made me feel so light and happy, how could it not be real? And yet, how could my feelings be true love when we'd only known each other such a short time?

The goblet said love was a choice, but it didn't seem like I'd chosen this. My attachment to Donovan had crept up on me, saturated me without permission. I felt weak, powerful, and a dozen other sensations all at the same time. Could real love do more than that to a person's emotions?

I told myself I would only shut my eyes for a second to rest them, then I'd go lay down in the back.

Donovan and I woke up when my sisters' footsteps sounded on the stairs. We pulled away from each other, both disoriented. He turned on his side and pretended to be asleep.

I got to my feet, wobbling, just as Rosamund emerged through the trap door. The other princesses followed her, giggling and talking about the evening. If they had paid attention, they might have wondered why I was standing so close to Donovan when they came in, but they were busy relaying the compliments the princes had given them.

"Frederick said my eyes shined like two stars."

"Hubert said the glow of my skin put the moon to shame."

I walked over to join them.

Jason's head rose out of the bowl of water, and then he hopped up on the rim of the basin. "Excuse me, ladies," he called. "Could I ask a favor? I need one of you to kiss me."

My sisters' discussions immediately stopped, and they turned to stare at me. "Why haven't you kissed him yet?" Rosamund asked.

"I did. Twice. It didn't turn him back into a human."

Several of my sisters gasped in surprise. Others gaped at me. Moving in one body, they drew closer to me, making a huddle of silky ball gowns around me. Beatrix put her hand on her chest in horror. "That means his love for you isn't *true* love."

Wait, was that what it meant? I'd been blaming myself for not loving him enough. Was it actually his fault for not loving me enough? "He thinks maybe one of you could break the spell."

My sisters exchanged glances again. A few of them looked

smug at the possibility. "He thinks he loves one of us more than he loves you?"

I shrugged. I couldn't really explain that Jason didn't realize it had anything to do with love. In my time period we read stories about princesses kissing frogs to turn them human again.

Jason jumped down from the basin and hopped along the edge of the dressing table. "Ladies, please, it will just take a moment of your time."

Catherine eyed him archly. "And who, sir, do you implore for a kiss?"

Jason hopped closer to her. "You'll do."

Catherine gave a laugh and sashayed over. "Truly, I never suspected. I fear my heart is spoken for, but I will bestow a kiss on you, nonetheless." She bent down, kissed Jason on his snout, and stepped back. I held my breath and hoped it would work.

Nothing happened.

My exhale was drawn out in disappointment.

Jason lifted one hand to check his status and swore. He waved his hand in Elizabeth's direction. "How about you? This time on the lips. Maybe it has to be on the lips."

She took a step back, fiddling nervously with her necklace. "Perhaps I shouldn't. Percival might not approve."

"Percy? He's my bro. He won't mind. Trust me."

She took mincing steps toward him. "Well, if you insist." She pursed her lips, hesitant, then bent and dropped a quick kiss on Jason's lips.

He slowly opened his eyes.

"Sorry," I said. "You're still a frog."

He put one hand to what would have been a forehead if frogs had foreheads. "Why isn't this working?" He surveyed my sisters. "You *are* real princesses aren't you?"

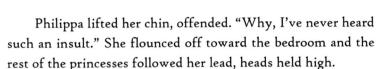

Philippa lifted her chin, offended. "Why, I've never heard such an insult." She flounced off toward the bedroom and the rest of the princesses followed her lead, heads held high.

"Can you imagine the impertinence?" Mathilda said, gathering her skirts. "Questioning our paternity? 'Tis a good thing Father isn't here to witness this vulgarity."

"Darn straight," Darby said. "There'd be some frog shish kabob going down."

"If Father was here now," I muttered, heading to the bedroom too, "the least of our problems would be explaining a talking frog's questions about our lineage. Can someone untie me? This corset is like a mini prison."

For the next few minutes we sat at our dressing tables unpinning our hair. Jason hopped from one table to the next, apologizing. "I wasn't insulting you. I'm just trying to figure out why I'm still a frog. You, the one in the pink dress. It's Clementia, right?" He leapt onto her table, scattering stray pins. "How about a kiss? I bet you could break the spell. You look like you've had a lot of practice kissing."

Clementia let out a humph and shook her brush at him. "If you weren't a poor woodland creature, I would strike you forthwith."

Jason hopped away from Clementia and sprang onto Isolde's table. He sat up as straight as he could and cleared his throat. It sounded like a cross between a cough and a croak. "I know I don't look so great now, but where I'm from, the ladies love me. I'm a big hit there."

"With your manners," Isolde replied coldly, "I'm sure you've been given many big hits—all by angry fathers."

Once our hair done in simple braids, my sisters and I moved into our closets to take off our gowns. We left the door ajar to let more light in. I hadn't expected Jason to follow us inside, but almost immediately, he appeared in front of the door. "One of you must want to kiss me—"

Penny shrieked and held her skirt against her body. "Peeping Tom!"

Philippa had just taken off her slippers. She threw one in Jason's direction. "Out, cad!"

"But I only—" Jason started. The second slipper hit the floor and would have bounced into him if he hadn't hopped away.

"Silence!" Rosamund hissed. "The guards will hear you!"

Before she finished the sentence, a knock sounded on the outer room's door, and a guard called, "Is all well inside?"

The princesses had undressed quickly before, but now the sleeves, bodices, and skirts came off in a blur of color and frantic swishes of silk. Rosamund finished pulling on her nightgown and hurried toward the door. "Everything is as it should be," she called to the guard. "I had a nightmare and yelled in my sleep. That's all. We are well and accounted for."

"Unlock the door from your side," the guard called. "I'll check to make sure nothing is amiss." We heard the sound of the outside bolt sliding across the door.

"No need." Rosamund said. "My sisters still sleep, and I don't wish to wake them. Go back to your post. In truth, nothing is amiss."

The princesses were making so much noise hanging up their dresses and putting away their slips, corsets, and underskirts, I didn't expect the guard to buy Rosamund's explanation.

"Methought I heard a man's voice." the guard said.

"That was Prince Donovan," Rosamund assured. "He

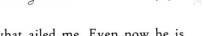

heard me call out and asked what ailed me. Even now he is searching the rooms to make sure nothing snuck inside."

"Ah," the guard said. He now had an explanation for the rustling coming from the room. "Very well then."

He slid the bolt back across his side of the door. We let out breaths of relief—and not just because our corsets were finally off. As Penny pulled on her nightgown, she sent me a dark look. "You shouldn't have brought Jason here. If he's discovered . . ."

"He's a frog," I said. "How hard can it be to hide him?"

I finished changing, then picked Jason up and carried him to my dressing table. "Once it's morning, I'll ask around the castle to see if anyone knows how to break a fairy's curse. We might find a way. Until then, you need to stay hidden from the king, okay?"

Jason squatted in an angry frog stance. "I'm not happy about this."

"If you remember, I warned you not to touch the goblet."

"Being turned into a frog is only part of it." His throat sack pulsed in and out. "What do you see in the invisible guy?"

"Is that a trick question?" I peered into my pitcher to make sure it had water. It did. I gently lowered Jason inside.

He floated on the water, legs and arms outstretched. "I heard the two of you talking about your pasts. Why would you want a guy with a criminal record when you could have a guy with a multimillion dollar record deal?"

I titled my head, not sure I understood. "Are you saying you have feelings for me?"

He gazed at me with his big, googly eyes. "At first I didn't think I did, but when you sat on the couch with Donovan, I hated it. I feel like, well, maybe I'm in love with you after all."

Not this. Not only did I have a frog problem, I had a

forlorn frog problem. Could I have done anything else to mess up Jason's life? I bent closer to the pitcher. "The love isn't real, you know. You only feel this way because my fairy godmother cast a spell on you."

He floated there in the water, unmoving and miserable. I tried again. "Your real girlfriends are way more impressive than me—models, rock stars, actresses. I'm no one important . . . just a girl from Kentucky."

"I know," he said. "And that makes it even worse. How can I ever introduce you to my friends? I can't. I'll have to keep you a secret."

I stopped feeling sorry for him then. "Be sure to stay out of sight," I reminded him, then went to my bed, settling in for what little sleep was left. As soon as I shut my eyes, I heard a small voice with an Irish accent near my ear. "So, judging by the fact you're lying about, I take it you didn't get the goblet tonight?"

I opened my eyes. Clover stood on my pillow. He wore his rumpled Team Sadie T-shirt over his other clothes. It had a small footprint on it, as though he'd pulled it off his floor and put it on.

"No," I whispered. "I didn't get the goblet."

"How's Donovan getting on?" Clover asked. "I have, er, a friend who has a bit of money on him."

Sure he did. I pulled myself up on one elbow. "Clover, are you betting against me? Seriously?"

He let out a grumble and pulled a piece of paper from his pocket. "Well, it isn't as though I'm paid much for being a fairy godmother assistant. And what's the use of having insider information if you don't put it to use?"

I pointed to his shirt. "You're supposed to be rooting for me."

"I am. I am. I'm betting on the lad is all."

Clover unfolded the paper and took a pen from his pocket. "These are the things Miss I'm-too-busy-gabbing-with-friends-to-check-on-my-charge wants me to ask you: Did Donovan abscond with the goblet?"

"No," I whispered.

Clover wrote something on the paper. "Did you hear the goblet's answer to the queen?"

I looked upward, remembering. "It said, 'You mistake in trying to find what comes forth from human minds. Listen to fair wisdom's voice. Love's not a feeling. It's a choice.'"

Clover put his pen to the paper again. ". . . a load of gibberish about love . . ." He wrote for another moment. "Last question. Did Jason kiss you?"

"About Jason . . ." I straightened, suddenly hopeful. Clover might know how to break the curse. "Queen Orlaith caught him with the goblet, and she turned him into a frog. She said true love's kiss would break the spell, but I kissed him twice, and he's still a frog."

Clover wrote on the paper again. "Yes, they kissed."

"How do I de-frogify him?"

"I've no idea. Well, I'm done here. I'll be seeing you tomorrow."

"Wait!" I leaned toward him, hand out, pleading. "Is that all you're going to say?"

"Ah—I nearly forgot." Clover made a check on the paper before folding it. "I believe in you, Sadie." He tucked the paper into his pocket. "Me and thirty percent of the betting fairy population." With that, the leprechaun vanished.

I lay back down on my pillow with a moan. Chrissy was right. Her assistant was completely worthless.

Chapter 24

I'm not sure how long I slept. Too soon, the door to our bedroom swung open and the guard announced, "His Royal Highness, the King!"

A moment later, the king and queen swept into the room. Even dressed in heavy brocades, the queen had a light, fluttering walk. She went to one bed and then another, pulling back blankets. "A new day is upon us," she cooed. "Meet it with grace and fortitude, my daughters."

The king strode down the room between our beds, carrying a walking stick that he rapped against the bed poles. "Up with you! Line up in your bedroom today. Let's see what mischief you've been at!" I rolled over and groaned. Why were these people up at the crack of dawn? Really, what was so important that they had to do it at first light?

The king rapped his stick against my bed especially hard, and I pulled myself from my blankets, yawning. My sisters were already retrieving their slippers. They made a show of gasping as they turned their slippers over this way and that, as surprised as if the footwear had turned into cucumbers. I grabbed mine and stumbled to my place at the end of the row. Donovan had come in and stood near the door, stretching. Madam Saxton smoothed her hair, tucking stray pieces into her cap. Her eyes darted around the room, guiltily.

The king stopped in front of our line. It's hard to pull off a stern and foreboding look when you're wearing what essentially are poofy bloomers, but King Rothschild managed it. Even his wrinkles looked disapproving. "Hold forth your slippers for examination."

The king, then the queen, walked down our line inspecting each pair.

"Worn, worn, worn, worn," the king muttered unhappily. "Worn, worn, worn, worn." His voice grew louder the farther he went. "Worn, worn, worn . . ." He stopped in front of me took my slippers from my hand and turned them over in his. "Only a trifle worn." I hadn't danced, and I'd come back early. My slippers were just a bit scuffed and dirty on the bottom.

The king eyed me warily. "Yesterday when your sisters' slippers were worn, yours were damp and near destroyed. Today, your slippers once again differ from the others. Pray tell, how is this so?"

I shrugged and shook my head as though I had no words to describe this phenomenon.

The king's eyes narrowed. "Were you with your sisters all night?"

I couldn't answer that question. I bit my lip and blinked innocently. "You're angry because my slippers aren't worn?" Questions weren't lies. "I thought you didn't want our slippers to be worn. Shouldn't you be glad?"

The king gripped my slippers hard, waving them at me. "I thought nothing could bother me more than knowing my daughters are nightly up to some secret tomfoolery. But lo, I was mistaken. It irks me more to know that while your sisters are doing whatever it is they do, you're up to mischief of your own." He dropped my slippers on the floor and stalked over to Donovan.

"Well, Young Prince, what say ye? Do you know what my daughters did last night to wear . . ." He glanced back at me. "What *most* of my daughters did to wear out their slippers?"

Madam Saxton apparently wanted to be as far away from the king and the discussion of last night as she could be. She went to Rosamund's dressing table and straightened it.

Donovan rubbed his chin, thinking. "Good King, I would not tell you my theory until I am sure it is the right one. I require one more night to solve the mystery."

The king let out a grunt. "'Tis fortunate you require only one more night, as that is all you have. Tomorrow morning when I come, I shall bring the executioner with me."

The queen strode over to Donovan, wearing her ever-present smile. "And I shall bring the priest, for I'm sure you'll have the answer we seek." She put her hand to her chest. "It will be so lovely to see our dear Sadie wed. We'll be thrilled to have someone we can call a son at last."

The king grunted again, obviously less thrilled than the queen.

Donovan put on one of his usual confident smiles. He looked particularly handsome like that, standing tall and straight, a secret humor in his eyes.

"I ask one more favor of you," he said. "Do you have a library, a wizard—someone that knows how to break fairy curses?"

The queen's hand flew to her throat in alarm. "Have our daughters fallen prey to a fairy's wrath?"

"It's a possibility," Donovan said solemnly.

I held my breath, hoping the king and queen knew a way to help Jason.

The king walked down the row of princesses, still regarding us. "Other suitors have considered the possibility of a fairy curse. We've placed fairy wards in the room. Iron. Bread. T'was to no effect."

Donovan gave a small agreeing bow. "That is why I need to study the matter further."

Madam Saxton poured water from Rosamund's pitcher into her basin, then moved to Beatrix's table and did the same. Why hadn't I considered the housekeeper might help us wash up in the morning? I should have hidden Jason somewhere else, somewhere safer. If the king didn't finish grilling us soon, Madam Saxton would reach my pitcher and see a frog inside it. I went through the possible outcomes in my mind.

Madam Saxton would see the frog and kill it. This would be bad.

Madam Saxton would see the frog and question us as to why it was there. My sisters would leave the explanation up to me and my nose would end up growing a foot long. This would also be bad.

Madam Saxton would see the frog and before she could kill him, Jason would plead for mercy or perhaps a kiss. Again, bad.

I cleared my throat. "Madam Saxton, you don't need to help us with our washing. We're happy to do it ourselves."

The king turned to me, disapproval weighing his brows downward. He'd been talking to Donovan about fairies, and I'd interrupted. "You speak out of turn in the presence of your father and king? That is twice the disrespect."

Madam Saxton halted her motions, waiting to see if the king had directions regarding my request.

I fidgeted with the lace on my sleeve. "I meant no disrespect. I was only trying to be helpful." Specifically, I was trying to help Jason. And myself. "Anyone who has kept watch in our room all night should be allowed to go and rest in her room."

The queen nodded in agreement. "I'm sure Madam Saxton must be over-weary."

Out of the corner of my eye, I saw Jason leap up and cling to the rim of my pitcher. He'd heard my remark about washing up and peeked over to see what was happening.

If the housekeeper or my parents looked in my table's direction, they would see Jason. I sent him a psychic message to drop back down and hide.

Apparently Jason had no psychic abilities. Instead of returning to the pitcher, he jumped out altogether. He landed on the dressing table with a splatting sound.

The king turned back to Donovan to speak to him, but the housekeeper heard the noise. She gawked at the table and gasped. "Gracious! What is *that* doing in here?"

All heads turned to see what had startled her. The king's head. The queen's head.

"Heavens," the queen said. "A huge toad."

"Impossible," the king declared, then he saw it too. It was hard not to see Jason. He leaped from the table onto the floor.

A couple of the princesses screamed, which was totally unnecessary since they knew he was in the room. The housekeeper picked up the broom from the hearth, held it above her head, and went after Jason.

"Don't!" I yelled, running toward her. "Don't hurt him!"

You'd think she'd have listened since I was a royalty, but no, she swacked the broom down right next to Jason.

He let out a croak and leaped out of the way.

"Stop!" I shouted. The word was lost in the noise of princesses shrieking.

To their credit, many of them were yelling the same thing I was—for Madam Saxton to stop. Others were just screaming, which really didn't help.

Jason was also screaming, but his small voice didn't rise above the din. Madam Saxton brought the broom down again, this time near a dressing table. A jar of pins rattled in protest.

Jason leaped around the room with such vigor it almost looked like he was flying. One moment he was on the floor, the next on a table, then on the back of a chair. I chased after him, trying to grab him.

"I've got him!" Donovan shouted. He took off his cap, held it like it was a butterfly net, and rushed toward Jason's flying form. Mid-leap, Donovan swooped the hat over the frog. He brought his hands together to close the cap, then tucked one hand behind him and held out the cap to us with a flourish.

I gulped, wondering what Donovan was going to do with Jason. Should I tell the king and queen of Jason's enchanted prince status? Perhaps they would have pity on him. Perhaps they would help. Maybe Jason could think of a story about his identity and why he was here that wouldn't reveal where the princesses went each night or who they danced with.

But if he couldn't . . . if he didn't even try . . . if the king found out about the secret now, he'd find a way to close the door to the fairy realm, and Donovan and I wouldn't be able to go back for the goblet tonight.

Worse still, would the king consider Jason the prince who'd solved the mystery? If that happened, then he'd be required to marry one of the princesses, and I would be his choice.

The only thing I could think of that would be worse than

being stuck here with Jason as a husband was being stuck here with Jason as a frog husband.

Donovan took a step closer to the housekeeper. "Would you be so good as to put this fellow outside?"

The housekeeper hurried over and took the cap from Donovan, making sure to keep the cap tight so the frog didn't escape.

I bit my lip. How would we find Jason again? Madam Saxton could put him anywhere on the castle grounds. And what if she didn't put him outside? What if this was one of those centuries where frog legs were a delicacy?

The king held out his hand for the cap. "Let me see the creature. It couldn't have come this far inside on its own volition, and I hardly believe one of my daughters would have taken the thing for a pet."

He regarded us, checking for contradiction.

At his side, the queen tut-tutted the idea. "The girls are too well-bred to drag a revolting toad inside."

"I . . . I . . ." I tried to find a way to phrase my confession without lying. I couldn't say I'd found the frog outside and wanted him as a pet. What could I say?

The king opened the cap and stared inside, perplexed. He turned the cap inside out. It was empty. The whole room let out a collective gasp of wonder.

My gaze went to Donovan. He winked at me, and I realized I'd just seen him do another magic trick.

"How can this be?" the king asked, shaking the cap as though it would explain itself if he throttled it enough.

The queen lifted her skirt and scanned the floor. "The toad vanished?"

The princesses lifted their skirts as well, each searching for a sign of green. Kayla whimpered with worry.

"Magic," the queen breathed out. "This is more proof of it." She let out a sob and hugged Kayla sympathetically. "My poor, poor girls. We must do something! We are beset with strange magic."

Madam Saxton put her hand to her mouth, as distraught as the queen. "The fairies have cursed our poor princesses. What if none of them can marry? The kingdom will be bereft of heirs."

At the phrase, "What if none of them can marry," several of the princesses sniffled, two broke into tears, and Clementia cried out, "Don't say we shan't marry, Papa. That would be too cruel."

The king tossed Donovan's cap onto the floor. "Stop your wailing at once. Why would fairies curse my daughters? What have I ever done to provoke the fairy realm?"

Rosamund stepped toward him, shoulders square. "Perhaps we're cursed because of the war—because you refuse to recognize the royal families of the rebelling provinces."

She was, I knew, trying to turn the situation into something that would benefit her prince—all of the princes. The other girls agreed with her at once, chiming in that King Rothschild should grant the defeated royal families a few concessions.

The king waved a hand to stop them. "Bah! What care the fairies of the rights of mortals?"

He had a point there. None of the fairies I'd met cared about my rights.

"And what do they mean by this magic—disappearing toads and worn slippers? If any of the fae realm wish something, let them come and speak of it."

"Well said, Sire." Donovan gave him a slight bow. "Still, I think it would be wise if I could study the matter. Do you know of any wizards or books that deal in magic spells?"

The king gripped his walking stick, poking it at Donovan's cap one last time. "We've no wizards here. Such men only make mischief. But if you'd like, you may search the castle's book collection. We've writings aplenty on every subject." He held up a finger, emphasizing his words. "You've only one day left. Read quickly."

At that the king strode out of the room, an air of authority trailing him as though it had been an actual robe.

The queen didn't follow. In a low voice she told us, "I'll speak to your father about the rights of the provinces." In a burst of motherly care, she squeezed Clementia's hand, then stroked Isolde's cheek with trembling fingers. "My poor cursed darlings. I would switch places with you if I could. Then you could be happy, and I would endure worn slippers for the rest of my days." She gave a little sob, kissed Darby and Catherine's foreheads, then hurried to the door, her shoulders shuddering with grief.

Madam Saxton left the room as well, our wash basins forgotten. "Toads in the castle," she muttered. "What will be next? Snakes I suppose. And badgers after that."

As soon as the door clicked shut, Donovan sidled up next to me. "I have the most wicked desire right now."

"No," I said, "You can't bring snakes and badgers into the castle."

He grinned. "But it would be fun."

The princesses gathered around us, taking mincing steps in case Jason suddenly appeared on the floor. "What has become of . . ." Clementia cast a guarded look at Donovan. ". . . of the frog?"

A muffled voice came from somewhere inside the folds of Donovan's jerkin. "Is it safe to come out now?"

Donovan reached around to the back of his jerkin and

produced a bullfrog. Jason's throat sack pumped in and out so fast his body rocked with the motion. His eyes seemed to swivel independent of each other. "Is the whacko with the broom gone?"

"A talking frog," Donovan said, as though he hadn't known this fact beforehand but wasn't surprised such things existed. "No doubt the poor fellow is the victim of a magic spell, and you've taken him in to help him."

Several of the princesses nodded. "His name is Prince Jason," Rosamund admitted. "But don't ask us to say more than that."

Beatrix and Kayla crowded around Donovan's hand. "We're so glad you're safe," Kayla said.

Beatrix took Jason from Donovan's hand and stroked her finger along his back like he was a lost puppy. "How did you manage to hide him?" she asked Donovan. "We saw you capture him in your hat."

"I did it like this." Donovan reached into the pouch on his belt and held up a coin. With one swish of his hands, the coin disappeared. He held up his empty hand, then reached out and pulled the coin from Beatrix's ear.

She laughed and took the coin, turning it over in her hand to examine it. "What sort of magic is this, sir?"

"That was so cool," Penny said, coming closer. "Do it again."

"Try it on me," Catherine chimed.

Really, they would have made him stand there making coins appear and disappear all day, if I hadn't dragged Donovan away.

"Go check on the goblet," I told him. "I'll take Jason and anyone who will help me to the library. We'll see if we can find anything about turning frogs back into humans."

Chapter 25

As it turned out, all the princesses wanted to help. I would've liked to think this was because they were nice people, but they may have worried that one day one of their princes would do something to tick off Queen Orlaith and they would be in the same boat.

Everybody wants a handsome prince. Nobody wants a frog.

We took our breakfast up in the king's library. It was a large room with gleaming wooden shelves that reached the ceiling. I hadn't expected to see so many books, hadn't thought King Rothschild was the literary type. Rows of books spread along the walls, worn leather covers next to colorfully painted volumes. A sliding ladder stood at the end of the shelves, tempting us to search on the dusty top shelves.

We ignored the history, etiquette, and law tomes and pulled out anything to do with medicine or magic. I took an armful, stacked them by a couch, and settled in to read. The first volume was entitled *Restoratives for Common Ailments*. I doubted the author counted froghood as a common ailment, but you never knew. Princes were frequently turned into animals in fairy tales.

Next to me, Clementia flipped through a book about wizards' spells. "It seems true love is the cure for many an ailment. I don't know why it didn't work this time. After all, your love is true enough to bring you together each night."

Obviously not. Or maybe the problem was more complicated. Love wasn't curing the fairies' trees. Could love have lost its magic power? Or perhaps true love differed from romantic love. Jason thought he loved me. He didn't really, though. Otherwise he wouldn't want to hide me from his friends.

I didn't want to hide Donovan. Although, come to think of it, I did want to hide his police record. Was that just as bad? Did you have to love everything about a person to truly love them?

My mom thought sports were a waste of time and nagged my dad if the ESPN was on too long. Dad thought Mom spent money on things she didn't need, and sometimes he acted like a martyr when he paid the credit card bills. But wasn't every couple like that?

How could I judge other people's feelings when I wasn't sure what real love was myself? I rested the book on my lap and watched Jason. He was perched on the top of Kayla's chair, saying something that made her laugh.

"What is true love?" I asked out loud. "Does it take years? Or can it develop in an instant?"

Catherine casually turned a page. "It doesn't take years. I had known my darling Leopold for only one night when I came to love him."

Beatrix, who sat in a chair on my other side, added, "I knew I loved Frederick the moment he asked me to dance. When he took my hand, I could think of nothing but him."

Mathilda and Philippa nodded in agreement. Rosamund put down one book and picked up another. "I tread more carefully in matters of the heart. Geoffrey wooed me for an entire month before he won me."

All of my sisters were smiling, lit up with happiness by the thought of their princes.

"But how do you know it's *true* love?" I pressed.

Beatrix sniffed, offended, and turned a page with extra force. "Of course what we feel is true love."

Rosamund straightened. "Would we risk our father's wrath every night otherwise?"

Maybe. It didn't take much to invoke the king's wrath. Having any sort of fun probably invoked his wrath. "I wasn't implying your feelings aren't real," I explained. "I'm just wondering about love in general."

Beatrix's expression softened. "You know it's true love because his name on your lips tastes like honey."

"You know," Elizabeth said, "because your soul soars at the sight of him."

Darby let out a low whistle. "You know because he looks hot even when he's wearing dorky half-pants and stockings."

Hmm. Couldn't I have said all those things about Jason before I got to know him? I didn't feel that way now. "The Queen's goblet said love was a choice. What does that mean?"

Catherine held her book down. "If the goblet said such a thing, it knows little of love. One doesn't choose love. It chooses you—like cupid's arrow striking your heart."

"I didn't want to fall in love with Prince Edgar," Isolde put in. "I thought to be an obedient daughter and marry whomever father picked." She smiled dreamily. "But when Edgar murmured my name in the moonlight, I was lost."

Everyone chimed in, agreeing they too had meant to be the most dutiful of daughters until struck down by the forces of love. And I was left unsure about any of it. I didn't feel lost when I was with Donovan. I felt . . . found. Like he had found a part of me I'd forgotten long ago.

Was I just responding to the first guy who'd ever really taken an interest in me? Was I rushing into things? Would either of us feel the same when we got home?

I dwelt on these questions while I skimmed restoratives for coughs, warts, toothaches, fevers, and something called apoplexy. Not long afterward, Donovan came in the room. For a moment my soul soared at the sight of him. Which meant maybe my sisters knew what they were talking about after all. When had the goblet ever fallen in love? It wasn't a choice.

He sat beside me on the couch. While pretending to look at my book, he told me about his meeting with the goldsmith. The man had assured him the work on the cup was progressing and would be ready after supper. Right on time.

Donovan grabbed a few books and opened one. "Find anything useful?"

"Not unless Jason develops heartburn. Then I'll know to feed him curds and whey."

Donovan nodded. "I guess he won't have to worry about any spiders that sit down beside him. They'll just be appetizers."

"I heard that," Jason said. He hopped further away from our couch, affronted.

I finished two more medical books, then read one on fairy

origins. One theory claimed the fae folk had been angels who long ago fought on Earth in a holy war, but when God called them to come back, they delayed and were locked out of heaven. I doubted that theory was right. Queen Orlaith wasn't at all angelic.

After a couple hours, I abandoned being ladylike and lay on the floor. It was how I always studied. Donovan joined me, and before long, everyone was sprawled in front of the fireplace.

Most of the servants couldn't read, so we hadn't asked anyone else to help us. Besides, it would have been hard to explain the presence of a reading frog— or one who kept sidling up to princesses and asking for a kiss.

As he hopped past me for the twentieth time, I said, "For future reference and your next girlfriend's sake, girls don't like it when you hit on their sisters."

Jason paused in front of my book. "I'm not hitting on your sisters. I'm trying to break the curse."

"I believed that the first time you kissed them, and even the second. Now it's just a pathetic ploy for attention."

Jason humphed and leaped over to Darby, hopping onto the pages of her book. "Come on, sweetheart, give me a kiss. I think your love could change me."

"Just watch," Donovan whispered. "Those will be the lyrics of his next song."

"Actually, those were the lyrics of his last song."

Darby made a shooing motion at Jason. "I already kissed you. Anyone who wants more time with my lips has got to spring for a meal and a night on the town."

Donovan shut his book, finished with it. Our stacks were dwindling, most books now lying in discarded heaps. He stood up, brushed off his pants, and held out his hand to help me up.

"Your sisters can search through the rest. You have other things to do."

I didn't have to ask what. I had to practice being stealthy, graceful, and quick—something I'd never accomplished before. It seemed pointless to think I could pick up those skills in a few hours, but I had to at least try. I followed Donovan out of the room.

• • •

We took two goblets, a pitcher of water, and several napkins from the kitchen. I led Donovan to an empty sitting room, knowing where it was even though I hadn't been there before. More proof, if I needed it, that my princess life was beginning to erase my modern one. Donovan set one goblet on a table and, with more optimism than he should have possessed, gave me the other goblet to keep in my pocket. "Make the switch," he said. "You need to do it soundlessly, fast, and without spilling anything."

For a half an hour I tried to live up to his optimism. I could manage two of his requirements, but not all three. If I was fast and soundless, I ended up spilling water. If I was soundless and steady, I wasn't fast.

Finally I sat down in a chair, devoid of optimism or anything resembling it. Donovan mopped up the water from my latest spill and showed me how to do it again. He made it look easy. "When you over-think it, you're too slow. The movement has to be natural. Automatic. Like riding a bike."

"I crashed a lot on my bike. Broke my arm, in fact."

"That was the old you. The new you is graceful."

He motioned for me to stand up, then made me do the exercise again and again.

After two dozen failed attempts, I managed the switch once, then twice. In my overconfidence, the next time I attempted to switch the goblet, I tipped it over. The cup rolled to the floor with a loud clank, splashing water everywhere.

Donovan picked it up and set it back on the table. "Try again."

I refilled the goblet and did. This time when I grabbed it, I was fast and soundless but a few drops of water fell out.

"Nearly perfect," I said.

Donovan shook his head, unsatisfied. "A few drops of liquid will leave spots on Queen Orlaith's table. If she notices those, then poof! You're the latest amphibious addition in the household."

I opened and closed my hands, stretching my fingers. I could do this. I had done this perfectly twice. Okay, granted, I'd done it wrong the other times, but I was getting better. Hopefully. Or maybe I was just getting lucky. Maybe anyone would be able to manage it right a couple times if they tried enough.

I reached for the goblet, silently lifting it from the table. I held the cups below the table line to hide them, poured the water from one into the other, and set the second goblet where the first had been. Not a drop spilled.

"Too slow," Donovan said. "Do it again."

I wanted to stamp my foot in frustration. Instead I pulled the goblet from my pocket the way he'd taught me: a subtle sweep of my hand that didn't draw attention. "You know, some guys know how to compliment a girl. Didn't you hear what my sister's boyfriend said when they came in? Frederick said Beatrix's eyes shone like two stars."

"That's a compliment? Stars are burning piles of gas."

While tilting my head conversationally, I picked up the goblet from the table. "And Hubert said the glow of Mathilda's skin puts the moon to shame."

Donovan smirked, refusing to be impressed. "The moon is pocked with gaping craters."

I poured the water from the queen's goblet into the other. Still keeping my gaze on Donovan, I replaced the second goblet, sliding it onto the table without a clink. I slipped the first goblet into my pocket. "You're not much of a romantic, are you?"

His smirk spread into a full blown grin. "Okay, here's a compliment. With moves like that, you'd make a decent pickpocket."

"Ah, thanks. My parents would be so proud."

He took my hand and pulled me to him, interrupting my practice schedule to show me that, yes, he was a romantic after all.

When it was time to dress for supper, I could make the switch right about seventy percent of the time. Of course, being able to make the switch smoothly wasn't going to do a lot of good if we didn't have a distraction. We'd counted on Jason singing to the queen. Donovan didn't seem too worried about this glitch.

"If Jason is still a frog," Donovan said as we left the room, "he can sit on the table and beg Queen Orlaith for mercy. That should cause a distraction."

"Yes, but it won't solve Jason's problem. We've got to find a way to change him before we go to the twenty-first century."

"I think being a frog suits him."

"He's a star. Don't you think fans will notice if he's a frog?"

Donovan shrugged. "He can do lots of radio interviews."

I hoped when I went up to my room to change my sisters would tell me they'd discovered a cure for Jason.

No such luck.

My sisters sat at their dressing tables, silently getting their hair done, an air of disappointment hanging around them as thick as their perfume.

My lady's maid helped me into a dark green skirt and bodice, then wove matching ribbons into my hair. When she finished, Rosamund excused the servants. I knew she wanted to talk to me about Jason.

I turned in my chair to face her. "Where is he?"

In answer to my question, Elizabeth took a goblet from the fireplace mantel and tipped it onto my dressing table. A frog waddled across the top and slumped in front of the mirror.

"What's wrong with him?" I asked, worried.

"Nothing." Rosamund said, straightening the lace on her sleeves. "He's just being dramatic."

"We gave him a curing potion we thought might help," Beatrix clarified.

Jason glared at her, his lips pursed. "They made me drink something with crushed newt."

"Sadly, it proved an ineffective remedy," Rosamund said.

Darby checked her reflection and adjusted her necklace. "He's been carrying on about it ever since."

"Crushed newt," Jason repeated.

"Frogs eat worse," Beatrix said and flounced back to her table. "It won't hurt you."

My sisters finished the last of their pre-dinner preparations and headed toward the door, lining up from oldest to youngest. I still sat at the dressing table watching Jason. He lay limply by my hair-brush, head down, eyes closed. I assumed he'd fallen asleep and wondered if it was healthy for a frog to sleep out of the water. Would he dry out?

As I pondered whether it would be unforgivably rude to pick him up and plop him into a pitcher, he opened his eyes and stared mournfully at me.

"I'll bring you something back from dinner," I said.

He didn't answer, didn't move.

The last of my sisters was nearly out the door. I should go too. I stood, hesitant to leave him. He looked so miserable.

"Well, besides the crushed newt potion, are you doing okay?"

His head sagged. "I'm small, warty, and hideous."

"I don't think those bumps on your back are actually warts."

Jason turned and put a hand to the mirror, touching his reflection. "Over a million posters of my face sold last year. I was on covers of teen magazines around the world." He let out a sad croaking sound, probably a sob. "Now look at me." He hung his head and continued to make pitiful squeaking sounds.

My guilt flared up again. If I hadn't wished him here, he'd still be back in the twenty-first century mocking other hopeful singers and putting his butt through its usual strenuous work routine.

I patted his back gently. "You need to stop staring in the mirror. Look at something else. And look on the bright side. When we go home, you'll have an easy time hiding from your fans."

He made more croaking sounds.

I remembered the locket Chrissy had given me, and I pulled it from around my neck. "Here. Pretend this is a mirror." I opened it up and propped it on the table in front of him. "See, that's who you are on the inside."

Jason gripped the sides of the locket, holding his portrait. "Look at me. Look at how awesome I was."

"Again, it's what's on the inside that counts. That's the moral of those frog prince fairy tales, right?"

He stroked the locket with a green finger. "I had the greatest smile. I miss me." He let out a wistful sigh, blinked at the portrait with liquid eyes, and kissed it.

The table creaked, shivering and groaning as Jason's weight shifted. One moment he was a forlorn green frog awkwardly kissing his portrait, the next he was a teen idol in Renaissance clothing crouched on my table.

I should have known all along he would end up breaking the spell that way. After all, Jason loved himself the most.

He gawked at his hands, turning them in front of his face in wonder. Like a shot, he jumped off the table and turned toward the mirror. "I'm me again!"

I shushed him, hoping no servants were passing by in the hallway. The last thing I needed was for the king to find a strange man in our bed chamber.

Penny and Darby must have heard him. They peered back into to the room to see what had caused the commotion. When they saw Jason, they sighed happily. "Oh, that's so adorable," Penny cooed. "It's true love, after all,"

"Sweet," Darby said. "Now get him out of here before someone sees him, 'cause I ain't answering questions about why there's a Briardrakian prince hanging out in our room."

"We've totally never seen him." Penny agreed. She took Darby's arm, and the two of them disappeared down the hallway.

I strode to the tapestry and took out the key hidden there. "They're right. You need to leave."

I went to the fireplace and inserted the key into the notch, just as Rosamund had done the last two nights. With only a nudge on my part, it slid open, revealing the landing.

Jason didn't move. "Where am I supposed to go? I don't know the way back to the lake. I rode in your pocket all the way here."

He had a point. "Wait for us on the stairs. We'll leave for the lake at bedtime."

He took slow steps toward the opening. "Bring me a lot for dinner. I'm starving."

I gestured toward the door. "Okay. Go."

"Something good," he emphasized. "No cow tongue or sheep stomachs or any of that other crap they pass off as delicacies here." He went through the door mumbling, "Seriously, there are no decent places to eat in this century."

I slid the fireplace closed, glad it was easier to do than it looked.

"So," a voice came from behind me. "Sneaking guys out of your room?"

I spun around, startled. Chrissy stood there, wearing her Team Sadie T-shirt and a flouncy blue miniskirt that made her wings glimmer with blue highlights. She held her wand loosely like it was a drumstick.

I put a hand on my pounding heart. "You just scared me to death."

She smiled, unworried about my health, and sashayed closer. "I hear you and Jason kissed last night. Twice. How romantic."

"He was a frog at the time."

"Well, it can only get better then, right?"

I motioned for her to walk with me away from the

fireplace, in case Jason could hear us. "I'm not kissing him again."

Chrissy raised an eyebrow. "Have your eye on someone else?"

I blushed. Was I that transparent? I didn't want to tell her about Donovan. He was supposed to be my competition, and I knew she wouldn't approve.

Chrissy put her hand on my arm sympathetically. "I know Kailen is the hottest guy you've ever seen, but don't pin your hopes on him. He's not into mortals."

"Oh." Relief. "Okay."

"Besides, he's way too cocky." Chrissy tossed her long pink hair off her shoulder. I would have looked ridiculous swishing my hair around like that. On her, it was graceful, natural. "A few months ago I was at a party with this buff elf guy, and Kailen and a couple of his friends came in. The first thing you know, Kailen was swaggering around, showing off for the girls—making vines snake around the elf guys, stuff like that. My date said something along the lines of, 'Real men don't wear wings,' and the next thing I knew he and Kailen were brawling like drunken frat boys."

"Really?"

"And then after my date stormed off to have his teeth fixed, Kailen asked for my number."

"That *is* cocky."

Chrissy folded her arms. "He never called." Another head toss. "Really, I hate it when guys treat me like a trophy."

I had no idea what to say to that. She'd actually given Kailen her number after he'd beaten up her date?

"Anyway," Chrissy said, returning her attention to me, "I wanted to check in, give you a pep talk, and remind you that even though I've got tons of things to do tonight, I'll once again be eagerly waiting to hear that you've got the goblet." Her wings opened and closed. "It's your third night here. Exactly what are you waiting for?"

"I'm going to take it tonight."

"Good. And you should look your best while doing it." She brushed a piece of lint off my shoulder and then, still unhappy with my appearance, snapped her fingers. "Much better."

I glanced in the mirror to see what she'd done. I was now wearing makeup, including deep red lipstick.

"Remember," Chrissy said, "I can't go on Queen Orlaith's land, so you have to make it through the forest and out onto the meadow before I can take the goblet. Call me as soon as you pass the last tree. Once it's in my hand, I'll send you and Jason wherever you'd like." She gave me a cheering smile. "I bet he takes you to some posh Hollywood party."

"I'll call you as soon as I pass the last tree."

"Awesome." She flicked her wand and sparkles spun in the air around her. "Oh, and after you steal the goblet, keep clear of stray vines. You don't want to end up as plant food." The sparkles fountained around her until she disappeared.

I watched her go and wondered which part of the last conversation was supposed to be a pep talk.

Chapter 26

That night, when my sisters and I went down the stairs to the fairy realm, Jason walked beside me, holding my lantern. I'd stopped waiting for him to be chivalrous, and I'd forced the lantern on him, telling him I needed both hands to hold up my skirts in order to lessen the chance I'd trip and plunge to my death.

"After the queen asks her question," I whispered to Jason, "Offer to sing her a song—your apology for the unfortunate misunderstanding last night. Keep her eyes on you. When you've finished singing, apologizing, and groveling in general, look at me. If I touch my hair, that means I've got the goblet.

"Tell the queen you still haven't recovered your stamina after being a frog, so you and I are making an early night of it. We'll need to get out of Queen Orlaith's domain as quickly as we can."

Jason switched the lantern from one hand to the other, nervously wiping his palms on his jerkin. "How come I have to be the distraction?"

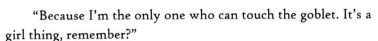

"Because I'm the only one who can touch the goblet. It's a girl thing, remember?"

"Why can't Donovan be the distraction?"

"Because he's invisible."

"He could make something float."

"We want her diverted, not suspicious."

Jason scowled and lowered his voice to a hiss. "If Queen Orlaith catches you, she'll change us both into something horrible. No, thank you. I've already done time being repulsive."

Behind me, Donovan let out a disbelieving cough. "Is that sentence over?"

I kept my attention on Jason. "We have to take our chances. You don't want to stay here, do you?"

Jason made exasperated grumbling sounds as he thunked angrily down the stairs. "You never should have wished me here."

"You think?" I snapped, tired of his complaints. "I could have used that wish for something useful like, oh I don't know . . . anything else in the world."

I held up one hand to stop him from protesting. "I know there are hordes of girls who would love to be in your presence no matter how whiny you're being, but I've realized I'm not one of them."

He sputtered at that. "You're insulting me, when all of this is *your fault*?"

From behind us, Donovan whispered, "I think you should ask the queen to turn him back into a frog."

Jason turned the lantern to the sound of his voice, scattering light up the stairs. "Keep hiding, punk. If I see you, I will totally take you down!"

Donovan didn't answer.

Jason waved a finger in his direction. "That's right. You're not so tough now."

I put my hand on Jason's arm and turned him the right direction. The princesses had stopped descending the stairs and were staring curiously at him.

"Who are you shouting at?" Penny asked, holding her lantern higher so its circle of light increased.

Jason dropped his hand. "Um, no one." He cleared his throat. "I just do that sometimes. Yell randomly." More throat clearing. "It's a guy thing."

I slipped my arm through Jason's arm. "He's fine now."

The other princesses sent a few more puzzled looks in Jason's direction, then turned and went down the stairs again, murmuring things. Probably none of it complimentary. Jason and I followed more slowly. "And that," I whispered, "is why you can't win an argument with an invisible man."

Jason shot Donovan an angry look over his shoulder, then picked up his pace. "I don't know why you *like* him, let alone *trust* him."

I wasn't going to let the conversation turn in that direction. Especially not with Donovan listening. "Don't worry about him. I'll get you home or die trying. All I'm asking you to do is sing for the queen. I'll do the rest."

Jason's gaze went to me, surprised. "You'd die for me?"

"Well, it's not part of the game plan, but it's a possibility."

Jason remained quiet for a few moments. The light from our lantern spilled down the stairs, one white marble step at a time. Finally he said, "I'm sorry I've been hard on you. I know you didn't mean to screw up my life."

Donovan snorted at that. Apparently he didn't think much of the apology.

"It's okay," I said, both to Jason and Donovan.

After that, Jason and I made small talk. At first it was forced and cold, but after awhile things thawed out. We talked about what we would do first when we got home. Jason was going to book a relaxing vacation in the Caribbean. I was going to come up with a good excuse to explain my three-day disappearance to my parents. And then I was going to think of things to do while grounded, because there was no way on earth my parents would buy any excuse I gave them.

Donovan didn't say anything. Maybe he didn't want to blow his cover. Or maybe he was thinking of his probation officer. How much trouble would he be in for disappearing?

A couple of times while we walked through the forest, the branches of trees swayed in a way that made me suspect Donovan was pilfering more fairy wealth. After we'd passed through the diamond trees, I heard Donovan's footsteps at my side, then felt something heavy slip into my pocket. When I checked to see what he'd put there, I found three small branches, a gold, silver, and diamond one. "For me?" I asked. Earlier, he'd given me some gold leaves. I hadn't expected more.

"You should get something from your stint in this fairy tale besides Jason's undying love."

"Thanks."

The princess procession reached the lake. Jason's boat sat on the shore exactly where I'd left it last night. The other princes stood by their boats, waiting, and cheered when they saw Jason, human and well. Several came up to clap him on the back and rib him about his time spent as an amphibian. Geoffrey, Rosamund's prince, predicted he'd be the quickest rower, since he'd been lounging around with the princesses while the rest of them had worked vigorously.

That prediction proved false, but Jason wasn't bothered—

at least not much—by being last again. This time he knew our boat was heavier due to an invisible stowaway.

"I don't see why I have to row the whole way," he grumbled. "Why can't Mr. Invisible take a turn?"

"Because," I said patiently, "it would look odd if the oars appeared to be moving by themselves."

Jason pulled at the oars, halfheartedly trying to catch up with the other boats. "You're not invisible. Whatever happened to equal rights?"

I relaxed against the side of the boat, listening to the slosh of the waves. "They haven't been invented yet."

Jason spent the rest of the ride to the pavilion alternating between complaining about being shanghaied into the past and predicting our doom. I mostly tuned him out and talked to Donovan.

Once we got to the pavilion, Jason spent a while at the refreshment table, filling his plate, and then filling it again. I should have eaten too. I should have enjoyed what was possibly my last meal, but my stomach wanted no part of it. I stood next to him, nibbling at flower petals I didn't taste.

Kailen wasn't around again tonight. Good. One less pair of eyes to watch us. Rosamund and Geoffrey came to the table for drinks, flushed from dancing. I took Rosamund aside. I had an irrational desire to fix this fairy tale. I didn't want to disappear back to my own century and leave my sisters' story unfinished.

I used my body to shield her from any passing glances and slipped the silver, gold, and diamond twigs into her hand. "Put these in your purse, and give them to Geoffrey before the ball ends. He needs to come to the castle, pretend to be a suitor from a distant land, and show the twigs to father as proof he's solved the slipper mystery. Geoffrey will choose you as his bride, and he'll inherit the kingdom."

Rosamund's gaze darted to the queen's table to make sure we weren't being watched. "Such a thing is impossible. Father would put a stop to our ball and never let our sisters see their princes again. I couldn't marry Geoffrey knowing that by doing so I'll ruin my sisters' chances for happiness."

She pressed the twigs back at me. I didn't take them. "Trust me about this. He'll let the princes marry the princesses. Probably insist on it, in fact."

"He won't. You know his stubbornness."

"Yes, but I also know he loves us. It will outweigh his stubbornness." I was suddenly sure of this fact, which was a nice bit of knowledge to have. In the story, the princesses wed and lived happily ever after. Despite his gruffness and threats, the king wanted his daughters to be happy.

Rosamund still looked unconvinced, but she slipped the twigs into her purse. "Mother did say she would talk to him about restoring the provinces' rights."

I nodded at her. "Mother will bring him around."

Rosamund pressed her lips together, thinking. "She might be a willing ally."

"Absolutely," I said.

Rosamund smiled, suddenly hopeful. "I'll ask Geoffrey his opinion of such a plan."

After that, Jason decided he wanted to dance and led me out on the floor. As I waltzed to the swaying sounds of the fairy music, I kept surreptitiously checking the clock, watching as the hands made their way around the face. Eleven came. Then eleven thirty. Eleven forty. Eleven fifty. With every passing minute, my heart beat faster.

I both wanted midnight to come and dreaded it. I wondered where Donovan was. He told me when I switched the goblets, he'd be near the table. Ready to help me if I needed it.

When the clock struck twelve, Jason and I danced our way toward the queen's table. She pulled a vial from her gown took the lid off, and poured the liquid into the goblet. Fear tingled up my back. My palms felt sweaty. It was almost time to make the switch.

Queen Orlaith picked up the cup, swirling it as she spoke. "Magic cup within my hand, make me wise to understand. I've bathed my trees in love's sweet air, yet even so, their boughs are bare. They've soaked up light from love's true kiss. They're watered by such tears of bliss. What need they more to grow and thrive? Tell me the key to save their lives."

The answer from the goblet came quicker than it had the other nights, as though it was weary of answering. "How can one show what you won't see? How can one tell what you won't be? Love is a tree, love is a river. Love is the gift and not the giver. True love becomes eternal, when offerings make love supernal."

She put down the cup, her expression fierce in its frustration. We had to make the switch before she locked the goblet back in the box.

I moved closer to Jason. "This is it. Ready?"

Instead of answering, he stepped over to the queen's table, swaggering as he walked. If he was anxious, he didn't show it. Perhaps that's what happened when you were constantly in front of cameras. You became immune to nerves.

The queen barely glanced at us. She fingered the goblet's stem, repeating its words, muttering bits of it like a chant. "A tree. A river. What is both tree and river?" She turned the goblet absently. "Roots spread out like rivers. One finds water the other gives it. But love is the gift not the giver. Water. What does water have to do with love?"

Jason bowed. "Your Majesty, please forgive me for last night. I only meant to refill your cup. In my land, guys do that for girls."

Her gaze flickered to him. "You're a mortal. Tell me, how does your love differ from that of the fairies?"

He shrugged. "I don't know. I've never loved a fairy." He gave the queen a wink. "I could give it a try, though."

One shouldn't joke with fairy queens, especially frustrated ones. She gave him a look that could have dropped the temperature by ten degrees.

"Insolent, barbaric creatures," she muttered. "They're as weak as wind-blown leaves. How could their love be strong enough to matter?" She waved her fingers in our direction, dismissing us. "Go dance. Your apology is accepted."

Jason bowed again. "May I sing for you, Your Highness? My music is the only gift I have that's worthy of a fairy."

When he said the word "gift," Queen Orlaith's gaze swung back to him. She seemed to grab onto the word, hold it up and consider it. "Yes, sing about love. Sing to your princess." She gestured to me. "You sing too."

Me? As though stealing a goblet wasn't hard enough—now I had to do it while carrying a tune.

Like he'd done before, Jason gave the queen a name of one of his songs. *Love for Two.* She tapped her wand to the table, and the opening stanzas of Jason's song filled the room. A change from the slower beat that had been playing. The swirling couples adjusted their pace, laughing as they tried to keep up.

Jason held out his hand to the queen, serenading her. "I don't want four solo measures. Don't need three part harmony. Just the two of us, living our sweet duet."

I heard the words, but I didn't. I was completely focused on the goblet sitting in front of the queen. It was a bit shorter than the one I'd brought. The base was thicker, the rim more delicate. How could switching them possibly fool the queen? And yet what other choice did we have? If I didn't steal the goblet tonight, in the morning my father would demand either an explanation or Donovan's execution. This was our last night.

I reached into my pocket, mouth dry, heart battering against my chest. I pulled the fake goblet from my pocket, holding it low, hidden beneath the edge of the table.

The queen was watching Jason tolerantly. Probably contemplating all the flaws of mortal love. Her goblet sat in front of her, waiting. My free hand shook. How could I make this work if my hand was shaking? And yet I held the false goblet in my hand. In about thirty seconds it would be my turn to sing. The queen's attention would swing to me.

I felt Donovan's hand brush against mine, give it a squeeze. I knew it was his way of saying he was there, that he believed in me.

Soundlessly, I reached for the queen's goblet and grabbed the stem. It felt cold in my hand, hard. I kept my gaze on her. If she glanced at me, her eyes would be drawn to mine, and hopefully not see what I did with my hands.

I pulled the goblet toward me, held it below the table, and poured its liquid into the fake goblet. In my hurry, I clinked one goblet into the other. Fortunately, Jason's singing covered the noise. He was almost done with his part. In another moment it would be my turn.

I placed the false goblet back in front of the queen, slipping the real one into my pocket. Only then did I breathe, which was a good thing since the song was about three seconds from my part. For two of those seconds, I couldn't recall the words to the song. Ditto for one second.

Jason stopped singing and motioned to me. The queen's gaze turned in my direction. I bluffed my way through the first few notes with an improvised, "Oh yeah . . . Baby . . . Baby."

In my defense, those are the lyrics to a lot of songs.

Then I remembered the real lyrics. "You see someone different in me. You see the person I'm trying to be . . ."

The queen watched me placidly. Her gaze wandered to the other dancers, to their attempts to keep up with the beat. They were failing, but enjoying themselves, laughing at their less-than-perfect efforts.

I finished my verse, and Jason and I sung the chorus together. The queen lazily reached across the table for her goblet.

I tensed, had to force the next line out. She was going to notice it was fake. How could she not? She'd stared at the same goblet for nights. I kept singing—reminded myself I hadn't noticed when Donovan used different coins in his trick.

She picked up the goblet, about to drink from it. And that's when I realized our mistake. Even if the queen didn't notice the goblet looked different, she might notice it tasted different, felt different on her lips. I should have waited until she'd drunk all the elixir before I made the switch.

I did the only thing I could think of. I drew in a breath, bent over and sneezed on the goblet.

The queen set the goblet down, repulsed, and wiped the back of her hand on the table cloth. No napkins sat on her table. Apparently fairies didn't need them.

"My apologies!" I picked up part of the table cloth and

dabbed it to her hand. As I tugged at the tablecloth the goblet toppled, spilling the remaining elixir. Some of which dribbled onto her dress.

She grabbed the goblet, stood up, and wiped the liquid off her dress. "Stupid girl!"

I shrank back from her. "I'm sorry that I'm so clumsy." It was the truth in general, if not in this specific incident. "Clumsiness is part of being a mortal. Like sneezing. And coughing. And sometimes rashes and cavities." Probably overkill, but I was nervous.

Still glaring at me, Queen Orlaith put the goblet in the middle of the box, tapped the table with her wand, and the box closed around the goblet, locking it up.

Mission accomplished.

The queen surveyed the crimson stain on her dress with anger. "This isn't a mortal drink I can dissipate with a flick of my wand. This is fairy nectar. And you've . . ." She muttered something unintelligible that may have been fairy cursing. "Go!" She waved her hand at Jason and I. "Go dance. I need to see to my dress." She sent another glare in my direction, just in case I hadn't caught the meaning of the first one.

I curtsied, keeping my eyes on the ground. When I looked up again, she'd vanished, gone off somewhere to change.

I straightened, relief pouring over me so thick and quick I nearly felt dizzy with it. I had done it. I'd stolen the goblet.

Donovan spoke near my ear. "Brilliant."

"I'm not good at a lot of things, but I know how to be clumsy."

Jason edged across the ballroom. "Let's go."

For once, all three of us agreed. Donovan and I followed after him, weaving our way around mingling couples.

Chapter 27

Donovan sat behind Jason in the boat, hands on the oars, helping him row so the boat would go faster. Jason leaned into the effort. "How come you never helped row earlier?"

"Because I figured you needed the exercise, oh Prince of Pop."

I was too tense to listen to them argue, let alone try to stop them. The goblet felt heavy in my pocket. A golden piece of danger. I kept glancing over my shoulder, half expecting to see Queen Orlaith storming after us. I also worried some gigantic creepy seaweed hand would reach up out of the lake, grab me, and pull me under. Nerves. I was *so* not cut out for the criminal life.

When we reached the other shore, I hauled my skirts up and climbed out of the boat, not caring that it wasn't a graceful disembarkment. My slippers sank into the wet soil. I didn't care about that, either. I ran to the posts where the lanterns waited.

I had only taken a few steps when I heard the birds. At

first they were just a faint, distant cawing. I grabbed a lantern and turned to Jason, who was coming up behind me. I supposed Donovan was somewhere near too.

"Come on," I told them and headed toward the trail.

The trees seemed darker than normal—taller. Their branches moved in the wind, limbs swaying. I hurried into the forest anyway. Birds erupted from the trees, scattering into the air. Some circled upward like smoke, their cries slicing into the night. Each caw sounded like the word 'cup'!

I stared at them, a cold dread spreading over me.

"What's wrong with the birds?" Jason asked.

Donovan's voice came near my side. "Are they saying, 'cup'?"

I hadn't been the only one who heard the word in their calls. I swallowed hard. Somehow the birds knew I had the goblet. They must be like store alarms that went off when shoplifters took something. We'd tripped a magical alarm.

Without another word, we set off in a sprint. The lantern jiggled in my hand. I worried I would knock the flame out and we'd be stuck wandering the forest in the dark, but I didn't slow down.

The birds circled upward above us, a dark tornado of wings flapping in alarm. "Cup! Cup!" they cawed. I waited for them to dive, to swarm down pecking and clawing at us. I scanned the trees for a loose branch I could use as a club—anything, any sort of weapon.

Then with one mind, the birds beat off toward the lake, an angry fluttering mass, swooping and calling.

"They're flying to tell the queen," Donovan said. He took the lantern from my hand so I could run faster. "Hurry!"

Jason led the way. Donovan ran between us, the lantern

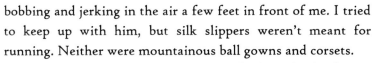

bobbing and jerking in the air a few feet in front of me. I tried to keep up with him, but silk slippers weren't meant for running. Neither were mountainous ball gowns and corsets.

How long had it taken us to walk through the forest? Fifteen minutes? Perhaps twenty? It shouldn't take long to run the distance. Five minutes, ten, tops. Could we make it to the meadow before Queen Orlaith found us?

Donovan must have checked on me and seen I was falling behind. He slowed his pace. He was choosing to stay with me rather than escape without me. Part of me wanted to hug him for being so selfless. The other part wanted to yell at him to get away while he could. I pushed myself to run faster so he could too.

We passed the diamond trees and went through the ones made of gold. Against the lantern light, their bare branches seemed like rows and rows of jagged spikes. The wind picked up, flooding through the forest in a way that made the boughs lash up and down. It was only the wind, I told myself. The trees weren't really shaking their branches threateningly. They weren't reaching out for me with spindly fingers.

As I ran, the goblet slapped against my leg. My slippers had no traction and I kept stumbling, tempting an all-out fall. We passed by the last of the gold trees and fled through the silver. The wind blew bits of dust and bark, making it hard to see. Five minutes, I told myself, I was only five minutes from freedom.

As we rounded a bend in the path, I slid and pitched forward. The only nice thing about running in a ball gown with a huge poofy skirt is they do a decent job of breaking your fall. This advantage unfortunately is counteracted by the fact it's impossible to get up quickly once you've fallen. I cursed and struggled with my dress. Donovan heard me. The light bobbed back to me. I felt his grip on my hand and he pulled me to my feet. "Are you okay?"

"Yes." I didn't bother to brush myself off before taking off in a run again. "Whoever named these shoes 'slippers' got it right. That's what they do."

A pine branch whipped out, striking my neck and chin. I pushed it away and kept running, hands raised in protection. A few feet later another branch swept down in front of me. This one larger. It caught on the lace of my sleeve and yanked me backward. I pulled frantically at the branches, ripping the lace to free myself.

I sprinted forward again, breathing hard. A few moments later, another branch swung into the path in front of me. I dodged out of the way, barely managing to avoid it. "The trees are trying to stop us."

Actually not us, *me*. Either the trees didn't see Donovan and weren't smart enough to figure out the bobbing lantern wasn't levitating by itself, or they knew I had the goblet and were only charged with stopping me. It's hard to judge how smart trees are.

"Hurry!" Donovan called. His voice was nearly lost in the angry howl of the wind and the answering moan of branches.

I ran faster, listening for the sound of the birds. They would come back, and when they did, they would lead Queen Orlaith to us.

I couldn't see Jason up on the path anymore. The other princes could say what they wanted about his lack of rowing ability, but when it came to running through a creepy forest, the boy could put on some serious speed.

How much longer till the trees thinned and we could see

the meadow? A minute? Three? I was panting, and each deep breath I drew came in sharp contact with the corset. Donovan slowed his pace so he wouldn't get too far ahead.

"I'm holding you back," I said. "Run up ahead and call Jade Blossom and Chrissy. By the time you work the deal out, I'll be there."

"I can't leave you. We've only got one light."

"Go. I can see enough to stay on the path." The moon was bright and the magical trees had a glow that faintly illuminated everything around them.

Donovan didn't say anything. He didn't run ahead.

"The sooner we call our fairy godmothers, the sooner we'll be safe from Queen Orlaith."

The light remained in the same position, a few feet ahead of me. I knew Donovan though, knew what to say to make him go ahead. "When the birds come back, they'll probably search for the lantern. I'll have a better chance of making it through the forest if they follow you instead of me."

Donovan said something, maybe swore in frustration. I couldn't quite tell. The wind howled angrily, tossing his words away before they reached me.

But my request had the desired effect. The light bounced away from me and down the path. Donovan was fast—should-be-in-track fast. Had-practice-outrunning-the-police fast.

I chased after the light, watching it grow smaller. A few moments later, it went around a curve and blinked out of sight. I was alone. Alone in the near darkness with flailing branches that struck at me.

Twice more tree limbs swung down and caught on my dress. I had to break off the gripping twigs to free myself. Each moment I expected to hear the call of the birds overhead, circling the forest to find me. Perhaps they were already above me, leading the queen to my location.

Where did the forest end? Why couldn't I see it yet? Had the queen put a spell on it so it never ended? Perhaps I would eventually fall down exhausted, and then the trees would grab me in their branches and hold me fast.

I ran on, tired and panting from fear as much as exertion. And then the trees thinned, and I saw the grey shimmer of moonlight on the meadow ahead.

I was nearly safe. When I passed the last tree, I would be out of Queen Orlaith's land.

A few steps later I could see people: Jason and Donovan talking with Chrissy and Jade Blossom. A nightlight glow surrounded Chrissy, and her wings glimmered on her back. Her hair was no longer pink, but a blonde that shone with intertwined starlight. The modern clothes were gone, replaced by a pale flowing dress.

Jade Blossom stood next to Chrissy, dark hair laying down her back in sleek waves. Her glow had a blue cast to it, and veins of green ran through her wings, gleaming. Jason stood facing the fairies, his shoulders rising and falling with each breath. Donovan had taken off his cloak, and he stood in front of the fairies, turning so he could check the forest. He was waiting for me.

I pushed myself to go faster, willed myself to sprint the rest of the way. We were nearly safe. We just had to complete the deal with our fairies and then we could go home. Home. I wanted to see my parents so badly it felt like a physical ache lodged in my heart.

I should have noticed Donovan's tense stance and his angry expression. I should have guessed what it meant, but I was too glad to see the fairies. I didn't pick up on the tone of the conversation until I came within earshot.

"Absolutely not," Jade Blossom said. Her eyebrows lifted in disbelieving peeks. "However, if you give me the goblet, I'll see what I can do to help the others."

Chrissy turned a triumphant smile on Jade Blossom. "Your guy is trying to swindle magic out of you because he doesn't have the goblet." She fluttered her hand, shooing him away. "Nice try, Donny. No goblet, no dice."

"Look," Jason cut in. "I'm the innocent one in all of this. I didn't do anything to deserve being here, but I still helped get that cup. Somebody had better send me home."

Donovan glanced at the path and saw me coming. Relief washed over him. "Sadie!"

The wind let out an offended sounding howl, slashing tree branches in my direction one last time, but they were too late. I passed the last tree and stumbled up to everyone.

Donovan took me by the arm, supporting me. "Show them the goblet. Tell them we're working together."

"We are," I panted to Chrissy. I pulled the goblet from my pocket and held it up.

Chrissy let out a squeal of happiness. Jade Blossom licked her lips. They both wanted it.

"The price has changed." I had planned on saying this with confidence, firmness. Instead I just tried to get enough air in my lungs between words. "You have to send all of us back to our homes."

Jade Blossom's wings flared open, fast, haughty. "The arrogance of mortals. You don't set the price—not when Queen Orlaith's servants swarm the skies on their way to find you." She turned her glare on Donovan. "You had skill and invisibility. How could you let this girl best you? How could you let her drag you into a hopeless partnership?"

Donovan stepped protectively closer to me, as though worried Jade Blossom might strike me.

Chrissy pressed her hands together in a clap of discovery. "How sweet. He's fallen in love with her."

Jade Blossom's mouth fell open, and she let out an indignant cry. "Of all the underhanded tricks!"

Chrissy's wings flapped happily. "Love trumps skill and invisibility. My mortal wins."

Jade clenched her wand, anger making it tremble. I was afraid she was about to curse someone, but instead she let out a humph and disappeared. All that remained of her was a falling trail of green glitter where she'd stood.

"So," Chrissy said in a cheerful tone that didn't match our surroundings. "The good news is Jade Blossom doesn't get the goblet. The bad news is I don't have enough magic to send three of you to the twenty-first century."

My heart stuttered. "What?"

She shrugged apologetically. "I did tell you I'm only a fairy godmother in training. I have restrictions on what I can grant mortals."

The birds were coming. The rumble of their cries sounded from somewhere over the forest. Donovan pointed to the goblet. "We know how much your people want this cup. In order to get it, you have to send *all* of us back. That's the deal."

Chrissy returned his gaze steadily. "I'd help you out if I could. Really, it would be much easier to wave my wand than stand here and argue with you about it, especially when Queen Orlaith and her minions are about two minutes from reaching us."

Jason nervously switched his weight from one foot to the other and searched the sky. "I don't want to be a frog again."

"Magic is being rationed," Chrissy went on. "The trees are dying here, and they're not doing so well in my land either. I had to cut corners on your wishes as it was."

I knew it. If Queen Orlaith hadn't been about to converge on us, I would have had a thing or two to say about that.

"There must be a way," I said. "Borrow some magic. Call someone."

"There's not enough time." Chrissy raised her wand, glimmers of magic running along its edges. "Choose who to take with you."

Jason nearly pounced on me. "She's taking me." He gripped my arm. "You promised."

I looked at Donovan, hoping he had another solution.

"Take us somewhere safe so Sadie can decide," he said.

Chrissy shook her head. "Queen Orlaith already sealed off the area." Her voice was as calm as if she was talking about some inconsequential weather front moving in. "I have enough magic to get myself and two other people out of here— preferably to send you to your final destinations." She glanced at the sky over the forest. "You have about a minute and a half left to decide."

Jason tugged on my arm. "You said you would get me home or die trying."

I had promised, but I wanted to take Donovan. I had to. I stared at him and gulped.

"It's okay," he said. "Go. I'll be fine."

I saw our entire future slipping away. All of the things Donovan and I planned to do together when we got home. It was gone. "No," I said.

"Yes." Jason gripped my arm harder. "Listen to Donovan on this one."

Donovan pointed a finger at Jason. "You're not getting off that easy. You've got to promise you'll do whatever she asks. You'll help her with her singing career. You'll let her open for your concerts. You'll take her to prom."

"Prom?" I interjected. Why would he think I wanted that? I hadn't even wanted to dance with Jason at the midnight ball.

"It will cause a sensation," Donovan explained. "The tabloids will love it. It will launch your career."

"I promise," Jason said, nearly yelling. "Now give the fairy the goblet."

Donovan pulled the invisibility cloak up so it covered his shoulders. He smiled, his eyes locking on mine. "You've got the most beautiful voice I've ever heard. The world needs you. You're going to have a great life."

He was trying to make me feel better, but each word stabbed me with regret. I didn't want to do what I knew I had to do. I couldn't see another way, though. Only two of us could go.

Jason hung onto my arm like a human anchor, so I didn't walk to Chrissy. I tossed her the goblet. Well, technically I threw it at her. After all, there's a fine line between toss and throw.

She caught it easily enough, plucking it from the air before it smacked her in the stomach. "Who do you choose?" She examined the goblet, turning it eagerly over in her hands. The glow around her grew brighter and her wings lifted in excitement.

"Jason and Donovan go," I said. "I stay." It had to be that way. I couldn't strand Donovan here. Not when his brother needed him. Not when Queen Orlaith was coming, looking for vengeance.

Donovan's eyes flew wide. "No!"

"You're smart, clever, and good," I told him. "The world needs that sort of person more than it needs singers."

He stepped toward me, but it was too late. For once, Chrissy did what I wanted. Lights sparkled and flashed around us. Like a concert, I thought. An auditorium full of fans taking pictures.

I heard sounds of creaking and popping coming from the forest trees. Perhaps they were leaning in for a closer look at what was happening. Perhaps they were reaching for the goblet one last time, trying to grasp hold of it. The lights faded and I stood alone. No, not alone. The shriek of birds coming from above let me know they'd found me. Any moment now Queen Orlaith would arrive.

Chapter 28

I didn't run, couldn't. The birds swooped down, swirling around me, ravens and owls alike, a whirlwind of flapping wings. "Girl! Girl!" the ravens shrieked. The flap of their wings sounded wrong - too loud, like thunder rumbling across the sky. With each pass they tightened their circle until I felt like I was in the eye of a hurricane. They smelled of dirt and steel, of sword blades that had yet to be drawn. I held my hands in front of my face to keep them from diving in and pecking me.

"Stop!" a voice yelled. The queen's.

The birds pushed upward. Several black feathers littered the ground near my feet, dropped in the frenzy. The birds flew back into the trees, disappearing like smoke vapor.

No, they hadn't all vanished. One large black raven sailed across the sky toward me, cutting a slash in the moon's silhouette. The queen watched it with a sigh.

In a flash, the bird transformed. One moment its wings were outstretched and gliding, the next Kailen dropped down in front of me, elegant and muscular. He was dressed in his usual black, but his hair wasn't smoothed back in a ponytail like it had been at the dance. It was loose around his shoulders and the ties of his top were undone as though he'd been relaxing somewhere and hadn't bothered to do them.

"Well, our thief is revealed." He eyed me smugly. "What do you have to say about that, Mother?"

"I shall apologize to you at length later." She stepped closer, eyes firm and hard in her pale face. Her red lips were vicious, nearly snarling. "Right now I only have one thing to say." She leaned toward me, her face inches from mine, and enunciated her words with icy resolve. "Where is my goblet?"

I was trapped. Any sort of escape was hopeless. I could only face my punishment with dignity. I stood straight, chin lifted, but my hands trembled at my side, quaking traitors. "It's gone. I'm sorry. I had to trade it so my fairy godmother would take Jason back home."

I left Donovan's name out of it. No need to drag him into this.

The creaking, popping sound came from forest again. Out of the corner of my eye I saw Kailen staring into the forest, puzzled by the noise.

"Deceiver," the queen hissed. "Mortal trash. I invited you to my ball as an honored guest and laid a banquet before you." She took hold of my arm and yanked me toward the forest. I planted my feet but it didn't matter. With her magic, she was strong enough to drag me wherever she wanted. She strode along the path at a fast pace. I stumbled after her, listening to her accusations.

"I brought you to a place humans only dream of glimpsing, and you repay me thusly?"

"I'm sorry. I had no choice."

"No choice?" Her nails bit into my arm. "'Tis true enough. Mortals by nature are selfish, greedy liars."

The accusation was too much, especially since Queen Orlaith had stolen the goblet from another fairy queen. I nearly pointed out I'd just been used as a tool in fairy intrigue, but I didn't say the words. Part of me hoped Chrissy hadn't completely deserted me. Surely a lingering sense of responsibility would draw her back here. It was better not to direct Queen Orlaith's wrath that way. Instead I said, "You only invited us to the ball to feed your trees."

"Oh, you will feed my trees, my dear." She pulled me harder, making me stumble. "Your blood will water their roots."

"Mother!" Kailen said, appearing at her side. "The trees—look at them."

Queen Orlaith's gaze shot to the silver trees up ahead. She gasped and stopped so quickly I almost ran into her.

I followed her gaze to see what had startled her. The silhouette of bare branches had changed. No longer did their arms reach upward like smooth candelabras. Buds had opened. New leaves shimmered in the moonlight, sleek and stretching.

Queen Orlaith let out another gasp, a happy one, a cry of joy. She let go of me and reached out to the trees like she wanted to caress each one. "At last."

I took a couple of cautious steps backward, wondering how far I could get away before she and Kailen noticed. As it turned out, not far.

Kailen's eyes returned to mine, questioning and sharp. "What caused the trees to grow?"

I had no idea . . . was too worried to puzzle it out. If I

pretended to have answers, they would keep me alive. But how could I pretend? I couldn't even tell a small lie.

"The fruit," the Queen murmured. "Perhaps it too has ripened." Her voice grew more certain. "Yes, it may have." She strode over and took hold of my arm, hard. "Did your love trigger the trees to grow? What did you do?"

I stared at her unspeaking. The answer came to me, drenched with all sorts of unpleasant implications.

I had sacrificed my future for Donovan's. That had been the act of love that finally made the trees grow. It was the reason the goblet had told Queen Orlaith only mortals' love would work. Fairies couldn't sacrifice for each other that way. They were magical and immortal. What could they sacrifice?

I couldn't tell Queen Orlaith any of this. If she thought sacrifice made her trees grow, what would she require from mortals next? She would most likely endanger the princesses to make their princes sacrifice for them.

I wouldn't bargain for my life, not if it meant putting others in danger.

"How could I know anything about your trees?" I asked. "I'm just an unimportant mortal. Carry out whatever sentence you're going to give me."

The silver trees' branches popped and creaked—the same noise I'd heard earlier. As I watched, the outlines of more leaves unfurled and grew. I had sacrificed again, and it had taken effect.

I pressed my lips together, afraid to say more. I didn't want the fairies to guess what I knew.

The queen's grip on my arm tightened. She yanked me closer as though she could read my secrets in my eyes. "You did something. You will tell me everything, or you will suffer."

The irony of her threat didn't escape me. "If you have to torture someone to learn about love, you won't understand it."

Near my side, Kailen paced impatiently. "I'll check the trees at the pavilion and see if their fruit is ripe." As he spoke the last word, he spread his wings. With his smooth black feathers, he looked more like a dark angel than a fairy. He shot away, vanishing over the treetops so quickly I couldn't tell whether he'd stayed a fairy or transformed back into a bird.

The queen glanced at me, then at the sky, undecided. She pursed her lips unhappily. "I'll go with my son." I felt her uneasiness more than heard it. She wanted to be there when he checked the fruit.

Perhaps she was one of those ultra-controlling people who couldn't delegate important tasks, or perhaps she had reasons not to trust Kailen. Whatever the case, she dropped hold of my arm.

For one hopeful moment I thought she might free me, that she was so happy to have the trees growing again, she'd spare me whatever punishment she'd planned.

"No, little thief," she said, guessing my thoughts. "You won't flee. You've still things to tell me."

The ground stirred beneath me, shifted, rumbled. Two long brown snakes slithered from the ground, grabbing my ankles. I jerked away, but couldn't free myself.

The creatures clamped around my feet so firmly I lost my balance and fell forward. I hit the ground, palms stinging. The snakes slithered up my legs, holding me. No, they weren't snakes—they were roots. Thick, winding roots.

I cried out and pulled at them, kicked. One broke, then the other ripped off. I tried to get up, but a dozen more roots emerged from the ground, pushing through the dirt like creaking fingers. A root slashed across my neck and pulled me backward. As I struggled with it, several more roots crept over my legs. Others took hold of my arms. "Don't do this!" I called to the queen. "Your trees are growing. Let me go!"

She didn't respond, just watched the plants twining and twisting around me. They left muddy trails along my dress and skin, dark slashes that looked like dried blood. The roots pinned me on my back, then limb by limb extinguished my thrashing.

The root around my throat tightened. I was trapped, sewn to the earth. Even before the roots stopped moving, sprouts poked up from the ground around me. Green tendrils stalked upward. They thickened as they grew, turning into a tangle of branches.

The queen smiled in satisfaction. I caught one last look of her pale skin and dark flowing hair, then leaves and branches blocked her from my vision. My gaze met only leafy darkness.

The queen's voice drifted downward. "I'll come back when I've harvested the fruit. We shall have a long talk then."

"Mercy is part of love," I called. "Show some. For your trees' sake, if not for—" Before I finished, a root slid across my mouth, cutting off my words.

If the queen heard me, she made no response. I imagined she'd left, gone to check on her fruit and her son. I struggled against the roots, straining against their grip. They didn't budge. I couldn't even shake the leaves on the branches. If the plant tightened its grip on my neck a bit more, it would cut off my air altogether.

The plant won't kill me, I told myself. The queen wanted to talk to me. She wanted me alive. I'm not sure she successfully conveyed this to the plant, however. Maybe it didn't have a clear understanding of the nature and purpose of the human throat in the whole breathing process.

The branches around me shifted and settled, waiting for the queen's return. I shifted my head to make it easier to breathe and tried to calm down. I needed to calmly assess my situation. I was smarter than a plant. Perhaps I could think of a way to free myself.

My assets: a human brain.

My disadvantages: I had no tools, and I couldn't move or speak.

Not a lot to work with, any way you looked at it.

The bush had small, heart-shaped leaves—the same kind of plant that grew everywhere in the forest. I had the horrifying fear the queen would forget where I was. I also feared she wouldn't.

Would it be better to die here, forgotten and starving, or to die in whatever creative and no doubt painful way the queen used?

Out in the forest an owl hooted. Branches rustled in the distance. Perhaps from the wind. Another noise. Someone called my name. No, I was imagining that. It was just the wind.

The call came again, low and insistent. "Sadie!"

Donovan. It was his voice. He'd come back. Part of me surged with anger. He was supposed to be in the twenty-first century—out of danger. What was he doing here? Why hadn't Chrissy done what I asked? My sacrifice was for nothing.

The other part of me wanted to cry with relief. He'd come to help me. I called his name. It choked out of my mouth, no louder than a hoarse whisper.

"Sadie!" he called again, closer now. He was walking nearby. Perhaps on the path. Would he notice a new bush where nothing had grown before? Probably not. What was one more bush in this forest?

"Donovan!" I could still only manage a rustle of sound.

"Sadie!" The sound came from farther away. He'd passed by me, hadn't heard me.

Tears stung my eyes. I couldn't do anything to get his attention. "Donovan!" I called, knowing the word would be swallowed in the breezes that rippled through the trees.

"Sadie!" He was walking away.

Panic and anger mixed inside of me. It wasn't fair. "I'm here," I whispered.

"Sadie!" He stopped, listened, but made no sign he'd heard me. "Sadie," he said sorrowfully. He was losing hope.

"Find me," I murmured, and then realized how he could. I turned my head, tilting it in Donovan's direction.

"I hate singing," I choked out, and felt the prick of my nose growing. "I hate chocolate, hot showers, and indoor plumbing. I love homework, chores, and being trapped by freaky, magical plants." Each lie brought a sharper pain to my nose, partially because it grew, partially because it scraped against the plant. As my nose knocked into the branches, they shivered, creaked. Made some noise.

"Sadie?" he called, and there was a question to it. He'd heard something.

"I love the mean girls at school, and I care about their opinions. That's what friends are: people who want to tear you down and see you fail."

My nose kept growing. It pushed twigs and leaves out of the way.

"Sadie?" Donovan called, worried. "Where are you?"

"If I get back to my real life, I'm going to obsess about the viral video of myself. Why care just about the mean girls in high school, when I can care about mean people across the nation? Strangers who see a bad moment in my life are in a perfect position to judge me. They've never done something stupid. They've never made fools of themselves. In fact, everyone's life out there is perfect except for mine."

I heard Donovan's footsteps coming closer. "Sadie, if you can hear me, do something. Let me know where you are."

"I don't want you to find me," I said. "I don't care if I die here. I don't love you."

My voice got choked. This time not from the root, but because I knew the truth. I did love Donovan. I had to, because my nose grew when I said I didn't. It was real love after all.

Donovan let out an exclamation of surprise. His footsteps hurried closer. The branches above me creaked, parted. At first I saw nothing, and then Donovan pulled the hood off his invisibility cloak.

He peered through the crisscross tangle of leaves. "Well, I've got to give you credit. You know how to get a guy's attention."

I'd never heard such beautiful words. "Hurry," I whispered. "The queen is coming back."

He pulled his sword from its sheath. "Shrink your nose so I don't accidentally hit it." He walked around the bush and hacked at the branches entwining my feet.

It was hard to recall all the lies I'd uttered. My opinions had been a jumble of panic. "I love singing, chocolate, and indoor plumbing, clearance sales, cats . . ." I must have hit some of the right things. My nose shrank.

Every time Donovan hit the bush, the whole thing shuddered. Bits of bark and leaves rained down on me. I squeezed my eyes shut. "I hate homework, chores, the song *Hotel California*, alarm clocks . . . oh, I remember . . . freaky magical plants that trap people." Each truth made my nose feel less taut, less painful. The scratches were disappearing with the length.

"I hate mean girls, and I don't care what they think. I'm not wasting my time worrying about their opinions." I doubt Donovan heard my confessions. His sword sliced through the plant again and again, chopping away the foliage. "I don't care about that stupid viral video or what anyone thinks of my audition."

When he'd cleared the branches above me, he slid his sword, flat end down, under the roots that wound around my arms and legs. Using the blade like a letter opener, he cut through them. They popped and broke, releasing their grip.

"I wanted you to find me." My nose was nearly back to its normal length. "I don't want to die here."

Donovan took my hand and pulled me to my feet. "I second that. Let's go."

I had one more lie to straighten out. "I love you," I whispered. With those words my nose shrank the last bit.

He did a double take. For a second, his expression showed nothing but shock, and I contemplated all the ways this moment could turn really awkward. "What did you say?" he asked.

"Nothing . . ." I didn't want my nose to grow so I added, "that can't wait until later."

Donovan seemed to agree. He pulled me toward the meadow. "Chrissy is waiting for us. She'll take us home."

"She came back too?" Of course she had. How else could Donovan have gotten here? Chrissy must have borrowed magic from someone, and Donovan had volunteered to search Queen Orlaith's land for me. The thought filled me with warmth, with energy. I used that energy to run faster.

Chapter 29

The advantage of sprinting through the forest without a stolen goblet shoved in your dress is that the birds don't rat on you in squealing alarm. The only sound I heard was our footsteps and panting breaths.

The trees thinned. I saw Chrissy in the meadow, floating a few feet off the ground. Her wings fluttered in agitation. "Hurry!" she called to us. "Kailen is coming!"

I glanced over my shoulder. A dark shape was gliding over the forest—not a bird. Kailen flew in his fairy form. I had no idea how he knew I'd escaped from the bush, but he held his twisted wand outstretched as he scanned the trees, looking for me.

I pushed myself to go faster. We only had a few more trees to pass, and then we'd be out of Queen Orlaith's lands. Donovan could have pulled ahead. He stayed beside me, though, matching his pace to mine.

Chrissy flew a couple of feet closer, then stopped, held

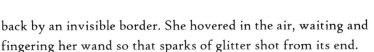

back by an invisible border. She hovered in the air, waiting and fingering her wand so that sparks of glitter shot from its end.

We were almost to her.

"Hurry," she called again. "I can't come on Kailen's land, but he can come here."

Yeah, I remembered that detail from the last time Queen Orlaith had captured me and dragged me back to her domain.

Chrissy swished her wand and a swirl of sparkles hovered and twirled at the edge of the boundary, illuminating it for us. Freedom was so close, just a few sparkles away.

"Stop!" Kailen yelled from the tops of the trees. He'd spotted us.

I ran faster. The border was only a few steps away.

"By fairy law," Kailen called, full of indignant authority, "the girl is my prisoner." He spoke to Chrissy not to me.

Donovan and I sprinted across the border. It felt like running into a shower of glitter. I waited for the lights to brighten, for Chrissy to take us away. She didn't. We ran to her, and she did nothing except twirl her wand and eye Kailen— watch his black wings carrying him toward us.

"Let's go," I breathed out. I wanted to add, *don't you dare turn us over to him*, but I was panting too hard to say it. So I stared at her with a ****correlated expression.

Chrissy didn't even glance at me. Her wings slowed until it looked like she was lazily hanging in the air. "The girl is my charge. That gives me the right to help her." Her smile was smug, almost flirty. "We can't expect mortals to obey fairy law."

Kailen landed on the ground, tucking his wings behind him. His eyes fixed on Chrissy. "I can expect *you* to obey it."

"You can expect it," she said, definitely flirting now, "but you'll be disappointed."

And with that, lights flared around us . . . lit fireworks, surrounding us in white flashes. A whoosh of air pulled me upward.

When the lights cleared, we stood in a hotel room—my old hotel room—the one where I'd first met Chrissy and Clover. My suitcase sat where I'd left it near the closet by the bathroom. Pieces of glitter from Chrissy's first visit still lay on the floor. The only difference was that now Queen Orlaith's goblet stood on the dresser next to the TV. It seemed out of place there, a gleaming fairy relic aside a cheap plastic remote.

Donovan blinked to adjust his eyes and looked around. He let out a relieved sigh when he saw we were in the right century.

Chrissy opened a gauzy purse that appeared on the end of her wrist and slid her wand inside. "That will teach Kailen to ask for my number and then forget about me." She snapped the purse shut in satisfaction. "I bet he remembers me for a long time now."

Donovan put his hands on his hips and took a deep breath. "Could you have cut that escape any closer? We were running for our lives, and you stopped for witty banter with the enemy?"

Chrissy glided over to me, still glowing with triumph. "Here's a pearl of wisdom from your fairy godmother: Never waste the chance for a dramatic exit, especially if a hot guy is involved."

I was too overjoyed to be mad at the way Chrissy dragged out our departure. I threw my arms around her in a hug, which is sort of hard to do when the person you're hugging has huge wings. "Thanks for returning for me."

Chrissy patted my back reassuringly. "That's what fairy godmothers are for: helping you and dispensing pearls of wisdom about hot guys."

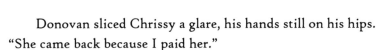

Donovan sliced Chrissy a glare, his hands still on his hips. "She came back because I paid her."

"What?" I pulled away from Chrissy and turned to Donovan. The last time he made a deal with a fairy, it involved stealing a powerful goblet from an enemy queen. "What did you pay her?" My gaze returned to Chrissy's, already pleading, already dreading.

Chrissy folded her arms. "Don't look at me like that. He cashed in a wish, and I gave it to him."

"He cashed in . . . what?"

Donovan reached into his pocket and pulled out three sticks he'd cut from the queen's trees. One silver, one gold, and one missing the diamond that had been there.

He held up the diamond branch. "The wish fruit ripened just as we left. That meant I had a magic wish. I wished you would come back home."

Chrissy smiled benevolently. "Some fairy godmothers wouldn't have had the courage to grant that wish. Fortunately, your fairy godmother is exceptional. And if the UMA contacts you with a customer satisfaction survey, please remember to use that wording. Exceptional."

I'd forgotten Donovan had a branch with unripe fruit, and now I laughed at the way it worked out. My sacrifice sending Donovan home had ripened the fruit, giving us the extra magical wish we needed. And the sweetest part was he'd used the wish to save me. "Exceptional," I repeated.

Chrissy walked to the dresser, an extra bounce in her step. "Well, that's another project successfully completed. Clover wasn't able to sabotage my attempts, no one died, and I retrieved a powerful relic."

She picked up the goblet from the dresser and surveyed it

with approval. "Let the Fairy Godmother University acceptance committee say I don't deserve to be admitted now."

She held up the goblet, making a toast. "This should put my job as an insomnia fairy to rest. Pun *so* intended."

I didn't point out that Donovan and I had played a large part of retrieving the goblet. "Is Jason back to his regular life?"

Chrissy fingered the goblet, still admiring it. "I left him at his dressing room at the *America's Top Talent* arena, surrounded by gift baskets."

Good. His natural habitat.

I looked around again, noting the hotel room's unchanged state. "How long have we been gone?"

Chrissy checked her watch and scowled. "Beetle dung. It's been half an hour. I thought for sure I'd gotten the stopping time thing right this go 'round." She let out a dramatic sigh. "Oh well, I'm still exceptional."

Half an hour. Not long at all. My mother was probably still at the store. No one was panicked or worried sick about my disappearance. I wouldn't have to come up with some convoluted explanation no one would believe anyway.

"About Jason," I said, drawing Chrissy's attention back to me, "is he still in love with me?"

"Yes, but he'll get over you quickly. Jason never stays in love with the same girl for long." As though anticipating a protest, she added, "You never specified a time length."

And I was glad now I hadn't. "That's fine. I don't want him to be unhappy."

Donovan grunted in a way that made it clear he was less concerned with Jason's happiness.

"What about the princesses?" I asked. "Will they be okay?"

Chrissy gestured toward the bed, and for the first time I noticed a picture book lying there. "See for yourself."

I glanced at the cover. *The Twelve Dancing Princesses.* The illustration showed dancing couples swirling through the fairy pavilion—my sisters. I picked up the book and flipped it open. An illustration showed a man coming to the castle in soldier's clothing. Not Donovan. Prince Geoffrey. I smiled and turned pages, watching my sisters and me getting ready for bed, stepping down the stairs, waltzing. The prince I danced with didn't look like Jason. He looked like Donovan.

I flipped to the ending and saw my sisters waltzing with their princes again—this time at the castle ballroom in wedding attire. The king and queen overlooked the celebration, the queen with a pleased expression, the king—well, in the time I'd known him he'd never looked happy, but he at least looked satisfied. It did have a happy ending.

I turned back to the picture of Donovan and me dancing and held up the book so he could see it.

He took a step closer to examine the picture. "That's not how it happened."

"I know," Chrissy said without glancing at the book. "Sometimes you have to improve the story. How would it look if the youngest princess ditched her prince and ran off with a thief? You don't want to be responsible for traumatizing children, do you?"

I took Donovan's hand and gave it a squeeze. "Actually, I like that ending."

He pulled me into a hug. Saying goodbye was going to be hard. Phone calls would be a poor substitute for seeing each other.

After a moment, I pulled away from him and turned to Chrissy. "When are you taking Donovan home?"

She stopped examining the goblet and gave me a disbelieving look. "Take him home? I already did that once. Then he wished to get you and bring you here." She made a sweeping motion that took in the room. "Voilà. We're here. My job is done. And remember, I did it exceptionally."

"Donovan lives in Ohio," I protested. "We're in St. Louis."

Chrissy's wings opened and shut slowly. "That's why humans invented the bus system."

"It's okay," Donovan said, resigned.

But it wasn't okay. "He's on probation. He's not supposed to leave his state."

Chrissy rolled her eyes. "I already explained to you that magic is being rationed."

The words triggered my earlier complaint. "Yeah, about that. You said you cut corners on my wishes. You knew all along you hadn't given me what I wished for, didn't you?"

I'm not sure why I pressed the issue. It wasn't like I wanted her to give me extra magic. I'd had enough of wishes. I guess I just wanted her to admit I hadn't been unreasonable or crazy when I complained about being the Little Mermaid and a dancing princess.

Chrissy raised her chin in an affronted way. "I gave you exactly what you asked for. The only corner I cut was that instead of giving you a new singing voice, I gave you the voice you'll have after you practice a few years." She waved her hand airily. "Moving your talent up a few years took less magic."

My hand went to my throat. "This is my real singing voice?"

"I know. It's amazing what practice will do, right? You might want to remember that in other aspects of your life. Like dancing."

She opened her purse and set the goblet inside. Instead of shrinking to fit in the purse, the way her wand had, the purse grew until Chrissy was able to shut it.

As I watched her, I caught site of my reflection in the mirror. Streaks of dirt crisscrossed my arms and face. My gown was rumpled, dirty, and torn. Bits of twigs and leaves littered my hair. My mom would wonder what I'd done while she was gone. How would I explain it?

I wiped at my hair, knocking bits of debris from it. "Now that you're done being my fairy godmother, my nose won't grow anymore, right?"

"Right," she said cheerily. "Feel free to go back to your normal dishonest self." She pulled her wand from her purse and gave it a twist. Sparkles fluttered around her like fireflies paying their homage.

"Clover will probably show up eventually to check on your progress. Tell him I said he's a slacker and he missed all the good parts and he's fired. Again." She gave us one last smile, then disappeared in a swoosh of sparkles and glitter.

I stared at the spot where she'd stood. I suppose Chrissy had that effect on people. You had to stare, even after she left.

"So," Donovan said, running a hand through his hair. "I guess I'd better check the bus schedules."

"Do you have to leave right away?"

"I doubt I'll be able to. How often do you suppose the buses go to Ohio?"

My purse sat by the door. I dug my phone out and handed it to Donovan. "There's one way to find out."

While he looked up the schedules, I took clothes from my suitcase and went into the bathroom and changed. I undid my hair, brushed as much dirt out of it as I could, and cleaned my arms and face with a washcloth. I hung my gown in the shower. It was the only place it would fit. Hopefully my mom wouldn't look inside before we left.

When I finished, I went and sat on the bed beside Donovan. He had the internet open to bus schedules. "A bus to Cincinnati leaves in four hours. I can transfer to Hamilton from there."

"Will you get in trouble for being away?"

"No. If anyone notices I'm gone, my brother will cover for me." Donovan handed me my phone. "It's hard to believe we're back, isn't it?"

"Things will be different for you now," I reminded him. "You've got silver and gold."

"And you," he said. It was a question more than a statement.

"And me," I agreed. I liked being needed, being loved. "Which reminds me, no matter what you made Jason promise, I'm not going to prom with him."

Donovan smiled. One of his smirks. "I bet I could sneak out on your prom night. After all, I do own an invisibility cloak." He leaned over and dropped a kiss on my lips. "Can you come to Ohio for my prom?"

"You're sure you want to show up with the girl whose upchucking video goes viral?"

He grinned. "I'll find a way to live with the infamy."

Donovan slid his hand across the back of my neck and kissed me again. He smelled of the woods, of that strange jasmine scent that hung there. His lips were warm against mine, soft, and perfect. Everything felt perfect. We were home again. I wrapped my arms around his neck and pulled him closer.

A moment later, the hotel door swung open and we jumped apart, startled. My mom stood in the doorway, a grocery bag in her arms. Her gaze went from me to Donovan and her mouth dropped open.

"Oh, hi Mom." I tried to sound casual even though I knew I was blushing. "This is my friend, Donovan. Donovan, this is my mom."

Mom didn't move. She may have gone into full-blown shock.

Donovan cleared his throat uncomfortably. "Nice to meet you, Mrs. Ramirez."

"Nice to meet you too." Mom's expression said, where did this guy come from, and why were you kissing him?

I gulped nervously, grasping for an explanation to his presence here. "I called Donovan and told him about my audition disaster. He was in the area, so he stopped by to make me feel better."

It was a good thing I could lie now, since I had a feeling I was about to do a lot of it. "Donovan lives in Hamilton, Ohio," I added to fill the silence. "I made him miss his bus back home, so he was checking to see when the next one left."

Mom finally came out of her shock. She smiled stiffly and set the grocery bag on the bed. "Well, it's always nice to meet Sadie's friends."

She eyed Donovan more thoroughly, clearly wondering at his Renaissance era clothing. The scabbard and sword at his side probably didn't reassure her that he was a guy her daughter should be kissing. "So," she said slowly, "how did you two meet?"

Despite what Chrissy thought about my proficiency in lying, I couldn't think of a plausible explanation.

Thankfully Donovan spoke before I had to. "We met online at a forum for people auditioning for America's Top Talent. We've been texting and calling each other for, um . . ." He turned to me to supply a time period. He had no idea how long I'd planned on auditioning for the show.

"Weeks," I said.

"Weeks," he agreed. "It seems longer."

Mom sat in the corner chair, her eyes sharp on us. I was afraid there was disapproval in that sharpness. If she didn't like Donovan now, she wasn't going to be happy when she found out he had a police record. "You sang at the auditions too?" she asked him.

"I did a magic act." He gestured at his clothes as though this explained them. "I make things disappear, do a little sword play, that sort of thing. I didn't even make it into the finals."

"Oh, I'm sorry." Mom didn't sound it. She sounded worried. "Are you planning on going into show business?"

"No," he said. "This was more of a bucket-list thing. I'm going to college in the fall. Business major."

Mom brightened at the word college. "That's nice. Where are you going?"

"Wherever Sadie decides to go."

Mom arched an eyebrow at me. "Are you going to college?"

"Yes," I said.

And I was as sure about it as I sounded. After everything I'd gone through, I didn't feel the rush to jump into the spotlight. Or maybe I just didn't need the validation anymore. I could take a few years to find out who I was before I let the music industry define that for me.

"I still want a music career," I said, "but college will be a good thing. Maybe sometime I'll want to teach music."

Donovan nodded. "You should take accounting classes. You're going to need to know how to handle all the money you'll make." To my mom, he added, "She has the most beautiful voice."

"I know." Mom sat back in her chair, finally relaxing.

It was probably Donovan's endorsement of college and my change of heart about getting a degree that brought about the change. She had decided he was a good influence on me.

"I keep telling Sadie this audition doesn't mean anything," Mom said. "She won't even remember it in a few years."

"Oh, I'll remember it," I said, and laughed.

Mom smiled and then laughed too. I knew she thought Donovan had accomplished what the ice cream could never do—made me feel better about bombing my song on camera.

But it wasn't just Donovan. I had swum to the bottom of the sea and met merpeople. I'd walked through trees made of silver, gold, and diamonds. I'd learned to waltz, been a princess, and danced for fairies. I'd almost drowned and I'd fallen in love.

A few minutes ago, I thought I'd never see my world again, and now I was back. It put a viral video in perspective.

Mom dished out ice cream for us, and we talked until it was time for Donovan to catch his bus. Mom and I drove him to the station parking lot. She waited in the car, while I walked Donovan inside and said goodbye.

When we reached the line at the counter, I pulled my wallet from my purse. "You'll need money for a ticket." Gold and silver filled his pockets, but he couldn't use that here.

Donovan shook his head. "Don't stress it. I'll use the invisibility cloak to get on the bus."

I took money from my wallet and held it out to him. "I'll worry less if I know you're traveling the legal way."

He tilted his head in disbelief. "I just chopped you out of a killer bush, saved you from evil fairies—and now you're worried about whether I'll be okay on a bus?"

"Yeah." I kept holding the money out.

He took hold of my free hand and gave it a light squeeze. His hands felt rough in mine, rough and warm. "You don't have to worry about me. I have a lot of experience taking care of myself."

"I know, but I'm going to worry about you anyway."

He finally took my money. "Okay." He tucked the bills into his pocket, then lowered his head so his forehead touched mine. "And by the way, I love you too."

I glanced up at him, surprised. "What?"

"Nothing . . ." he said with a grin, "that we can't talk about later."

I took hold of his hand again. "I think now is later."

He laughed, pulled me closer, and gave me another kiss.

Chapter 30

The video of my audition went viral faster than I'd imagined. I had one day at home, one day of normal life, before the show aired. After that, the internet went crazy. At first it was a montage of my performance. Then a meme popped up, and people tacked the footage of me heaving onto other videos so it looked like I was throwing up in response to a myriad of things. Political opinions. Celebrity fashions. Jason's latest music video.

Donovan actually made that one. He took a clip of Jason singing, "Do you want me, baby? Do you think I'm the one?" and then cut to me throwing up in front of Jason. The video had a million views by the end of the day. I didn't know whether to laugh or yell at Donovan for thinking the whole thing was funny.

It was easy for him to see the humor in my ill-gotten fame. He didn't have to go to my school. For a couple days, it seemed like the entire student body had nothing else to do except make comments about my performance or walk around the school pretending to vomit.

I tried to be a good sport. I said things like: "Just doing my part to put our town on the map," and "The judges got it wrong. Projectile vomiting *was* my talent."

A few people were extra nice, which sort of surprised me. The girl at the locker next to mine hadn't spoken to me all year, but when she saw me, she said, "Don't listen to the jerks here. At least you had the courage to walk out onto that stage. Most people at this school wouldn't do that."

I nodded philosophically. "Which is why most people at this school still have their dignity."

She laughed, and didn't look away. "You've got a good sense of humor. I don't know why you've always been so quiet."

Because I'd been afraid I would say the wrong thing. Because I'd been afraid people would criticize me. Because it was easier not to draw attention to myself. The upchucking video pretty well blew that strategy out of the water. Now I had to speak up for myself. And I found I wasn't that bad at it.

After a few days had passed and everyone else had moved on to other entertainment, Macy and Brooklyn strolled up to me in the hallway.

"How's your singing career going?" Macy asked.

I kept walking to my class. "Better than yours. At least people know who I am."

"I'd rather not have that sort of fame," Macy said.

Brooklyn wrinkled her nose. "I wouldn't want a singing career."

"Then you're in luck," I said. "You'll never have one," and I turned to walk into my class.

That day after school, *The Tonight Show* called my parents and asked if I could perform my song on Friday's show. It was ironic that such a horrible experience on one show led to an invitation from a bigger one. I wasn't sure whether Jimmy Fallon wanted to give me a chance to redeem myself or whether he was expecting me to fail again in an equally entertaining way.

I accepted without hesitation.

I flew to New York with my parents and spent the next afternoon rehearsing with the band. The musicians were really nice. After they introduced themselves, one of the guitarist said, "Hey, I know you'd rather be famous for something else, but don't feel bad about those videos. A lot of singers would pay for that kind of exposure."

"Then it's too bad I couldn't sell it to them." I only half meant it. I knew I would come through all of this stronger. I already was.

The guitarist took extra time to talk with me during rehearsal and suggested changing a few notes and adding some chords in my song. He was right. The song was better that way.

With his permission, I jotted down the changes so I could add them to my music back home. "I guess I still have a lot to learn about song writing."

"Nah," he said. "Revisions are just part of the game. You've got talent. Keep using it."

He didn't have to compliment me. I was only a high school kid here as a novelty. But it was nice that he did. It proved that not everyone in the business was like Jason.

That night when the cameras turned on and the band started playing my song, I was still nervous— petrified really— but I knew I could do it.

The intro music sounded smooth, professional. I took a deep breath, opened my mouth, and the notes flowed out clear and flawlessly. This time while I sang, I didn't picture Jason. I saw Donovan's cool blue eyes, his mussed hair, and his smile that tilted up at one side.

My voice was strong and beautiful, even if I did sound a little too happy about unrequited love. I couldn't get that wistful tone of longing that had been there when I practiced in front of Jason's poster. I was too un-unrequited.

When I reached the part of the song I'd choked on during the America's Top Talent, the audience leaned forward in their seats, one collectively-held breath. My voice slid upward effortlessly, and I lengthened the note just to show I'd conquered it. The audience burst into applause, drowning out my next few words.

With the band at my back, and the audience breathing in the music, singing felt magical. In a good way. I was wrong about not wanting the spotlight. I could live here.

When I sang the last note, the audience cheered their approval. I didn't care that they'd probably all seen my video and laughed at it. They were applauding now. They were clapping for everyone who'd made a fool of themselves and didn't let it stop them from trying again.

I took a bow and strode over—no heels to worry about today—to the guest chair. My nerves came back in force then, throbbing through me. I'd known all along I could do the song. Talking in front of the camera was another matter. Donovan had spent an hour with me on the phone, practicing possible things to say.

I shook Mr. Fallon's hand. Smiled big. "Before you interview me, I want to make sure—you can edit out anything embarrassing I might do, right?"

He waved away my comment. "Listen, you were so good, I think I'm going to throw up. It just seems like the thing to do."

The audience laughed, and my nerves melted away.

I sat in the chair, ignored the cameras aimed in my direction, and answered his questions. It went by in a blur. There was more laughing, more clapping. He shook my hand again and said, "You're a talented young lady. I can tell you have a great career ahead of you."

After the show broke for commercial, Mr. Fallon gave me the thumbs up. "You just killed it in front of eight million viewers. Not bad for someone who hasn't graduated from high school."

He was right. This wasn't bad at all.

The next surprise happened that night at the hotel room. My parents and I had a luxury suite, compliments of the show. I'd just taken a book out to the balcony when Jason Prescott called my phone.

"You're alive!" he said as soon as I answered.

"Yep. Last time I checked, that was my status."

I couldn't tell if he was happy or just surprised. "I thought you were stuck back in the Renaissance," he said. "I thought the fairies killed you. I've spent the last two days writing a song mourning your loss."

"Sorry. Still alive."

"Why didn't you tell me you'd escaped?"

"Well, I don't have your phone number. How did you get mine?"

"I got it off the forms you filled out for *America's Top Talent*."

Oh, that's right. I had given them my personal information.

"How did you get away?" Jason asked.

"Donovan and Chrissy came back and rescued me."

"That's good." A pause. "She was hot, your fairy godmother."

Apparently Jason was progressing just fine in falling out of love with me. "I mean," he went on, "I never pictured fairies that way, you know?"

"I never pictured them like Chrissy, either." I'd imagined them to be nicer. Like the harmless little old ladies in Disney movies. Chrissy, I was sure, would never use the words "Bibbidy-bobbidy-boo."

"I felt so bad about leaving you there," Jason said, "especially when those videos came out mocking your audition. I told the show they shouldn't air your segment, but they said the rest of the show wouldn't make sense if they didn't."

"Yeah, well . . . that's the important thing."

He completely missed my sarcasm. "It's their most watched episode so far. Although that might be because I was a guest judge."

"Great." I slouched in my chair. "Glad to hear it."

"Anyway, I've been bummed because I thought you died, and then—wham—the TV starts running ads about your appearance on *The Tonight Show*. Totally cool. How did it go?"

"Really well. You can see it tonight."

There was a moment of silence. I decided that meant it was time to end the call. "Well, sorry you thought I died and everything. I'm fine. Thanks for checking."

"When is your prom?"

"What?" The change in subject was so abrupt, I wasn't sure I'd heard him right.

"I promised Mr. Invisible I'd take you to prom."

I'd forgotten about that. "No need. Donovan is taking me."

Jason let out an offended huff. "You'd rather go with the invisible guy than me?"

"He's my boyfriend now, and he's not invisible anymore." Neither of us was. "But if you want to fulfill your promise, you could sing at my prom."

"You want me to perform while you dance with another guy?"

"It would be good publicity for you," I pointed out. "You came off kinda mean in those viral videos. You know, famous rock star crushes poor hopeful's dream so brutally that she's ill on stage."

"It wasn't like that," he said.

"Actually it was exactly like that."

"I gave you constructive criticism."

"You told me I didn't practice enough."

"That's constructive."

I tapped my fingers against the armrest. "You promised Donovan you'd do anything I asked, and I'm asking you to sing at my prom."

Jason let out a martyred groan. "Okay. Just this once."

"Well, that's normally how many times people do prom when they're seniors. However, I'm going to Donovan's prom too. I'm sure the people at his school would also love to hear you."

"One prom," Jason said.

"My fairy godmother could always change you back into a frog, you know."

"Fine," he muttered. "Both proms."

• • •

My prom was first. Donovan got permission to come and rented a limo. Normally I would have told him not to spend the money, but it turns out pocketfuls of silver and gold are worth a lot. Donovan not only had enough money to go to college, if he wanted, he could buy his own house near campus.

His problem was he could only sell off a gold leaf at a time or people would wonder if his newfound wealth had come about by illegal means. It's hard to explain where you suddenly got hundreds of thousands of dollars worth of precious metals from.

I had my own souvenirs tucked away in my closet: gold and silver leaves Donovan had given me, the pearl bracelet, and a fallen wish that would only ever be a diamond. Someday I might sell them—maybe when I was a poor struggling musician—until then, I would keep them.

When I stepped out of the limo in front of the hotel where prom was held, the paparazzi were waiting. Camera flashes went off around me, illuminating the area with splashes of light. Reporters jostled each other to get closer, holding mikes in my direction. "What do you think about Jason performing at your prom?" one asked.

Another called, "Are the two of you friends now?"

Then it seemed everyone was shouting questions at me. "Are you going to pursue a singing career?"

"How has this affected your life?"

For twenty minutes I answered them while kids from my school skirted around us, eyeing the cameras. Donovan stood by my side, protectively close. He kept his hand on my arm as though he thought he might have to bat the reporters away. Actually, I began to wonder if he would, since they showed no sign of letting us pass.

Finally, Jason and his body guards came out to rescue us. Or maybe Jason came out because he wanted to ensure the reporters got pictures of him with his arm draped around me, demonstrating we had no hard feelings. It was difficult to tell those sorts of things with Jason.

After a sufficient number of pictures had been snapped, Jason's bodyguards cleared a path into the hotel. Once we went inside, the hotel security kept the paparazzi from following us through the lobby.

We walked into the ballroom, Jason retook the stage, and the crowd cheered to have him back. I'd never seen so many starstruck people. Even the guys at my school who had sworn Jason was no big deal grudgingly clapped. Several girls looked nearly hysterical with happiness.

Hard to understand, since Donovan was hands down the most handsome guy in the room. We danced song after song. We even waltzed a few times.

Some of my classmates gave us odd looks as we waltzed passed them, circling the perimeter of the room. A few whispered and laughed. I didn't care. Waltzing was fun. And it reminded me of the first time Donovan and I had danced together back at the castle.

Other people watched us enviously. A few clapped for us, and one guy called out, "Do the salsa next!"

"We'll have to learn that," I told Donovan.

"Right. Then we can do it at my prom."

Throughout the night, we mostly stayed on the dance floor. This was partially because I liked dancing with Donovan, liked watching him move to the rhythm. And partially because every time Donovan and I left the floor girls accosted me, asking about Jason. *How well did I know him? Were Jason and I ever going to hang out together? If we did, could they come along?*

Um, no. After his stint as prom entertainment, if Jason and I ever got together, our conversations would not be ones I'd want anyone else hearing. Undoubtedly they would include fairy queens, dancing princesses, frogs, and mermaids.

The girls I ate lunch with came over to meet Donovan. I knew they were curious about this hot guy I'd shown up with, a guy I'd never mentioned before. They probably thought I'd hired a male model so I'd have a date.

"How did you two meet?" one asked, her gaze bouncing between us.

Donovan gave her his trademark smirk. "We're both underworld spies. We met at a spy convention."

"That's not true," I said. "I'm a spy, and Donovan is a paid assassin. We met in a Mexican prison."

"Ah, prison," he said. "Those were the good old days."

Then we told everyone the story we'd told my mom. We met when we'd tried out for America's Top Talent. Donovan told that part wistfully. "If only I'd thought to upchuck on Jason's shoes, I could have been the one on *The Tonight Show*."

"There's still time," I said. "You can throw up on his shoes tonight."

Donovan nodded. "I'll put it on my to-do list."

Toward the end of prom, Jason called me up to sing a duet with him. "We've done this song before," he told the crowd. "It's going to blow you away."

We sang *Love for Two*, the song we'd done for Queen Orlaith. And it was good. Jason and I blended well, even if he did like to show off a little by meandering through the chords.

My classmates stared at me with surprise and awe. I think they were awed because Jason said we'd sung together before, not because my voice impressed them. But whatever. Donovan smiled while I sang, and his smile lit up the whole room.

When we finished our duet, I returned to Donovan. Jason sang a new song, one with a tune I recognized from Queen Orlaith's pavilion. It wasn't as mystical or melodic without the musical instruments that evoked the elements, but it was still pretty.

Donovan and I swayed to the music. I liked the smell of his aftershave and the way he looked in his tux—polished and handsome.

"This is a nice dance," Donovan said. "Even if there aren't glowing pillars, a fountain, or a spread of chocolate flowers."

"I miss the chocolate. I'm tempted to nibble on your boutonniere."

He tilted his head questioningly. "Does this place seem hokey after being in a fairy court?"

I glanced around the room at the crowds of sweaty teens, at the hotel lighting and plain walls. "This is much better than the fairy court . . . because I'm dancing with you."

He grinned at me and we kept dancing.

From: The Honorable Sagewick Goldengill
To: The Department of Fairy Advancement

To the Esteemed Department,

I am in receipt of student Chrysanthemum Everstar's extra-credit report and have reviewed it thoroughly. I, like the rest of the Seelie Court, rejoice in the return of Queen Titania's goblet. I applaud Miss Everstar's creative use of wishes and commend her desire to return our beloved leader's possessions to their rightful place.

However, I can't condone Miss Everstar's reckless methods. She didn't seek, let alone receive, permission to embark on a mission with possible profound and long-reaching consequences.

Our sources in the Unseelie Court report a high degree of hostility forming there, especially since Queen Orlaith and Prince Kailen feel the sting of being bested by a fairy godmother in training.

I believe accepting Miss Everstar into Fairy Godmother University at this time would be a particularly bad political move. It would be, as they say, Not only chopping down the tree, but using the wood to build more axes.

I suggest we give Miss Everstar another assignment—something simple to keep her out of trouble until tensions die down. Perhaps you could find her a charge with an easily-cured affliction, such as an overabundance of warts, body hair, or optimism. Miss Everstar should be able to easily clear up any of those things.

With staid regards,
Sagewick Goldengill

About the Author

When asked what she wanted to be when she grew up, Janette routinely said she was going to be a princess. This was mostly because she wanted to wear a tiara and a poofy ballgown. Also, a handsome prince sounded like a good idea. She was quite sad when her siblings informed her that in order to be a princess, their father had to be a king. And he wasn't. He was a professor of Business Administration at WSU.

Thus, Janette learned early on that career expectations are easily dashed.

Since the princess gig didn't work out, she opted for a much more practical career—writing. She has written twenty-two novels and sold over a million copies of her books.

Although she has no experience with fairy godmothers, mermaids, or secret balls, the insomnia fairy frequently shows up at her house.

CPSIA information can be obtained at www.ICGtesting.com
Printed in the USA
LVOW07s1612231115

463837LV00001B/97/P